MY PERFECT
WIFE

BOOKS BY CLARE BOYD

Little Liar
Three Secrets
Her Closest Friend

CLARE BOYD

MY PERFECT WIFE

Bookouture

Published by Bookouture in 2020

An imprint of Storyfire Ltd.
Carmelite House
50 Victoria Embankment
London EC4Y 0DZ

www.bookouture.com

ISBN: 978-1-83888-168-9
eBook ISBN: 978-1-83888-167-2

There are people who have money and there are people who are rich.

Coco Chanel

CHAPTER ONE

I had been told that the beat of our hearts slows down when we look out to sea. As I soaked up the view in front of me now, I believed that. There was a shine to the heavy swell, as though it were keeping calm and carrying on today. With a shiver of pleasure, I zipped my fleece right up to my chin and pulled my wet hair into a bun.

'I'm gutted you're off,' Jason said, handing me a complimentary custard cream with my cup of tea.

I jumped up to sit on the counter of his beach kiosk. 'Thanks.' I dunked my biscuit. 'It'll be okay.'

The sun slipped behind a bank of clouds and the wind whipped the water into crests of white, sending the waves diagonally into the shore. Cradling my paper cup, I brought my attention back to the seven children in my charge, whose goose-bumped little bodies I had helped re-clothe after our swim. They were hunched at a picnic table on the grass; a raggedy bunch, wolfing down bacon sandwiches from brown paper bags.

'How long d'you expect to be away?'

'Don't know. Six months? Be back after the summer, I hope.'

He split his custard cream in two, scraping the filling with his teeth. 'We'll go bankrupt round here without your trade,' he said.

I laughed. 'More like you'll be quids in.'

'Nah,' he replied modestly, unable to accept thanks for the free sandwiches and biscuits he provided for the kids every Saturday. He scratched one of his knees, exposed by the shorts he wore all year round.

'I'll try to get back one weekend to see them and have a swim, once Dad's shown me the ropes and I've settled in.'

Jason sighed. 'If I moved back in with my old man, we'd probably kill each other.'

'Dad and I will be fine. We get on now.'

'Now?'

'We *still* get on, I meant.'

Both of Jason's eyebrows rose, but I was saved by a cackle of laughter from the picnic table. I changed the subject, burying my head in my rucksack. 'Check out the house I'll be working at.' The pages of the magazine were now crumpled from water damage, which would infuriate my mother. For two years she had kept it in the cabinet, out of direct sunlight, away from the risk of tea stains. Like a family photograph album, it was brought out only occasionally, mostly to show off to her new friends.

Jason moved his head closer to the photographs. 'You are *kidding* me.'

'Mum and Dad grew that garden from scratch.'

He pointed to the title of the article. 'Jekyll and Hyde?'

'I guess they mean it's got a two-sided personality – the pretty, fluffy borders and the modern hard stuff, like the geometric hedges.'

'Sorry to be funny, but the house looks a bit weird, if you don't mind me saying.'

I laughed. 'I don't mind. It's not my house.' I turned to the second page of the four-page spread. 'That's them. Lucas and Elizabeth Huxley.'

'She's fit.'

My eyes flicked away from Elizabeth and onto Lucas, whose face I had looked at on these pages more often than I had seen him in the flesh. Lately, anyway.

'I used to sneak through the hedge and swim in their pool when I was a teenager,' I confessed.

'Like a mermaid,' he murmured.

I was tempted to tell him the rest of the story, but it would have set a precedent. There was something comforting about having a secret that only one other person in the whole world knew about. Nursing it had become second nature.

'God, I used to want their life so badly.'

'Before you met me, you mean?'

I brought the rim of my cup up to his and said, 'Yes. And cheers to that!'

'Cheers!' He took a loud slurp. 'Who needs champagne?'

Amy emerged from the toilets with one of the children. Her short corkscrew curls had knotted into electrified clumps, just as they had done all those years ago when she'd come over to me in the school canteen queue wearing her skirt rolled too high and non-uniform pop socks. She had asked me to buy her the Wotsits she had been eating.

'Uh oh, it looks like Full Monty's at it again,' Jason said under his breath, nudging me.

My attention snapped back to the table, where Reese had dropped his pants. Before I could reach him, he was shaking his seven-year-old dangly bits at the other children. There was a cry of 'Gross!' from a girl in a pink hoodie, probably more out of habit than disgust.

'Come on, Reese, no, no, no, up they come,' I said, tightening the elastic waistband of his tracksuit. There was the faint whiff of wee.

He pulled them down three more times before I managed to persuade him to sit down again and drink his juice box.

'He's trouble, that one,' Jason said.

'Not really,' I said, remembering the conversation I'd had with Reese in the sea earlier.

He had nodded at the hazy strip of land in the distance, sculling to stay afloat, and said, 'You ever swum out to that bit of ground?'

'I haven't, Reese. But I'd like to. Not sure I'm fit enough yet.'

'My dad said I couldn't do it neither.'

His black eyelashes had blinked droplets of seawater down his cheeks. I had looked right into his bloodshot eyes and regurgitated someone else's words: 'You can do anything you want to do, Reese. *Have* anything you want. *Anything.*' Then I had told him to straighten his legs when he kicked.

At the picnic table, Reese swore loudly, bringing me back to reality. I winced at the sound of the four-letter word coming from his young lips.

'Total bloody angel,' Jason said, winking at me and handing Amy a cup of coffee.

I laughed. 'If you met his father, you'd see why he's like that.'

'You should meet *my* old man,' Jason snorted.

'And you were an angel when you were his age, were you?' I teased.

Jason was about to remonstrate when Amy cut in. 'Jase, you're wasting your breath, mate. Heather loves all those little shits,' she said with a smile that suggested she loved them too. The very fact that she came out to the windswept beach to swim with me and the little shits every Saturday, as my unpaid sidekick, was testament to that.

'I do love them,' I said.

I was determined not to cry or hug the children when I said goodbye to them, knowing they would laugh at me. There would be no tear-jerking thank-you cards from any of them. Reese had been the only one to express his appreciation, in a drawing he had made. Smudged in places, it was a portrait of me with excessively

long limbs and floor-length green hair, ''Cos I didn't have orange.'
I was stretching my legs and arms into a star shape next to the pool
that belonged to St Catherine's School for Girls, which justified its
charitable status by offering its facilities to the local sports charity
on Saturday mornings. Next to me Reese had drawn seven yellow
star-shaped stick children. Lots of stars. That was how I saw all
the children I taught, including the St Catherine's girls, the more
privileged of my students, whom I had been teaching full-time
on weekdays for the past three years. Their lives had been turned
upside by the school's closure last month, just as mine had.

I gathered my wetsuit and towel. 'We'd better go. If I don't get
them home on time, I'll be late for Dad,' I said.

Amy and I said goodbye to Jason and bundled the children into
the minivan. On the journey, two of the girls began screaming at
each other in the back. It was hard to tell if they were excited or
furious. There had been a time when these fights would terrify
me, but we had learnt to stay out of it, until blood was drawn.

'I can't concentrate with that racket going on, you two!' Amy
yelled from the driver's seat.

They ignored her and we continued on our route, dropping
six out of the seven children home.

'You do think I'm doing the right thing, working with Dad,
don't you, Ames?' I asked, taking a packet of crisps out of the glove
compartment and offering it to Amy. It wasn't the exact question I
had wanted to ask, but it was close enough to represent the doubt
that lurked inside me.

'Definitely. Absolutely one hundred per cent. One *hundred*
per cent,' she insisted, nodding hard. The van swerved a little.
'Whoops.' She straightened the wheel and asked, 'Which is the
turn-off to Reese's again?'

Reese's house was last. Always last, poor Reese, I thought.

I pointed to the next turning on the left. 'I've been wanting a
change of scene.'

'And that place you'll be working at looks awesome,' she added, referring to the *House & Garden* article.

Part of me wished I hadn't shown the article to anyone. It made my move look glossier than it was.

We drove in silence until we pulled up outside the row of pebble-dashed terraced houses: one of them was Reese's, two were boarded up. The curtains were still drawn. I took him to the front door and rang the bell.

As we waited for the door to open, Reese shoved a Snickers bar into my hand and said, 'I didn't nick it.'

A tear escaped.

'Thank you, Reese,' I said, bending down to give him a hug he stiffened for. 'Check around the back to see if your dad's in the kitchen.'

He ran off and back again, shaking his head. My heart sank.

Biting at the red-raw skin under his bottom lip, he said, 'It's all right, I'll climb in the back window and wait.'

'No you will not,' I said. 'Come on. Let's get a cup of hot chocolate at Mirabelle's like we did last time and wait for him together.'

He rubbed his hand over his thick loo-brush head of hair, mimicking his father, and shrugged. Reese was a boy of few words, but he had a look on his grey freckled face that suggested he was full of all sorts of words; words that he might spend a lifetime holding back. I understood that face.

On the way to Mirabelle's with a silent Reese, I held back my fury. Reese's father was useless and Reese deserved better, but there was nothing I could do about it. Not now. Not now that I was leaving and giving up on him and the other children.

In the café, he began jumping up and down in his seat. Then he began to climb onto the table. I coaxed him down, scrabbling in my bag for a pen and paper for him to draw with. *House & Garden* dropped out.

'What's that?'

'Want to read it?'

He grabbed the magazine and flicked through the pages, strangely calmed by what must have seemed other-worldly. I winced when he came to the article about the Huxleys. Elizabeth's beautiful eyes gazed up from the page, smiling benevolently at him from inside her perfect bubble life. I wanted to cover her face with my finger.

'Look at that wanker,' Reese said, pointing at Lucas. 'His missus looks proper stuck-up.'

I held back a chuckle. 'Mind your language,' I said, without much conviction.

He shrugged and sucked his teeth. 'She does, though.'

'I'm sure she's very nice,' I said with a wink. Then I felt guilty for encouraging such unkindness. If Lucas had fallen in love with this Elizabeth woman, she was bound to be lovely inside and out.

My car door creaked with rust as I shut it before running back up the stairs to the flat to grab one last thing. Rob was lying on top of the duvet watching sports clips on his laptop while I packed the car.

'You keep coming back in because you don't really want to go,' he said.

'You got me,' I replied, rushing around searching for my blue goggles.

'Or maybe you just don't care,' he said sulkily and clicked on a new clip. Angry rock music blared out. Over the noise, he added, 'Maybe this is your way of leaving me.'

'Don't be silly.'

He slammed his laptop shut and chucked the blue goggles in my direction – the goggles I would have little hope of using.

'I don't want you to go,' he said. 'It's only money. We'll find a way. The takings at the bar will pick up. It's not too late.'

I looked at him, at his crown of white-blonde hair, textured like straw from sea salt and too few showers, and his once mischievous blue eyes that were now tired and hung-over. I knew very well – as well as I knew every inch of him – that he did not mean what he had just said. He understood that we had no money left. Since St Catherine's closure, we had lost our only source of income. My small pot of savings had run out and Rob's new bar on the high street was months, if not years, away from turning a profit.

'Dad was expecting me two hours ago. I have to go,' I said, kissing him.

'Stay,' he whispered, pulling me into his lap.

I wanted to stay. Momentarily, wilfully, I put aside the fact that I had cried with relief when my father had offered me the job of covering my mother's leave at Copper Lodge, saving us from rent arrears. But I could not forget about my mother, who was already miles away in Galashiels, caring for her dying sister. When I thought of her, I knew I had nothing to complain about. With a huge effort I said, 'You know I can't,' and pulled myself up. My father needed me as much as I needed him. 'It's not just about the money,' I reminded Rob. 'Dad can't keep on top of that garden without Mum.'

'He could employ someone else.'

'The Huxleys are fussy about who works there.'

'Your dad's fussy, you mean.'

'It's not his fault Aunt Maggie's ill.' I took my goggles and headed for the door.

'He doesn't deserve your help, if you ask me,' he mumbled.

'What?' I stopped in the doorway, wondering if I had heard right.

He did not repeat it. Instead he said, 'The lodger had better be tidy.'

I was on the cusp of telling him how much it hurt my feelings when he criticised my father, but before the words came out, I noticed a drawing on the fridge. It was Reese's picture of me and my little stars by the pool. I pulled it out from under the magnet, unzipped my rucksack and slipped it into the pages of *House & Garden*, which I had sandwiched in between my two horticultural encyclopedias, attempting to flatten out the buckling. I vowed not to look at the photograph of the Huxleys again before starting at Copper Lodge.

Then there was a traffic jam. Gridlock, engines off on the motorway.

Unable to think about anything else, I pulled the magazine out of my rucksack and reread the article that accompanied the photographs. In direct contrast to how the sea made me feel, my heartbeat sped up. The journalist, Tara Sandeman-Fitzroy, described the house and garden as 'a balance of order and rebellion'. She wrote about Elizabeth 'brushing her hands over the flower heads of the soft borders, talking through a shy smile, seemingly unaware of her ethereal beauty', while 'in the house, Lucas seems to command the architectural space with his charm and energy', and that it was no surprise that 'an invitation to their annual summer party is the most sought-after in Surrey's social calendar'.

I put the magazine back in my rucksack and reminded myself I had been employed at Copper Lodge to do a job. For Dad. That was all. I wasn't there to flit around the daisies and dream of being invited to the summer party, like Cinderella. Six months. Head down. Pay the rent. In and out. And back to my happy, fulfilling life in Rye with Rob. Simple.

CHAPTER TWO

Elizabeth Huxley pulled her turtleneck high to her jawline to make sure her throat was hidden. The ribs of cashmere pressed into her skin like wire. The day was too warm for wool of any kind, but she was fed up of covering her bruises with her cotton scarf. The light material needed constant attention when it unravelled or flapped or tangled.

In the kitchen, Agata was clearing away the children's cereal bowls. When she saw Elizabeth, she handed her a stack of letters. She had sifted out Lucas's mail, leaving Elizabeth with catalogues, charity leaflets, free local magazines and, of course, Lucas's instructions for the day. Today there was also one large white envelope that was addressed to both Mr and Mrs Lucas Huxley. Elizabeth pulled it out.

It had already been opened. There were two Post-it notes stuck to it. Lucas had scribbled on one in his looping cursive, *Have a think, darling*, referring she assumed to the contents. She put the envelope and the other letters down on the worktop. She would have to eat something before tackling what she knew was in it.

'Lucas didn't eat his grapefruit?' she asked Agata, seeing it still in the fridge.

'I made him some ...' Agata pointed at the jar of her home-made granola, which sat in an exact line of identical jars filled with pasta or oatmeal or rice.

'Ah.' The sound stuck in her throat. She would have said thank you, for being kind, but talking made it sore. A glass of water soothed it.

'Grapefruit is, you know …' Agata mimed a thumbs-down and sucked in her cheeks to suggest malnutrition. 'We need muscle,' she smiled, squeezing her small bicep, which flexed when she reached for the granola.

Elizabeth smiled. 'I don't want muscles,' she said, sitting down with her grapefruit at the breakfast bar.

Agata was on the other side of the long bank of kitchen units, shooting up and down the narrow space, unloading the dishwasher, polishing glasses, tidying the fridge. The girl's pencil-thin ponytail cut through the air, left to right, right to left, as she dashed around in her clean white trainers and high-waisted jeans. The squeak of her rubber soles on the concrete floor was grating. Elizabeth wanted to tell her to stop moving, but knew it wasn't normal to ask such a thing. *It's such an effort to be normal*, she thought.

Slowly she picked through the segments of grapefruit. Each cold slice as painful to swallow as the last.

The breakfast bar separated the two of them. It should have been appropriate, as though Elizabeth were sitting behind an executive desk: a boss in charge of her employee. But it didn't feel right in a domestic setting, in her own home. Being a boss had never felt right to Elizabeth. It didn't suit her temperament. And she had grown fond of Agata.

She studied the girl, assessing her skin tone and physique for signs of health and vitality, just as she would scrutinise Isla and Hugo's lithe, naked little bodies before bath time or around the pool. She tried hard to be dispassionate, like an MRI scanning her for anomalies. She noted the sallowness of Agata's olive skin, with a breakout of spots on her chin, and the ever-growing strip of dark brown at the roots of her hair, even thinner at her hairline than at the brittle, bottle-blonde tips. Under her brown eyes, which were pretty but too close to her nose, were dark hollows, pockets of emptiness. The accumulation of poor sleep was becoming obvious. With a shabby, useless sort of guilt, Elizabeth wondered what she should do about it. She played with the segment of grapefruit in her bowl, allowing it to slip and slide off her fork.

'Where are Isla and Hugo?' she asked, noting their empty cereal bowls.

Agata snapped a glass jar shut. The sudden noise made Elizabeth jump.

The girl pointed left. 'They play ...'

Elizabeth smiled at the thought of her two children playing happily together.

On cue, there was a thundering of feet and they exploded out of the corridor that led from their bedrooms.

'Hugo hit me!' Isla wailed.

'She cheated, Mummy!' Hugo retorted.

'Stop fighting, you two,' Elizabeth said calmly.

'But MUM!' they both protested at once.

Elizabeth turned back to the hard work of her grapefruit. 'Not interested.'

'Let's go. Mummy doesn't care,' Isla whispered to Hugo, rummaging in Elizabeth's handbag for a handful of sweets. Elizabeth pretended not to notice. Isla's words stung, but she smiled when Agata winked at her. It had been Agata's advice to disengage from their fighting, to not take sides. The idea of not seeking justice for one or the other of her children, of not finding a victim or a perpetrator, had been a new approach, different to her husband's need to pin down the culprit. It took willpower to stay seated, to resist seeking Isla out to kiss her face, to give her another handful of sweeties, to remind her she always cared.

'Lucas say to meet you at five o'clock today in ...' said Agata, pointing out of the window towards the outbuilding in the garden.

The mossy tiles and tumbledown brick of the old barn was the only blip on the horizon of their expansive sightline across the Surrey Hills.

'Oh, I'd forgotten,' Elizabeth murmured, pushing her half-finished breakfast away.

'And these, yes?' Agata's eyes were on her as she pushed the stack of post in front of her.

Elizabeth focused on the white envelope. On the second Post-it, Lucas had written, *Just a little reminder to call Bo Seacart about the summer party!* She removed both sticky notes and put them aside. The postmark on the envelope was a red shield with *Channing House School* written across it. Her stomach flipped. She handed the junk mail to Agata. 'Bin these, will you?' Agata dried her hands on the dishcloth and took them.

Gingerly Elizabeth opened the envelope and pulled out a school prospectus and a letter. It read:

Channing House School for Girls
Tilford Road
Hambledown
Hampshire
HO27 2NS

Dear Mr and Mrs Huxley,

We are very pleased to inform you that we have found Isla a last-minute place in our Junior House, commencing in September 2020, following her academic assessment and interview last month.

As discussed over the phone, I have included details of our 'sleepover weekend' in July of this year, to which Isla is warmly invited. This is highly recommended for our prospective young boarders, but not compulsory. These weekends are designed to be a fun and educational experience for the children. They enable us to build an all-round picture of your child academically and socially in preparation for her start next term. It will also be an important opportunity for your child to get a feel for Channing House, to meet fellow students and find her way around our grounds.

We require you to confirm Isla's place and fill out the attached medical form and send it back to us as soon as possible. If there are any questions, please don't hesitate to call.

We very much look forward to welcoming you both on our open day on Friday 5 June.

With best wishes,
Mrs Anne Hepburn
Headmistress, Channing House School

Elizabeth dipped into her handbag and stuffed two fruit sours in her mouth. She chewed slowly. Her gums smarted and her throat ached. She stared at the laughing faces of the young students in the glossy prospectus: playing hockey, playing tennis, studying hard at desks, laughing by the fire, sitting cross-legged on their duvets reading books in their bright little dormitories. She tensed at the thought of Isla in one of those pine bunk beds. Who would comfort her in the night if she had a nightmare? Perhaps it would be a housemistress with a towelling dressing gown and an unfamiliar face-cream smell. Or the eight-year-old girl in the top bunk whose tears had dried already. Or nobody. Maybe nobody would come to pull her covers over her and kiss her on the forehead.

She wanted to scribble a Post-it back to Lucas: *PLEASE NO! NO! NO!*

She left the letter on the side, then ambled over to the bank of glass walls and leant her shoulder against the chilly, trunk-like concrete post that had been the architect's nod to brutalism. Too brutal for Elizabeth's tastes.

'Could I have a hot lemon this morning, please?' she asked Agata.

While Agata boiled the kettle and sliced the lemon, Elizabeth looked out. From this position, she had the feeling that their house was crouching, lying low in the landscape, hiding behind the tall, sparsely placed oak and birch trees. The edges of the patinated copper roof at the top of the windows sliced off the sky and the slate tiles of the patio, laid across the concrete foundations, sucked up the natural sunlight. The thick, dark mahogany doors weighed down the doorways either side of their open-plan kitchen-diner.

Last year, when the build had been finished, Lucas had taken Isla and Hugo to see it before they moved in. Isla, only six years old at the time, had mistaken the roof for gold. In spite of the green oxidation that covered it now, both Isla and Hugo continued to describe it as a golden house, but Elizabeth could only see the tarnish.

How arduous and expensive the process of building a house had been. The day the floor-to-ceiling glass panels had arrived on site to the wrong specification, three centimetres out. The week it had snowed, preventing the concrete being pumped into the floor, delaying the rest of the build, costing them more money, meaning they were unable to afford to renovate the pool, tennis court and barn. The day they had found a crack in the concrete posts.

She couldn't help grieving for Lucas's parents' bungalow, which they had razed to the ground. It had been his childhood home, stuffed full of life and memories. Its replacement, this upmarket single-storey showpiece of glass and concrete and copper, was, to Elizabeth, a money pit that reflected their architect's talents and her husband's insecurities. But Lucas would call her a philistine. He would laugh about her being unambitious and she would not be able to deny it. Her mother had said the same about her. Yet their disappointments in her were idealistically opposed.

Elizabeth's mother, Virginia, with her perfect diction and layers of uneven hemlines, had taught both Elizabeth and her brother Jude that being poor was noble. In her mother's eyes, living for the theatre – living in poverty – was proof of her authenticity and integrity as an actor, or a voice coach, as she later became. In Elizabeth's eyes, being poor meant scrabbling under sofa cushions for bus fares and shoplifting nail polish from Boots.

Looking around her now, she still couldn't believe what she had. Never would she forget what she hadn't had. The ex-council flat in the high-rise in Ladbroke Grove where she had grown up had been warm, most of the time, but the lift to the fifteenth floor had smelt of urine and had broken down every week. Elizabeth had had school shoes that fitted, but she had worn the same jumper and jeans outside of school for so long her friends had begun to notice. One year, for a whole term, they had eaten baked beans on toast for their supper every night, sharing one can between three. If they ever went out to eat, others paid. While Elizabeth's father came and went as he pleased – as an actor himself – her mother paid the rent and survived on her own, her pride steeped in martyrdom and melodrama.

Lucas had represented the antidote to this gentrified struggle. They had met at a house party thrown by a mutual friend who was at SOAS with Lucas. Clutching warm wine in a plastic cup, transfixed by his handsome face, Elizabeth had struggled to hear him over the tinny nineties hip hop, but she had understood enough to know he had strong, old-fashioned values. He was a man who believed in the traditional family. A man who promised to take care of the woman he married. A man whose ambitions included a well-paid career and a family to provide for. A man who had been unapologetically clear about what he wanted, which had become – on that very night – what Elizabeth wanted too. The job her mother had found for her, working in a kiosk at the Barbican, had not suited her. A career in the arts had not been what she had dreamed of. She had not been passionate and motivated like Virginia. But at that party, she had found a man with enough of both for all three of them.

Later, after a day of doing very little, she put her book on the coffee table and thought of the letter that she had stuffed into the drawer. Her fingers reached around her neck and pressed on the bruises. The dull answering pain was a comfort. The bleak days of last week moved inside her again. If she lost her daughter to that school, she would only have herself to blame.

From her place on the sofa, she could see the blanket of green fields rolling out to the horizon. From afar, the terrain looked flat and the horizon reachable, as though you could walk there in an old pair of trainers, with no possessions, as though the world around them was accessible to all. Yes, she was free at any point to walk out of the door, hand in hand with Isla and Hugo, and across the horizon. But where would she walk to? What would she do? She looked out, further away, stretching her sight. Through the hazy blur of the horizon, the earth slid down, down, away to the unknown, where human feet were walking through their lives, anonymous and unfamiliar to her, busy and full of purpose. She couldn't imagine that any of them were struggling, like her, with the pointlessness of it all. Quickly she wound up her thoughts, running them back up and over the horizon to the safety of her home, to her garden, where she loved to spend time with her children.

But Isla was going to be taken away from here, from her home, by a housemistress in a sensible skirt. Isla was her firstborn, her baby with the funny blonde curls either side of her big cheeks. And Copper Lodge was her place of security. Every day, Elizabeth wanted to see her running around, wild and uninhibited. Every single night, she wanted to make sure her warm little body was snuggled into her pink Pusheen bed in her own room. Every morning, she wanted her to wake up with a kiss from her mummy. Every single day of her precious childhood, Elizabeth wanted her here with her in the proverbial four walls of family life.

'Agata, hand me that letter from Channing House, will you?' she said with purpose. And she took the white envelope, tore it up and stuffed it in the bin.

In that euphoric moment, she didn't care one bit how Lucas would react. Not one bit.

'Elizabeth, please, you must go. He said five o'clock,' Agata urged, almost pushing her outside.

Her heart sped up as she watched Lucas's approach in the distance. She had been instructed to meet him at the barn at five. It was six minutes past. He was coming to find her.

CHAPTER THREE

Throughout the two-and-a-half-hour journey up to north Surrey, I let a stream of old footage of the good times with my father play out in my mind. The smell of wet wool as he carried me over bogs on our long hikes; the taste of the pies we would eat together in front of the rugby on Saturday afternoons; the feel of his huge hand on my forehead when I was ill; the sound of his singing in the two-inch-deep bath on Sunday mornings.

Having arrived in Cobham three hours and twenty minutes late, due to Reese's hot chocolate and a traffic jam, I did not feel hopeful about his mood.

Winding up Bunch Lane, I slowed down as I passed Copper Lodge, but as always, I could only get a flash of glass through the trees. It was set back too far from the road to see properly.

I drove into Connolly Close next door. My father's white van was parked up outside their red-brick bungalow. The house, and five others exactly like it, had sprung up on the wooded strip of land next to the Huxleys' plot in 1981, when Huxley Senior had changed the boundaries and sold it to crooked developers. The local residents, some of whom were still alive, had never recovered from the loss of the rare slow-worms and the lesser-spotted woodpecker; nor could they pass the estate without a sniff of disdain about the ugliness of the architecture.

I blew out a shot of air, releasing some of the dread, readying myself to go in; then I remembered my hair was down. Quickly I pulled a band out of my pocket and wrapped it into a bun. Dad did not approve of my long hair, which my mother had never let me cut. It was one of the few battles she had won. It had been prettier when I was young. It should have been auburn, but was now tinged green from its overexposure to chlorine. In spite of its length, it needed very little maintenance. A weekly brush in the shower with some conditioner was enough of a fuss for me. I should have cut it shorter. I wasn't sure why I didn't. Maybe I kept it long for Mum. The rest of me I ignored almost completely: a flannel, a toothbrush, a pot of cheap face cream and a Vaseline lip salve was all I needed. There was a stub of an eyeliner pencil embedded in the lining of a wash bag somewhere, and an old dried-up mascara, but they were never used.

I pulled my suitcase out of the boot and wondered if Dad had waited to eat, in spite of his warnings that there would be no food for me if I wasn't on time. Seven sharp was teatime.

'Dad?' I called out as I walked in.

His huge form emerged from the kitchen and approached me for what was neither a kiss nor a hug, but more of a touching of shoulders, our toes far apart from each other. I sucked in his familiar smell and held onto him for longer than he wanted me to.

'Sorry I'm late,' I said. Now that I was working for the family business, right where he had always wanted me, maybe he would let it go.

He scrutinised the wall clock above our heads. I had missed his strong face, his square jaw and his endearing ears, which stuck out a little, too small for his large head.

'I was late too, as it happens. Mr Huxley wanted me to look at that damned tennis ball machine,' he said.

'Is that what gardeners do these days?'

'It's what gardeners do at Copper Lodge.'

I followed him into the kitchen. The usual rush of cleaning fluid and mothballs wasn't there. The house smelt of cooking and damp wool. I looked out for old pizza boxes, empty beer bottles or squished-out cigars, anything to suggest that he hadn't been coping without Mum. Aside from a cable-knit jumper dripping from a radiator, the room was clean and tidy. There was nothing sinister to the naked eye.

He sat down. 'The mugs are in the bottom cupboard now. Your mum changed things around before she left.'

I took out two mugs, switched on the kettle and plopped in the tea bags.

'How is Mum?'

'Very well,' he sighed.

'And Aunt Maggie?'

'Hanging on in there.'

I imagined how hard my mother was working to keep my aunt happy and comfortable in the last months of her life. I stared out of the window at her garden, neglected by Dad. Tall, spiky weeds pushed through the rose bushes; the purple buddleia, six feet high, shadowed half the small patch of overgrown grass, which was covered in moss patches and dandelions. It was strange to see it so unloved.

This garden, their house, had been Mum and Dad's dream. They didn't see the ugly bungalow that the sniffing residents saw. Represented in every brick was proof of how they had come up in the world. They had worked hard for their home and its spot in one of the most expensive areas in Britain, in north Surrey's sought-after commuter belt, five minutes' walk from a train that sped into London in forty minutes. The house, bought off plan with a little help from the Huxleys, had cost them more than it should have, considering its size, but they had aspired to this better life. The deprivation of the rural town of Galashiels, where they had both come from, was their past. Connolly Close was where they had arrived, down south, surrounded by affluence. The fact that the mortgage had crippled them every month was beside the point. If they stood at the entrance to the close, they would see the markers of others' success, reminding them that their sacrifices – one child, no holidays, few clothes or meals out – had been worth it. Their next-door neighbour, Alan, was a City lawyer with a sporty Audi. In the house opposite, an estate agent – 'so handsome' – lived with his young family and their chocolate Labrador puppy. Four doors down, at the bottom of the close in the big house with the electric gates, was a property developer, Mr Turns. It was a long way from home, and Gordon and Sally liked it that way.

'It's looking a bit wild,' I said.

'Your mum planted some tomatoes in the lean-to, do you see?'

'I'll make a salad with them.'

'They're a bit green still. I've got some tinned carrots if you want some with your spaghetti.'

At first I thought he was joking. Then the charge of a memory surged through me. A dented can, with its torn white and orange label, rolling back and forth on the lino. A salty, slimy taste in my mouth; his shouting drowned out by the thrum of blood rushing through my ears. 'No thanks,' I said.

'Your mum said you must eat your vegetables.'

'I'm not twelve!'

He opened the can and poured the contents into a saucepan. 'You need to eat properly, Heather.'

'Sure, okay, I'll have a few,' I said. I would bend to him in the way I never did as a child, hoping it would make a difference.

I remembered his lessons back then: how grateful I should be for every crumb – or tinned carrot – on my plate. How those crumbs equalled the blood, sweat and tears of their sacrifice.

So many lectures. So many mistakes.

I had left a fingerprint smear on the paintwork in the lounge and they accused me of taking the walls that housed me for granted. I had lost a sock from my sports kit and they lectured me about how hard they had worked to pay for every thread of clothing I wore. I had asked for £3 extra pocket money for a school trip and they retold stories about their childhoods of paper rounds and glued shoes and meat-free stews. And what about the poor souls who turned up at the Salvation Army soup kitchen every Sunday!

My sense of inadequacy ran thick in my veins still. I strived to be like them, but they were a hard act to live up to.

So I ate my slimy carrots, forcing back a retch with each mouthful. I felt his attention on me completely, though his eyes were on his own bowl.

We ate in silence mostly, with the odd throat-clearing and a failed attempt at some weather chat and a sad story about one of the poor souls at the soup kitchen, where he and my mother still volunteered. Shouldered by guilt, I pictured swathes of time with him and his heartbreaking stories, and was weighed down by sadness.

'I've recorded a documentary for us,' he said.

'Cool.'

'It's about the agricultural history of Missouri.'

The episodes of the second series of an American comedy that I had been looking forward to watching on my iPad would have to wait, for months, possibly.

'I'll just unpack first,' I said.

As I squeezed through the crack of the bedroom door, stopped by my suitcase on the floor behind it, I felt uneasy. The walls had been washed clean of the Blu Tack remnants of my posters and the windowsills were clear of my old teddy bears, but the childhood memories lingered in the air like they had been suspended in jelly. The walls seemed even closer together, the bed smaller, and the view out of the window – if a hedge could be called a view – was more limiting than ever. I remembered how much I had hated that hedge. How the evergreen leaves had looked the same all year round, trimmed and shaped and stunted into a waxy, boxy barrier against the expanse of world beyond it. Immediately behind it had sat the Huxley Seniors' 1970s bungalow, long and thin on its five-acre plot. Now, Copper Lodge dwarfed its original footprint. My heartbeat spiked off the chart at the thought of seeing it in real life tomorrow.

I sat on the soft bed, and had begun compressing my grown-up clothes into the tiny wardrobe when a stack of purple and yellow exercise books fell out. Feeling the need to cheer myself up, I leafed through my Year 4 English book, smiling at my messy handwriting, and came across a story that gave me an unexpected lurch in my stomach.

My House

The house next door is bigger than my house. It is long and thin and has lots of windows. It has a big massive garden and a swimming pool because they are rich. I can see the water is sparkly when I look through the hedge. I really want to swim in the pool but Mummy and Daddy said I am not allowed. Mummy said that if I work hard I can live in a big house and she said that without hard work nothing grows but weeds but I don't want a big house and I like weeds. Daisies are weeds and I think they are so pretty. When I grow up I want to swim all day and not work and wear daisy chains and I want to live in a big house too.

Good effort, Heather! ☺ Remember the exercise was to write about your own house. Use more descriptive words. What colour was the house? How many storeys does it have? Who lives there? (2 house points)

Unnerved, I stuffed all four exercise books under the bed and changed into my pyjamas.

After brushing my teeth clean of the taste of carrot, I sat in front of Dad's tiny black-and-white television to watch the solemn documentary about America's Midwest. The narrator droned on. I wanted to hurry him along to the end, so I could go to bed and wake up and go to work, desperate to get the first day over and done with, too sick with curiosity to wait any longer. My stomach rolled over, turning inside out and upside down. As the minutes ticked by, I became more and more nervous and excited about the prospect of seeing Lucas Huxley again. It was going to be impossible to get to sleep tonight as I played over how I would simply say hello.

CHAPTER FOUR

Elizabeth watched Lucas approach the house. He was wearing his tennis whites. As white as the torn-up letter from Channing House in the bin by her feet.

She picked up her mobile, pressed Bo Seacart's number and listened to the tone from New York ring and ring in her ear.

'Please pick up,' she said, mostly to herself. She was eking out a few more moments of hope, wanting to please Lucas, earn one of his proud smiles. The strange coldness inside her, like a rod of ice, could be melted by one of those smiles.

Her failure to action both of his simple Post-it note requests – to speak to Bo Seacart and send the forms back to Channing House – sent a stinging feeling to the back of her eyes. She regretted her overhasty ripping-up of the letter. The prospect of confessing to Lucas set her blood pumping too fast through her body. Her fingers jittered and she dropped the phone. The ringtone cut out.

Picking it up, she nipped outside to meet Lucas head-on.

'Hi,' she called out.

'Hi,' he said, smiling. 'Everything okay? You look harassed.'

He always said this when she was late. On their first date he had said it when she had turned up to the restaurant late, having been thrown off a broken-down 148 bus. Huddled under an umbrella, with her dress sticking to her knees, she had been soaked through and freezing cold, but she had said she was fine. Throughout dinner, she had worried about how she would pay for the meal and had felt the scratch of the price tag on her ribs, praying that the rain hadn't ruined her chances of taking the dress back to Jigsaw the next day. The Mayfair restaurant had included the prices on Lucas's menu only, which had been a great relief to her. She had been too broke to be a feminist, to insist on going Dutch or make a point about the chauvinistic menus. Two years later, in his wedding speech, Lucas had admitted he had re-ordered a cut-up credit card to pay for that meal.

'Sorry I'm late. The time slipped by,' she said now, nestling into him to hide the worry on her face.

He dropped his tennis bag on the bench as they passed and made a call. 'Gordon! If you're swinging by the bench at any point, could you take my rackets back to the house? Only if you get the chance. After you've fixed that bloody ball machine. Thanks, mate.'

He hung up and wrapped both arms around her as they walked. She felt his dampness and the contours of his muscles. She glanced up at him, analysing his features for clues to his mood. He looked very handsome today. There were days when she couldn't see it. His colouring was unusually sensitive to his moods. Angst about work could suck the health out of his skin, painting purple under his eyes, turning his hair from gold to brown. This afternoon, he was beautiful, which boded well.

'I thought he fixed the ball machine yesterday?' she asked, completely disinterested in the ball machine, but wanting to stave off his inevitable questions about Bo Seacart or Channing House.

'He did. It jammed again.'

The gulping of the old pool filter could be heard through the thick clouding of the hedge as they walked past. She was about to suggest a swim, when she remembered he had a dinner meeting with an American financier at his London club this evening.

'What did Bo say when you called? Are they coming?' he asked.

She pulled away and hooked her hair behind her ears. 'I haven't spoken to her yet.'

'Didn't you get my notes?'

Elizabeth's gaze wandered along the pathways that flanked the packed, vibrant borders, over the dancing heads of the flowers in the meadow and across the Surrey Hills as she thought up her lie.

'I've been trying all afternoon but I haven't got through. Walt's assistant said she'd gone to the house in the Hamptons.'

She wasn't sure why she hadn't attempted to reach Bo earlier on in the day. She regretted that she hadn't tried harder. It was a problem of hers, being lazy. She watched other women juggle full-time motherhood and successful careers without any help, and wondered how they managed it. Hours seemed to pass her by and nothing of merit was ever achieved. Lucas was the one who achieved.

'Have you tried her there?'

'I don't have her number and her assistant wouldn't give it out.'

None of this was true. It might have been, had she tried.

'And you remembered to send the forms to Channing House?'

'Yes,' she said, in a panic.

'Where are your shoes? There might be glass in the barn. You need shoes, Elizabeth,' he said gently. Again his phone was at his ear. 'Agata, could you please do me a big favour? Might you be able to bring down Elizabeth's shoes? You're a superstar, thank you.'

As they waited for Agata at the door to the small barn, Lucas stood with his legs wide and his hands in his pockets, casting an eye over the building.

Elizabeth followed the trail of his gaze over the tumbledown structure. Moss was holding the tiles together. The old brick walls were being supported by climbers. But through his eyes, she could see its potential.

'Piotr will need to repoint this,' he said, peering in through the grime of a window. 'And he'll need to enlarge this opening. Walt loves light. He's obsessed.'

'What will happen if I can't persuade Bo to come?'

He looked down at her. A hint of fear flashed up in his solid blue eyes.

'If they don't come, it means the deal's off.'

'It's really that serious?'

Lucas untucked his T-shirt from his shorts, like a man in a suit might loosen his tie. He laughed, a slightly false laugh. 'You know how he rolls. If he doesn't like me, he won't trust me, and if he doesn't trust me, the partnership deal goes up in flames.'

Four years ago, Elizabeth and Lucas had visited Bo and Walt Seacart for supper at their penthouse, where talk of a Seacart–Huxley partnership had first begun. They had sat around a low coffee table on cushions and eaten Goan curry out of wooden bowls. The price tag was still on the bottom of Elizabeth's – $375. Lucas had been squashed in between a Portuguese screenwriter called Tito Dantas and a documentary essayist called Jed – just Jed – who made films about the effects of architecture on social cohesion in modern-day Eastern Europe. Lucas had been keen to talk to Walter, who had been distracted by conference calls to clients in Uruguay, and he had struggled to find conversational common ground with the other guests. Had they talked about finance and economics, he would have been a fountain of knowledge, but he lacked a frame of reference for the discussions of the intellectual elite. Socially he was fun and smart – street-smart – and charming, but he rarely read books, except blockbuster thrillers on holiday; he only ever watched films to the end when he was strapped into his seat on a plane and he only bought art for his walls if he thought it might make him money. In the end, Tito Dantas and Jed had talked across him, allowing Lucas to slip away unnoticed. He had found Walt in his study. They had drunk whisky together and discussed the growth prospects of Lucas's property portfolio, in which he wanted Walt to invest.

'Of course he likes you,' Elizabeth said.

She genuinely believed that Walt Seacart had fallen for Lucas's charms on day one. Shortly after the New York dinner party, Walter had been in touch about carrying out some preliminary due diligence on Lucas's company with a view to investing. To celebrate, Lucas had not bought champagne or called a friend to share the good news; he had instead read up on modern architecture and decided to build their copper-roofed house. In many ways, he was a grown man who had not grown up. Elizabeth had been attracted to that boyish vulnerability when they had first met.

She stepped forward to kiss his lips. '*I* like you.'

Lucas allowed her a short kiss and cupped her face. 'You're my secret weapon. We're so near to closing this deal. If Bo likes us, *he'll* like us, and then we'll be so rich we won't know what to do with it all.'

Elizabeth could not see the merit in having more. She imagined being as rich as Bo Seacart, and pictured herself living Bo's life, padding barefoot across the mahogany floorboards of her Upper East Side penthouse apartment, sipping fennel tea in silk yoga trousers and headscarf – Bo had a knack of tying a batik turban over her blonde hair and looking dizzyingly beautiful – walking her two sausage dogs through Manhattan, eating her professional chef's superfood salads, buying the right kind of art and furniture to fill their many homes: a beach house on Long Island, a hideaway in Costa Rica, an apartment in Sydney, where Bo's mother now lived, and a 262-foot matt-black superyacht moored in Mykonos. But she was exhausted by the idea of managing all those homes, which would be empty most of the year. And if she wore a turban and walked sausage dogs, she would feel utterly ridiculous. But she understood what drove Lucas, and that was enough for her.

'Here's Agata,' he said. 'You're a darling, Agata, thank you.' His eyes followed the girl as she walked away. 'Has she lost weight?' he asked quietly.

Elizabeth refused to acknowledge his question and kept her head down to tie the laces of her white sneakers. A sharp pain shot from ear to ear. A doctor had once explained to her that this pain was a sign of stress or an oncoming migraine, rather than a brain tumour.

Lucas said, 'Let's take a look inside, shall we?'

'Gosh, this is a mess,' she said, peering in.

The floor was covered in hazards. Rusty nails were sticking out of wood panels. Glass shards shone from under piles of leaves. Old tools lay in a corner that might not have seen daylight in a hundred years.

Carefully, she followed him in, inhaling the smells of damp concrete and mulch. Through the window at the back of the building, she could see Agata and Piotr's parked caravan.

'You really think you can get this done before the fourth of July?' she asked.

Lucas clapped his hands together. The noise made Elizabeth jump. 'I want *you* to be the one to get it done before the fourth of July.'

She managed a smile through the swirl of panic that gathered in her chest. 'No. No way.'

'Yes way. I want you to project-manage Piotr on the renovation and be in charge of organising the summer party this year.'

'It's too soon, Lucas.'

'Elizabeth, the negotiations on the deal take up every second of my energy.'

'But I can't do all this *and* the party. Not by the fourth. It only gives me eight weeks.'

'Piotr knows what he's doing. And you used to love the party-planning every summer. You can do it standing on your head.'

She pulled the sleeves of her jumper down. 'I did used to love it.'

'Okay, then. Good.'

Without delay, Lucas sped through a list of requirements for the renovation and she tapped them into her phone, wishing she had a pen and paper. His expectations of her, of everyone, of everything, of life, were so high, it was hard to keep up.

'Slow down. It's too much,' she said.

Lucas sighed, and she felt useless before she had even begun. Raising his eyes to the cobwebbed rafters, he put his palms together as if in prayer and rested them on his lips. Then he spoke.

'If you manage this for me, we can maybe forget the idea of Channing House. Find a day school for her.'

'Are you serious?'

'Yes. Deadly. If you can handle it, it'll prove you're better. Then we won't have to explain ourselves to anyone.'

'And you think I can do it?'

'Yes, I do. It's smoke and mirrors, Elizabeth. That's all. Smoke and mirrors.'

'Smoke and mirrors,' she repeated, nodding.

'You're game?'

'Yes. I'm game,' she said, trying to sound convincing.

'Good. Okay then.'

'Shoot.'

He smiled at her and continued. 'For maximum light, I think we need the existing glass pantiles to be converted rather than filled in.'

Unable to type as fast as he was talking, she pressed the voice record button. When he had finished, she said firmly, 'I'll talk to Piotr as soon as he's back from London.'

'Good. You're great with him,' he said, stooping under the door frame to go outside.

She thought of Piotr and his strange face; his poor English, his brusque manner, his sour smell. He was a man from beyond the horizon, who had once had both feet planted into that sloping-away other-world.

'And then we've got outside to think about,' Lucas added.

Elizabeth followed. She said, 'Sally can do one of her beautiful flower borders here.'

'God, haven't I told you? Sally's going to be away for six months. Gordon is bringing in Heather, their daughter, to work in her place.'

'Heather? Really?' Elizabeth's mind swirled with this news. She had not met Heather Shaw, but she knew enough about her to feel immediately on edge. That familiar pain shot across her skull like a laser. A few months had passed since her last migraine, and she hoped this wasn't the beginning of one. She feared the crushing pain that would radiate through her forehead and pound behind her eyes, disabling her until she would be forced to retreat to a darkened room; but even more terrifying were the hallucinations and disquieting visions that often accompanied them.

Pressing two fingers into her right temple, dulling the head-ache, stopping the spiral of unpleasant thoughts, she asked, 'Is Sally all right?'

'Her sister's unwell, sadly.'

Perhaps it was the temporary loss of Sally, in her bobbled jumpers and pearly pink lipstick, that bothered Elizabeth more than the idea of Heather working here. Elizabeth did not like change, and Sally had been a constant and friendly presence in their grounds. For two decades before Lucas had inherited the plot, the Shaws' green fingers had worked the soil, managing and tending to their design of the structured topiary and the looser seasonal plantings.

'I'll talk to Gordon about the borders,' she said, zipping along the front of the barn, determined to stay focused, noting the tangles and weeds, anxious about them. Thinking aloud, she said, 'Gordon is better at the maintenance side of things, but I'm never sure his design skills are up to much.'

'That's a bit harsh,' Lucas laughed.

'Oh, you know what I mean,' she said, knowing that he did. 'How do you want to manage the finances? Do you want to top up my housekeeping account? Or would you prefer it if I came to you to ask for cash?'

'I'm not sure it's a good idea to put all that money into your account like we did on the build.'

Elizabeth's palms sweated. 'God, I was such an idiot.'

'We'll do it in cash where we can, I think. Just to be safe. Or you can ask for my credit card whenever you need to make a transaction.'

'Okay,' she agreed, feeling better.

'Right, I'm off,' he said. 'I won't be late.'

'Don't forget to say goodbye to the kids!' she called after him. Lucas, who loved Isla and Hugo very much, would not intend to neglect them, but when he was fired up about work, he disengaged too easily.

'Good luck party-planning!' he called back.

The summer party was her opportunity to fix what she had broken. It was an incentive to get going, to stop moping, to keep Isla at home. She would persuade Bo and Walt Seacart to stay as their guests, manage the build on the barn conversion and help Lucas to seal the Seacart–Huxley investment deal. Their house and garden would be her new place of work.

She thought of Gordon and Sally's daughter turning up for her first day tomorrow. She breathed while counting down from twenty and found a strawberry bonbon loose in her pocket. Chewing slowly, she promised herself she would keep it together. Not even that would derail her.

CHAPTER FIVE

My first day at Copper Lodge had arrived. To please my father, I had woken up half an hour early to make some real Scottish porridge, which I hoped would be as good as Aunt Maggie's.

The rigmarole of my aunt's method was only for the dedicated. I had watched her make it: stirring the steel-cut oats and whole milk with a wooden spurtle, always clockwise with her right hand, fearing the Devil would come for her if she changed hands or direction; round and round for half an hour, adding the essential pinch of salt, letting it simmer and bubble. She would put a pot of cream in the centre of the table for the family to dip into while we ate, always standing up, which my mother thought was bad for the digestion. When my father had been young, batches of this godly porridge had been poured into a kitchen drawer, left to cool and cut into slices. Every morning, he and his sister had taken a slice wrapped in brown paper and eaten it for breakfast on their way to school.

This morning, my porridge had turned out stodgy and lumpy.

Dad ate each mouthful of this *un*godly offering with stalwart persistence, in silence. I made myself some toast and feared that I had inadvertently conjured the Devil.

We gathered our fleeces and sandwich tins and walked next door.

My toes and fingers tingled with nerves. Never before had I been officially invited onto the property; never before had I spoken to Lucas in the company of others.

'Have you switched your mobile off?' Dad asked me.

'Yup.'

'And the toilet in the camper van is out of order, so they've allowed us to use the one in the main house.'

'What camper van?'

'A Polish couple live in the grounds. The girl looks after the kids and her boyfriend is a builder. He's going to work on the barn conversion.'

'Wow. Any other staff I should know about?'

'That's it. Us and them.'

'Us and them,' I murmured, wishing that I wasn't meeting Lucas again as his employee, his gardener. I was then deeply ashamed of myself for thinking it. My father was proud of his position and his work, and so was I.

'And remember, if you're ever invited into the main house, take your muddy boots off.'

'What's Elizabeth Huxley really like?' I whispered as my father pressed the code into the sliding gate. Up until now, I had resisted pestering him for titbits of gossip, cautious of giving myself away, but the anticipation of meeting her overrode my previous restraint.

'She's our boss, and that's all you need to know.'

'But is she nice?' I persisted.

He sighed, speaking quietly. 'I don't know. Rich people are different.'

I chuckled. 'You don't really believe that, do you?'

'Money changes people.'

'On the surface, maybe.'

'Just be polite when you meet them today.'

'Why wouldn't I be?' I said, goose bumps running across my skin.

Behind an enclave of tall poplar trees near the main road, my father opened up a wooden garage that must have belonged to the original house, where the tools, the lawnmower and larger machinery were kept. We left our sandwiches on the workbench and headed up to the main house. The magazine photographs had not prepared me for how impressive it was in real life, or for its unusual style. It was modern and low-slung, and stretched across the width of the garden, almost camouflaged. Its green copper roof allowed the round concrete pillars and shiny glass walls, unnatural and man-made, to settle into its environment. I could see right through the timber frame to the meadow and green landscape beyond, as if it were an apparition of a building, a distortion of molecules. The architect's mix of materials was clashing at first, yet as my eye adjusted to its design, to its unfinished quality, I began to appreciate the juxtapositions. Its beauty spoke in whispers to a knowing audience. Like a beautiful woman who dared to arrive at a party wearing sneakers and no make-up, there was an aura of arrogance, of separateness.

I gulped in the details, in awe of how perfect it was.

The garden – my parents' creation – complemented the modern architecture. I remembered my mother's sketches and their original plantings. After years of maturity, it was more beautiful than ever; award-worthy. They had added a structured hedge design that guarded the loose planting in the beds, stepping up to the task they had faced after the build.

I remembered visiting the more traditional garden that had belonged to Mr and Mrs Huxley Senior. Every year they had allowed hordes of locals to mill around the beds and along the paths at the Surrey open garden event. Mr Huxley had spoken to the punters about the garden as though he had designed it himself, which had not bothered my parents. Creating it had been enough for them. This garden was their first child, their entire focus. I had always accepted that my father loved it a little more than he loved me. In spite of the many challenges it threw their way, it certainly never answered back like I had.

But every swirling petal and shuddering leaf belonged to Lucas Huxley, and my initial wonder was toned down by the anxiety I now felt about seeing him.

'Ready?' my father asked, towering over me as I knelt in the flower bed.

'Yup!' I said, expecting another task.

Since this morning, he had been teaching me how to use the tools to trim the hedges, how to mow strips across the lawn, how to chainsaw the wood correctly, how to dig holes big enough for the route systems of an avenue of trees, how to weed around swimming pools and tennis courts. He had even shown me a brick wall that he had laid and a fence that he had built. At Copper Lodge, he turned his hand to anything they asked of him: fixing outbuildings' roofs, digging trenches for cabling, realigning garage doors, grouting patio flagstones, unblocking drains. There didn't seem to be enough hours in the week ahead to make a dent in the long list of tasks we had been asked to complete. It didn't faze me. Hard work equalled peace of mind. Anything was better than fretting about money in the middle of the night.

'Lucas is home and he's keen to say hello.'

My stomach flipped. I had been so busy, I had almost forgotten.

'Cool,' I said, brushing off the soil from my hands, feeling very uncool.

'It'll only take five minutes and then we can head off home.'

I straightened, and walked stiffly up to the house, swallowing repeatedly and wiping my sweaty hands up and down my jeans, blowing on them, wanting to cool them. I tried to remember how to breathe.

A woman a few years younger than me with peroxide-blonde hair was waiting for us by the floor-to-ceiling sliding windows. As I took off my muddy boots, I looked around at the interior.

It was the same airy, sparse room that I had scrutinised so often in the copy of *House & Garden*. The slate and glass galley kitchen was at the back, adjacent to the sitting room area of low leather sofas. There were hardwood partition walls hung with modern paintings like splatters that stopped where the ceiling vaulting of beams began. However impressive it was, the reality of the house reminded me of viewing rentals with Rob. The estate agents' details always promised us the perfect flat, but when we viewed them in 3D, they were smaller than we had imagined, and had smells and aspects that changed them for the worse. It wasn't that I disliked the interior of Copper Lodge; it was simply less soulful than I had imagined. There was a sinus-clearing rush of cleanliness, and sharp edges everywhere. The chilliness from the concrete underfoot seemed to rise through my bones and into my head.

'I am Agata,' the young woman said, in a strong Polish accent.

'Hi.' I put my hand out, and she took it for a moment, absorbing its tremor.

'He's in the …' she began, pointing to a door, twisting her peroxide ponytail into a knot before undoing it again and repeating the process. She was so thin, she looked like a pretty child with malnutrition. Her eyes were close together, appealingly so, but they were deep-set, haunted. Her cheeks were covered in a layer of fine downy hair.

'The study?' Gordon said.

Agata nodded and handed us a pair of fluffy grey slippers each.

'I'm fine in socks,' Dad said, sniffing. But I took mine, too nervous to say no.

'I just get …' Agata said, darting into the kitchen and pouring some frothed milk into a cup of coffee. 'For Lucas.'

My father and I followed her through a heavy brown door into a narrow corridor that was darker than the rest of the house. The walls were panels of polished wood decorated with more paintings. Too many, I thought. But I was no judge.

Before Agata had a chance to open the middle of three doors, Lucas burst through it, almost bouncing. 'Hello,' he beamed, ruffling his loopy blond curls and blinking his long, fair eyelashes rapidly at us as though he hadn't seen human life in years.

Blood collected in my heart and it thumped, once, as though announcing the arrival of a big important feeling. He looked even more handsome than I remembered. As a younger man, he had had shorter hair and a rangier body, but now his hair curled behind his ears, like an earnest boy's, and his broad shoulders and olive tan spoke of wealth and a good life. I was reminded of how commanding his height was, and of the small mole high on his cheekbone, perfectly placed, where an artist might draw it. I wanted the door to shut again, allowing me to re-present myself as a completely different person. A magnificent person who had sophisticated conversations up my sleeve, and clean clothes. Appearing in front of him as normal old me was agonising.

'I'm Heather,' I said inanely, and then stuck my hand out for him to shake.

He took it. His touch could have melted me clean away. 'I'm Lucas,' he said, grinning, holding my hand for longer than an employer should.

My father cleared his throat, a small frown twitching in one eyebrow.

'Let's walk and talk while we wait for Elizabeth,' Lucas said, charging off.

Agata came up beside him to hand him his coffee. He took it and drank it with one small sip and two gulps. As he walked, his long limbs had a swinging, striding confidence. I shuffled along behind him, trying to keep up in my ridiculous slippers.

We shared eye contact for a split second as he spoke over his shoulder, and I doubted my heart could withstand the shocks of electricity.

'Where's Elizabeth, does anyone know?' he asked, taking his mobile out from his shorts pocket. Before any of us had a chance to answer, he was speaking into it. 'Hi, darling. Gordon and Heather are here to talk about the borders around the barn, remember? … Ha! Don't worry, we'll wait for you.'

Agata looked at me briefly.

'Agata, you make the best coffee in the world,' Lucas said, leaving his cup on the breakfast bar and adding, 'Tell Elizabeth we'll be down by the barn.'

My father and I followed him into the garden.

Lucas slowed down, hanging back to walk next to me along the pathway. 'How's your auntie doing?' he asked, dropping his voice. His eyes matched the clear sky behind him, as though he were born to complement it.

'Much better now that Mum's there.'

'We'll miss her. But thrilled to have you on board,' he said, speeding up ahead again. His nervous energy was infectious. I became excited about an unidentifiable adventure ahead, and eager to follow.

'Thanks,' I said.

We passed the laurel hedge. It had grown to twice its original size, but I recognised where I was immediately. The water gulped at the filter. The feel of the pool water was a sensory memory that raised the hairs across my arms.

'Through there is the swimming pool, but then you probably remember that,' Lucas said.

'Dad never let me near it,' I replied coolly, glancing at my father, the blood coursing through my veins.

My father looked up, missing again what he had missed in the past. 'That laurel's due for a trim,' he said.

Lucas caught my eye and I silently willed him not to talk about the pool again. There was a playful *Dare me!* glint in his eye. My cheeks flamed.

'We really need Elizabeth,' he said, grinning. 'She had some ideas for the border, apparently.'

My face cooled, but before we reached the barn, he stopped and pointed at the delicate pink and white flowers that drooped behind the box hedge. 'What are those called again?' he asked me.

I gaped at him, startled by his audacity, then fired out my answer like a pupil asked to stand up in assembly. 'Bleeding hearts.'

'And the Latin?'

'*Lampro*—' my father began.

'*Lamprocapnos spectabilis,*' I cut in.

'You know your stuff.'

My father cleared his throat. 'Aye, she does.'

'Are you going to take over your dad's business here?'

'I retrained,' I said, flushing; it was a thorny subject between me and my father. 'I'm a swimming coach now.'

Lucas stared at me as though I had told him I was an astronaut. 'I'm glad,' he said before walking off.

Dad grabbed me by my belt loop and held me back. 'Why is he glad?' he whispered.

'Dunno,' I said, shrugging, looking down at my feet and hurrying to follow Lucas to the old barn.

We stood in a line in front of it, my breathing rapid as though I had been running. I was in the middle of the two men, feeling giddy, sensing right to my bones the different energy of both, the power emanating from them; recognising their lifelong influence on me.

I chewed the side of my tongue and admired the picturesque old barn, holding back a rising glee, hoping my father would not ask too many questions later.

Lucas checked his watch again, sighing. 'Elizabeth will be here any minute.'

The magazine photograph of her came into my mind. After years of imagining what she was like in person, I felt suddenly impatient to meet her and frustrated that she was late.

We went around to the back of the barn, where a man was up a ladder chipping out loose mortar from between the flint bricks. But I was distracted by an abandoned camper van parked under the shadow of a crooked tree. The vehicle was incongruous, an irregularity in the grounds, and I was quite shocked by the sight of it. It was run-down and lopsided due to a flat tyre. The windows were green with moss and grime. Then I noticed a pair of black boots next to the fold-out steps up to the door, and I felt uneasy. I did not want to believe that this heap was the camper van my father had talked about this morning, where Agata and Piotr lived. Surely the Huxleys would not allow anyone to sleep there while there were spare rooms in the huge, luxurious house a few yards away.

'Hello, Piotr! When d'you think you'll be done with the repointing?' Dad called out.

At first I thought Piotr was hunching over, until I realised his shoulders were set in a rounded, cowed hook over his narrow hips, like he had been carrying two heavy pails of water all his life. His baggy T-shirt did not hide his sinewy arms.

'Hello,' he said in a thick accent, ruffling the stiff spikes of his hair. 'I spend … London … two night … I finish this next day … no, no, sorry … the week next.'

Lucas looked to my father, who said, 'You're working two days in London next week, is that right? So you'll be finished with this next week. Yes?'

Piotr studied my father's lips as though they might offer up the answers after they had stopped moving. Finally he said, 'Yes.'

'Great. Thanks, Piotr,' Lucas said, looking at his phone. 'Great work. So, once he's finished the pointing, you can get on with the borders. Elizabeth has some—' he began. Then, 'Elizabeth! Darling!'

From around the corner, Elizabeth appeared. She was smaller than I had imagined, much shorter than Lucas, but their colouring was alike: a blond, blue-eyed brother and sister rather than husband and wife. Her short gold-spun hair was swept into a side parting. A sea-wave curl across her forehead was lacquered, tamed and tucked behind her delicate ears. Her diminutive soft features and sleepy eyelids gave her face an old-fashioned prettiness. She didn't seem to belong to real life. More suited to a black-and-white film or a Man Ray photograph, there was something watchable about her, something that made me stare, something that caused a sting of terrible envy, and fascination.

'Tell them about your vision,' Lucas said, gazing at her. 'She's going to transform this shit-heap for the Seacarts, aren't you, darling?'

Elizabeth offered her hand. 'Heather. Hello, I'm Elizabeth Huxley.' She held a smile for me, with seeming effort, but her fingers crushed my knuckles together. 'Bo and Walt Seacart will be staying here as our guests at the summer party,' she explained.

'Ah,' I said, imagining I should know who the Seacarts were.

'Do pass on our warm regards to your mother. We miss her here already.'

'Thank you, I will,' I replied, but I did not feel her warmth.

'Right, I'm off,' Lucas said. 'I'll be in my study if anyone needs me.' He sped away, tapping at his phone.

As soon as he was gone, Elizabeth dropped her smile and Piotr climbed back up his ladder.

'Tell me what you want in these beds,' she said. Her manner was disinterested enough to be rude.

My father's arms remained crossed over his chest. 'Lucas told us you had some ideas, Mrs Huxley.'

Elizabeth visibly shivered. 'You go first, Gordon.'

Dad began a monologue about the creative tension between the formal hedge structures and the more exuberant plantings;

how the spring flowers and plants were currently being replaced by summer flowering ones; how the colour in the long borders should complement the strong shapes of the perennials, bragging about what already existed instead of helping her to decide what should be planted. In response, Elizabeth stifled a yawn. I could tell that neither of them knew what to do about the beds. There was a passive, distant tension between them that I didn't understand, as though they had once been angry at each other but had given up actively showing it. Nervously I spoke up in my mother's place, wondering if she had mediated between them before.

'Perhaps some yellow colours here would look good against the brick. Something like a "Canadale Gold", or some spiraea "Gold Mound"? And then some tall shots of colour, purple flowers maybe, to break it up, like the *Lupinus polyphyllus*?'

Elizabeth handed me her phone and said, 'Show me what they look like.'

On her screen saver, there was a black-and-white photograph of her and her two children, round-cheeked and fair-haired, pressing kisses onto her while she laughed. The sparkle in her eyes surprised me, and I wondered where it had gone today.

I searched for images of each flower online and showed her.

'Hmm. Gordon, what do you think?'

Holding my breath, I waited for my father to respond, fearing I might have spoken out of turn, undermining him on his territory. His large finger passed back and forth across his bottom lip. 'Yes, that could work.'

'That's settled then. If you could price it up for us?' Elizabeth said. 'Obviously Lucas will have to sign off on it.'

'You realise we won't be able to plant anything until the renovations are finished, Mrs Huxley? When are your guests due?' my father said.

Elizabeth looked at him and then away, at Piotr, who was further up his ladder, chipping away at the cement.

'The fourth of July,' she said. 'If they arrive at all …' Her gaze seemed to melt away.

I was already intrigued by the Seacarts, about why they commanded this level of attention to detail. Any guests staying at our flat in Rye, however loved they were, would be lucky to get an extra pillow for the couch.

'Eight weeks away. That gives us plenty of time to order anything we won't have time to grow.' Dad nodded.

'Hmm?' she murmured.

It seemed we had lost her.

On the way to the garden centre, Dad was whistling. I didn't want to spoil his good mood, but I had many questions.

'What's the story with that camper van, Dad?'

'Put your feet down,' he said, taking his hand off the wheel to hit my boot, prompting me to remove them from the dashboard.

'What's it doing there?'

'I told you this morning. Agata and Piotr live in it.'

'No way.' I refused to believe that Lucas would allow anyone to live like that.

'Yes way.'

'You're saying that they live full-time in that thing?'

'Piotr works on a construction site in London two nights a week, but Agata lives there full-time.'

'It isn't fit for anyone to live in.'

'Did you go inside?'

'Course not.'

'How do you know it's not fit to live in then?'

'You're saying it might be like a wee cosy love nest inside, like a George Clarke small space?' I cried, incredulous.

'Who's George Clarke?' he said irritably.

'Never mind.'

Through a tight jaw he said, 'It's none of our business. Agata and Piotr can choose to live how they want.'

'They're *choosing* that?'

'There are plenty of jobs for someone with Piotr's skills. They don't *have* to work for the Huxleys.'

There was a pause. 'But why wouldn't the Huxleys put them up in their massive house?'

'It's none of our business,' he repeated, cranking the van into fifth gear. The tools rattled in the back as we charged up the motorway.

Grumpily I mumbled, 'Lucas had better be paying them well.'

Without warning, my father's mood turned. 'Of course he bloody well does,' he hissed.

Shocked by this switch in him, I clung to the side of the bench seat. The traffic queue arrived at our bumper and he slammed on the brakes. I jerked forward. We were now stationary.

'How dare you judge those people for how they live?' he hissed.

'I wasn't judging them.'

His voice grew angry. 'Your problem is you've had everything given to you on a goddam plate.'

'Dad, please. I didn't mean to sound like … I do know how lucky I am,' I said.

My cheeks were smarting, as though he had struck me. I knew that ingratitude riled my father more than any other vice. A few years ago, he had taken me to watch the demolition of the Red Road flats in Glasgow, where he had grown up. 'That was ours, at the top,' he had said, pointing up. In the fierce wind, we had craned our necks to stare at the six twenty-eight-storey buildings wrapped in red tarpaulin, lurid against the white sky, emblematic of the social housing failures of the 1960s – and of my father's brutal childhood. He had described the coffin-like lifts and the views to Ben Lomond from the top; the suicides, and how the asbestos in the walls had killed his mother. As the buildings had collapsed to dust, he had stared on, steely-eyed, squeezing my hand until I thought it would drop off, insisting, as his father had done before him, that the flats were better than the slums they had moved from. He had been aggressively proud and deeply sad, and for the first time, I had understood the deprivations of his upbringing.

'Then remember this: we're a whisker away from living in that thing with them. Get it? Your mum and I are too old to look for other work. We've been there too long. We couldn't cope with the upheaval of starting on a new garden. Or working on smaller gardens. It'd be back-breaking for us, especially for your mum.'

'The Huxleys would never let you go.'

He ignored me, continuing on one track. 'Your mum loves that garden. It's her whole life.'

'I know that.'

'And there isn't a damned thing we can do about that Polish couple. They have food on their table and a roof over their heads. I'd call that a good start.'

'Sorry.' I stared out of the window. My hands were sweating. I squeezed up against the door. The landscape blurred through my tears.

He parked up outside the garden centre. As I sat there fiddling with the elastic of my jacket, he put his arm around me and kissed me on the side of my head with a clumsy burst of affection. He had not embraced me for years, and I tried to appreciate it, but my return hug was stiff. I felt dirtied by his attempts to woo me back, and as off-kilter as that camper van had been.

He opened the van door and turned back to me before jumping down. 'Don't look so glum. I know you mean well, love, but Agata and Piotr do all right, believe me.'

My thoughts rewound, and I contemplated Elizabeth Huxley. Having met her, I wasn't so sure about her. She had been cold towards my father today, and oddly separate. *Money changes people,* my father had said. Perhaps he didn't like her and was protective towards Lucas, whom he had seen grow up in that garden. As an adult, Lucas had been loyal to him, and as far as I was aware, my parents had been treated like family members.

And then there was me. How had he treated me?

A lost image came to mind, of his torso, blue-white from the water, gliding through pockets of air as he twisted to the surface. I closed my eyes, trying to hold on to the memory, see more than the flash of him.

'The camper van's probably nice inside,' I murmured, deciding I might check for myself tomorrow, hoping there would be a cosy, well-maintained interior, clinging to my certain belief that Lucas would look after his staff properly.

If I discovered otherwise, I feared it would cast shadows over my deeply settled understanding of who Lucas was; and I didn't want to doubt him, as it would call into question what had happened between us all those years ago, when I had been a starry-eyed girl who had hung on his every word.

CHAPTER SIX

With the phone at her ear, Elizabeth listened to the series of long beeps from the States, and her stomach fluttered. This was the vital first phase of Project Party. Droplets of water rained down on her. She looked on from her sunlounger at Isla and Hugo playing in the pool with Agata.

Bo answered. 'Elizabeth, honey, can I call you back in two?'

Elizabeth's heart sank. It was the third time in as many days that she had tried to get hold of Bo. If she couldn't talk to her today, Lucas's dream of getting the Seacarts to come to their summer party would be over.

'Sure, sure, I'm on the mobile,' she said, and hung up, unwrapping a sweetie and placing it on her tongue.

Without Bo, there would be no point to a party. If there was no party, there would be no deal. If there was no deal, Lucas would be angry with her. If Lucas was angry with her, Isla would go to boarding school in September. If Isla went to boarding school … Piotr came through the gate, halting her catastrophising. She brought her knees up to her chest. Damp patches formed under her arms.

After he had disappeared into the pool shed, she loosened the scarf around her neck and watched her children play. She could not expose her own body in a swimsuit yet. The bruising on her neck was at the yellow stage, looking worse than it had when it was at its most painful. If the children saw the marks, they would ask her how she'd hurt herself.

The pool water moved and shone, but under the surface many of the mosaic tiles were missing and the grout was mouldy. The children didn't care. Their glee rang through the air as Agata sprayed them with the water gun. Elizabeth noticed her beaming at Piotr when he emerged from the shed with a circular saw, and she realised it was the first time she had seen the girl smile in three days.

Piotr said something to her in Polish, and she wiggled her hips at him. Her belly-button ring jingled in the hollow between her hip bones. Elizabeth watched Piotr's eyes on his girlfriend's body and remembered Lucas's comment about her weight. Was it normal for him to notice? How much else did he notice about her?

Her mobile chirruped, saving her from her thoughts. She took a deep breath, heady with relief, and picked up.

'Hello?'

'It's Bo. Sorry about that, Elizabeth. My dog-walker just arrived and I had to pay him.'

'No problem at all. How are you?'

'Actually, super-positive at the moment. How about you, honey?'

Elizabeth watched Hugo lose his balance on the loose paving slab at the deep end. The dilapidation of the pool was her fault. They had not been able to afford to renovate it after the overspend on the house build. Forgetting she was on the phone for a second, she sucked in her breath, ready to dart over to him. Hugo corrected himself and performed a perfect dive.

She let her breath out. 'Quite well really.'

'You don't sound so sure.'

Elizabeth smiled. 'I'm quite sure.'

'I can never tell with you British.'

She decided to broach the subject of her call straight away. From the handful of times she had met Bo, Elizabeth had gleaned that she did not like sycophants, and she would be too astute for rambling diversions.

'I was calling to find out your plans for London. I heard horrible rumours that Walt might be cancelling his trip in July.'

Bo's accent took on an English twang. 'Tell me about the weather first.'

'Quite lovely. The sun is out for a change and the kids are back from school and swimming in the pool. I'm going in for a dip in a minute.'

'Oh, you're so cruel. I'm stuck in the hot city when we should be by the ocean.'

'Why are you still in the city?'

'One of Walt's functions.' Bo sighed. 'He's being such a jerk about it. I'd have kicked up a stink if I didn't have to catch a friend's exhibition anyhow.'

'There's a Basquiat exhibition on at the Barbican in the summer. It'll be worth seeing when you're here. You and Walt *are* coming to the UK, aren't you?'

There was a pause.

'We're not clear on that yet.'

Elizabeth's chest tightened.

'You got our summer party "save the date" email, didn't you?'

'I did. But most years we go to the Hamptons on Independence Day weekend.'

'Maybe we'll have some red, white and blue fireworks in your honour.'

'Sounds fun,' Bo murmured.

'Benjamin Healing will be there,' Elizabeth coaxed, wondering if someone like Benjamin Healing could ever be persuaded to leave E7.

Bo laughed. 'Will your brother be there?'

'Of course. They're still great friends.'

Elizabeth had first met Bo at a Benjamin Healing exhibition sponsored by J. P. Morgan at the Max Wigram gallery in London. Bo had attached herself to her side and fired off questions about her brother, Jude, whose talent she had recognised when she'd seen his oil painting triptych exhibited alongside Healing's work. That night, Jude had sworn too much but had spoken about his work with elegance and intensity, and Bo had liked how handsome and socially awkward – and how poor – he was. Elizabeth's hope that the Seacarts, who were renowned collectors, might buy her brother's work had been dashed when Bo had put her little red dot next to one of Healing's paintings. It had disappointed her that Bo had bought into the dealers' hyperbole about Healing and bowed under pressure from Walt.

At the end of the night, Jude had not sold his triptych and Elizabeth had offered to buy it herself.

'You'd be doing it out of sympathy,' Jude had said.

'Not at all. I think they're the most beautiful paintings I've ever seen.'

'Then you can have them.'

'That's silly. I'll pay for them. You're broke.'

'I don't mind being broke.'

'I insist on giving you what they're worth.'

'It'll be Lucas's money.'

'Technically.'

'It's your birthday next month. I'll wrap them up for you.'

He had, and they were still wrapped up. And they were now worth a lot of money, which gave Elizabeth an idea.

'You know we're selling Jude's triptych,' she told Bo. As she blurted it out, she felt a twinge in her heart. Those paintings were her most precious possessions. She loved them more than anything she owned. But she loved Isla more.

Bo leapt on it. 'Are you *kidding* me?'

'Lucas is having them valued this week,' she said, even though Lucas had forgotten they existed.

'You're serious, right? I never forgave myself for listening to Walt at the Wigram. Walt's tastes are so Republican, it drives me nuts. That lame Healing painting's in our john now. It does nothing for me.'

Bo's rejection of Walt's Texan conservatism and her spurning of her own Martha's Vineyard upbringing – albeit not her inheritance – was everything to her. She wore her nonconformist image as a badge. It gave her credibility and integrity in the art world, setting her apart from the WASP housewives she spoke so scathingly about.

'They're here on the wall,' Elizabeth lied. 'You could take a look at them when you come to the party. I'm sure Lucas would prefer to make a private sale.' Lucas would sell his grandmother to ensure his deal with Walt Seacart went ahead, she thought.

'Let me get my diary,' Bo said.

Waiting for Bo to return to the phone was exciting. Elizabeth knew she'd read her correctly. Bo meditated in silk rather than Lycra; served up her Downward Dogs at the Harbour Club rather than the incense-infused yoga centre downtown; threw charity lunches to help the poor rather than question Walt's offshore accounts; forced her son to go to Harvard rather than let him travel the world with his guitar. She would want Jude's paintings more than ever now that the triptych – which she could have picked up for a couple of thousand pounds five years ago – had proven investment potential *and* was on sale.

'I'm going to do it in the shallow end!' Isla cried.

Elizabeth's attention shifted vaguely to the pool while she thought about how she might break the good news to Lucas when he returned from London later. Then her mind wandered to the renovations in the barn. Her mood board included a cream woodburner, tongue-and-groove whitewashed walls, a Scandi-style sofa, a gallery bed under the skylights, a cow-hide rug. Her brother's three paintings on the wall, like a promise.

'No, Isla,' Agata said.

'You're too chicken, chubby buttons!' Hugo taunted, diving in with the expert of a child many years his senior.

'Not there,' Agata said, wading at speed towards Isla, who hovered, dripping, on the side of the shallow end, bending into a crouching position for her dive. Elizabeth had a fleeting worry about the creases in her daughter's stomach and promised herself she'd give her fewer sweets.

'That's not how you do it!' Hugo laughed.

Bo's voice returned into Elizabeth's ear. 'I guess I could move that … and that …'

Elizabeth laid her head back against the cushion, held her breath and dug her nails into her palm, imagining Bo as the wind beneath Walt's superyacht's sails and Walt as putty in Bo's namaste-pressed hands.

'Walt and I could do with some fun, I guess. The Bridgehampton party scene is lame these days.'

Feigning an afterthought, Elizabeth said, 'Obviously you'd stay here in our guest house. Piotr can drive you up to town. And the roses will be in full bloom.'

There was a long pause. As she dared to hope that Bo would confirm, she heard Isla and Hugo's altercation grow louder.

'You know, between me and you, honey, I can't stand all the hot dogs and the flag-waving,' Bo continued. 'I'm a terrible American.'

'Come to the UK and escape it then. We can have a midnight swim with Benjamin Healing and Jude to sober us up,' Elizabeth teased, amazed that she was capable of such shameless manipulation.

There was a spluttering scream from Isla.

Elizabeth shot up from her chair. Isla's body bobbed to the surface. The water turned pink around her contorted face. Her mouth twisted for air. Deaf to Bo's next question, Elizabeth dropped the phone, tore off her sweater and ran, jumping in with her jeans still on. Piotr had come out of nowhere and dived in with her.

Isla flailed and splashed, and Elizabeth gulped down water, spluttering it out as she dragged her daughter out of the pool, helped by Piotr, whose bare skin met hers fleetingly.

On the side, Isla's head was on Elizabeth's thighs. Safe. Alive. Trickles of watery blood from what looked like a small cut on her forehead wove down her cheek and onto Elizabeth's jeans. Drips from Piotr's face splashed onto Elizabeth's bare arm as he bent over her. His chest heaved. Elizabeth took her eyes away.

'You must have hit your head on the steps. You're okay, my darling, you're okay,' she soothed, pulling Isla up into a hug, feeling the shuddering of her body, skin against skin. She buried her face in her daughter's neck. Through the chlorine, Isla's hair smelled of strawberry shampoo. She inhaled it and kissed her daughter just in the spot where it tickled.

'Stop it, Mummy!' Isla giggled, wriggling free.

'Here, have this, for the shock,' Elizabeth said, handing her one of the mint humbugs from her wet pocket, taking another herself, offering the remaining two to Agata and Hugo.

'Sorry, Piotr,' she said. His eyes left hers to trail down to her neck. She felt the bruises throb under his gaze.

'She could have drowned, Mummy!' Hugo cried, a little too gleefully.

'She okay. Your mummy is a hero,' Piotr said.

Hugo's little face became serious as he sucked on his sweet. Agata took his prescription goggles off and wrapped him in a towel. Elizabeth bunched another towel carefully around her own neck.

Her panic and shock dissipated. The memory of her abandoned phone call to Bo charged back into her mind. Her handset lay by the sunlounger. She could not let go of Isla yet. For certain, the line would have been lost when she dropped it. Bo would have moved on, to another acquaintance, another party, another painting, another million-dollar deal, and Elizabeth would have failed Lucas.

'Come on, let's get a plaster from the house.' She stood, leaving her phone on the grass, and held on to Isla, who walked woozily next to her.

Leaving Piotr behind, the group shuffled through the small gate that was cut into the laurel hedge. Out of nowhere, a tall, lanky young woman with a trail of auburn hair ran up to them.

'I heard the scream all the way from the meadow. Is everything okay?' she asked, panting.

Heather's skin was pink under the freckles of her cheekbones. Her almond eyes darted across each child's face. Her lashes – rust-coloured like her hair – fluttered wildly when she saw Isla's forehead. Her beauty was enhanced by the concern in her eyes. The kindness there distracted Elizabeth, for a moment, from what she knew about her.

Gathering herself, she pulled Isla closer and replied, 'Just a little graze.' Then she moved on, leaving Heather behind.

'Who was that pretty girl, Mummy?'

'The new gardener,' she replied, unable to utter her name.

They were quiet as they dripped into the house. While Elizabeth and Agata searched for a plaster, Isla lay on the sofa in her wet costume. Elizabeth let it go.

'I'll look for the plasters, Agata. Could you sit with her and make sure the blood doesn't drip anywhere. You're drier than me.'

After searching through the drawers in her sodden jeans, a little shaky still from the shock, she concluded they had run out. 'I'll pop to the shops.' It would give her a chance to call Bo back to explain.

'Elizabeth …' Agata began. 'I have …' She pointed outside, towards the barn.

'You have some in the camper van?'

She nodded. 'Me go?'

'I'll go. You stay with Isla.'

On the way to the van, Elizabeth detoured to the poolside to retrieve her phone. She noticed the four sweet wrappers floating on the surface of the water, fluttering, catching the light, like real gold but precious to nobody.

She pressed Bo's number. She would explain what had happened. It went straight to voicemail. She waited for the beep and then left her message. 'I'm so sorry about that, Bo. Isla hurt herself in the pool. She's fine now. Do call me back to talk about the summer, if you have a chance.'

But as soon as she hung up, she had the feeling that the moment to persuade her had passed. The more pressing issue was Isla's injury, which Lucas would immediately suspect was Elizabeth's fault. It would be true that she hadn't been concentrating, that she had neglected to keep her daughter safe. This failure drained her. Walking the last few feet to the camper van left her quite breathless.

The door swung loose on its hinges, and she noticed how dilapidated the van had become since Agata and Piotr had arrived three months ago. She hesitated, then trudged up the two narrow steps; a bag of rocks on her back in the form of the confession she would make to Lucas later.

Inside, the ceiling was low. She sucked in her breath and covered her nose and mouth. The smell of air freshener could not hide the reek of mould and toilet odour. Moss edged the windows, inside and out. The interior decor was dingy in dirty brown and mustard, ingrained with many years of dirt. Everywhere she turned, she saw broken hinges, loose metal strips and taped-up drawers. A rolled duvet was stuffed beneath the foldaway table, and two thin pillows lay across the seats. By the small tin sink Agata had placed a vase of pink blooming 'Red Dragon', which had been sown by Gordon in the meadow at the bottom of the garden. In this context, the flowers looked spiteful. Their beauty could not spread cheer in such a cold, sunless place. It was not a home, it was a health hazard.

Elizabeth felt sick when she compared this cramped existence to how she and Lucas lived only a few yards away. She reminded herself that it was not her fault that Agata and Piotr had refused to live in the house beyond that first week. And it was true that Agata spent most of her time working, while Piotr often left for London early, with his head-torch beam bobbing out of the gates, returning home too late to care where he laid his head. Nevertheless, for the few hours that they slept in this dirty space, Elizabeth could not imagine how their weary minds and bodies found rest enough to work hard day after day after day.

She shuddered and found the box of fabric plasters in one of the two broken drawers under the sink, then hurried out of the van.

Much to her annoyance, Heather Shaw was there again, removing the ladder from the back wall of the barn.

'Oh! Hello,' she said. She fumbled with the ladder, straining with its weight under one arm.

'Isla needed plasters,' Elizabeth explained, strangely humiliated, as though caught out where she wasn't supposed to be.

'I hope she feels better,' Heather said, glancing beyond Elizabeth at the camper van under the tree.

Elizabeth wanted to explain to her that Agata and Piotr would be moving into the converted barn after the party. But she didn't. It was none of Heather Shaw's business.

Up at the house, Elizabeth tended to Isla. She felt awkward around Agata and was unable to look her in the eye. If she had acted on her true feelings, something might have tumbled loose inside her. She might have burned down their camper van and begged the young couple back into the warmth of their home. But she put her sympathy away for now; a problem she couldn't currently solve. Agata had refused their hospitality and was staying in the van of her own free will.

Her immediate problem was Isla, whom she would teach to dive. It seemed of utmost importance, all of a sudden, that the little girl should perform a dive as well as her younger brother. Elizabeth did not want Isla to live in Hugo's shadow for the rest of her life. If she tried harder, she had the potential to be just as sporty as her brother, just as capable.

'Let's go back in the pool, Isla,' she said. 'I'm going to teach you to dive myself.'

'No!' wailed Isla, pulling at Elizabeth's towel. 'I'm too scared to swim!'

Agata's mouth fell open. Her eyes were fixed on Elizabeth's lurid bruises. The towel had fallen off one shoulder.

Pointlessly, Elizabeth pulled it back into position. 'Agata, will you take them back to the pool while I change into my swimsuit?'

An hour later, after watching too many of Isla's belly-flops, Elizabeth gave up. The sun was dropping and their teeth were chattering. It had been a futile exercise. She had sought equality for Isla in the wrong arena, at the wrong time, projecting onto her a need of her own. Empowering her daughter with the same skills as her male sibling would not counterbalance her own sense of inadequacy next to Lucas. It had been unfair on Isla, and it had taken away none of the dread she felt about telling Lucas she'd made a mess of inviting Bo to the summer party.

When Lucas finally arrived home, the two children were at the breakfast bar, showered and in their pyjamas, eating sushi rolls, headphones plugged in, screens on. Elizabeth was behind her laptop, chewing a salted liquorice, searching for companies that specialised in pool renovations. The wobbly paving stone was going to be her excuse. She planned to exaggerate the dangers of leaving the pool in its current state and insist they fix it. Implicit in this demand would be a veiled accusation: Lucas's refusal to spend money on the pool had been negligent and played a part in the unfortunate mishap that had led to Isla's accident, and to the transatlantic hang-up and the potential fallout with Bo. If she tapped into his guilt, he might not be so disappointed in her.

The sleeves of his white shirt were rolled up and a London tabloid was tucked under one arm. He smelt of a new aftershave, which made her smile. He was endlessly buying them, cluttering up the bathroom shelves, never able to settle on one that he liked. Never had she seen him dishevelled from his commute like the other men she would watch piling out from the train station, looking sweaty and grim.

'Here, I brought you this. I know you like the magazine bit,' he said, placing the newspaper on her keyboard, kissing the children on their foreheads, saying hello to Agata.

Neither Isla nor Hugo reacted to his presence: Hugo giggled at his screen and Isla passed a hand over the plaster, which Lucas didn't notice.

'Thanks,' Elizabeth said, closing her laptop to flick through the magazine and fret quietly.

'Anybody want one of these?' Lucas asked, offering two cans of Coke to Isla and Hugo.

Their attention shifted. Screens and headphones were abandoned.

'Thanks, Dad!' They grinned at each other. Lucas never allowed them to have sugary drinks and usually frowned at Elizabeth when she gave them sweets.

Agata handed Isla and Hugo plastic glasses with ice. She raised one of her pencilled eyebrows at Elizabeth, seemingly as surprised by Lucas's gesture as Elizabeth was.

He leant casually into the worktop and passed Agata two beers. 'Will you open these for us? I never know where you squirrel away the thingamajig.'

Agata opened the beers and handed one to Elizabeth. Before Elizabeth had a chance to begin her convoluted excuses about the wobbly tile and Isla's split forehead and the abandoned handset, Lucas whispered in her ear, 'Come on, let's go for a swim.'

He tugged her hand and she let him lead her into the night and down to the pool. But she could not relax until she knew why he was not asking her about Bo. 'We haven't got costumes,' she said.

'Who cares?' He was pulling her to him, kissing her and undoing her jeans as they walked.

The water was lit up bright blue. It would be cold.

After he had peeled off her jumper, he felt in her back pocket and pulled out her phone.

'Oh look, a missed call,' he grinned, handing it to her, tugging his trousers off.

Elizabeth's stomach flipped. A missed call from Bo Seacart.

'I'll listen to it later,' she said, bending down to take her jeans off.

'Go on,' he said. He removed his watch, even though it was waterproof. 'Put it on speaker,' he added.

She stood opposite him, face to face. She wanted to cry, but did as she was told, pressing the speaker button to hear Bo's message. Lucas unbuttoned his shirt. Silvery watermarks shimmered over his face, masking his expression. She couldn't read his features. His lips were pink and wet. He was like an angel, with his blond curls and big eyes. Her feelings for him were heightened, as intense as they could get, less love than reverence. Bo's voice message came between them.

'Oh Elizabeth! I heard *everything*! You were *so* awesome and brave. Oh my, her scream was just *horrible*! It was the most awful thing I ever heard, and when you said she was okay, oh my God, honey. What a super mom! Saving your little girl like that. I'm off to the Harbour Club now to recover from the trauma. Can't wait to hear all about it in July. My assistant is booking our flights right now! But I'm sure Lucas has told you by now. Bye for now, honey. Namaste!'

Elizabeth pressed end. 'You knew?'

'Walt called me this evening,' he said, unclipping her bra, kissing her neck tenderly over the bruises. 'They're coming to the party, Elizabeth! The deal is moving forward thanks to your brilliant idea of throwing in your brother's paintings as incentive. Not to mention your heroics today.'

Elizabeth laughed, mostly to herself. 'Walt would have called you anyway,' she said.

The last of their underwear was left on the side. They held hands and ran and jumped into the water, screaming with the shock of the cold. He held her tight, pulled her under, their nakedness slippery and other-worldly. His unflustered, contained appearance of before was gone, replaced by a wild excitement. The sex was heart-stopping. The broken mosaics left small cuts down her back. Her bones were chilled. The pads of her fingers shrivelled. She was dizzied by him, tumbled, unaware of where his feelings stopped and hers began.

They walked back up to the house shoulder to shoulder, their fingers entwined, dressed again in their clothes, which clung to them in patches. Elizabeth felt exhilarated, victorious. She could think of only one thing: Isla's boarding school place. This was the moment to broach it. The perfect moment.

'I've got a confession to make,' she said.

'Uh oh,' Lucas said, clipping his Rolex back onto his wrist.

'I tore up that offer letter from Channing House.'

He stopped walking to stare at her, but a smile played on his lips. 'You did?'

'I really want to keep Isla at home for just one more year. I think I can do it. She needs me.'

'You do seem better. This party has given you a focus, hasn't it?'

'I am better, I really am. I'm so sorry I worried you, and poor Isla … but I feel I can handle anything now. I haven't even had any migraines this month, and when I saw the Isla in the pool today … I thought … oh my God … I …'

He held her chin and pressed his finger on her mouth to stop her talking.

'I'll call Mrs Hepburn tomorrow and tell her we don't want the place.'

'Really?' she cried.

'Really.'

She threw her arms around him and buried her face in the crook of his neck. She was off the ground. He had lifted her up and her toes dangled as he walked on. Both of them were laughing. She wrapped her legs around his waist. As he carried her up to the house, she rested her chin on his shoulder and looked out across the hills. The lights of London twinkled at her in the distance. As long as she was in his arms, she had no desire to put on her old trainers and walk towards them and over the horizon.

Later that night, in bed, she couldn't sleep. Her mind switched back and forth. One minute she was obsessing about finding a last-minute day school place for Isla; the next she was imagining mood boards for the barn renovation and the party. Briefly she fell asleep and awoke again in the middle of the night, still thinking.

Her alarm clock read 2 a.m. Then she noticed that Lucas was gone from their bed. She crept out of their room and along the corridor to find him. The kitchen was empty. His study was dark. Through the window of the hallway, she checked that their cars were still there on the driveway.

Before heading to the family bathroom, where they kept the medicines, wondering if he had woken with a headache, she noticed that the sliding window to the garden was open a fraction. She froze. Something told her she should not go outside. The spectral image of the unsteady camper van loomed out of the darkness and imprinted itself on her eyelids. She rubbed her eyes, erasing the thought.

In bed, she pulled the covers over her head. She'd told Lucas she was better. She hadn't been lying. She had believed that she was. *Yes, I am better*, she said to herself, over and over as she fell into a light, fretful sleep.

CHAPTER SEVEN

I was jiggling around, crossing my legs and pretending I didn't need the toilet. Every time I needed to go, I cursed my weak bladder. Going inside the house meant seeing Lucas and resisting the urge to ask him direct questions about the camper van. Holding back my feelings on this subject was wise if I wanted to keep my job. Until I knew more, I would try very hard to be polite and open-minded.

Agata was vacuuming under the cushions of the sofa when I came in. I had to wave at her to get her attention. Her legs got caught in the tangle of the cord when she tried to turn the hoover off.

'Sorry,' she said. The closeness of her eyes and her small mouth, like a rosebud, exaggerated her shyness. Her clothes were less demure. She had the style of an American teen, with her white teeth, peroxide hair and stone-washed jeans. I noticed a hole where a nose ring might have been.

'Sorry. I didn't mean to interrupt you. I'm just going to the toilet, if that's all right.'

'Yes, yes.' She pointed in the direction of the bathroom door, which she knew I had used every day I had worked there.

Before she switched the vacuum cleaner on again, I whispered, 'Is Elizabeth here?'

Her expression changed. A shadowed thought seemed to run across those close brown eyes of hers, which I thought looked redder than usual. She shook her head and glanced over her shoulder, before giving me a quick nervous smile. It was a small moment but it signified an alliance.

Feeling childish, trying to build on the moment between us, I made a big deal of slipping and sliding across the polished concrete in my socks, making out that I was on a surfboard.

Agata let out a brief, skittish laugh. 'Dangerous,' she tutted. Her smile could not hide the unease underneath.

'When is the toilet in your camper going to get fixed?' I asked, fishing for information, for an invitation even.

She shrugged and returned to her vacuuming.

While I was sitting on the toilet, I looked around me at the hexagonal black tiles and antique gold taps and the matching green bar of soap and felt a sudden and shameful pang of envy for everything the Huxleys had. I did not feel proud of myself for it, and quickly swiped it out of my mind, chiding myself, hoping it was not the reason I was fixating on the camper van. *If you search for fault*, my father had always said, *you're bound to find it*. And if I had, it was the only anomaly in the midst of perfection.

I flushed the antique chain and chuckled at the words that were embossed on the cistern: *Crapper's Valveless Waste Preventer No. 892*. Grinning, I made a mental note to tell Rob that I went to the toilet on a real crapper every day. The soap that I lathered on my hands smelt delicious enough to eat. There was another bottle next to it with what looked like Roman numerals on the label. Greedily I took three large pumps to try it. It flew out too fast, blobbing all over me and the sink, turning out to be hand cream. In a minor panic, I wiped it off the surfaces with wads of toilet paper, leaving fig-smelling white smears everywhere. My hands were so over-moisturised, I couldn't turn the tap off. While I held it with a towel to twist it closed, I heard voices coming from the living room. I leant my ear to the door. It was Lucas and Agata. My heart missed a beat. Opening the door a crack, with as little sound as possible, I listened in. I was rewarded by the tail end of a sentence.

'… ask you to do something you don't want to do, please tell me, okay?' Lucas was saying gently, with an edge of anxiety. I didn't hear Agata's response. He added, 'Promise?'

I felt a tickle in my throat and knew I couldn't hide myself any longer. 'Hello, sorry, just using the toilet,' I said, coughing, stepping out, conscious that I might smell like a perfumery.

They were sitting next to each other on the low sofa. His arm was around her shoulder and her head was bent low. They did not flinch or pull apart when they saw me.

Unfazed by my sudden appearance, Lucas said, 'Agata's not having a good day.' He handed her a tissue. Seeing his kindness stirred up a familiar sense of how he had once been towards me. A blond curl fell over the mole on his cheek when he looked up at me. Blood rushed to my head. I forgot how to speak.

Agata blew her nose and stood up, 'Thank you, Lucas. I work now.'

My only focus was on my boots by the window. The floor under my socks felt slippery, like thin ice. As I tied my laces, my fingers quivered. Adrenalin was firing through my veins. I dared once to glance up, hoping to catch his eye. He was at the fridge, humming, and Agata was pushing the vacuum cleaner to the other sofa.

As I hurried out, leaving one lace undone, I heard Lucas say casually, 'I'll take lunch in my study, Agata. And help yourself to some of this Brie. It's bloody delicious.'

My presence had been already forgotten.

I turned the soil in the newly dug flower bed, slamming the spade into the hard ground. The sun burnt the back of my neck: the spot where Lucas's arm had hung over Agata. When I stopped to rest, to wipe my nose or push a piece of hair back into my cap, the past came rushing back in. I reminded myself that the tremble in my fingers up at the house had been my body's reaction to the memory of Lucas, not the reality of his handsome face, of the mole that accentuated his high cheekbones, of his dark blue eyes. I kept digging, harder and faster.

A few feet away was the gate snuggled into the laurel hedge, where the stone path ended and the flagstones of the pool terrace began. The repetitive gulp of the water in the filter tormented me further, pulling the present away like the draw of a wave.

The hedge scratched my arms and my towel got caught on a bramble, but I made it through and out into the Huxleys' garden. As I dashed along the pathways, I grabbed the heads off a couple of poppies. Poppies were my father's favourite and I hated them with a passion that equalled their colour.

When I came to the pool, I was disappointed. I had imagined it would be sparkly and spotless, with smart tiles, a diving board and bath-like warm water. The steel steps wobbled as I got in. A mosaic tile came loose and twirled to the bottom. The chill of the water stopped my breath and I paused before fully submerging. But once I was in, I was in, and I let out a little cry of exhilaration. I doggy-paddled to the far side, barely keeping my head above water, and then returned. Soon I was attempting lengths, trying front crawl, but my head was out of the water. I didn't know how to breathe properly. Choking, ineffective, I was getting tired, but I wouldn't stop swimming, not until I hated my father a little less.

It was just becoming dark when I heard the sound of a man's laugh.

'I'm off to the garden centre. Need anything?'

I jumped. It was my father's voice. He had come out of nowhere, disturbing my reverie. I felt the spade, solid in my hand, and steadied myself upon it.

'No thanks,' I said.

'Looks like you need a swim to cool off!' he said, reading my mind.

As he strode off, I wanted to chuck the shovel to the ground, run to the pool and jump in, but I dug on; dug and turned and dug and turned, trying to rid myself of the tangles of my memories.

The water was close; I could almost taste it, like a slippery temptress luring me in with gentle watery sounds.

My favourite strip of sea near Rye would be rolling into shore without me, over two and a half hours away. Neither of my parents went near the water. The closest beach at Worthing was an hour and fifteen minutes away from Cobham by car. Our start time at the Huxleys was 6 a.m., and we would finish at 7 p.m., leaving me no time on weekdays to swim. At the weekends, every penny of my hourly rate would have to be saved in an envelope rather than wasted on petrol.

I wondered if Lucas and Elizabeth would ever grant me official permission to use the pool to keep up my fitness. There would be irony in that, after years of sneaking through the hedge and jumping into its unheated water while the Huxley Seniors were away. I remembered how the shock of the cold had opened my eyes to the thrill of the world that awaited me, shimmering and glittering in the sunlight; beyond my solitary childhood, beyond that waxy hedge.

A quick peek, I thought. Maybe dip my toes in. For old times' sake.

I left my spade sticking out of the ground and opened the squeaky gate.

The blue and white mosaics wobbled through the crystal-clear water.

I dipped my hand in. The ripples tinkled and shimmered.

Nobody was around. I would be hidden by a thick hedge at the bottom of the five-acre garden. I would never be discovered.

Dad had left for the garden centre. Elizabeth and the children were out somewhere. Piotr was in London. Agata was making lunch for Lucas, who was in his study, working hard, straining his blue eyes at the screen, making more money than he needed.

Just a quick dip to cool me off, to bring him back to me. Just two minutes of that feeling again, in and then out.

I stripped down to my underwear, hooked my toes over the lip of a tile and hovered above the glistening surface, splitting the water with a dive. My limbs drove me like a machine to the other end. I plunged my head under to turn my body around in the silent world, cut off from the air and noise and confusion of the outside. The chlorine was bitter at the back of my throat and the water ice cold but like silk over my skin. It felt more expensive than any water I had ever swum in. The weeks deprived of this feeling had been torture.

Back then, as a girl, Lucas had taught me how to feel this good, to know euphoria and freedom.

'Is that ... you? From next door?' the Huxleys' son asked.

I scrambled to the side and spluttered a no, leaving a puddle on the stone slab at my fingertips. He laughed again.

Too startled and worn out to risk swimming to the steps, I shuffled along, gripping the edge, kicking my feet beneath me to stay above the surface. When my foot felt for the first rung of the ladder, the Huxleys' son said, 'Hang on a sec, no need to get out. I'll give you a few pointers so you don't drown next time.'

Blinking away the blur of chlorine, I watched him undo his wristwatch, strip down to his shorts and perform a perfect racing dive. His beautiful blond hair blackened and slickened under the water. He pounded to the shallow end, where I stood shivering and rubbing my stinging eyes. His muscles ran with rivulets. His irises were as blue as the water.

'Lie on your tummy,' he instructed me. 'Kick your legs. Keep them straight. That's right. Good girl. Well done.'

I did as I was told, and he held me around the middle and manipulated my limbs into swimming strokes. At his touch, tingles rolled through my body from the tips of my toes right up into the roots of my hair. Under his tutelage, I let go of my scratchy home life, feeling as though I was turning from a child into an adolescent in the space of that one dusk-lit hour.

As I thrashed out more lengths, I reminded myself of how far I had come. My new life with Rob was everything to me now. I slowed my strokes and swam to the edge, ready to get on with the garden: I was grateful to Lucas for the job – and nothing else.

Then I heard the squeak of the gate. I plunged under the water again and swam to the other side in a panic, hoping whoever it was would leave. My stupidity came crashing in on me. I was trapped, like a fish in a tank, swimming in circles. A dark form shimmered through the water, peering downwards. If it was Lucas, I contemplated drowning rather than facing him. Unable to hold my breath a second longer, I rose, spluttering into the sunshine. It was not Lucas.

'What the hell do you think you're doing?' Elizabeth said.

'I'm so sorry,' I muttered, shooting out of the pool, chilled by the air, exposed in my black underwear. Head down, I followed the ground to my clothes. Water pooled at my feet as I tried to untangle them.

Her pretty eyes bored into me. 'This isn't *your* pool,' she stated.

I forced my wet legs into my jeans and gulped my heart back down my throat. I would be sacked. Perhaps both my father and I would be sacked. I couldn't believe what I had done. I picked up my socks, wondering how I could have risked everything for two minutes in the water.

'What were you *thinking*?' Elizabeth asked.

I could say I had fallen in.

I could say I was rescuing a small animal or a piece of jewellery.

I could prostrate myself at her feet and beg for her mercy.

I could feel the drips wiggling down my cheeks.

'I wasn't thinking,' I replied, utterly humiliated.

She was so close to me, I could see the pulse in her throat. Her expression changed, as though her anger was a thin veneer that had melted away.

'What are those? How did you do that?' she said. She twisted both my arms outwards.

I pulled them away and rubbed at the healed scars. Mostly I forgot they were there. I put on my T-shirt. 'They're grazes from the lane ropes at the lido. I was training for a long-distance swim.'

She smiled, unevenly. 'That's why you're swimming now? You're training for something?'

I should have lied; she seemed to want me to say yes. 'No,' I said. 'I was hot and I just … I'm sorry.'

She moved even closer and whispered, breath sugary sweet, 'I *know* about you.'

My stomach rolled. 'I …' I faltered.

'You can go now,' she said, raising her chin. 'But I'm afraid I'm going to have to talk to Lucas about this.'

I put my cap on, grabbed my boots and rushed away down the path to the meadow, where I jumped over the low wall and ran as fast as I could into the long grass. I felt dizzy and sick by the time I had slowed to a walk.

I lay in the tall flowers, and picked one of the bendy, floppy poppies, waiting to hear my father calling me for lunch. My hair was splayed out, drying in the sun.

When I finally heard Dad's voice, I tied up my hair and hurried to the wall.

His familiar face was reassuring. He was holding the Tupperware box filled with our home-made chicken sandwiches. I found his sticky-out ears and reliable stride endearing, but seeing his trusting smile, I wanted to fall back into the meadow grass and sink into the earth.

We looked out across the South Downs as we ate.

'Arthur turned up last night,' my father said, staring down at his sandwich before taking a bite.

I swallowed my first mouthful with a dry throat. 'That's a relief,' I said, genuinely happy that the lonely alcoholic at the soup kitchen was alive and well. 'Where had he been?'

'On a bender, of course. Don't know why I ever believe he'll go sober.'

I asked more about poor, lonely Arthur, who wore bicycle clips on his trousers even though he didn't own a bike, touched that my father and my mother had developed such deep attachments to the regulars at the soup kitchen.

Before I knew it, lunch break was over. And I had not told him what I had done. While there was still hope that Elizabeth would calm down and forget to take it further, I would be cowardly. I could not bear to watch Dad's face fall, knowing that he and my mother would suffer because of my selfishness.

Later that night, I called Rob, hoping for some sympathy. The walls were thin so I whispered the whole story, omitting the feelings Lucas had dragged up inside me again. The strange emotional ties to the past were unwarranted and unwanted, and unfair on Rob; he didn't need to know.

At the end of my tale, he stayed silent. 'Rob?' I said, checking he was still on the line, fearing he had read my mind.

'That was a really stupid thing to do,' he replied.

My skin flushed. I shouldn't have been surprised by his reaction. 'I know,' I said.

'If you lose that job, we'll be in the shit again, and I won't be able to make a proper go of the bar.'

I spoke quietly. 'The other week you were telling me not to go.'

'The other week I hadn't spoken to my accountant.'

'Oh.' I rubbed the bottom edge of my lip. 'I didn't know. Not good?'

'I don't wanna talk about it.'

A ring-pull cracked off a can. There was a pause as he took a sip. A tin of lager, I guessed.

'Do you think they'll sack Dad, too?' I whispered, terrified of how Rob would answer, as though his reply would solidify our fate tomorrow.

'They might,' he said.

I groaned. 'What have I done?'

He laughed, but it wasn't light-hearted. 'Shit, Heather. You're mental, you are.'

'It's so stressful working there.' I cleared my throat of the tears that were coming on. 'Small things become big things, you know?'

There was a pause while he took a swig of his drink.

'Listen to us, whispering down the phone like teenagers,' he said, burping.

'Why are *you* whispering?'

'TRUE! I CAN SHOUT AS LOUD AS I LIKE!' he roared.

'Shh. You'll burst my eardrums.' I snuggled down under my duvet. 'Tell me something to help me get to sleep.'

'I've got a raging boner. What are you wearing?'

'Thick greying flannel pyjamas with holes in the armpits.'

'I've still got a raging boner. That's how much I miss you.'

I reminisced about last weekend, when Rob and I had lain in bed for longer than usual on Sunday morning. The sun had streamed into the whitewashed room and the shells I had threaded on a string and hung from the curtain rail had rattled in the breeze of the open window.

'Why don't I come down to see you this weekend?' I suggested.

'Saturday nights are our only busy nights,' he said.

It was a rejection and it felt like a punishment. I said, 'Yeah, I guess the petrol costs a fortune. I'm not sure the car will even make it.'

'Another weekend, babe, okay?'

'Sure,' I said.

Last year, when Rob had forgotten my birthday, I had complained to my mother about the lack of romance in our relationship, questioning whether we were right for each other. In response, she had described how Dad's habit of microwaving cold stewed cups of tea had always infuriated her, but that she had learnt to accept his foibles, as he had accepted hers. She believed this acceptance was the ultimate romance and dismissed my concerns that Rob's oversight was symbolic of a deeper ill between us.

'You should see the crappy van that Agata and Piotr live in,' I said.

'It can't be worse than that VW we rented when we first met.'

He was referring to the holiday in Wales where I had told him I loved him for the first time and he had suggested we move in together as a way of pooling our money.

'Maybe it's not that bad,' I laughed, knowing that the camper van at Copper Lodge was far worse that the VW in Wales.

'We should do that again next year.'

'Yes.' I sighed wistfully, wishing we could go now.

Misunderstanding my sigh, he said, 'We don't have to.'

'Honestly, I'd love to. I'm just tired. This is all much harder than I thought it would be,' I admitted.

There was a loud rustling of Rob's bed covers and then a grunt.

'I warned you about their type, didn't I? Posh twats. I said they'd lord it over you. Remember?' he said.

'Yes. I remember.' But it was Elizabeth's words that launched themselves into my mind.

I know *about you*, she had said. *I* know *about you.*

As I said goodbye to Rob, I thought about Elizabeth and what she knew, and went to sleep certain that the Huxleys would terminate our contract at Copper Lodge tomorrow.

CHAPTER EIGHT

'It really was shocking to see her there,' Elizabeth insisted, remembering Heather's beautiful eyes gazing at her. 'In her underwear!'

The corner of Lucas's mouth twitched. He slugged back his espresso. 'You know I used to let her swim in the pool when it was Mum and Dad's.'

'But she was a kid back then. And she works for you now.'

'She was probably just—'

His mobile buzzed.

Before he picked up, he said, 'You're getting distracted, Elizabeth. You need to focus on the party. Everything's about the party. Leave Heather to me. I'll deal with her.' Then, into the phone, 'Hello? Yes, uh huh. Go ahead, George.'

While he listened to what Walt Seacart's assistant was telling him, he sifted through the sample invitations that Elizabeth had placed in front of him, checking the back of each design for the name of the stationers and its price.

When he came to the card decorated with gold strawberries, Elizabeth tapped on it and whispered to him, 'Isla really wants us to use this one.'

It was by an artist and renowned local stationer, Mary Billingshurst, whom a smart mother at school had recommended. Yesterday, Elizabeth and Isla had taken a trip to see her in her Arts and Crafts cottage.

'Mummy, this is the best one, you *have* to have this one, *please*, Mummy, please,' Isla had begged. They had been standing in Mary's workshop. The bright, cluttered space had smelt of turps and sawn wood. Mary had been behind the counter, quietly painting. She had worn an eyeglass and had thick veins on the back of her steady hands. Her designs were displayed on shelves. Each was unique and expensive.

'Let me have a look,' Elizabeth had said. The sample had been painted with two exquisite gold-and-red embossed strawberries in the top centre. The tiny flecks of pink, like seeds or confetti, looked as though they had been blown across the calligraphy. She imagined Bo Seacart's eyes widening in admiration and Jude's arty friends wowed by the understated craftsmanship, but when she had seen the price tag, she had gulped back her shock.

'Darling, I'm not sure Daddy will go for this one,' she had said quietly.

Isla had responded loudly. 'But you *promised* I could choose and now you're not letting me!'

Smiling apologetically at Mary, Elizabeth said, 'Shush now, darling. Don't be sad.'

Isla had crossed her arms and turned her mouth down. 'You never like anything I like.'

'That's not true, poppet.'

'It is true! I got you those dangling earrings and you never wear them!'

'I do wear them.'

'You and Daddy just think I'm stupid!' she had said, hanging her head and biting her nails.

'Isla—'

'You never listen to anything I say because you think I'm stupid. And I am!'

Elizabeth had dropped onto her haunches, eye level with her daughter. 'No. You are not. You are clever and beautiful, and you must believe in yourself. Daddy and I love you everything about you, and we love you very, very much.'

'Promise you'll order these then,' Isla had sniffed, handing her the invitation.

Elizabeth had pushed her daughter's blonde tresses behind her ears and promised she would try to persuade Daddy.

Now Lucas hung up the phone and flapped the gold strawberry sample in Agata's direction. 'Do *you* like these, Agata?' he asked.

Elizabeth wondered if his trip into the garden last night had anything to do with his interest in Agata's opinion now.

Agata's face remained impassive when she said, 'Pretty.'

Irritated, Elizabeth snatched the card from Lucas. 'Shall I order them?'

'We can't afford them,' he replied, shrugging at Agata as though apologising to her. 'What's happened with the caterers?' he added.

'Sarah Smith's coming at nine thirty.'

'Who the hell is Sarah Smith?'

'The lady who makes the amazing macarons,' Elizabeth reminded him.

'Shit. I'd forgotten. I'm on a conference call until ten. Can she wait for me?'

'I can handle it on my own, Lucas,' she said, dumping three supersize packets of cola bottle sweets onto the work surface, breaking them apart noisily, tipping them into the jar, which was running low.

His phone rang and it was George again. Mary's gold strawberries were back in his hand and he was studying the price on the back while grunting *hmm, yes, hmm* to George.

Elizabeth literally crossed her fingers. Lucas moved on.

'Any of these three,' he mouthed, waggling three dull art deco samples from a Sloane Street stationer.

'What about Isla?' she whispered, picturing her daughter's heartbreaking tears.

Into the handset he said, 'Hold on a sec, George, will you?' He pressed hold. 'When this deal goes ahead, we can buy her a field full of real gold strawberries, okay?' Then he left the kitchen to continue his conversation with George in the garden.

In the build-up to 4 July, Lucas's mood had been increasingly buoyant, bullish almost, in spite of the fact that Walt Seacart was being over-scrupulous about the full due diligence process, suggesting there were inconsistencies in the accounting practices of Lucas's company, questioning its original five-year plan, under-mining its projections and sales forecasts and nit-picking over insurance policy audits and the terms of the lease on a commercial property in his portfolio. On the surface, Lucas seemed convinced the deal would go ahead. But every single night he interrogated Elizabeth about progress on the party-planning, asking her to take her through every decision she had made. He would then remove his Rolex and instigate sex, sometimes twice over, and Elizabeth pretended to want it, accepting the pattern: the less control he had at work, the more he wanted at home.

Agata smoothed a hand over the sample. 'Shame,' she said.

'Isla is going to be so upset,' Elizabeth said. She stirred her coffee, worrying about the meltdown her daughter would have.

When Lucas had finished his call, she asked him, 'Final decision?'

'The others will bankrupt us,' he said. He settled at her side and opened his iPad to read the newspaper.

'Never mind,' she laughed.

She was pretending she didn't care; pretending she didn't care that he never deferred to any of her decisions. Ever.

She was sure he could have afforded the invitations if he had wanted to.

'I'm leaving for yoga now,' she said. 'I'll be back in time for Sarah at nine thirty.'

'Namaste,' he chuckled.

'Namaste,' she returned, holding her hands in prayer and bowing to him.

Throughout her yoga class, she had experienced a crushing feeling in her ribcage. She had taken the long way home, needing to find some space to breathe.

With six weeks to go, she was trying her best to stay focused and positive, but her stress levels were rising exponentially, exacerbated by Lucas's inability to delegate. He had given her the responsibility but lacked faith in her, which was the worst of both worlds.

At least Piotr had been respectful, and was on schedule. He had finished the repointing on the barn and had brought in two Polish men to help him gut the inside, preparing it for the installation of the pre-built oak mezzanine. The new windows were arriving next week. The new bed and coffee machine were ordered. Renovations were going according to plan, but somehow she couldn't believe it would stay that way. Anxiety about making a mistake plagued her.

Now she was late for Sarah. It was 9.34 and Lucas was calling her already.

But she needed more time. More space. Enough space to stop herself from opening the car door and jumping out into the ditch, letting the car run off into the distance while the ringing got further away, and quieter, until it was gone altogether. Until *she* was gone.

On Lucas's fifth call, she picked up. 'Hi.'

'Hi, darling. You know Sarah's here already?' he said.

She slapped one palm on the steering wheel and then composed herself. 'Sorry. There were temporary traffic lights at the A245 junction.'

'I was worried.'

'My phone was on silent. Sorry.'

There was a pause.

'I thought you weren't picking up because you were upset about the invitations.'

'No. I understand.'

The car banged over a pothole.

'I'm getting Jude's paintings out of storage this week.' He knew how much she cared about this.

'Oh good,' she said, feigning indifference.

'Did you hear me get out of bed last night?'

She pressed down her window for some air. 'No? Did you?'

'I went for a swim.'

'In the middle of the night? How funny.'

'I'm stressed about this deal. I can't sleep.'

'I didn't realise. You seem so upbeat about everything.'

'I'm trying to be.'

He had sounded genuine. 'It'll all be worth it in the end,' she said, softening. It was a relief to muffle her suspicions, just as she had done last night, by pressing the pillow over her head, blocking out the noise of the shower.

'When it's signed, I'll buy you a sports car.'

She remembered a story he had told her about his housemaster at boarding school. 'You don't need to prove anything to me, or to anyone,' she said.

'I'm not that boy any more,' he snapped.

She regretted bringing it up. 'Okay then. I'll have a Ferrari, please,' she joked.

'Done.'

Before reaching home, he called again.

'I just wanted to say I'm really proud of how you're coping with the party and stuff. I'd never get through all this without your support.'

'I'm enjoying it,' she said.

She increased her speed to sixty mph on a lane more suitable for thirty and thought about how fast she would be able to drive in a Ferrari.

She reached home in one piece and parked her car next to Sarah's old Audi. Through the glass walls, she could see Sarah sitting at the kitchen table and Lucas standing nearby. Before going inside, she watched them both for a minute. Lucas was throwing his arms in the air, holding court, and Sarah was laughing. Sarah might guess that Lucas was a type: the finance guy who was happy for his wife to get on with the silly business of party-planning.

'Sarah, hi! Sorry, the class ran over,' Elizabeth said, joining them.

'No, no, don't be silly. Agata and Lucas have been looking after me,' Sarah said.

Lucas said, 'I'll be back when I'm done with this conference call. So sorry to be rude, Sarah. Are you sure you're okay waiting?'

'Of course,' Sarah said, lifting her baby out of his pram and letting him dangle in the air as she smiled at Lucas.

'Hello, James,' Elizabeth said to the pretty child, who was red-cheeked and snotty on Sarah's shoulder. She pined for the days when Isla and Hugo were that age. At the back of her sock drawer she kept the muslin cloth that she had draped over her shoulder all those years before.

James began wailing. Agata passed Sarah a warmed bottle.

'I wish I'd breastfed,' Sarah said.

'My boobs used to spurt into Isla's eyes and make her scream,' Elizabeth said.

Sarah laughed. Elizabeth joined in, wondering if it was laughter, or the lack of it, that had been the reason why she had wanted to employ Sarah. At the school gates, she had fantasised about being her friend. Going for coffee and seeing French films together.

The last time she had been out with another woman, without Lucas, had been two years ago. She remembered the cheap pizza restaurant and the tart red wine. She remembered how luxurious it had seemed and that Lucas had waited up for her to ask her how the evening had gone.

'Everyone told me it would be easier with the third,' Sarah said.

'I don't know how you do it,' Elizabeth said.

'I'm so tired I'm just horrible to everyone all the time, even to myself,' Sarah said, slumping.

In spite of a decade of experience at a top patisserie in Paris, Sarah now had the definite look of a scruffy down-home mother of three, as though she had been one all her life. She had a narrow pale face, partly hidden by a thick chunky fringe, possibly hacked off with kitchen scissors. But her smile made up for the dreariness of her appearance, always playing at her lips like mischief itself.

'They go to school in the end, remember,' Elizabeth said. 'I even managed to read a book this month. A proper novel from cover to cover.'

'Next you'll be telling me you have sex with your husband!' Sarah laughed.

'At least once a year!'

Elizabeth's hand passed over her throat.

'Now I'm *really* jealous.' She reached into the bottom of the pram. 'But I can bake at least. Try one.'

She handed Elizabeth two pastel-pink boxes wrapped in dark silk ribbon. *Elizabeth and Lucas Huxley* had been printed in elegant white italics in one corner of each box. Elizabeth took a sharp intake of breath. 'How lovely.'

'I can personalise little going-home presents for all your guests too, if you like. Maybe truffles?'

Elizabeth checked the clock. It was ten minutes to ten. Ten minutes until Lucas would be finished on his call. 'Look, Sarah. I have to explain something before I try one,' she said.

Sarah bounced James on her knee and waited for her to go on.

'Lucas is … how can I describe it … a bit of a traditionalist. He likes to know what he's spending his money on.'

'He's worried it'll be going on some scruffy mum who bakes out of her kitchen, right?'

'He'll take a bit of persuading,' Elizabeth admitted, reaching into the cupboard for a box of macarons from a famous patisserie in Knightsbridge. The lettering – *The Brompton Cross* – was splashed across the box, modern and garish in hot pink.

Sarah looked at her searchingly. 'Please tell me you're not going to compare mine to Brompton's?'

James stopped gurgling and inspected his mother's face.

'I know it's a risk. But yours are better. When he tastes them alongside theirs, he won't be able to doubt me – doubt *them*, I mean.' If Elizabeth wanted to win this battle, she had to work doubly hard for it.

'I think it's professional suicide, but hey, you know your husband better than me.'

Elizabeth checked the clock again. Five minutes.

'Why doesn't Agata take James for a walk around the garden? Give you a breather?'

Sarah blew out her cheeks. 'You don't have to ask me *that* twice.'

Agata pushed James away in the pram minutes before Lucas strode into the kitchen at ten o'clock exactly. Elizabeth's shoulders rose and her heart hiccuped.

'Hello! Hello!' Lucas bellowed, clapping his hands. 'My mouth is watering.'

Elizabeth handed him a fork. 'I'll make coffee.'

'So, I've heard you're the best in town,' he said, leaning across the counter on his elbows.

Sarah straightened her skirt and smoothed her hair, shifting from one foot to the other. 'Well I don't know about that,' she said, and handed him one of her boxes.

He undid the satin ribbon and popped a green macaron into his mouth, closing his eyes as he chewed. Sarah seemed mesmerised by him, jumping slightly when he blinked his eyes open. 'Not bad at all.'

Elizabeth placed a coffee on the side and brought out the box from the Brompton Cross. 'To compare.'

Lucas raised an eyebrow and took one. 'Not as pretty as yours, for starters.'

When he had finished his mouthful, he said, 'Okay, Sarah Smith. My assistant got me a twenty per cent discount at Brompton's already. Can you be competitive on your pricing?'

Elizabeth was shocked by his cool lie.

Sarah handed him her brochure. 'Yes. I think you'll find I can.'

He scanned it with expert speed and threw it on the counter. 'Looks good. Welcome to the madhouse!'

'Ha! Thank you!' Sarah's tired eyes were stretched wide.

Taking up his coffee, he said, 'By the way, darling, will you find Gordon and Heather and tell them to pop in and see me sometime today?'

'Sure,' Elizabeth said, watching him walk away, wondering what he had in mind for Heather.

'And don't forget to order the invitations today. We're already pushing it time-wise.'

Returning to Sarah, Elizabeth said, 'I think you just pulled that off.'

'*We* did,' Sarah replied with a grin, holding her coffee mug up to Elizabeth, who clinked it with her own.

'To rainbow macarons!'

'To the party!'

Elizabeth was high on the success for about five minutes. As soon as Sarah was gone, the long to-do list unravelled in her mind. She needed to order the DJ and find a company for the marquee and the drinks van, and pin down the menu with the caterers, and so many other things. Absent-mindedly, on the way out to the garden to find Heather – whom she guessed might not have a job by the end of the day, which she thought might be a good thing for everyone – she grabbed a sample invitation from the kitchen counter and began scribbling a list on the back with one of Hugo's crayons.

CHAPTER NINE

As I placed the first clump of peonies into the hole, I spotted Elizabeth heading in my direction. She was sucking on something, a sweet perhaps. Her small, light steps, her unreadable prettiness gave her the air of a younger woman, younger than me, a teenage girl even, who had not engaged with real life quite yet.

The water lapped noisily from behind the hedge, like a rushing broil in my ears. The trowel escaped from my sweaty palm and the rocky soil flicked into my face, stinging my eyes. I stood straight, light-headed, spotting an envelope in her hand. It might be a termination letter, or a contract that she would rip up in front of me and scatter in the soil at our feet.

'Heather, can I have a word?'

'Sure,' I said, adjusting my cap, pulling it a little lower over my eyes.

'Gosh, you look peaky. Are you feeling okay?' She pushed a wave of her golden hair back from her forehead.

'I'm fine. I think.' I stared down at the envelope.

'Do you want to see?' She held it out. 'It's the invitation Lucas wants. Boring, isn't it?'

It was a white card with a crease down the middle and scribbles on the back.

'You don't like it?' I said, ambivalent, wanting to sound neutral, wondering if it was a trick. If she and Lucas were about to sack me,

I wondered whether she would be capable of engaging in chit-chat about an invitation. But she was hard to read, nervy always. She might want to avoid a confrontation, play good cop to Lucas's bad.

'I hate it.' She slipped it back into the envelope, adding, 'Lucas wants a word with you and your dad.'

'When?' I gasped, unable to hide my dismay.

'Now. Will you find Gordon for me?' Her baby-blue eyes blinked at me. 'I'm off to look at marquees with the kids. I'll be back later. If you're still here.'

She left me clutching the trowel. For a moment, I was too frightened to move. Looking for my father would be like walking a gangplank of my own free will.

I found him in the barn, helping Piotr lug a rusty lawnmower outside.

'Lucas wants to see us.'

'Really?'

His surprise increased my terror.

'Is that unusual?' I asked him.

'It must be about the party,' he said, dusting off his hands.

I looked over at pale-faced Piotr, who had stopped work to stare at me. His eyes were hidden under a noon shadow. Sinews were carved into his arms like drawings of a superhero in a graphic novel.

On the way up to the house, my father's silence was a wall that blocked out any ideas of a quick confession about my illicit swim.

Lucas Huxley's study was small but immaculate. The desk faced the floor-to-ceiling window. His chair swivelled rhythmically, his suited knees jutting out like angular instruments. Buried intently in his work, he didn't seem to notice we were there. He continued to read the document laid neatly in front of him. The back of his head moved from side to side, as though he had no peripheral vision, back and forth across the lines of text like an old typewriter. At the end of the page, he swept one hand through his golden curls.

'Hi! Sorry, you two. If I don't finish this now, I'll lose my thread,' he said, holding his finger up to us, continuing to read.

My socks left damp marks on the concrete. Agata had spared me the humiliation of the slippers. I tried to stand evenly on both feet, ready for the verdict. The material of my T-shirt clung to the front of my body. I kept plucking it away. Dad pulled my cap off my head just before Lucas turned to us.

'Do you want to sit down?' he said, pointing to the two-seater leather bench to the left of his desk.

We sat down and he swivelled his chair around.

My father's thick, brutish thighs were almost knee to knee with Lucas's long, lean legs. Our trousers were caked in mud. Flakes sprinkled the floor at our feet. I twisted my fingers into contortions.

'You both look terrified!' Lucas laughed, fiddling with the links on his wristwatch. I remembered the digital Casio he had always left by the side of the pool before getting in.

In the soft summer light, the mole on his cheek had given him a kind of feminine beauty. I wondered if the image of us in the pool together flashed before him now, as it did before me.

I turned up at six o'clock, as arranged. He was already swimming lengths. The rotation of his arms worked the muscles in his back, defining them. Did he know I was watching him? I whipped off my towel and hurried down the corner steps into the shallow end, desperate to submerge my legs in the water, wishing I had started shaving them, like Amy did now.

He reached the end and stood up, flicking his hair out of his eyes, smoothing it back. His torso was tapered at the waist, slim and toned.

I had not been this close to a man's unclothed chest before. His form was different to those of the boys at school – which were either skinny or fat – and its strength, its hardness appealed to me.

'What did you tell your parents?' he asked.

'They think I'm revising.'

'They won't check?'

'No,' I said. My parents would be having their bath, sharing two inches of brown water, chatting about the Huxleys and the weather and their plans for the garden tomorrow. Their routine after work never changed.

I asked him the same question about his parents.

'They like me using the pool when they're away,' he replied. 'But they don't know you're here, obviously.'

I became aware of my own semi-nakedness and I rounded my shoulders to hide myself, self-conscious about my rapidly developing body. My chlorine-eaten swimsuit was threadbare and billowed at the stomach.

'Let's begin,' he said. 'Copy me.' He fell back and floated like a plank with his arms and feet spread wide. His toes, his thigh muscles, his groin and his pectoral muscles protruded above the surface. 'Hold your breath and be still.'

I lay there with the water blocking my ears; suspended, rocked, transported. A series of droplets splashed on my cheeks. When I opened my eyes, Lucas was looking down on me. I shot up, choking, forgetting I was in water; sinking, scrabbling to stand, realising I had floated into the deep end. He grabbed hold of me, one arm supporting my shoulders and the other under the crease of my knees. 'I've got you.'

I coughed out what I had swallowed. The water was choppy around us.

'Sorry for startling you.' He smiled down at me.

I lay across his arms, my heart beating wildly.

'You okay now?' he asked, releasing me.

I nodded.

Then he reached out and pulled a wet tendril of hair away from its chokehold around my neck. 'I don't want to have to tell your dad that I drowned you,' he laughed.

I guessed this was why we were really here in his study. Because of who I had been to him back then, rather than what I had done wrong now.

I dragged as much air into my lungs as possible, to prepare.

'I want to ask you a favour,' he said.

'A favour?' I blurted. Lucas's lips parted in a small, questioning smile, and I wondered if he knew about the swim. There was a dance in his eyes that suggested he might.

My father cleared his throat. 'Anything at all, Mr Huxley.'

I tried to keep a straight face.

'Elizabeth's brother is an artist – I don't know if you knew that.'

My father nodded his head.

'I didn't know,' I said.

'Jude Woods. Have you heard of him?'

The name rang a bell. 'I think I have,' I said, surprising myself.

'Well, a few years back he gave us three large paintings that we've been keeping in storage in Guildford, but now we want to get them out and mount them in the barn. When it's finished, of course.'

'How can we help?' my father asked.

'Well, the trouble is, the BMWs are too small to transport them, so I thought your van might do the trick.'

'Yes, we can do that for you.'

'Any chance you could squeeze it in this week? Elizabeth is extremely anxious about them – they're rather special, you see – and she thinks the lock-up is damp. I've promised her it isn't, but anyway, we're keen to get them back into the house as soon as possible,' he said, holding both arms of his swivel chair.

I grinned, biting back a laugh of pure relief. 'Of course.'

'Great stuff. I'll text you the address and the code for the lock-up.' He rubbed his hands together. 'You wait till you see them. They'll blow your mind. They're of the sea, you know,' he said pointedly, looking straight at me.

'Cool,' I said, trying to sound nonchalant, immediately intrigued by the paintings, wanting to ask why such valuable art had been kept in a storage unit for so long. I held my tongue.

He turned to my father, 'When do you think you can get down there?'

'Is tomorrow morning okay?' my father asked.

'You're literally lifesavers, thanks,' Lucas said, eyes glinting.

As I closed the door behind me, I snuck a glance of him through the gap. He was staring out at his garden, at his kingdom, distracted from the papers that had so absorbed him before; his mind on the paintings of the sea perhaps.

Once we were at a safe distance from the house, my father said, 'Millionaire problems, eh?'

I chortled. 'It's all relative, I guess.'

'Like we don't have enough to do.'

'Come on, Dad. It'll be a change of scene.'

He scratched his head. 'If you say so.' And he laughed.

I threaded my arm through his and we walked, united, down to the bottom of the garden, where he left me at the flower bed by the pool.

As I worked, a fresh smile crept back onto my face. I was over-joyed that my father and I still had a job. I couldn't wait to tell Rob. Elizabeth's brother came to mind. His name, I now remembered, had been featured in an online *Guardian* article about emerging artists returning to the traditions of the Old Masters by painting in oils – they were apparently making a comeback on the art scene and selling for small fortunes. Normally I wouldn't have clicked into an article about art, but the photograph of the seascape painting had been arresting and had drawn me in.

On the front of the bag of peony bulbs there was a stock photograph of an elaborate explosion of pink petals. Their beauty was shamelessly extravagant. They reminded me of Lucas. I pushed the misshapen bulbs into the ground. An earthworm slid out from the side of one hole. Absently I watched it writhe before covering up the last bulb with soil. The flowers would take years to grow. Their full glory lay in wait, latent, full of potential, like Elizabeth's brother's paintings, which had been buried in a dark storage unit for years. Lucas's excitement about bringing them out again had been palpable, rousing my own curiosity. Unlike my father, I enjoyed going to see art exhibitions, mainly at local galleries – not that I ever told Dad that – and I felt thrilled to be part of uncovering a famous artist's paintings tomorrow. Especially as they depicted the sea. It felt like a present I couldn't wait to unwrap.

CHAPTER TEN

'Where would you like it?' Gordon huffed. Elizabeth thought it was typical of him to be a martyr. The canvases weren't heavy, just long and awkward to carry. He had far harder tasks to contend with in the garden.

'Just there's fine,' she said, pointing to the concrete pillar where it could lean for the time being.

Heather hovered while Gordon went out to their van for the second painting.

'Would you like to see it?' Elizabeth asked.

'Yes please,' Heather replied, glancing over her shoulder. 'Lucas told me how amazing they were.'

'Did he now?'

Elizabeth was too nervous to care that Lucas might have been flirting with Heather instead of telling her off about the swim. Her heart fluttered at the thought of setting eyes on her brother's paintings again. Her fingers jittered over the packaging, hovering there, feeling ill-equipped to peel it back.

'Do you want some help?' Heather asked, reaching out.

Elizabeth stepped in to stop her. 'Please don't.' The shock on Heather's face shamed her. *Sorry*, she thought, but she didn't say it out loud. She was too overwhelmed by the task in front of her.

The storage unit had not been climate-controlled and she worried the paintings might have been laid on top of each other, or even left underneath heavy bric-a-brac. She placed her hands on the crackling bubble wrap and slid them along the ridge of the frame. The masking tape had come away from one corner, tearing the sticker in two: *Blue No. 1 by Jude Woods.*

When it was revealed, she heard Heather gasp, 'Wow.'

The tall panel jutted out of the wrapping-strewn floor, larger than life, a portal to a blue seascape. The interplay between the bold, wild strokes was breathtaking: the bleeding of light into the sea, the dense churn at the tip of the prow of a dinghy, the block of yellow shoreline. Her eye was swept back and forth across it like the tide itself.

'I love the sea,' Heather murmured.

The two of them stood there mesmerised until Gordon came in, nonplussed.

'Here's the next one,' he said, and off he went for the third.

Together, this time, Elizabeth and Heather unwrapped the second canvas panel, titled *Blue No. 2.* It was a continuation of the first, moving further away from the shore, into choppier, moodier sea. Elizabeth's mind flew over the jagged, angular peaks of froth, fell into the troughs of green-blue and got tangled in the twist of seaweed that led her eye off and away into the distance.

When Gordon brought in *Blue No. 3*, her stomach lurched. She could see that half of the brown paper had been torn and was flapping open. There was no bubble wrap to protect it.

There was a sharp white scratch mark, roughly four inches long, across one corner.

She touched it, to verify what she saw, and then cried out, tearing away the rest of the paper. Two more marks had damaged the centre of the stormy oil painting. The deeper shades of blue, cut with black and sprayed with white, raged from the canvas as though it knew it had been defaced.

'I don't believe it,' Elizabeth rasped. The air was high in her lungs as though there were arms around her, squeezing her breath up and out. Unable to contain her fear, she turned on Heather. 'It was you, wasn't it? It was *you*. *You* did this.'

Gordon stepped towards her, remonstrating, and Elizabeth turned away from Heather and flew at him. She wasn't sure whether she wanted to kill him or feel his strength in a comforting embrace, but both fists met his chest, striking his breastbone once, like it was a door she wanted to get through. He took her wrists and gently pushed them down by her sides. 'We found it like that, Mrs Huxley,' he said.

Tears ran down her cheeks. '*He* did it,' she murmured.

'Who? Do you know who damaged them?' Heather asked, sounding near to tears herself.

Elizabeth drew back, gathering herself. 'I don't know. Why would I know?' she said, hearing the sudden chill in her own voice. She wiped a finger under each eye to get rid of her tears.

'But you said "He did it", like you knew,' Heather continued.

'*Jude* did it. He painted this, and now it's ruined.' Elizabeth stared at Heather and Gordon, who were pillars side by side in front of her; pillars she hoped might disintegrate if she closed her eyes. When she opened them, they were still there.

'You can go now. I'll deal with this,' she said, turning away from them, feeling their conspiratorial doubt ganging up on her as she walked away.

She called Jude straight away.

'Are you free for a coffee today?' she asked him.

'You're in London?'

'Not yet.'

'Everything okay?'

'Can I meet you in your studio at one?'

'Okay,' he said with a question in his voice.

'See you then,' she replied, putting the phone down quickly.

There was a tug of love and fear in her belly. As a child, her happy place had been sitting on the sofa with him, shoulder to shoulder, eating Monster Munch, watching after-school television and deciding which of his pictures they should send into the BBC art competitions. Upsetting him frightened her. She had learnt as a girl that men disappeared when they were upset.

The large oak warehouse doors of Jude's studio were solid and handsome, decorated with bottle-green stained glass in the panes along the top. Against the decrepit brickwork of the industrial courtyard, they were pieces of art in themselves.

'This is a nice surprise,' Jude said, heaving the doors closed and clicking the padlock shut.

'Yes,' she said, guessing it would not turn out to be nice at all. 'Where shall we go?'

'Are you sure you don't want a cup of tea here?' she asked, double-checking. Part of her would have preferred to deliver the bad news in private.

He groaned. 'I need to get out. My latest piece is doing my head in.'

'How about a bagel from that place you took me to last time?'

'Perfect. We'll find a park bench.'

They zigzagged through the strange mix of Victorian conversions and low-rise prefabricated apartment blocks of Shoreditch, crossing the scruffy, busy Kingsland Road and on through the five-storey red-brick tenements of Arnold Circus. The walk was familiar and comforting, reminding her that this city ran in her blood, and that she could leave her identity at Copper Lodge behind. Walking next to Jude, past the chained-up bikes and the graffiti, inhaling the bus fumes and shouting over ambulances, was like coming home.

She even enjoyed the occasional stare from strangers. They were an incongruous pair. Nobody would guess they were brother and sister, or even friends: a Home Counties housewife and an east London artist.

As children, everyone had assumed they'd had different fathers, a fact that their mother had neither confirmed nor denied. Back then, both of them had had long scrubby hair, which Virginia had never brushed and had allowed to grow right into their eyes. Jude had often been mistaken for a girl. As an adult, Elizabeth had tamed her own hair, but Jude had left his the same. His large blue eyes still blinked through the dark mop, until he shoved it back to see better, opening up his charming, boyish face.

Elizabeth had never wanted her little brother's face to show anything other than permanent happiness. Yet here they were.

They turned into Brick Lane and the bagel shop came into view. They joined the queue that had formed outside and along the pavement. Two pigeons pecked at the rubbish that had spilled out of a split bin bag. Elizabeth watched the birds and gathered sentences together in her head. When she finally started her confession, she spoke so loudly, the two pigeons flew off and the couple in front of them turned round.

'You're not going to like what I have to tell you,' she said.

'What am I not going to like?'

She continued in a whisper. 'It's quite bad news.'

His whole face stretched into a grimace of alarm. 'What's happened?'

Realising she had launched in too heavily, she backtracked and explained about the damage to the painting, talking in breathless bursts, feeling her heartbeat increasing.

When she had finished, he said, 'To be honest, I'd forgotten those paintings even existed.'

Elizabeth knew this couldn't be true. 'You're not angry?'

They shuffled forward, almost at the door. The smell of warm dough hit her.

'Paintings get damaged all the time in storage or in transit,' he said.

'Really?'

'What do you want?' he said, cupping his hands through the shop window to see the various tubs of fillings on offer.

He seemed unperturbed by her news, but she couldn't relax. Maybe she didn't trust in his nonchalance. When he was worried about her, he stopped sharing his true feelings. Was he worried about her now?

'But aren't you upset?' she asked.

He laughed. 'Do you want me to be?'

'No! But it's ruined!'

'I can fix it,' he said.

She held her breath, suspending his offer in her mind like something precious held high. On an out breath, she said, 'Is that really possible?'

'I'd have to take a look at it, but by the sounds of it, I'd be able to patch it up, good as new.'

Then came the relief, rushing through her whole body. 'Really, Jude?'

'Yes.' He indicated the woman behind the counter, who had asked them something. 'What do you want?' he said again.

Elizabeth ordered a plain bagel with cream cheese and Jude ordered a hot salt beef with mustard. She grinned at him. 'You are the best, you know that?' she said.

He grinned back. 'Yeah. I know.'

With their warm paper bags in their hands, they walked to the church gardens and found a bench to sit on.

'Do you want me to transport the canvas to your studio?' she asked.

'I'll come down to Copper Lodge and have a look at it,' he said. 'Then I'll get to see those two little mischiefs.'

The prospect of his visit – so rare these days – unlocked a rush of love and gratitude in her heart. 'Thank you, Jude.' She left the parcel of food on her lap and began to cry, releasing some of the recent pressures.

Jude put an arm around her.

'Shh, shh, Elizabeth. It's only a stupid bit of oil on canvas,' he soothed.

'Sorry, I'm okay, really I am.' She wiped her eyes with a paper napkin and looked up to the white, meaningless sky, trying to find something to focus on. There was a plastic bag high in a branch. She watched it billow and flap, and imagined a gust of wind dislodging it and sending it flitting across the sky to end its journey in a vast, stinking landfill. Her tears receded. Her self-pity was pathetic. 'I'm so up and down these days. I'm probably perimenopausal. Some women do get it in their early forties,' she waffled, knowing how high-pitched and silly she sounded.

They unwrapped their bagels in silence.

'Are you still seeing that woman?' he asked.

She screwed the napkin into a ball. 'I don't need to *see* someone every time I get a bit upset, Jude,' she returned, irritated. Then she added, 'Except maybe a beautician about these wrinkles.' She squinted at him to accentuate her crow's-feet lines, but he didn't laugh.

So she bit into her soft, still-warm bagel and asked him to tell her all about the struggles he was having with his latest work. Anything to avoid talking about doctors.

Elizabeth was poised at her computer, ready to order the dull art deco invitations that Lucas had wanted. She fiddled with the edge of the credit card that he had given her. Her eyes were dried out from crying with Jude, but she felt significantly less burdened inside.

She hesitated over the stationer's order form, blinking at the screen. The notion of writing to Mary Billingshurst to commission the expensive gold strawberry invitations was a temptation she was trying to resist.

Sabotaging thoughts like this one had multiplied in her mind throughout the afternoon. There had been various decisions to make and yet she had been deliberating about all of them, leaving emails unanswered: flute or coupe glasses? Cream or white tablecloths? Tomato salad or cucumber and strawberry? These frivolous details were important to Lucas, but the options were piling up inside her, cramming her brain, ready to spill out and shatter into pieces with no party to show for it.

She had to break the impasse by ordering the invitations. It was essential she send them out six weeks before 4 July.

Still she prevaricated. She thought about Isla's tantrum yesterday. She had wanted to drop Lucas in it and say 'Daddy *does* actually think you're stupid. Join the club!' But she hadn't. She had swallowed Isla's blame and withstood her small pummelling fists.

After seeing Jude this morning, she felt buoyed up, and a little rebellious.

The cursor flashed in the address box of the stationer's website. The little line ticked patiently, waiting for her to fill in the blanks. It would do anything she asked of it, just as she would for Lucas.

There had been a time, many moons ago, when her mother had accused her of being spirited and wilful. Virginia had laid down rules and Elizabeth had broken them. That bolshie child was still inside her somewhere.

But she knew the hand-painted invitations were an unnecessary expense and that the Sloane Street stationer was the safe, conventional bet. To afford this party, Lucas had been loading up his credit cards, consolidating loans and managing their money meticulously, eking out its value to ensure they could hire or buy the highest possible quality for the lowest possible price.

Mindful of the tight budget, she began to type in her details.

Then the white scratch on Jude's painting flared across her eyelids, like lightning across the painted sea, and she stabbed at the delete button. Lucas had been responsible for the damage to her paintings, and she felt a surge of anger towards him.

She clicked out of the website and opened up her emails.

As though the cursor had come to life and taken charge, the letters of Mary Billingshurst's name appeared, forming a blue, underscored destination for her email. She clicked into the main body of the message and carefully worded her order.

Before sending it, she double-checked the finished email, and then triple-checked it. Her heart rose into her throat as she tapped send to confirm the order of one hundred and fifty gold strawberry themed invitations.

Shortly afterwards, she received an email from Mary asking her to call with her credit card details. With the full knowledge that there would no longer be enough left on this particular credit card to pay the deposit on the marquee, she read out the long number on the front.

She was shocked by what she had done, but not shocked enough to change her mind over the coming days before the invitations arrived.

Lucas's voice on the phone cut out repeatedly.

'Stop rustling those packets, you two!' Elizabeth cried out, trying to decipher Lucas's broken-up instructions through their crisp-eating in the back of the car.

She gleaned he needed her in London by 8 p.m. She was to meet him at the Berkeley private members' club, where Sam and Poppy Stone would join them for dinner.

Elizabeth had never met Sam and Poppy Stone before, but she remembered writing their address, *One Hyde Park, SW1X*, underneath their names on one of the small white envelopes. Their gold strawberry invitation would have landed on the doormat of their exclusive home in the heart of Knightsbridge, where the apartments cost twenty million pounds, give or take a few hundred thousand.

Meeting a billionaire like Sam Stone might have interested Elizabeth years ago, when she and Lucas had first met. She might have wanted to know how he had earned his money, how he spent it, where he holidayed, whether his skin had the glow of wealth or his eyes shone with the secret to an easier life. She might have convinced herself that he was more interesting than the average person, like meeting a celebrity, an exotic creature, someone her mother would have scoffed at.

Now she was in a taxi from Waterloo station to Berkeley Square, passing one of the four-storey houses in Mayfair that Lucas had once promised he would buy her. She remembered him saying it after she had admired its Georgian windows, and how she had exhaled with a sense of relief. She had been in love with Lucas, and had begun to view her mother's disdain for the wealthy as a perverse inverse snobbery, a prejudice even. There were different ways of living, she had thought, and she had decided on one that she thought would suit her better. By choosing Lucas, a lifetime of money worries would be over. Little had she known that Lucas would worry about money just as much as her mother had, albeit in a different way. The hardships weren't there, but the focus on finding money was as all-consuming. Appearing wealthier than they were took skill and dedication. Borrowing off the back of his assets and juggling debts had become a twenty-four-hour preoccupation. And Elizabeth had begun to learn from him. For instance, to solve the problem of the shortfall on the credit card for the marquee deposit, she had tricked him into giving her more housekeeping money this month.

Smoke and mirrors, darling, smoke and mirrors.

At the Berkeley Club reception – Lucas had negotiated a discount on their membership in exchange for recruiting five new members a year – they knew her by name.

Lucas was sitting in the corner of the bar, on a circular green velvet banquette. There was a martini waiting for her on the table. She was relieved that Sam and Poppy had not yet arrived. When he saw her, he stopped circling the cocktail stick in his own drink. 'Wow,' he said, looking her up and down and whistling. She was wearing a silk wrap dress in midnight blue that she knew he liked. His approval gave her a thrill.

She slipped in next to him, relishing the smells of good food and the sound of ice on cut-glass tumblers. The low lighting made everyone look beautiful. The shadows across the glass of the ornate antique mirrors, heavy and overbearing around the room, reflected infinite muted versions of the huge chandeliers; of prosperity and luxury. Everything he had promised her.

The first sip of her martini went straight to her head.

Lucas stroked her leg through the slit of her dress, high up her thigh. She wished they could find somewhere to have an illicit kiss. No more. Just a kiss, like teenagers.

'Sam's running late. But it gives us some time.' He popped the gin-soaked olive into his mouth.

'What's he like as a person?' she asked. 'Sam, I mean.'

'He's a bit of a prat, if I'm honest. He pretends he's self-made, but all the investments he's made have been off the back of Poppy's dad.'

She tried not to drink her martini too fast and said, 'I'd always imagined that only Russian oligarchs and Saudi oil-men lived at One Hyde Park.'

'His business partner is a Russian oligarch.'

She laughed. 'And Poppy? Do you think we'll get on?'

'I haven't met her. Are they coming on the fourth of July?'

'They haven't RSVP'd yet.' Elizabeth thought again of the invitations that Lucas had not sanctioned.

'How many are we up to?'

'Twenty yeses and two noes.'

'Who are the noes from?'

'The Arnolds – they're going to be in Perugia – and your sister can't make it. But Benjamin Healing is confirmed.'

'Who's he?'

'An artist.'

'Do we have anything by him?'

'No.'

'He was on your brother's list?'

'Yes. Jude's driving him down. They're good friends. He's pretty hot right now.'

'*Should* we own one of his pieces?'

'You didn't like his work when we saw it at the Wigram a few years back. Too many lines, you said.'

'I remember now.' He stopped a waiter and asked for more olives. 'Make sure you tell Poppy your brother will be there. She's impressed by that crap and I really want them to come.'

'Poppy and Bo are friends, aren't they?'

'That's why we're here.' Lucas dropped his voice, 'There they are.' He stood up to wave them over.

Sam Stone looked much younger than Elizabeth had imagined him to be. He was small, with a squashed face, as though a spade had flattened his nose to the side and forced his eyes further apart. He was underdressed, wearing trainers and a short-sleeved black sweatshirt. Poppy was a few inches taller than him and far too thin, in an elegant cream chiffon blouse. The severe points of her nose and cheekbones contrasted almost comically with Sam's boneless features. Her name conjured a smiley, fun girl. On first sight, Elizabeth gleaned that Poppy was neither.

'Lucas?' Sam Stone said.

'Sam. Poppy. Great to see you. This is Elizabeth, my wife.'

Sam held Elizabeth's hand. 'A pleasure to meet you,' he said, kissing her on the cheek.

They settled at the table and ordered two whisky highballs, which reminded Elizabeth of a novel she had once read about a couple living in 1960s suburbia whose loveless marriage was propped up by highballs – until the husband began murdering his wife's lovers.

Sam yawned, almost lying down on the banquette. 'I need a pick-me-up.'

The yawning continued, frequent and undisguised, and Elizabeth wondered if he might fall asleep. Next to him, Poppy crossed one arm across her ribcage and locked her hand at the other elbow, as though barring entry.

'We're a little jet-lagged, I'm afraid,' she explained.

The two men began their talk about business.

Elizabeth and Poppy tried to make conversation of their own. Elizabeth wasn't sure why it was such hard work; whether it was her fault or Poppy's.

During their starters, she broached the all-important question. 'Can you come next month?'

'Where?'

'To our party.'

'The invitation! We got it today when we dumped our bags.' Poppy slipped her hand into her clutch bag, brought out the gold strawberry card and waved it in the air.

It caught Lucas's eye. He stared, mesmerised, stopping mid-sentence. Elizabeth couldn't swallow her mouthful. She wanted to snatch the invitation from Poppy's hand.

'I was going to tick this for you now,' Poppy said, pushing her half-finished plate aside. 'Saves me having to post it. Have you tried Paperless Post yet?'

A reply to that question never made it out of Elizabeth's mouth. One look from Lucas told her to keep very quiet. A sick-making heat spread across her cheeks.

Poppy ticked the box for 'Yes, we're coming!' Unaware of what she had revealed, she scribbled along the line that asked for allergy information. Elizabeth could make out *vegan*, *dairy-free* and *gluten-free*.

'Such *beautiful* invitations,' Poppy said. 'But the stationer doesn't have a website. I checked on the way here. You must forward me her number.'

She handed the RSVP card back to Elizabeth, who swiftly put it away in her handbag, into which she wanted to vomit.

'I will, of course. I'm so pleased you can come,' she managed, avoiding Lucas's eye.

Sam said, 'I hope there'll be dancing!'

Poppy stabbed at the roast aubergine on her plate. 'You don't want to witness that, believe me,' she said, smiling at Elizabeth for the first time. Elizabeth attempted to smile back, but her lips had forgotten how.

She tried her best to be entertaining and light for Sam and Poppy, but her thoughts were taken up by the invitations.

Lucas had booked a driver to pick them up from outside the club. The car had slippery leather seats. Elastic pouches were stocked with high-end magazines for the passengers. Chilled water bottles glowed in the neon-lit drinks holders.

Elizabeth climbed into the back. Lucas sat in the front. The driver, who wore a suit, pulled out into the traffic. She was relieved it wasn't Piotr.

'Successful night?' she asked Lucas, testing the waters.

He didn't respond.

She leant forward and repeated the question. Again he didn't respond. She sat back and reached into her handbag for some liquorice.

'Matt, how are the kids?' Lucas asked the driver.

Throughout the journey, Lucas talked to Matt or read on his phone. He did not speak to Elizabeth, nor did he look at her.

She continued to chew on her sweets.

When they undressed in their bedroom at home, she tried again to talk to him about the evening. She offered snippets of her conversation with Poppy, lacking the courage to bring up the invitations. To everything she said, a muscle in his jaw twitched, but it stayed locked.

Lying next to him in the pitch black, in the silence, she feared that she did not exist at all.

The next day, late morning, she knocked on the door to his study.

Standing in the doorway, she said bravely, 'I am so sorry I didn't tell you about the invitations, Lucas. Isla wanted them so much. It was emotional blackmail. She thinks everything she does is stupid. Or she thinks we think that.' She was rambling now.

He scratched his cheek, cutting across his mole.

Finally he replied, 'You knew we couldn't afford them. It takes us way over budget and the credit cards are all maxed out.'

'Oh God, I'm so sorry.' She plucked at the sleeve of her sweatshirt, trying to think up an explanation without tangling her words. Blood rushed through her ears. She heard Agata next door in Hugo's room, tidying, and she decided she should go and help her, anything to escape her own shame and regret.

Lucas rubbed his face, 'Darling, do you think you might be struggling? You've been doing so well, but you can tell me the truth. I won't blame you for feeling overwhelmed.'

A lump rose up her throat. 'No, seriously, I can handle it,' she said.

'You're sure it's not too much? First the scratched painting, and then the wrong invitations?'

She picked at the edge of her thumbnail, fighting back the urge to counter his accusation about Jude's painting. 'I made a terrible decision about those invitations. When I was writing them, I started to hate them.' She had imagined everyone opening them at the breakfast table and sniggering over them as they drank their morning coffee. Tears rushed into her eyes again.

'Well come on now, don't look so sad. I'll find a way to pay for them. And Jude's coming down to fix the painting. It's all going to be okay.'

'Isla was happy about her gold strawberries at least,' she murmured.

He cleared his throat. 'Speaking of Isla, it's the parents' orientation day at Channing House the week after next, isn't it?'

Elizabeth's eyes dried as though a sudden wind had blown into them.

'But you cancelled her place,' she rasped, horror-struck.

'Well, after all this, it might be wise to keep our options open, that's all. Is that okay? Just to be safe? I couldn't handle the kids going through another ...' He trailed off and her knees gave way beneath her. He leapt up. 'Are you okay?' he asked, catching her under the arms.

'I'm ... I'm not feeling too well actually.'

He hugged her. 'It's for the best,' he said gently into her ear.

Elizabeth began trembling, as though she were cold. 'I was sure I was okay. I thought I was okay. I'm okay, aren't I, Lucas?'

'Shh, shh,' he said, just like Jude had. She remembered why all this had happened. Disorientated, she mumbled, 'Yes. Jude's coming to sort everything out. He misses the kids.'

'Lovely. He'll be a tonic.'

After a few moments, she recovered herself. 'Let's hope he can fix the damage,' she said.

Lucas let her go and returned to his desk.

Elizabeth left the study, bleary-eyed, passing by Hugo's open bedroom door. Agata stopped folding Hugo's T-shirt to stare at her. Sympathy pulled down her mouth; appalling sympathy. It stopped Elizabeth in her tracks. She hesitated at the door, tempted to collapse on Hugo's small bed, curl up under his duvet and unload her feelings onto Agata. But she raised her chin – though it felt heavy as lead – and walked on.

CHAPTER ELEVEN

I was up a ladder trimming the laurel hedge by the pool. Below me, Agata was sandwiched in between Hugo and Isla on an inflatable. Their legs were splashing about behind them. Agata was giggling at something one of them had said.

I moved the ladder a foot across and continued snipping at the infernal hedge, listening to their playing, both cheered by it and wishing I could join them. Their laughter was infectious and I realised I didn't hear much of it at Copper Lodge.

From the barn, the high-pitched screech of Piotr's circular saw split the air.

The saw stopped. I heard Elizabeth's voice and looked down. She wore a smart summer suit and large sunglasses.

My ladder clanged as I lost my footing. Her head snapped up towards me.

'Do be careful,' she said. Then she yelled, 'Isla! You need to get out right now and get ready for Channing.'

'No!' Isla wailed. 'I don't want to go!'

Agata remained on the inflatable. Her legs were not kicking, nor were her arms paddling.

'Agata, will you deal with this? Lucas is getting antsy about leaving,' Elizabeth said.

While Agata tried to cajole a screaming Isla out of the pool, Elizabeth removed her sunglasses and shouted up at me, 'Heather, would you come down a minute?'

Obediently, and reluctantly, I dismounted the ladder and joined her at the poolside.

Over the noise of Isla's full-blown tantrum, Elizabeth said, 'Will you look at Hugo's stroke? His teachers say he's a natural, but I don't know whether it's because we pay too much in school fees.'

'Sure,' I said, wondering how she could switch off from Isla's distress, wondering why she was dressed in a suit, and why, if Lucas was getting antsy about leaving, she had time to showcase Hugo's swimming.

'Hugo, darling. Show Heather your front crawl,' she said. 'She can give you some pointers.'

I waved hello at Hugo, who grinned at me from the side.

Piotr's circular saw started up again, obscuring what Agata was saying to Isla. I could make out Polish, angry Polish. Whether it scared or fascinated Isla out of her rage, I couldn't tell, but she followed Agata out of the pool. Their wet footprints left a path that swerved wide of Elizabeth and out of the gate.

'We're going to an orientation day at Channing House,' Elizabeth declared as we watched Hugo thrash his way through the water.

'She's moving schools?'

'She's going to board,' she said, clapping Hugo, who had reached the other side.

Hugo's swim, however impressive for a five-year-old, became irrelevant. '*Boarding* school?'

'Yes.'

I couldn't help myself; the words came out of my mouth before I could stop them. 'But she's only a baby!'

With a sharp flash of her wristwatch, Elizabeth slapped my cheek. I froze, electrified. It had been so out of the blue and so uncalled for, I couldn't believe it had happened. Too startled to react, I watched her hurry away on her tiptoes, her heels raised off the ground as though she were stepping through dirt.

Hugo stared up from the water, sculling to stay afloat.

'I think you'd better jump out and go on up to the house, Hugo,' I said.

Hugo splashed around for a bit while I stood there motionless.

'Come on, Hugo. Out you get.'

When he had gone, I picked up my clippers, which had fallen to the grass; I didn't remember them slipping from my hand.

The ladder was a safe place to retreat to, and I made my way up in a daze.

As I clung to the top rung, paralysed with an attack of vertigo, the wretched saw screeched again. I thought of Piotr working hard on the Huxleys' conversion and wondered if he had ever been slapped for getting it wrong. When I considered the injustice of it, my right boot inched down to the next rung. And then the left, and on down until I was standing on the grass again. They walked me up the shingled path to find my father and tell him what Elizabeth had done.

The screaming of the tool hurt my head as I passed the barn. I pictured Piotr bent double.

My father ducked through the low door frame. 'Heather, we need a hand.'

I stood dumbly, staring at him.

'Sometime before Christmas?' he said.

In that split second, I had a decision to make.

'Coming,' I said, walking towards him, lead weights for feet.

The strain of lifting the beam could have burst thousands of my blood vessels. Even Piotr's face was distorted as he heaved. We grunted and groaned as we dropped the beam where it needed to be.

'Thanks, love. Meet you on the wall for lunch in five minutes,' Dad said.

'Sure, see you there,' I said. I dared to look at Piotr. His eyes penetrated mine. I feared he had noticed the redness on my left cheek.

Unsure of what to do, I made my way back to the laurel hedge to collect my clippers. I thought about the consequences of confronting Elizabeth. It could destroy my parents' livelihood, force me and Rob into rent arrears and threaten my relationship with Mum and Dad forever. It wasn't worth it, but I couldn't help reassessing my position at Copper Lodge. What had the slap meant? What had it really been about? Yes, I guess I had been out of line, but had I deserved to be hit? Or had her reaction been an unconscious punishment for my past with Lucas? I wondered about how much Lucas had told her.

Deep in thought, I leapt back a step when I heard Lucas himself.

'Have you seen Elizabeth anywhere?' he asked me. His eyes seemed to have receded into their sockets, lost and vulnerable. His blonde curls, usually so neat, bounced about in mockery of the smart blue suit and tie that he wore.

'We were by the pool,' I replied.

'When?'

'About fifteen minutes ago?'

'She's just disappeared into thin air,' he said, shaking his head, staring at me.

'Have you checked in the barn?'

'I've checked everywhere.'

'Maybe she went out.'

'But the car's there. Any chance you could help me look?'

My time was owned by him. I would do anything he asked of me. But I didn't know how I would react to Elizabeth if I saw her.

'Sure.'

His smile had a sad edge. 'That would be so great, if you could spare the time.'

We searched, and he called for his wife repeatedly. 'Elizabeth! Darling! Elizabeth! We've got to go!'

We reached the meadow.

'This is a nightmare,' he said, stopping. 'We were supposed to have left for Channing half an hour ago.'

'You're looking around a new school?' I said, feigning ignorance, wanting to ask him why he would even consider sending his sweet seven-year-old to boarding school.

He squinted at me through the glare from the sun, cupping both hands over his brow to shelter his eyes. 'This is Elizabeth's fault. All this,' he said.

I stayed silent, confused, knowing it was more than he should have said. His arms fell to his sides and he began to walk back towards the house.

'Sorry. That was really inappropriate.'

'It's okay.'

'None of this is okay.' His hands were deep in his pockets and his eyes followed the ground as we walked. His energy had changed, as though he had given up hope of finding her. 'Why would she let the kids go swimming when she knew we had to leave?'

I put my hand to my cheek. I said, 'Hugo was showing me his stroke.'

'How ironic,' he said.

'How so?'

'You. Now. With my son. And back then, when I—'

'He's good,' I interrupted, blushing.

'Says the pro.'

'No,' I said modestly.

'I credit myself, of course.'

My heart leapt high in my chest. 'It was nothing to do with *you*,' I shot back.

He looked hurt. There wasn't time to rectify it and apologise. Elizabeth appeared from around the back of the barn, where the camper van sat. She was plucking at her skirt nervily, straightening it. Her cheeks were over-rouged. At least I thought they were, until she got closer, when I realised she was sweating. Her face was on fire, as though she had been running.

'Where have you been?' Lucas asked, desperate rather than angry.

'Just reminding Piotr to let the marquee people in at twelve. They need to recce the site.'

'But we've been looking for you everywhere!'

She checked her watch. 'Oh gosh, sorry, is that the time?' she said airily, pushing her hair off her forehead, avoiding eye contact with me. 'Is Isla ready?'

Her fey act didn't tally with her outburst at the poolside. I began to wonder whether I had imagined the slap.

'Isla's been waiting in the car for twenty minutes,' Lucas said. 'You *knew* what time we had to leave.'

She looked at me and blinked in slow motion. 'Lucas always wants to be five hours early for everything.'

'It's better than being five hours late,' Lucas said, storming on ahead.

'Sorry,' she mouthed, stroking her own cheek, as though she was apologising for slapping herself; biting her lip sheepishly, shrugging, and then trotting after Lucas.

I watched them go, incredulous.

Dad twisted the can-opener around the tin of mince. We had eaten mince and spaghetti every night for two weeks. Usually we would eat fast after a long day of physical work. Tonight, I would have preferred to go hungry.

The bowls were put on the table and they steamed in front of us. I listened to the latest gossip about the soup kitchen. How the Salvation Army had begun to take the spillover from London's homeless into their shelter in Guildford. About the sixteen-year-old who had been kicked out by her abusive mother, and how she had asked a lady at the bus stop for fifty pence to make a phone call and then been arrested for begging. And about an ex-tiler with depression who had been sleeping in the air vent of a building to hide from the police, fearing they would arrest him for vagrancy. He described tales of lives gone wrong, and their backstories of abuse and maltreatment. As we talked, I knew I should feel lucky that I wasn't one of those people, but I couldn't hold in what had happened to me for one second longer.

'Dad, something really bad happened today.'

He finished his mouthful by sucking in a dangling spaghetti string. 'Hmm?'

'You know I was cutting back the laurels by the pool?'

'Yes.' He placed his hands either side of his bowl. His head seemed to grow even larger.

'Elizabeth asked me to watch Hugo swim,' I began. 'And I kind of said something that offended her. And she slapped me.'

'She *slapped* you?'

'Yes.' I put my hand on my cheek.

He picked up his fork. 'No,' he said.

'You think I'm making it up?'

His fork was pointed at me. 'You obviously upset her. What did you say to her?'

'I was a bit shocked when she said they're sending Isla to boarding school, that's all.'

'So you were being rude.'

'I didn't mean to be.'

He frowned and began eating again. Through a mouthful, he scoffed at me. 'You've always been a hothead, with all your opinions.'

The bowl wobbled as I knocked it by accident, reaching for my water. 'It just came out.'

'I guess you want to keep your job? *Our* jobs?'

I sipped my water and tried to quell the rise of indignation. 'To be honest, Dad, I wanted to tell her to stick the job,' I mumbled.

He stood up, towering over me, pointing down at me. 'Careful what you wish for.'

I looked up at him. 'Sorry, Dad. I didn't mean it.'

'Just keep your head down, okay?' He wiped sauce away from his mouth with a tea towel.

I dumped the leftovers into the bin, now feeling guilty about provoking Elizabeth; about how judgemental and outspoken I had been. 'It's going to be awkward tomorrow. She's going to hate me now.'

'You think she cares about you enough to hate you?'

I shrugged, feeling very small.

He cleared his throat. 'Young lady, I do hope all this isn't to do with your feelings for Lucas.'

Mortified, I shot back, 'Feelings for *Lucas*?'

'A little bird told me you used to rather like him.'

The 'little bird' must have been my mother, who had once read Lucas's name on an open page of my diary. I had made her promise not to tell anyone and had trusted her to keep the secret.

'When I was a teenager!' But my face was bright red.

'He's very handsome, very wealthy and very kind. I wouldn't blame you if you still did.'

'For God's sake, Dad. Elizabeth's the one who's in the wrong here.' I left the dishes in the sink and hurried off to my room, cringing.

There was no air in my room. I opened the window, biting back the urge to yell at Elizabeth over the hedge, 'Sorry, okay! Just SORRY!'

It was my place to be sorrier than her. We needed her more than she needed us. That was the way of the world, and my ranting and raving about it wasn't going to change anything. It left me feeling powerless. So utterly powerless, I felt like giving up on being a good citizen altogether: finding some pot to smoke, drinking a bottle of gin on a park bench and sticking two fingers up at all the well-to-do passers-by. The thought of it cheered me up, and I went to sleep dreaming of an anarchic life, carefree, on the sidelines of society, and liberated from the Huxleys – in my head, at least.

CHAPTER TWELVE

The girls' bedrooms were in a wing of the old Victorian school building. There was a smell of furniture polish and stale uniforms. The floorboards creaked underneath the plastic carpets. Elizabeth, Isla and Lucas walked two steps behind the headmistress down a dark corridor towards a fire door. In Elizabeth's pocket, her mobile pinged with a text. She prised off Isla's hand to read it, knowing it would be a reply from Jude about the paintings.

Hi sis, can't do this weekend. Doing a talk at the Bilbao in Spain. I can do 20th?

Isla was walking so close, Elizabeth kept tripping over her as she texted Jude back.

The party's on the 4th. It has to be before then. How about next weekend, 13th/14th June?

'Everything okay?' Lucas said, under his breath.

'Yes. All good,' she replied, putting her phone away, crossing her fingers in her mind.

Mrs Hepburn opened the fire door to reveal a large room packed with pine cubicle beds and dressers. Elizabeth noticed a calendar pinned to the wall. A school crest headed each month. Every single day leading up to today's date – 5 June – had been carefully crossed out in thick red pen. The end of term was decorated with drawings of rainbow explosions and dozens of happy faces.

'We dislike the term "dormitory" as we feel it sounds a little stuffy. Isla would be sharing with four other girls in her first term,' Mrs Hepburn said.

Isla began to cry and Mrs Hepburn tried to comfort her. 'You'll make lots of friends, and soon you'll be telling Mummy and Daddy you don't want to come home.'

Elizabeth thought of the calendar and doubted it very much. She didn't like to see Mrs Hepburn's hand touch Isla's shoulder. It was Elizabeth's job to console her daughter, not a stranger's.

'We'll be back in a minute,' she said, taking Isla's hand and leading her along a never-ending corridor that reminded her of a scene in a horror film she'd watched about an orphanage that burned down with all the children inside.

They ended up in a stairwell of damp-smelling carpets and rendered walls. Isla sat down on the top step. Her head dropped forward and her little chest heaved with quiet sobs. Elizabeth sat down next to her.

'Have one of these,' she said, offering her a packet of Polo mints.

Isla didn't take one.

'I don't want to sleep here in this school,' she sniffed.

'But you liked the big swimming pool? And the amazing theatre? Didn't you?'

'A bit.'

'And all the girls seem very friendly.'

'They look very tall.'

'It's bound to feel a bit scary,' Elizabeth said weakly.

Isla turned her face to her and blinked her blue eyes and said, very quietly, 'Why don't you want me to live at home with you, Mummy?'

'Darling! I *do* want you to live at home with me!' Elizabeth cried, throwing her arms around her. *More than anything in the world*, she added silently.

'Is it because I'm naughty?'

Her heart rocked in her chest. 'Oh Isla! Is that what you think?'

'You want to live with just Hugo. But he's a telltale. He starts it, Mummy, but you never tell him off! And I don't mean to be bad!' She began to cry again.

'Sweetheart. That's not it at all. It's got nothing to do with how naughty or good either of you are. It's because you're the big girl.' She heard how ludicrous this sounded. Isla wasn't a big girl. She was a baby, just as Heather had said.

'I don't want to be a big girl.'

Elizabeth looked outside, through the high, narrow windows, and saw the trees bent out of shape, permanently altered by the wind that blew relentlessly from the sea. 'You'll always be my little baby Isla.' She hugged her daughter tighter.

'Why do I have to go here then?'

'Because it's a good school and …' Elizabeth's sentence trailed off.

'It smells funny.'

Tears filled her eyes and she laughed. 'It does, doesn't it.'

'Tell that headmistress I'm not coming then.' Isla put her head on Elizabeth's pulled-up knees.

'Okay, darling,' Elizabeth said, stroking her daughter's hair, wondering how she could possibly fulfil this promise.

When they returned to the bedroom, Lucas said to Isla, 'The rooms are nicer than they were in my day!' He laughed, then his phone rang. 'Sorry, I've got to take this,' he said, disengaging. Elizabeth wondered if these rooms triggered memories of his own school. From the stories he had told her, none of them would be good.

The loo cubicles, next door, smelt institutional. She noticed a baby toothbrush on the side of a basin, and then a pull-up nappy stuffed into one of the bins. She imagined the child hiding it from her friends or being made fun of for bed-wetting. Isla still wet the bed occasionally, when she was anxious about something. Would she be that child on her first night?

At this, something broke in Elizabeth. It didn't matter how plush the theatre was or how spectacular the swimming pool or how impressive the league tables; it didn't change the fact that this school was an institution. It didn't change the fact that Elizabeth would not be able to scoop Isla up in her arms and give her a warm, loving cuddle every morning and every afternoon, before and after school. Only at home could Isla get unstructured, untrained love on tap, taken for granted, shunned even, but unconditional. What else was Elizabeth there for if not to provide that every day for her day-dreaming, unconfident, sugar-addict daughter?

'No, I'm sorry!' she cried. 'No, no, no way. I can't do it, Lucas.' She grabbed Isla's hand and dragged her away down the horrid corridor. The Polo mints clattered to the floor.

A group of heroic girls with knobbly knees and skinny arms trotted past them in their baggy PE kits. Elizabeth stopped running and held her breath, trying to be as plucky as they were. Each girl said hello to them politely. Isla said hello back as Elizabeth tugged her along, almost off the floor, holding her breath all the way to the car, where Piotr was waiting.

Isla climbed into the front. 'Mummy didn't like that school,' she explained to Piotr, and reached for her iPad. 'She wants me to stay at home with Hugo.'

The computer game bleeped into the silence.

'I'm afraid I found the tour a little overwhelming, Piotr,' Elizabeth sniffed, searching the car's side pockets for her tin of boiled sweets. When she found it empty, she buried her head in her hands and her emotions flooded out.

Piotr reached into the glove compartment and popped a white pill out of a foil blister pack. 'Here,' he said, handing it to her. 'I have left. This. For you.'

She took it with a swig of water and pulled her phone out of her pocket. There, sitting on the screen, like a present, was a text from Jude.

W/e 13th good. See you then. ☺

When they arrived home, they found Agata dishing out cottage pie for Hugo. Elizabeth nodded at her briefly and told Isla to sit down for supper. Then she went straight up to the bedroom.

She shut the door and backed herself against the wardrobe.

Lucas was close behind her.

'That was totally bloody humiliating,' he said, sitting down on her dressing table stool, swivelling it in half-circles, head in hands.

Out of the window beyond him, distant plumes of bonfire smoke punctuated the expanse of farmland. She thought of the horizon.

'I don't want Isla to go to that school.'

He threw his head back and groaned. 'But we've been over it again and again!' The tips of his fingers whitened on his knees, as though he were holding himself down. 'How many times do we have to do this?'

'I'm capable of looking after her now.'

'And today proved that, did it?'

Elizabeth looked at her feet. Just socks, soft and vulnerable. *Sticks and stones may break my bones but words will never hurt me. Sticks and stones may break my bones but words will never hurt me.* 'But I'm not having bad thoughts any more.'

'Is that really true?'

Both Heather and Agata were pretty young women. Any wife would be wary. The bad thoughts had been within the bounds of normal. She was sure of it.

'I swear it's true.'

'I get scared,' he confessed.

'Don't be,' she said, but she understood why he might be.

The material felt soft around her throat. The yellow bathroom stool was a little wobbly on the marble floor. It reminded her of the useless tiler who had laid the slabs unevenly. Mundane thoughts like this flickered across her mind, but without anxiety. It was a blessed relief to think and not feel. Nobody could get to her; she would be gone and she would be free of the desolate feelings. Her children would not grow up to hate her. She would be forever loved. Though she did not feel grand or dramatic about the act. It felt lighter than life or death. She had the sense that she was walking out of a door and away from unendurable thoughts, away from life's expectations of her. Too high, too hard.

She had tied the cord onto the curtain rail, which was an oval chrome loop above the free-standing marble bath. Closing the curtain had been important to her, a pointless modesty that had been logistically complicated to arrange. She stepped up onto the stool and over the thick, expensive lip of the bath and let the noose take her weight. Its initial softness hardened to razor-sharp wire. It was agonising and petrifying as the air to her lungs was cut off, leaving her suffocating, her eyes popping out of her skull. Her legs kicked out for a surface to take the weight, to stop what she had started. By her own design, her tiptoes could not reach. The shower curtain flapped open.

A small figure in a white cotton nightie stood in the door frame: the angel who would save her.

He sighed. 'I'm worried about leaving you alone.'

'That's why you've been working from home so much?'

He shrugged and nodded. His voice became hoarse. 'I want to trust you, I really do.'

'Agata is here to help me.'

'Agata can't possibly understand what's going on inside your head!'

'But you don't either!' she cried, pressing her fingers into her temples. 'I'm telling you I'm fine but you won't believe me!'

Through the shower curtain, Lucas's arms enveloped her and lifted her up high, keeping her alive as he found a way to untie the cord. She coughed and vomited, and he wailed like an animal: about loving her, about the pointlessness of his life without her.

'This is my fault,' he said over and over again.

He brought her down to safety, right down to the floor, where they both collapsed. Elizabeth hid her face in his body and wept in his arms, choking and gasping. Her tears did not express regret or relief or love or gratitude, or even anger. They were tears of failure and humiliation. The shame of seeing Isla in the doorway was worse than death, proof to herself that she was a terrible human being. Proof that she didn't deserve to live.

'This is all my fault,' he said, seeing into her thoughts, echoing those words of before. 'I'm putting too much pressure on you. I'll get my assistant to take over the party.'

'No!' Elizabeth wailed.

'We've come so far since that night. I can't go back there. I just can't. None of us can.'

A memory came to her. Not of the night in the bathroom, but of before, way before. One of her mother's boyfriends, an actor, who had spent six weeks in their flat, had told her off for not cleaning her room. He had been drunk and he had picked up a pair of her dirty knickers and laughed at her, calling her a filthy bitch. The mortification had burned onto her cheeks. Now the accusations were different but she felt branded by that same feeling. Over a quarter of a century later, she felt like a useless, dirty child.

'You can't take the party away from me, Lucas. I'll prove myself to you. It will be incredible. Please,' she begged, fumbling around in her jacket pocket for her mobile. 'I'm calling the caterers now to confirm the menu. Jude's coming on the thirteenth to fix the painting. And almost all of his arty friends have RSVP'd. It's going well. It's all under control,' she said. Her hands were shaking. She dropped the phone.

He exhaled, then stood up and came around the bed towards her. He picked up her phone and handed it to her. 'Okay.' He sighed heavily. 'But you realise how important this is, don't you? To us? To our future? If you think you're not coping, or if the thoughts come back, you have to tell me, okay?'

Tears came into her mouth, making it hard to speak. She nodded. She had understood. 'I won't let you down,' she said.

'Leave all the school stuff to me then. I'll take that burden off your shoulders, at least.'

She imagined dragging Isla out of a rough sea, her little hand slipping from her grasp.

'I don't want to let her go,' she said, and closed her eyes tightly. 'I know how much you love her.'

'I'm a good mother,' she whispered, but she wasn't sure whether the words came out.

The metal chinks of his Rolex wristwatch rattled next to her ear as he held her face and kissed her on the cheek. 'I'll look after you,' he said. 'Whatever happens.'

It was a starry night. Elizabeth had looked out into the garden after hearing Lucas leave their bed. She tried to sleep. The bad thoughts she had promised him she wasn't having were constant whispers in her brain: *Lucas is having sex with Agata. Lucas is still in love with Heather. Lucas doesn't love you. Lucas is taking Isla away from you as punishment. Lucas is having sex with Agata. Lucas is still in love with Heather. Lucas doesn't love you. Lucas is taking Isla away from you as punishment. Lucas is having sex with Agata. Lucas is still in love with Heather. Lucas doesn't love you. Lucas is taking Isla away from you as punishment.* There was a dry, inflamed sensation on the skin of her throat, as though the unspoken muttering scratched there, trapped. She was hot, too. So hot. She got up again.

A light from outside shone eerily through the blinds, lighting her way out of the bedroom and to the kitchen, where she found the secret stash of pills.

She thought of the many different ways she could end the relentless circling in her mind.

There were two shotguns locked in the gun cupboard, brought out seasonally for clay pigeon shoots and for Lord Cecil-Johnson's annual pheasant shoot. The key was hidden somewhere in Lucas's study.

And a dressing gown cord hung in the bathroom.

Her fingers ran down the healed skin of her throat. She remembered how the softness of the towelling cord had become steel wire around her neck, and how her cheeks had bulged with blood.

A better way might be these, she thought, popping out a handful of beta blockers. The medication dosage was written in Polish. This morning Piotr had finally given her the whole box, fed up of being asked for one here and one there. The first of them had been given to her by Agata, who had, a few months previously, walked in on her having a full-blown panic attack in the bathroom and had diagnosed her instantly. Her dizziness and heart palpitations had been the same as Piotr's symptoms. Their doctor had prescribed the medicine for him in Poland, before they came to the UK, but he had never taken them and he never intended to.

Fingering the small round tablets in her palm, Elizabeth wondered how many of them she would need to take to block out the bad thoughts for good.

CHAPTER THIRTEEN

When my mother called for a catch-up, I wanted to spill my heart out to her. To tell her about Elizabeth slapping me, to confess to my resurfacing feelings for Lucas. And I wanted to tell her that I should not – *could* not – work at the Huxleys' a day longer. I was going home to Rye, to be with Rob. To hell with Dad! To hell with the financial consequences! To hell with Lucas!

Instead, I listened to her telling me about the smell of the dressings on Aunt Maggie's weeping ulcers, and about the ambulance call-outs in the middle of the night, and about how she'd tripped on a pair of slippers and spilled the bedpan that morning, and I knew I could not complain to her about anything.

'That sounds totally horrendous, Mum,' I said, running my fingers along the jagged wooden edge of my desk.

'You've got to enjoy every moment of your life, love,' she said wearily. 'Grab everything you want before it's too late.' The sound of her heavy sigh in my ear blew out reality, making room for the image of Lucas to fill my head.

'What are the doctors saying?' I asked quickly.

There was a strange clicking sound on the line, and then buzzing. Her reply was unintelligible.

'What did you say, Mum? You sound really far away. The line is terrible. Shall I call you back?'

'They've upped the morphine. Said it could be just weeks now,' she repeated.

If the sad fact of Aunt Maggie's death hadn't been there between us, I would have asked her to tell me how many weeks exactly. How many minutes, hours, days would I have to endure living alone with my father?

'I'm sorry, Mum. It must be so awful,' I said.

'Oh listen to me. All this self-pity and I haven't yet heard how you're getting on at Copper Lodge!'

There were many anecdotes I could have told her.

'I'm knackered all the time. I don't know how you do it.'

'Ha! Your father said you were struggling.'

'Did he?'

'Don't get your knickers in a twist. He said you're doing really well and that you're working very hard, but that you're a wee weakling. All skin and bone and pretty hair, aren't you, love?'

I chewed my lip. 'I wish you were home.'

'If I were home, that'd mean your poor Auntie Maggie had passed, God bless her. I'll miss her, I truly will, but I wonder if it should be sooner rather than later, to end her suffering.'

'Send her my love, won't you?' I said, trying to remember Auntie Maggie's face, which I hadn't seen since I was little. I could only recall the porridge ritual, and the blue curlers in her black hair, and the fact that Mum's face was a version of hers. I pictured my mother's eyes now, clear blue, and her freckles, like mine, and the short curls of dark grey hair over her ears. How her pearly lipstick was permanently bracketed by crescent smile lines above each corner of her mouth. The sensible jumper that she would tug down at the hips every so often, revealing a tiny hint of self-consciousness.

'You're down in the dumps, I can tell it,' she said.

'I'm fine. Just a bit tired.' I conjured Lucas's face in my mind, and my stomach flipped over.

'Why don't you visit Rob? Take a weekend away.'

'He's so busy. And petrol's expensive.'

'I'll sub you twenty quid for the petrol. Look in the pot in my bedside table. I imagine you and your dad could do with a break from each other.'

Hearing this, I wondered how much Dad had told her about our fight, how much she knew, or knew from his point of view.

'Maybe I will. I do miss him. And I want to see how Reese is getting on.'

'There you go. It'll cheer you up and you'll be right as rain for the new week ahead.'

The line began crackling again. 'Thanks for calling, Mum.'

'I'll ring again in a couple of days.'

The sun was low behind us. The air cool. The sea far out. The barbecue filled the air with purple woody smoke. Idly I watched Amy play Hacky Sack. We were expecting a crowd of friends to join us here on Winchelsea beach, and I tried to stop fretting about Reese, whom I planned to look for tomorrow before I left.

As I leant into the crook of Rob's arm, I thought about Reese's empty house. Seeing Reese, to reassure myself that he was well, was important to me this weekend. I had banged on his front door, through the cloth of a St George's flag, comparing its dilapidation with the extravagance of Copper Lodge. It was incomparable, like different countries, or different worlds. I wished Lucas could see the unbridgeable gap between Reese's life and that of his own children.

I sighed. 'I've missed this,' I said.

Rob kissed the top of my head. 'It's here every weekend if you want it,' he said with a petulant edge.

I did want it. I had always wanted it, from the moment I was born, as though leaving my mother's watery womb had never felt right.

*

I stretched my toe down from my chair. The stone was hot. I pulled it away again and swung my feet wildly, feeling the heavy air move through the hairs on my legs. My father's hand landed on my thigh.

'Stop fidgeting,' he said, resuming his chat with my mother.

The torn shreds of my croissant littered my plate. A curled crusty piece had escaped onto the table. I crushed it with my fingers into flaky crumbs and pressed some onto my fingertip.

'Stop playing and just eat it, Heather, please,' my mother said, before replying in hushed tones to my father.

I looked at them talking. Their own half-finished coffees and pastries sat untouched. Their mouths were turned down like sad people in cartoons.

Having noticed a dried prawn in a crack between the wooden slats of the table, I picked up my fork and began digging at it. The night before, we had sat at this same table, where I had tried my first ever paella. My parents had drunk a large jug of red alcohol with floating fruit in it. It had smelt sickly and their eyes had wobbled when they talked.

They were still talking. Always talking. I dreamed that they were planning a surprise for me, conspiring to buy me a big and exciting present. But no surprises or presents materialised. Ever.

The hotel pool sparkled at me. It was filled with children splashing around. But not me. I couldn't swim. The lessons were too dear, my parents said.

I felt hotter than I had ever felt before. I looked up at the blue sky through the wooden canopy. It burnt my eyes, even through my eyelids when I closed them.

A bee buzzed through the slats and headed straight to the pool. It landed and floated, spinning round and round.

Maybe I could float like the bee.

I slid from the chair.

When I reached the other end of the pool, I checked to see if my parents had stopped talking. They hadn't.

I jumped.

The water was a shock. It filled my mouth, my head, my throat. The more I tried to breathe, the less I could. I flailed and kicked and pulled, but the water disappeared through my fingers. My body dropped. I was losing the fight. There was a pain in my chest, and then a sound from above, like a muffled explosion.

A large dark form came at me through the water.

My arms were pulled out of their sockets. My body was yanked into the chest of a man in a white shirt, wet and gummy on my cheek. He smelt of aftershave and sweat. I spluttered and spat and cried on him as he carried me to my parents, who were running down the side of the pool towards me.

My mother scooped me from him, thanking him through tears. Her pearly lipstick was wet from where she had kissed me. 'You silly child,' she said.

'What were you thinking?' my father shouted.

I had been thinking that I wanted to swim. That was all.

Now I watched the sea and tried to make peace with my father's inability to see anything from my point of view. He preferred to trust in Elizabeth Huxley's character rather than mine. At home, before I left, I had pretended to accept it, folding my jeans into my suitcase with extra care. He had helped me pack and then microwaved me a cup of tea. On the surface of things, we had moved on.

Sliding into my view came Amy, kicking the Hacky Sack up in the air. Her legs were brown and endless.

'It doesn't make sense that she's been single for so long,' I said to Rob, lazily.

'It's because she's married to her job,' he replied.

'She does love it. I envy her that. Especially now she's styling celebrities and all sorts.'

He shrugged. 'It's intimidating to some guys.'

'That's ridiculous,' I said, irritated.

'Just saying what's true.'

'Then she's right to be choosy.'

Rob flexed his arm. 'You're *proper* choosy, aren't you, babe?'

I laughed, but stayed on the subject. 'Do you think Amy's lonely?'

'Nah.'

'Elizabeth Huxley is lonely, and she's surrounded by people twenty-four-seven.'

Rob sighed.

'What?' I asked.

'Nothing.'

'You sighed.'

'I'm not allowed to breathe now?'

'I can tell something's bothering you.'

'Forget it.'

'Seriously, Rob, what did I say wrong?'

He coughed. 'You're always going on about the Huxleys.'

'Am I?' I hadn't noticed. It seemed I had been talking about them but saying nothing.

'Yeah. And it's boring, if I'm honest.'

My neck felt awkward in the crook of his arm, and I pulled away and hugged my knees. 'They're complicated.'

I weighed up the benefits of telling him the full story. Opening up to Rob about Elizabeth hitting me was unlikely to be a cathartic solution to the problem. It would burden me with his reaction – overreaction possibly – rather than unburden me of the dilemma. He was unlikely to provide answers. I had survived the whole of my life without telling many people about many things. It had worked for me. I knew how to hold onto secrets.

'Complications that are none of your business,' he said.

'That's what Dad says.'

'He's right.'

'I know. I keep telling myself it's only a job.' I hugged my knees tighter.

'I wonder sometimes …'

'What are you getting at now?'

'Nothing.'

'If something's bugging you, just let it out.'

'Nothing's bugging me. Come here. You're so arsey sometimes.' He grinned at me, grabbed my arm and tugged me into a hug. We kissed our differences away. It was how we resolved our fights.

Amy arrived. 'No heavy petting on the beach!' she teased.

We pulled apart, laughing. Rob said, 'Let's get the sausages on.'

Amy and I chatted as we cut the buns.

'Rob's place has been heaving lately,' she said.

'The takings have been up,' Rob nodded.

Since the gastropub had opened on the high street opposite Rob's bar, business had declined steadily. His decision to open only between Thursday and Sunday had allowed him to stay afloat, just, for now.

'Have you been going down there a lot, Amy?' I asked.

'When I'm home, yes. Those open mic sessions are fun.'

'I don't want you two having fun without me,' I complained. As I said it, I realised it wasn't true. I did not mind at all that they might be having fun without me. For a moment, I pictured them together as a couple, and I imagined not minding about that either.

Amy shook her head vigorously. 'No, no, no, we never have fun without you. Ever.'

'Never,' Rob said, a little sulkily. He wasn't smiling like Amy.

'Good.' I swigged to the bottom of my beer and reached for another one.

The others arrived with music and vodka. With our windswept, beach-baked bodies now clothed in jeans and fleeces, we danced and laughed and caught up on each other's news.

It was four in the morning by the time Rob and I stumbled into the flat, trying not to wake Jake, the lodger. Rob was snoring before I had finished brushing my teeth. I hadn't been in the mood for sex, but I was disappointed that he hadn't tried. Especially considering how long we had been apart.

The next morning, I cooked eggs and bacon for our hangovers. It had not been an automatic process, as it had been when I lived here. Nothing was where I had kept it before. My dishes and trinkets were gone from the windowsill. The plates and utensils were in the wrong cupboards. It was like cooking in someone else's home.

Rob came into the kitchen after his shower. The water hadn't managed to wash away his bloodshot eyes.

'Oh, good girl,' he said tucking in. He wolfed the food down, hunched slightly, like a starved caveman.

'Last night was fun,' I said.

He shrugged. 'Suppose so.'

'Didn't you have a good time?'

'You were well and truly arseholed.'

'God, was I that bad?'

'You kept hugging everyone.'

'Nothing wrong with spreading the love.'

He licked his plate clean, like a bad-mannered child, then said, 'You know, Amy and I chatted a bit about marriage last night.'

I pretended to skim the newspaper headlines. 'You two will be very happy together,' I teased.

'Can we talk about this properly?' He put his hand over the newspaper.

'Sure.' I didn't want to look up at him.

'Could you stop reading?'

'I'll have you know I was reading about how female masturbation is coming into its own in pop music. It's really important stuff,' I said, stabbing at the photograph of a semi-naked pop star gyrating on stage.

He rubbed at his stubble as though mulling me over, perplexed by me.

'I just want you to think about it. I'm not proposing, *obvs*, but I want you to think about it as an idea. Amy said I should stop whingeing to her about it and talk to you directly,' he said, looking glum.

'I promise to think about it. But I have to get through this stint with Dad first, and after that I'll have to find a job and—'

'And after that you'll want to go to the Twin Falls in Hawaii, and after *that* you'll want to do the Great North Swim, and after *that* you'll want to save the lido from closure. There's always an "and after that".'

'You've forgotten the Moonlight Swim in Keswick. I want to do that too.' *And*, I thought, snorkel in the sea off the Izu peninsula, *and* compete in the Open Water Masters, *and* set up charity swim camps for children …

'Could you be serious with me for one flaming second?'

I sat up straight, deadly serious. 'I do want to do all those things, Rob. I don't see why I should feel bad about it.'

'What if I came with you?'

'If you want to come too, I'd love that!'

'Really? You would love me to come?'

'Yes, I really, really want you to come.'

Mischief played in his eyes. 'You hussy. You know, I think I can arrange that right now,' he said, undoing my jeans.

'I didn't mean that,' I chuckled, remonstrating. 'I need to go out again to find Reese!'

'You said it, not me,' he grinned, dragging me into the bedroom and closing the door.

*

When I left the flat on Sunday afternoon, Rob was in good spirits.

As I drove off, up the M20, I imagined him in our flat, our home, lying on the sofa, watching water sports on cable television or browsing YouTube for motorsport crashes. He would be happy. I had made sure he was happy, which gave me the feeling that I had done the right thing by visiting.

But I did not feel happy. I felt sad that I had not been able to find Reese. My wanderings around the wastelands of Rye had simply exacerbated my sense of rootlessness. After three more visits to his house, I had given up and roamed his local haunts. Everywhere I tried – the car park where he watched the teenage boys rev and wheelie their scooters; the supermarket playground where he smoked old cigarette butts from the grass; the fish and chip shop on the front where he met his friends; Jason's Kiosk, where he stole custard creams – all of them had been empty of Reese. Nobody, not even his neighbours, had been able to tell me where he and his father were, and I had given up.

On the road northwards now, the cool sea was disappearing behind me, further and further away. And the car became hotter and hotter as the sun beat down through the windscreen.

I was leaving a home that no longer offered me a sense of security, and approaching my childhood home that was filled with uncertain memories.

Willingly regressing, I slipped backwards in time, towards the pool at Copper Lodge and its temptations. For as long as I could remember, whispers from the other side of our hedge had coaxed me into their grounds; siren songs beckoning me towards a life that was within touching distance, a life that my parents forbade. I thought about how humiliated and resentful I had been when Elizabeth slapped me. But here I was returning to Copper Lodge to work for her and tug at my forelock. And to Lucas, who had once promised me the life that Elizabeth now had.

CHAPTER FOURTEEN

Lucas pushed a velvet box towards Elizabeth. She stared at it. A glare shot up from the glass table and forced her to squint. She did not want whatever was inside that box.

'Go on, open it,' he said, shuffling his rattan armchair closer to her.

She summoned the energy to reach forward and open the box, but the tennis coach, Tim, arrived, saving her the effort.

'I'll join you and Jude after the game?' Lucas said.

'Yes,' she replied, dredging up a smile.

Since the visit to Channing House, her capacity for light-heartedness was at a low ebb. She had been coasting, riding her days out, navigating Lucas's constant monitoring of her every move; striving to prove to him that she was stable, which made her feel quite *un*stable. The future stopped at the summer party. She couldn't see a day ahead of it, as though the calendar was black beyond 4 July. Any bid for her children's well-being or her own happiness was on hold. There was too much to do. Too much at stake.

'Enjoy!' she said to him, but he had already gone.

She left the velvet box and headed down to find her brother, who was swimming in their pool. The air smelt like holidays, the soil warmed after a blue-sky day, and she felt sanguine about her weekend with Jude, in spite of why he was here. She prayed that the painting was salvageable, and was eager to find out.

Jude pulled his lean body out of the water to reveal what Elizabeth called a farmer's tan. Brown arms, white torso. Never had he stayed still long enough to sunbathe. It wouldn't occur to him to take his T-shirt off in the sun to get an even tan. He didn't care what he looked like.

'I thought I could show you the painting while Lucas is playing tennis,' she said. 'You must be dreading seeing it.'

'A little.' He shook the water out of his scruffy black hair like a Labrador shaking its coat.

'Only a little?'

'When I give my paintings away or sell them, I lose connection with them. It's like they're someone else's.'

'I feel so awful.'

'For what?'

'You gave them to me and I didn't look after them properly.'

'Don't blame yourself. That'll upset me,' he said, drying his legs with a towel.

Moved by his forgiveness, she said, 'I've missed you.'

'Missed you too. And the kids. When are they back?' he asked.

'We've got an hour. Maybe you could make a start now?'

'Let's have a look,' he said.

She watched him try to pull his moth-holed T-shirt on. He put his arm in the neck hole and had to start again. 'Come *on.* Hurry up.'

'Okay, okay,' he said, hopping forward, catching his toe in a small rip at the knee of his jeans – they were old rather than designer – and tripping over the other trouser leg.

'You clot,' Elizabeth said.

Jude laughed. 'It's the dyslexia.'

'Of course it is,' she said, grinning.

Their mother had used his dyslexia as an excuse for everything that went wrong in Jude's life: when he failed to get into the local grammar school, when he had to retake his driving test five times, when he ran out of money in Chile. And when things went well for him, she used it too. When he had been one of only seventeen young artists to get onto the MA course at the Royal Academy, she had said, 'Oh, thank goodness for your dyslexia!' And the three of them had laughed.

Once he was dressed, Elizabeth took his arm and strode him up the lawn towards the house. The clop-clop of the tennis balls being hit back and forth between Lucas and Tim was like the tick-tock of time. She was reminded of the velvet box, which she had left on the glass table, and hoped that Agata had cleared it away. She didn't want Jude to question her about it.

He was ambling behind her, incapable of hurrying. At the barn, he nodded towards the noise of banging, where Piotr was laying the wooden floors. 'Can't I see inside?'

'Later, okay?'

'Everything all right?'

'Sorry, I just want to get the painting sorted. And I'm a little tired. Hugo had a nightmare last night. Then this morning Isla had a tantrum about her pink ballet leotard. Agata had forgotten to put it in the dryer so she had to wear her white one.'

'Poor Isla,' Jude sighed.

Elizabeth chuckled. 'You struggled with your ballet leotards too, didn't you, baby brother?'

'I swear it's scarred me for life.'

She let out a burst of laughter before pulling it back, unused to letting go. 'God knows why Mum put you through it.'

'Because she wanted to ruin my life?'

'I think she thought it would help with your coordination.'

'That worked out well.'

Elizabeth slipped her arm around her brother's waist. 'Oh Jude. I love you just the way you are. In fact, I can't wait for lots of little mini Judes to be running around tripping and dropping things exactly like you do.'

There was a comfortable silence as they strolled in synch up to the terrace.

Jude sat down on the rattan chair that Elizabeth had been sitting on earlier. The velvet box was still on the table. She imagined what was inside, perhaps wriggling with worms.

'What a view,' he said, leaning back into the chair.

'Come on! Inside. They're in the spare room.'

She now suspected he was procrastinating, less relaxed about the scratch across *Blue No. 3* than he was letting on.

The spare room was cool. She had pulled the blinds and instructed Agata to keep them down – and keep Lucas away. Any mention or sighting of the scratched painting triggered a bad mood.

The three paintings were propped up in a line against the fitted wardrobes. It was obvious which was the damaged one. Even in the murky light, the scratch stood out. Elizabeth pulled the blind up and held her breath, waiting for her brother's verdict.

'Oh bloody hell. Phew. Thank fuck for that.'

'What do you mean?'

'That's easy to fix. I'll go get my stuff from the car.'

'I knew you were worried!'

'I didn't want to upset you before I'd seen it.'

'Upset *me*?! Oh Jude, you're an angel,' she cried.

From her perch on the bed, Elizabeth watched Jude zone out from her and engage with his work. He filled in the indentation and mixed the blue hues, bit by bit building the colours onto a separate canvas. On and around the scratched corner he added the paint, layering the sea and sky with vigorous, bold brushstrokes. He repainted in the spirit of the piece, as though harnessing his original mood. When he had finished, the result was flawless. It was different, yet the same.

After Jude had cleared away his paints, they sat on the terrace to enjoy the warmth from the dropping sun. Elizabeth was glad that Gordon and Heather were not working today. The garden felt more like hers at the weekend. Heather was more conspicuous than Sally had been. For many reasons, she was less easy to ignore.

'God, this view is something else,' Jude said.

'You said that already.'

'I hope you never take it for granted.'

Elizabeth thought about that. She didn't take it for granted. It meant more to her than that. It was an extension of her; a sprawling setting for her adult self, similar to how London cradled her childhood.

'So, how have you been?' he asked, stretching out his legs and crossing them at the ankles.

Agata came out with a tray of chilled wine and olives.

'Thanks, Agata,' Elizabeth said.

'Thanks Agata,' Jude repeated, flashing a smile.

Elizabeth waited for the girl to leave before answering her brother, before evading his question. 'Lucas is really stressed out about this deal.'

'Is he ever *not* stressed out?'

She poured a glass of wine. 'Of course.'

Jude sighed. 'I'll take your word for it.'

There was a pause while they took in the view. The rumble of a plane filled the silence. Elizabeth reached for her pen and pad.

'Let's talk about the party. He'll be more relaxed after that.'

'Right.' He yawned.

'We're having a hog roast, macarons and pink champagne. Lil and Kat are DJing. And fireworks at midnight.'

'Lil and Kat? Sounds cool, sis. How many people are coming?'

'So far we have one hundred and twenty-one acceptances. Fifteen of them are your guests. Lucas wants to know exactly who they are and why they're coming.'

'Okay.' He yawned again and stretched his arms. 'Remind me who I asked?'

'Oh Jude. I can't believe you don't remember,' she said, exasperated. She read the first name on her list. 'Amis Yorke.'

'Amis Yorke,' he repeated.

'Yes. Tell me all about him first.'

'He loves rich people.'

'Is that all you've got?'

'Believe me, it's all you need to know.'

'Jude!'

'One of his paintings got into the summer exhibition at the RA. God knows how.'

'Okay. The RA, good,' she said, writing down the information next to Amis Yorke's name.

'Has Bennie confirmed?' Jude asked, his eyes fixing on the velvet box.

'Benjamin Healing, you mean?'

He nodded absently and then picked up the box. 'What's this?'

She snatched it from him and put it back on the table.

'Concentrate. Yes, Benjamin Healing is coming and he's bringing a friend. Does that mean he has a girlfriend?'

'No, he'll probably bring his trans lover.'

'What?'

'He … I mean *they* … they perform at the Box and wear tassels on their nipples.'

'Oh. That's nice,' she said, trying to be open-minded, wondering how she would break it to Lucas.

He laughed. 'You're so gullible!'

'Oh Jude! Be serious.'

'Why does Lucas care so much about who's coming this year?'

'I told you already. The Seacart–Huxley deal.'

'And they like artists, these Seacarts, do they?'

'They are the most important collectors in New York.'

He whistled. 'Wow. That must mean they're even richer than you.' He grabbed hold of the velvet box and held it in the air. 'I'm dying to know what's inside this.'

'Don't you dare!'

He rattled it.

'Don't do that!' She threw her arms up and then dropped her hands in her lap. 'You know what this reminds me of?'

'Nope.'

'The time I asked you to sneak that money from Mum, remember? After I'd spent all my salary on that stupid trip to Ibiza with Cassie.'

At twenty years old, Elizabeth had skipped two weeks of temp work to go to Ibiza with a friend who had owned a house out there. Once she had paid the rent on her flat-share in Stockwell, she hadn't had a penny left for food until she was paid, in ten long days' time. Jude, four years younger than her, had been living at home still and had access to the maternal purse strings.

'I got you that thirty quid, didn't I?'

'And my God I had to work for it. How many fag runs did I do for you?'

Jude grinned. 'It was fun seeing you squirm.'

Elizabeth punched his arm. 'This is different. This party is really important to me.'

'More important than needing thirty quid to eat?'

'Yes. Much more.'

'Okay. I'll stop behaving like an idiot and focus. On one condition …'

She raised her eyes to the heavens. 'Go on.'

'We see what's in that posh box,' he said, pointing at it.

Elizabeth clutched her head. 'Okay!'

She reached for it. It had a weight to it. There was no obvious access, but she knew how to open this kind of box.

'Oh my GOD!' Jude cried, staring at what was inside.

Glinting in the sun lay a clear blue sapphire the size of a two-penny piece, set into a pendant necklace. Diamonds were inlaid into the chain. Sparks of light shot out from the jewels – like tiny screams, Elizabeth thought.

Agata reappeared to refill their glasses. When Jude thanked her, Elizabeth noted her eyes on the velvet box, and felt embarrassed. Agata knew how little she deserved it.

Jude was agog. 'Lucas gave that to you?' he cried.

'This morning,' she replied, relieved that Agata had gone back inside.

'You don't like it?'

She put her sunglasses on and stared out at the horizon. 'It was his mother's.'

'It must be worth thousands of pounds.'

'I imagine it is. I'm very lucky.'

'How can you be so blasé about it?'

'Inside, I'm dancing with joy and gratitude,' she said.

'What's the occasion? I haven't forgotten your birthday again, have I?'

The corner of her mouth twitched with a smile. 'No, baby brother.'

'Then why the fancy necklace?'

'He wanted to cheer me up.'

Jude shuffled forward and placed a hand on her knee. 'I knew something was up. What's been going on?'

She braced herself for her confession. 'Isla's going to boarding school.'

He looked serious for the first time that day. 'What?'

Isla and Hugo came charging out of the house, running straight at Jude, semi-hysterical with excitement. 'Uncle Jude!' they screamed.

Jude scooped Isla up into his arms and kissed her hard on the cheek.

'I've got you, my little Isla. How's life, beautiful? How did you get so tall?'

Isla snuggled into his chest. 'I eat lots of broccoli,' she said, tugging her crop top down to hide her tummy.

'You won't want these then,' he said, presenting them with two Curly Wurly bars.

Hugo thumped Jude in the thigh. His little glasses were skewed. Jude plonked Isla down and pulled Hugo up.

'And hello, handsome boy,' he said, straightening the glasses.

'Guess what, guess what?' Hugo cried, his lisp obvious when he was overexcited. 'I'm going to swim for England!'

'For the county,' Elizabeth corrected.

'At five?'

'When he's old enough. His teacher thinks he's got some talent.'

Isla climbed back on Jude, pushing Hugo away. 'Uncle Jude, guess what? Guess what? I'm going to boarding school!'

That serious face returned. 'When *you're* old enough?' Jude asked, glancing at Elizabeth.

'She'll be starting next term,' Elizabeth said, picking up the jewellery box, smoothing her hand across the velvet. Anything to avoid looking at her brother's face.

'And I'm going to have my own tuck box!'

'That's very exciting, Isla,' he said, but the dead tone betrayed him. She dared to look, to see it. His hair was heavy over his eyes.

'Mummy, can we go swimming now?' Hugo said. 'I want to show Uncle Jude my dive and then go to bed *after*.'

'No, darling. It's far too late.'

'Those Curly Wurlys are going to melt unless you eat them,' Jude said.

Forgetting about swimming and boarding school, the two of them climbed up and sat either side of Jude on the arms of his chair to unpeel their chocolate bars. Hugo nibbled away elegantly, while Isla tore at her bar, leaving more chocolate on her face than around the caramel centre.

Jude stared at Elizabeth. 'Can I see the barn now?'

'Are you really staying for a sleepover Uncle Jude?' Isla interjected.

'I am indeed.'

'Awesome,' Isla said.

'It is awesome,' Jude agreed, winking at her, adding, 'Okay, you two, your mummy's going to show me around the barn.' He did a cartoon yawn and mouthed 'Booorrrrring' in a loud whisper. They both giggled. Elizabeth knew she should laugh along.

Out of earshot, as they walked, Jude hissed hotly, 'You can't actually be telling me that you're putting Isla away in some boarding school.'

'We're not *putting her away*. It's a lovely school.'

The red crosses on the calendar came into her mind.

'But she's only seven years old, for crying out loud.'

She clamped her hands to her thighs. Hitting Heather had only made her feel worse. She swallowed the lump in her throat. 'She'll be eight by the time she starts.'

'Oh, that's all right then, is it?'

'She's very grown-up for her age.'

'Are you *kidding* me? Has Lucas forgotten what *he* went through?'

Elizabeth regretted having told him those stories. Stories of seven-year-old Lucas calling his mother in tears from the housemaster's study, and his mother hanging up on him and the housemaster laughing at him. Stories of his housemaster cutting off his blonde curls while he slept, telling him his parents couldn't afford to send him to the hairdresser. Stories of his housemaster reading out his mother's letter at the breakfast table, dropping his t's and exaggerating his o's, badly imitating an East End London accent. Stories of his housemaster punishing Lucas for his scholarship and for his sweet looks and charm. When the housemaster had died – in an act of autoerotic asphyxiation behind a locked bathroom in the eaves of Winslow Junior House – Lucas had opened a bottle of champagne and got drunk. Too drunk. Angry drunk.

'Schools aren't like they were in the old days,' Elizabeth said to Jude, glad she was wearing her sunglasses. She didn't want him to see the fear and powerlessness in her eyes. 'They're much more understanding of children's emotional needs now. The headmistress was nice.'

Jude walked ahead a little and brushed his hair back. The low sun backlit his tall form and a chill rested over Elizabeth in his shadow.

'I know you and I know you don't want this,' he said, stopping.

'I have to think about what's best for the whole family.'

Jude's jaw clenched. 'How can it be best for you guys?'

'I haven't been coping too well.'

'You seem so much better. And you've got Agata, if things spiral again.'

'When you have your own kids, you'll understand.'

'No, believe me, I won't. Not about this.'

'Don't be like that.' His disappointment was unbearable.

'Have you told Mum? She'll go mad.'

'She'd already heard about the facilities there. The theatre is like a West End stage.'

'Isla is no actress,' Jude said.

They had reached the barn. 'Hello Piotr,' Elizabeth said. Piotr was on his knees. She looked around at the transformed space.

It took a few minutes for Jude to follow her inside. He ducked under the doorway.

'Hi, Piotr,' he said.

Elizabeth smoothed her hand across the dry plaster. 'We're going to paint it white, aren't we, Piotr,' she said, thinking about the white beta blockers that she had returned one by one into the packet.

Jude grunted.

'You see the mezzanine floor for the bed? Piotr built that!'

For a moment, it seemed that Jude had remembered his manners. 'Piotr, that's bloody brilliant work. Beautiful.' He stood at the bottom of the wooden ladder that led up to where the bed would be, but he didn't climb it. In a good mood, he would have.

'And this wall is where we're putting your paintings,' Elizabeth continued.

He swivelled around. 'Oh my God! You're going to sell them to that American couple, aren't you?'

'Bo has always loved them.'

'I want them back,' he said furiously.

'But you gave them to me.'

'I've changed my mind.' He began walking out.

She blurted out, 'If Lucas thinks I've screwed this up, he'll use it against me.'

Jude stopped in the doorway and turned back to her. 'What do you mean?'

Elizabeth bit down on the edge of her tongue. 'I don't want to let him down. You know what he's like.'

'I wonder if I do sometimes,' he said, scratching his head.

'Come on, Jude. Let's not squabble.' She smiled, but her heart was hammering in her chest. 'You've not missed them in five years!'

'Neither have you, by the looks of it.'

Jude joined Lucas on the terrace after his game. Lucas picked his brain for information about the London art scene – specifically the artists on the summer party guest list. He wanted to know who was coming and why, which emerging artists had been picked up by White Cube, Jude's dealer, the famous arbiters of the art world, and whether he should buy their work. He was one-track, which visibly irritated Jude. Elizabeth was still not sure what Jude's decision about the triptych was going to be. She could see he was preoccupied, still mulling it over, battling with the two sides of their argument. Dutifully he gave Lucas the details he needed for the guest list, but his smiles and teasing hadn't returned.

'You should do an art history course or something, Lucas. If you're going to start buying more,' he said.

Jude respected art collectors who knew about art, but he was scornful about rich people who wanted art as an investment only. Lucas mentioned the Paris salons of the eighteenth century – one of a few facts he had gleaned from a Christie's event sponsored by Citibank – and Jude explained the history, exposing Lucas's scant knowledge. Quietly, to Elizabeth, Jude admitted that artists needed their sponsors. These days, he slept on a proper bed and drank good wine, thanks to rich, ignorant collectors like Lucas.

*

He had only stayed the night for the children's sake. Or so Elizabeth guessed. She hoped there was a small part of him that had stayed for her too, but the triptych had not been mentioned.

At the car, as he said goodbye, he softened towards her. 'You can do what you like with those paintings.'

She exhaled, tears of relief welling in her eyes. 'Thank you.'

He frowned at her. 'You're looking after yourself, aren't you?'

'Yes, baby brother.'

'You deserve to be treated well.'

'I'm treated like a princess. I even get sapphire necklaces.'

He scratched one eyebrow. 'That's not what I meant.'

Elizabeth regretted her poor joke. She said, 'I'm the one who's the handful, believe me. God knows how he puts up with me.'

'He's a lucky man,' he said. Then, before closing the car door, he said one last thing. 'You know, if you think it's best that Isla goes to Channing House, then I respect that.'

For a split second, her heart stopped beating. It was one of the few big lies he had ever told her. She knew he would never respect her decision to send Isla to boarding school at seven years old.

Choking out, 'I appreciate that,' she stepped back from the car, crossing her arms over her chest.

She did not appreciate his forgiveness. It was worse than his anger. It meant he had acquiesced, like the rest of them. He had finally bought into the lie that she projected: that she could be bought for a sapphire necklace, that she had choices. It seemed he was finally convinced that her values were up for sale. It set a precedent in their relationship.

Up until now, Jude had been her ally, on her side when their mother judged her for making different life choices; on her side when old friends fell by the wayside; on her side when Lucas thought she had lost her mind. Her brother had stuck by her, always believing in her, always trusting that deep down she was the same girl he had grown up with, in spite of the lifestyle that spoke differently.

Now that she had complied with Lucas on Isla's schooling, it seemed Jude had lost all faith in her.

She could not lose faith as her brother had done. She would cling to the belief that change was around the corner, that Lucas would trust her again, when there was less at stake, when he wasn't living on the edge, risking his investments and his reputation. Around the corner, he would get what he wanted and achieve all he had dreamt of. He would lay to rest the taunts of his housemaster. Around the corner, she would think happier thoughts; say the right things, do the right things. Around the corner, the pressure would be off and they would find equilibrium. Soon. Around the corner and after the party.

CHAPTER FIFTEEN

'Why are we even doing this?' I sighed, twisting a screw into a bed frame.

'All hands on deck today. Only a week to go,' Dad said.

From our position on the mezzanine, I stopped to look down at the rejuvenated barn. The space was unrecognisable. Everything was white and clean. The white walls and clean white floorboards, the white woodburner in the centre, the large skylights. There were opaque white blinds on the back-wall windows that hid the camper van behind them.

'Why hasn't Elizabeth invited you and Mum?'

'Ha! What would your mother and I have to say to those people?'

'Quite a bit, if you ask me.'

'Nobody *is* asking you.'

It was a warning shot. I was irritating him. Every day I sensed that his patience with me was lessening, as though my presence had a cumulative effect on his mood. It reminded me of how I had felt as a child, how I had wanted to pack myself away from him. Staying quiet and invisible had been the best solution.

The silence was interrupted by Lucas, who appeared at the bottom of the ladder. I wanted to run.

'How's it going?' he asked.

I neatened my hair and wished I wasn't so hot.

'All good,' Dad replied.

'Just wondering if I left my watch up there?'

I scanned the floor, looking under the plastic wrappings and flat-pack instructions, wondering when and why Lucas might have had reason to remove his watch up here.

'Nothing here, Mr Huxley,' Dad said.

While my father's back was turned, as he continued to search, Lucas looked right into my eyes, conveying an unreadable feeling; a vulnerability or a need, I couldn't grasp which. His blue eyes were bottomless pools. Instinct told me he was using the watch as an excuse to see me. A childish excitement skittered through me. Forgetting who I had become and how far I had moved on, I wanted once again to dive in and save him from himself. It was a fleeting madness. I was not that silly girl any more and never would be again.

'No worries,' he said, leaving us to our bed assembly.

'Back to the real beds,' my father quipped after we had laid the mattress on the frame.

'Ha!' I said, following him outside, picking up one of the wheelbarrows full of 'Canadale Gold', spiraea 'Gold Mound' and *Lupinus polyphyllus*. 'I'll start around the back.'

I knelt at the beds and took my time with the planting, wishing I could control the recurrence of thoughts about Lucas that looped in and out of my mind.

After a couple of hours, I saw Agata dart around the barn to her camper van. It was unusual to see her here in the middle of the day. She seemed harassed, tugging her peroxide ponytail tight to her head as she ran.

'Hi, Agata!' I said, slapping my hands on my thighs to shake the excess soil from my gloves.

Startled, she stopped and looked down at me as though I were a dog who had barked at her. Then she gathered herself. 'Oh, hi.'

'How are the preparations for the party going?'

She blew out her cheeks. 'Everyone is …' She circled her finger around her temple to suggest they were all crazy, making me laugh. I couldn't have agreed more.

After she had disappeared into the camper van, I poured out the remaining water from my drinking bottle and knocked on the van door. Agata might be able to offer a diversion from the flower beds and also, possibly, some news about Elizabeth and Lucas's boarding school visit. I hoped to hear that it had been an aberration, that sweet Isla would be remaining safe at home.

'Yes?' Agata said, standing on the top step above me.

The noise of Dad mowing a pathway through the meadow for the marquee was in the background.

'Sorry, but any chance I could fill this up?'

She shrugged and stood aside for me.

As I ran the tap into the small metal sink, I could hear her opening and closing drawers and cupboards.

I turned the tap off. At my feet, she was on her knees looking under the small table. 'Lost something?' I asked.

She didn't reply.

'I can help you look if you like?'

'No,' she said, standing up. 'No, no.'

'Okay then, I'll leave you to it. Shout if you need any help.'

She waited for me to go before continuing her search, but just as I was leaving, I heard her exclaim something in Polish.

I nipped up the steps. 'Everything okay?'

She stuffed an object into her jeans pocket. A couple of metal links connected to a man's wristwatch flopped out. I recognised them instantly.

She tapped her pocket, shoving the links back in. 'I find it.'

I couldn't hold back. 'Whose is that?'

Her close-set pretty brown eyes blinked repeatedly. 'It's Piotr's,' she said.

I took a sip of water to hide how surprised I was about her lie. Pretending to make light of it, I grinned at her. 'Piotr has a Rolex?'

She shifted from one foot to the other and shrugged. 'Lucas leave it by the pool. I pick it up.'

'Why did you say it was Piotr's?'

'I not stupid. I know what you think,' she said, clicking her tongue.

'I don't think anything!' I hadn't *wanted* to think about what had first occurred to me.

'Elizabeth thinks …' she said, stopping, picking at her nail polish.

'What does she think?'

She shrugged again, her small shoulder bones poking the air by her ears. 'She nuts.'

'In what way?'

She deflected. 'You know, I from bad place in Poland. If I steal this piece of shit, my whole life is different. And Lucas buy another one.'

'You're not like that, Agata,' I said.

She looked out of the window. There was a view of the gnarled trunk of the tree. 'I am just stressed out,' she said, seemingly adopting an expression she had picked up from Elizabeth.

'Yes. Stress makes us do crazy things,' I agreed.

'Piotr's brother. He have a baby. We want to go see him, but is not possible.'

'Because of money?'

She shrugged, jabbing the watch further down into her pocket. 'We have money.'

I wasn't sure what she meant, whether she meant she *now* had money, thanks to the watch, or whether her statement had been a proud declaration of their financial self-sufficiency. Whatever the connotations, I didn't feel it was my place to get involved.

'I'd better get back to it,' I said, leaving her with her decision. I was not going to be the one who stopped her stealing from Lucas.

As I rolled the wheelbarrow closer to the hole I had dug earlier, I heard Agata hurry past me. The tiny purple flowers trembled as the warm breeze disturbed the air. I kept my eyes fixed on this last remaining plant. It sat there waiting its turn, ready for its roots to be placed in the composted soil, ready to grow. But I didn't move to plant it. In its pot, it was neat and separate, but as soon as I placed it in the flower bed, its roots would lace themselves into the soil, embed and entwine into life's cycle. Around me, the trees and shrubs whooshed in the wind. The world's chaos – its inexplicable miracles and its cruel blows – were beyond my control. When I looked at this pretty plant, hothoused for the structured bed, my hands became inert but my brain went into overdrive. I recalled those evenings that summer. Before every lesson, Lucas had removed his Casio watch and placed it on a white plastic chair. The memory of its metal face shone in my mind, vivid enough for me to feel I could reach out and touch it again. I wanted to place it back on his wrist and halt the momentum of suspicion. The more I thought about Agata and the watch, the less I believed that stealing it would ever cross her mind.

My thoughts began pedalling faster than I wanted them to, bringing disparate facts together, recalibrating memories, forming an impression of Lucas that was unthinkable. Ridiculous, in fact. I must be tired, I thought, or I wouldn't be inventing such mind-boggling theories. Stress was whirling around the grounds and it was getting inside me too.

But then I considered Elizabeth's unstable character and it seemed plausible that Lucas might seek comfort in the attractive young woman who cared for his children every day. It was common for men to sleep with their nannies, and Lucas was a risk-taker by nature.

Even so, I still couldn't picture it. Something was unconvincing about the two of them together. With the party ahead, and this purported deal so close, I couldn't fathom why he would gamble it all away for Agata.

I planted the flower, pressing the soil down around the stem, feeling the sensory pleasure of the springiness and softness of earth under my fingertips; connecting with nature. Calm and order settled over me. My heart rate slowed, just as it did when I looked out to sea. The party would be over and done with soon. Everyone's efforts would prove worthwhile. And if not? Would the world stop turning?

CHAPTER SIXTEEN

It was the morning of 4 July. Elizabeth was wearing a tracksuit. Her hair had been blow-dried and her nails manicured and her headache dulled by two paracetamol. Kneeling next to her at a large cardboard box were Jude and Agata, who were helping her to fill the glass tea light holders with candles.

There were five hours to go before Bo and Walt Seacart arrived, and eight hours before the party started. Elizabeth worried her head might spin off her shoulders.

Outside, the sun was shining and the marquee was erected. She had been checking the weather report every hour since yesterday morning. The sun icons had popped up each time, but she would not take it for granted. Her contingency plans for rain were in place. Fifty large branded umbrellas were stacked in a box for the guests to use between the house and the marquee, if necessary.

'It will be perfect tonight,' Lucas had whispered to her earlier that morning, panting into her ear after sex. It had been fevered and quick, up against the kitchen units in the barn. It wasn't the first time they'd had sex there. A week ago, before the bed had been erected by Gordon and Heather, he had pulled her up the ladder of the mezzanine and made love to her on the freshly painted floorboards. The tension in his performance had stretched the sinews in his neck and brought high colour to his cheeks, released only when he had climaxed. As soon as he had clicked his watch back on, she'd lost him to his thoughts again.

It will be perfect tonight.

He had chosen those words to reassure her, to prove that he had faith in her. But they had become a mantra of fear, driving her through the exhaustive list of tasks.

Everyone had too much to do. Everyone was sweating and harassed. Agata had taken twice as long to iron Lucas's shirt than usual and Elizabeth couldn't fathom why. She needed her to be on her game, more than anyone else.

Yet to arrive: twelve dinner tables and chairs, twelve bouquets for the tables, parquet dance floor and disco lights, Moroccan pouffes and low metal coffee tables, plus rugs, linen tablecloths and napkins, 120 champagne glasses, 120 wine glasses, 120 dinner and side plates, 120 pudding bowls. Yet to do: lay tables, hang the Moroccan lanterns, decorate and arrange the Moroccan lounge in the marquee, set out the occasional tables and the large beanbags for the hog roast buffet, arrange the logs and hay bales around the fire pit, roll out the carpets for the marquee, erect and light the bamboo fire lights, make the bed up in the guest barn, hang Jude's paintings, position the flowers, tidy up the house and garden. Due to arrive: hog roast caterers and drinks waitresses, Sarah with the macarons, fireworks display company, DJs.

'Oh!' Agata cried as one of the glass candleholders slipped from her grasp and smashed on the concrete.

'Agata! Be careful!' Elizabeth cried, clutching her chest, trying to slow her heart.

'Elizabeth, I not feel so …' Agata said. Tea lights rolled off her lap. Her hand covered her mouth.

'You don't feel so good?' Elizabeth asked, holding the back of her hand to Agata's forehead. Her skin was cold and wet. 'What kind of not well?'

'I think I …' Agata replied before throwing up into the cardboard box, covering all the tea light holders in lumpy yellow vomit.

Time froze. Elizabeth's low-level headache was dialled up a notch. She knew from experience that an oncoming migraine could cause intense confusion and difficulties discerning what was real and what was not. As she stared at the sick, she doubted for a second what she was seeing.

'You poor thing,' Jude said, helping Agata up.

'Oh dear!' Elizabeth realised the smell was very real. 'You're *definitely* not well!'

'Sorry,' Agata croaked.

'You need to go to bed,' Elizabeth said, patting her shoulder. 'Jude, you take her.'

Jude led Agata out of the house.

With absolute focus, knowing that Lucas must not see this mess, Elizabeth held her breath, picked a candleholder out of Agata's sick and began to wash it up. Then she moved on to the next and the next, and so on, until Jude returned from the camper van.

'They live in that shit-hole?' Jude said.

'Does she feel better now?' Elizabeth asked, refusing to acknowledge the problem of the camper van.

A frown set in on Jude's face. He picked up a tea towel to help her dry. 'I'm afraid she said she'd been vomiting all night.'

Elizabeth hated being sick herself and felt sorry for Agata, but her stress about the party smothered her immediate sympathies; the list of jobs to complete was too long.

'Is it a bug, or something she ate?'

If it was something she ate, Elizabeth reckoned she would feel better later and be able to help at the party.

'She wasn't making much sense. She was mumbling about wanting to go back to Poland to see her nephew or something. She said it was making her ill. Or the kid was ill? I couldn't work it out. There was a lot of Polish thrown in.'

'She's vomiting because she wants to go home?'

'No. She's genuinely ill. There's no way she'll be able to help tonight.'

Both of Elizabeth's hands flew up into the air. 'Now we're a man down! What am I going to do with the kids when everyone arrives?' Bubbles slid down her elbows and dripped onto the floor.

'Won't they be asleep by then?'

'Are you kidding me? Do you even *know* your niece and nephew? There's going to be a big grown-up party going on. They'll be hyper and Lucas will freak out if he sees them running about unchecked.'

She envisaged the children upending champagne trays and smearing canapés on the guests' dresses. And all her hard work coming unstuck.

'I can look after them,' he offered.

'Good try. No. We need you at the party.'

'What about Mum?' he suggested.

'It's the closing night of *Coriolanus*.'

'Lucas's parents?'

'They're too frail now,' she said. She experienced a surge of panic. 'Oh my God. What am I going to do? I can't handle all this on my own. I can't handle this.'

'Elizabeth, get some perspective here,' Jude said. 'It's just a party.'

'You have no idea. Literally no idea.'

Pacing, trying to think, time closed in on her, and she accepted she didn't have any choice but to calm down and solve the problem.

She dried her hands and scrolled through her phone for baby-sitters, skimming past various texts, mostly from guests. Some were asking what they could bring, or for directions; others were sending last-minute cancellations and their apologies.

The first babysitter she tried was Emma, but she was busy. Next she tried Victoria, Kate, Petra, Lucy and then Holly, whom the children barely knew. All of them had plans for their Saturday nights. The group email she sent to the parents at Isla's school was met with two replies, both suggesting a babysitter she had tried already.

Near to tears, she went out into the garden to get some air, letting Jude finish the washing-up. She wanted to give up all together, defeated at the final hour. Heather was hammering one of the sixty bamboo lanterns into the ground. An idea came to Elizabeth, and she hurried to her and tapped her on the shoulder.

As though disturbed from a daydream, Heather lost her balance and dropped the hammer at their feet. 'Sorry, I was in a world of my own!' she said, pushing up her cap and smiling.

'Heather,' Elizabeth said, catching her breath, picking up the hammer and handing it to her. 'I need to ask you a favour.'

'Sure. Go ahead.'

'What are you doing tonight, after you've finished here?'

'Nothing, why?' she said.

'Might you be able to babysit Isla and Hugo for us? Ten pounds an hour?'

'Yes, I can do that,' she answered.

Elizabeth resisted the urge to hug her. 'That's wonderful.'

'But what about Agata?'

'She's got a sick bug.'

'Oh. Poor Agata.'

'So awful.'

'Will the kids be okay with me?'

'They're very adaptable, and they've seen you around the place.' Elizabeth looked Heather up and down. 'Will you be able to go home with your dad and change? We'd quite like it if you could bring the children down to say a quick hello to some of the guests.'

Heather looked down at her clothes, as though noticing for the first time how scruffy she was. 'I'll definitely change.'

And then Elizabeth did actually hug her. 'I can't tell you how grateful I am.'

'My pleasure,' Heather laughed, scratching her forehead under her cap. 'Happy to help.'

Elizabeth had fixed the problem without calling on Lucas. In the countdown to the party, she moved on with a pumped-up feeling inside, inflated by a sense of purpose and fun. Every so often Lucas would emerge from his office to oversee the more important decisions, like the positioning of the floral arrangements or the place cards for the tables; when he failed to find fault, a rush of love for him came over her, strongly, like a dizzy spell and her insides churned with life.

Bo Seacart stood in the converted barn, stylish in buff against the all-white backdrop, like a celebrity in a magazine. The sun shone on her head through the Velux windows and warmed the room pleasantly.

'Open some windows in here, darling, will you?' Lucas said, joining them from the garden, ducking his head under the low beam. He was followed by Walt, who surveyed the brand-new conversion in a way that suggested he was looking rather than seeing.

Walt Seacart was a man of few words, of average height and average looks. His silver hair was cropped short into a crew cut and his cheeks were ruddy with broken veins. He looked half a century older than Bo, with his moist eyes and slack jaw, but in fact he was only eleven years her senior.

'It's charming, Elizabeth,' he said in his Texan drawl, revealing his bright white capped teeth.

'I'm so glad you like it,' she exhaled, adding, 'The coffee machine's here, and I've tucked two yoga mats there, just in case, and if you get cold, Piotr can light a fire.'

She showed them around, alert to Lucas's edginess, as though he was waiting for her to embarrass him. But Bo's attention was not on Elizabeth. She was staring at Jude's three paintings. It seemed her appetite for his work had not been blunted.

'My God. I'd forgotten how fucking awesome they are,' she exclaimed, dumping her monogrammed rucksack and pashmina on the Scandinavian button-back sofa that Elizabeth had found on eBay.

Elizabeth stood next to Bo to admire the paintings. Behind them, she could hear Lucas telling Walt about Jude's growing reputation as one of the hottest artists on the scene.

'It's your fault we didn't buy these at the Wigram, Walter,' Bo sniped.

Walter winked at Elizabeth. 'My bad.'

'Well, no matter. They're now officially for sale again,' Elizabeth declared.

'They are kick-ass, I'm dead serious. Phenomenal. I want all three for our new cabin in Maine. Or the beach house? Walt?' Bo said, turning to her husband. 'I'm not missing out on them for a second time.'

'How much?' Walt asked bluntly.

Elizabeth had not prepared herself for this question. 'I'll ask Jude for you. He had them valued recently,' she lied.

Lucas dropped his hands into his pockets. 'I'm sure we can agree a good price, in the light of Seacart–Huxley Investments.' And he laughed, knowing he was taking a risk by implying the deal was closed already.

Bo's almond eyes widened at her husband. 'Hear that, honey?'

'How about we include it in the contract? Make up for the surplus lease liabilities, eh, Lucas?' Walt drawled with a rare smile.

Elizabeth did not understand what a surplus lease liability was, but she understood that Walt was making an in-joke.

'You're on!' Lucas bellowed, clapping him on the back. 'Come on, dude. Let's crack open a couple of cold ones.'

As they filed out of the barn, Lucas winked at Elizabeth, and she brimmed with pride, knowing she was responsible for providing the cherry on the cake of the business deal of a lifetime.

But straight away, a twinge of concern about the party tightened her mood, reminding her that she could not be complacent. The evening ahead of her felt like the start of a long tightrope walk above a raging waterfall, where one misstep could be fatal.

CHAPTER SEVENTEEN

'What do you think?' my mother said, cocking her hip.

Dressed in a pink flowery skirt suit, she stood in the tiny space between the bed and the mirrored wardrobes. She had come home to see us, and to attend a Salvation Army fund-raiser tonight. Her curly brown bob was brushed and turned under, and her lips were painted pearly pink. There was wisdom and kindness in her face. Instead of babysitting next door, I wished I was going to the fund-raiser with her. That was how badly I didn't want to go to Copper Lodge. Not even a little bit of me had wanted to help out, but Elizabeth had looked desperate, and I had softened. At least the extra cash would help fix my car, which had been making strange whirring sounds.

'Oh Mum. You're gorgeous,' I said, leaping off the bed and squeezing her tightly. 'We've missed you.' I pulled away and straightened her skirt, where the petticoat had created static. In the brief silence, I wondered idly what her take on the wristwatch incident would be, interested to know whether Agata had struck her as the type to steal. Asking her would risk sending her down a dubious line of thought about Lucas. And I didn't want that to stick in her mind as it had in mine. I was trying hard to park that thought. Three streets away. No, even further. Out of town.

'It'll do for the golf club,' my mother said, putting her hands on her hips and grinning at me. I glanced over at my father, who was in the corner, buttoning his shirt.

'You scrub up nicely, Mrs Shaw,' he said. He was gazing at my mother as though a supermodel stood in front of him.

'I have to admit, it's rather nice to be dressed up again. I've been in the same jumper for weeks.'

'I bet I know which one,' I said.

'I'm sure you don't,' she tutted, puckering her lips, trying to stop the smile. My mother rarely went for more than a few minutes without smiling.

'The navy one with the bobbly strawberries?'

Mum chortled. 'Well, it's a cheery one, you know, for poor old Mags. I tried doing her hair and nails, you know, but honestly, it was such a silly idea. It made her look worse.'

'It was a lovely thing to do.' I reached out to touch my mother's care-worn hand.

She asked, 'Are you going to be okay tonight?'

I pulled my bathrobe tighter around my body and flopped backwards onto their marshmallow-soft bed. 'Yes. Fine,' I said, recalling the chaos of Copper Lodge, Elizabeth's restrained hysteria and Lucas's intense mood. By the time I had left, Elizabeth's voice had risen by two octaves and Lucas had shut himself away in his study. I was sure Elizabeth would have burst into tears if anyone had clapped their hands or snapped their fingers.

'What am I going to wear?' I asked.

Her father straightened his tie. 'Something sensible and clean. You're not a guest.'

'I *know* that, Dad.'

Mum laughed. She would always laugh to dispel tension between me and my father.

'I'll help you choose something nice,' she said, taking me by the hand and leading me along the corridor and into my room.

'How's Rob, love?' she said. She pulled out my only pair of smart jeans. 'You haven't mentioned him since I've been back.'

'He's okay,' I shrugged, tugging the jeans on. I had spoken to Rob twice over the past week. Both times had been brief and forced. Our chat about marriage had been there between us, lying low but not forgotten.

'It's difficult spending time apart.'

'It's not been easy,' I admitted.

Mum sat on the bed and smoothed her skirt over her knees. 'Lucas hasn't been a distraction, has he?'

For as long as I could remember, Lucas had been a distraction. A resident in the hinterland of my mind, representing a kind of distant, abstract alternative life. There lived the delusion that a tweaked chain of events might have brought us together: had I taken the place I'd been offered at Capel Manor horticultural college in London, we would have worked near each other and possibly met up. Had I remained at East Surrey College to complete my diploma, instead of wild-water swimming across Europe, I would have been living in Connolly Close the year he moved back home in his final year at SOAS. Had my father mentioned he was living next door again, I might have been galvanised to fly back from my beach-bum life with Frank in Hossegor a few weeks sooner to see him. And Lucas might not have gone to the party in London to fall in love with Elizabeth. If, if, if. But, but, but. But I couldn't tell my mother that.

'Lucas is not a distraction, Mum,' I said firmly.

There was no *what if*; only what there was now. And now, Lucas was not my reality. Whether he was sleeping with Agata or whether Agata was a thief, it was as it should be, and it was none of my business. Lucas was married to Elizabeth and I was with Rob, and I would never be unfaithful to Rob, however many problems we were having.

She handed me a white top to wear with my black jeans. 'Sorry. Just checking.'

My father interrupted us. 'Come on, Sally, it's five thirty already.'

At his command, she darted out. I trailed her as she ran around collecting her lipstick and keys and changing out of her slippers.

'Bye, you guys,' I said, adding, 'Be good, and if you can't be good …'

'… be careful!' my mother said, winking at me.

I waved them off with a sense of relief.

At six o'clock I was ready, half an hour early, and sitting in front of the television with a ham sandwich and a can of Coke. Before I had taken a bite, I spotted an old-style Fiat 500 zoom into the drive and I went out to see who it was.

Elizabeth's brother, whom I had met briefly earlier, popped up through the sun roof. 'Your chariot awaits.'

'To go next door?'

'I was on my way back from Boots and thought I'd scoop you up on the way.'

'Thank you. That's kind.' I smiled, gathering my things and getting in next to him.

'Isla and Hugo are wreaking havoc.'

In the plastic bag at my feet, I spotted extra-strength Nurofen. 'Who has the headache?'

The small car lurched off. 'My sister.'

He revved the engine and honked the horn as we left the close. I imagined Mrs Barnaby at number 23 poking her nose through her curtains and I leant back into the tatty leather seat to enjoy the three-minute ride.

'This is fun, isn't it!' he said.

I glanced over at him. He had wild dark hair and rosy cheeks and a crease of amusement at the corner of his mouth.

'I'm looking forward to hiding in the kids' bedrooms,' I said.

'Don't bet on it.' He parked up next to the Huxleys' two BMWs.

'What do you mean?'

He rubbed his hands together and affected a sinister accent. 'Lucas has vays of making people have fun!'

I said, 'I'm staff. I'm invisible.'

He chuckled. 'You are *far* from invisible.'

I didn't know how to take that. There was a long silence as we sat in the car staring at the house ahead of us. The flames of the lanterns flickered through the glass.

'Ready?'

'No.'

'Neither am I,' Jude said. 'Let's stay here.'

Elizabeth looked as though she were made of gold. She wore a dress of yellow silk, mid-calf and loose across one shoulder. Her eyes were smoky black. A wave of her hair was swept to the side, falling at her cheekbone, leaving the other side of her face exposed. Her necklace was impossible to miss. The drop of a blue jewel in the centre seemed to be winking at everyone in the room, saying, 'I'm around the neck of the most beautiful woman here!'

'Thank you for coming early, Heather.' She smiled at me and squeezed Jude's forearm with her skinny fingers, heavy with diamonds. 'Thank you for getting her.'

It was clear they had planned my early kidnap. 'No problem,' I replied, as did Jude. 'Jinx,' we said, again at the same time. We laughed. I liked his eyes.

'The house looks amazing, Elizabeth,' I said.

The windows were pulled wide, opening the house into the garden. The path was lit up by the bamboo torches that I had hammered into the ground earlier. Candles littered every surface.

Bouquets of pink roses and sunflowers and elderflowers filled every corner. Waitresses skittered about with trays. A harassed blonde woman arranged bright macarons into a rainbow shape on large silver dishes.

'You look stunning, sis,' Jude said, holding her hands wide as he admired her.

She twirled under his arm and they fell into a hug.

'Your mate Benjamin Healing's here. Will you go straight down?' she said.

He nodded goodbye to me, saying, 'When the little ones are asleep, I'm going to force a glass of champagne on you and make you dance.'

'I'd like you to stay if you can, just in case they wake up,' Elizabeth said to me.

Isla and Hugo leapt in front of us to offer up a tray of minuscule canapés. Two pastry puffs slipped off the edge. Isla bit Hugo, who then dropped the entire tray to hit his sister back. Elizabeth cried out, more tearful than angry, 'Now look what you've done! Please, you two! Stop it!'

I helped her to pick the food up from the floor, remembering that I hadn't managed to eat. It was quite tempting to pop one in my mouth, but I resisted. We shoved the canapés in the bin.

'Say sorry to Heather and Mummy, will you, please?' Elizabeth said to her children.

'Sorry, Heather!' the two rascals shouted in unison, looking less than sorry.

'Hello, Isla. Hello, Hugo. Do you want to show me your bedrooms?'

Elizabeth said, 'Why don't you find a story for Heather to read you while I show her the marquee.' She shooed them away.

'But we want to see it too!' Isla cried.

'Heather will bring you down later, after your bath. I promise,' Elizabeth said, tweaking Isla's nose. Then she popped open her clutch bag and handed them each a gold-wrapped sweet. 'Don't tell Daddy,' she whispered, kissing them both.

As she led me through the garden, I straightened a lopsided torch and cast an eye over the beds outside the guest house. The yellows and purples of the borders were pretty in the dying light.

'How is Agata feeling?' I asked.

'I don't know,' Elizabeth said.

A waitress approached with a tray of champagne. Elizabeth snapped, 'No, no, Heather isn't a *guest*.'

The low pink sun threw long shadows across the meadow of flowers, setting alight the petals, silhouetting the marquee, whose tent poles pushed up turrets of white canvas, resembling a fairy-tale castle. A thick red curtain was drawn over the entrance and pooled onto the seagrass carpeting. She pulled it back.

'Here we go, take a look. I wanted to show you before it's all ruined.'

Dozens of lanterns filled with tea lights dangled from the draped ceiling. The tables were arranged either side of the dance floor, adorned with gold cutlery and posies. Moroccan-style gold and silver pouffes were scattered around low metal tables in one corner. Two young women of roughly my age, in white tank tops and layers of gold necklaces, worked behind the DJ box. One bent over the vinyl turntables, which were plugged into a top-of-the-range speaker system, with an earphone pressed to one ear.

'Cool,' I said, peering in.

'Thank you,' Elizabeth said, and added, smiling, 'If you could bring the children down in about an hour, when the party is in full swing, and make sure you hold their hands. I don't want them running off and annoying the guests.'

There were only a few guests so far. They were not how I had imagined them to be. I had expected them to be typical of the Surrey housewife set: wives with floral dresses and toned arms and husbands in paisley shirts and ironed blue jeans. But I was surprised to see that Jude was talking to a man wearing a bomber jacket and neon trainers, holding the hand of a small, curvaceous woman in an all-in-one denim catsuit and red-soled high-heels. The woman teased her backcombed hair with her red nails and cackled at something Jude said.

Elizabeth led me away to the second clearing, mown into a perfect circle by my father, lit by more of my fire torches. There was a huge open fire pit and a hog roast being turned by a chef in a tall hat. A long table was laid out with wooden bowls of fruits and salads and breads.

'I thought a buffet would be more fun,' she said. 'And look down there, can you see? I've lit up the trees,' she laughed, pointing to the oak trees at the bottom of the meadow, which were now illuminated red and yellow and blue. 'Too much?' she added.

'No. It looks amazing,' I said.

'The fireworks are going to be started down there.'

As we made our way back up to the house, she said, 'Thank you for helping us to make it happen, Heather.'

'My pleasure,' I said, genuinely pleased.

More guests appeared and chattered behind us.

Elizabeth stiffened. 'Okay, Heather, you can go now. Isla will take you through the routine. Don't forget to put Hugo's glasses back in his case, otherwise he loses them. They know where everything is.'

Passing the guest house, I pictured Agata curled up in her cramped, damp van. The contrast between that hidden shame and the opulence of the party sent a shiver through me.

Before I left, I would bring her some food, as a gesture, even if she couldn't face eating it yet.

Isla and Hugo were soft and clean in their pyjamas after a bubble bath. Hugo stood on the yellow stool in the bathroom to look into the mirror. He flattened his hair to the side like a film star's. I straightened his spectacles and tightened Isla's dressing gown cord.

'Ready?'

'I'm tired,' Isla said. Her near-hysterical excitement of earlier had died down.

I pushed her damp curls back from her forehead. 'You don't want to go down?'

'I do!' she said, snapping out of it, grabbing Hugo by the hand and pulling him off the stool. 'I'll show you the way!'

Her confidence ebbed away again as we made our way down the path to the marquee. She slipped her hand into mine and stayed close. Hugo skipped in front and said hello to every single guest we passed, eliciting smiles and comments about how sweet he was.

I felt as shy as Isla did. The guests were impossibly sophisticated and intimidating, and my best jeans felt like rags. Even the guests I presumed were Jude's arty friends looked expensive with their designer glasses and animal-skin clutch bags. Beyond the fleeting patronising admiration the children garnered, I didn't know whether their once-overs of me were born of curiosity or distaste.

My desperate wish to avoid seeing Lucas at all costs grew by the second. As the crowds thickened, I kept an eye out for him.

'I want to find Daddy!' Hugo said.

'Your mummy said we mustn't disturb him,' I said.

'Your hand's sweaty,' Isla said, pulling away from me. I wiped it on my jeans and looked down for Hugo, but he had already disappeared.

'Where's your brother, Isla?' I asked her, panicked.

I swivelled around and then back again in response to a tap on the shoulder.

'Hello again,' a man's voice said.

'Jude!' I whispered, relieved. 'Hugo's darted off.'

His eyes lit up. 'The little monster. I'll help you find him.'

'I only took my eyes off him for a second,' I said.

'What trouble could he get into? It's only a party.'

I took the lead, swiftly weaving through the guests, my eyes dipped down to the level of his littleness, at people's skirts and slacks, tanned legs, shiny shoes.

Trouble was everywhere. I saw pale dresses and red wine; a hog roast over tall flames; candles dangling within easy reach; fireworks in the field, unmanned and poised to explode. Everywhere there were dangers for a five-year-old. Everywhere there were possible mishaps that would evoke Elizabeth's quiet wrath.

'Let's look in the marquee,' Jude said, taking Isla's hand, changing direction.

'Naughty Hugo,' Isla said gleefully, trotting next to him.

I followed them. In Jude's wake, heads turned. One woman's eyes widened for a second when she saw him. She nudged her husband. 'That was Jude Woods,' she said.

The music became louder. Over my shoulder I glimpsed Elizabeth in the distance near the house, moving slowly alongside an older man with a cane. They inched down the path, giving us more time to find Hugo.

Jude pulled the marquee curtain back and we cried in unison, 'There he is!'

Hugo was on the other side of the dance floor, in the arms of one of the pretty blonde DJs. He was clapping and singing, balanced on her skinny hip. His ears were covered in red headphones, bigger than his whole head, and his glasses had steamed up. Enchanted, I had no inclination to rush over to him and drag him away, however furious Elizabeth might be with me.

'Can *I* have a go too?' Isla asked.

'Come on then, I'll introduce you,' Jude said.

We made our way through the throng. A woman in a linen shirt and pearls was twerking. A man in a suit with a handkerchief in his pocket was knocking out an enthusiastic running man. They seemed to be having fun. I actually wished I could gulp back a glass of champagne and join in.

'This is Lil. And this is Kat,' Jude said. I shook the DJ girls' hands. Close up, I realised they were twins, with different hair-styles.

Lil fist-bumped Hugo. 'This rude boy is *fly*,' she shouted in a London accent laced with private school. 'What's *your* name, sister?' she added to Isla, high-fiving her.

While the two children were being given a lesson in DJing, Jude and I stood side by side surveying the dance floor. Behind the turntables, we were separate from the party. There was no sign of either Lucas or Elizabeth.

'Have you been having a good time?' I asked him.

'Um. Let me think. See that guy?' he said, pointing to a man in a paisley shirt shuffling awkwardly next to his wife, who was bouncing about in a knee-length leather mini. 'He's in the Forbes Top 100. He owns a superyacht mooring in St Bart's. And that woman,' he said, pointing to a blonde in a velvet suit, 'started a nail bar chain in the States that has just floated on the stock market for millions. Her country house is currently being rented out by Adele. And see him with the checked shirt?' He nodded to a bald man with protruding eyes. 'He's head of JCB in Russia and has just moved to Kent from West Sussex so he can afford land for his own airstrip.'

'Right,' I said. From the way he delivered the information, it wasn't clear why he was telling me. I hoped he didn't think I was the type of person who would be impressed by their wealth.

'The money on that dance floor alone could wipe out poverty in the UK,' he continued with a frown. 'These are not my people.'

Before I could think of an intelligent response that represented my like-mindedness, I spotted Lucas and lost the ability to talk.

His white shirt was neutral and classic, setting him apart from the guests, whose fashion choices marked them tribally. He could have been part of any social faction here: the London set, the green welly brigade, the art scene, the aristocracy. With one hand in his pocket and one through his hair, he scanned the room. Our eyes met and he headed straight for us, politely responding to the many guests who wanted to talk to him. With a shoulder squeeze or a heartfelt handshake, a laugh here and a flirtatious wink there, he worked the crowd like a famous footballer with a bank of fans.

'Hugo, Isla,' I said, finding my voice, 'I think it's time for bed.'

Both of them ignored me. 'Jude,' I whispered urgently, 'will you help me coax them away?'

Together we managed to prise them off Lil and Kat, bribing them with a rainbow macaron each.

I carried Hugo. The four of us circumvented Lucas, managing to escape outside without an encounter. Outside, Elizabeth caught sight of us and withdrew from a small unit of blonde women, who closed ranks after her departure. I prepared to apologise for the children's DJing, although I couldn't be sure she had witnessed it.

'Darlings!' she cried, tripping on a cushion that had somehow made its way out of the marquee. She bent to kiss both Hugo and Isla on the lips, and wiped off the lipstick smears, giggling like a schoolgirl. 'I heard you were naturals on the turntables!'

'I was just taking them up to bed,' I said.

'Wonderful, Heather. Do come down and get some food when they're tucked in, won't you?'

'And a midnight swim maybe?' Jude said, looking at me.

'A swim? Is that what you'd like?' Elizabeth asked.

A cool dip under the stars would have been sublime, but I was wary of Elizabeth's friendliness, knowing how easily she could turn. 'No, don't worry,' I said. 'I'm fine, thanks. I'll just watch a bit of telly.'

'Oh, don't be silly,' she said. 'It's a no-go zone for the guests and it'll be so much fun in the dark with the pool lights on. It's the least you deserve after helping me out tonight.'

'Thank you, Elizabeth. I'll see how these two go down.'

'Whatever you feel like. There are spare swimsuits in the shed,' Elizabeth said. She bent down to give the children hugs. 'Night, night, my beautiful poppets.'

Jude kissed his niece and nephew on their heads. 'Be good for Heather, won't you?' he said.

'I'm sure they will be,' I said. 'Bye, Jude. Thanks again.'

'Come down and find me as soon as they're in bed!' he called out.

As we pottered up to the house, with Hugo almost asleep on my shoulder, Isla said, 'I wish we could stay at the party.'

'Me too, little one,' I said, realising with surprise that I meant it.

Through the window of the television den, I could see the guests spilling out of the marquee into the meadow. The semicircle of light from the party glowed like a force field into the dusky evening sky. The noise of talking and laughing, and the pumping music, vibrated through the walls. I was amazed that Hugo and Isla were still asleep.

Having checked on them for the fourth time, I snuggled under the cashmere sofa throw, clicking through the channels with the television remote. I landed on a programme where a woman was in tears over her detox drink of boiled lemon juice and maple syrup. My stomach rumbled and rattled. Looking at my watch, I debated whether I was brave enough to venture out and find some food, and perhaps Jude. Then the door opened and Jude's head poked round.

'Those two worn you out?' he said.

I sat bolt upright. 'No, no,' I replied, swiftly switching off the TV.

'Fancy that swim?'

'I'm not sure.' My stomach rumbled loudly.

'After some food, maybe? Elizabeth said it was okay.'

I clutched my stomach. 'I'm so hungry I was about to start eating this blanket.'

'Come on then.'

On the way down to the meadow, Jude slowed at the little gate to the pool.

'We could watch the fireworks from the poolside. Those sunloungers will be the best seats in the house.'

There was a wooden sign that said *No Entry* hanging on the gate.

'Are you sure Elizabeth's really okay with it?'

'The party's going so bloody well, I don't think she'd care if I told her we were about to elope.'

'Jude, I can't.'

'Elope?'

'No, I mean, yes. Definitely no to eloping, but I can't go for a swim with you either.'

He stopped walking and turned to me with a grin.

'I know you're taken, Miss Heather Shaw,' he said. 'I'm trying very, very hard to make peace with that, but I promise, with all of my heart, as a true gentleman, that I will respect your boundaries. I just want to do something fun tonight. Everyone at the party is boring me to death.'

'What if the kids wake up?'

'We can use the baby monitor.'

I thought quickly. 'Okay,' I said, still not entirely sure it was a good idea.

Jude linked arms with me, companionably, and we walked along the pathway. He grabbed two glasses of champagne from one of the trays.

'Do you want to come with me to get the food?'

'No thank you,' I said, shivering at the thought of seeing Lucas.

'Happy for me to choose for you?'

'I'll eat anything.'

'Cashmere blankets?'

'If there's enough barbecue sauce.'

He and Elizabeth were so different, I thought as I watched him amble off towards the spit roast.

Before slipping through the gate, I looked over my shoulder to check that nobody was around. My heart stopped dead in my chest when I saw Lucas coming out of the guest barn. Fearing he had seen me, I backed into the hedge and waited for him to pass, then nipped through the gate.

The floodlights had turned the water a luminous blue. The shed by the pool smelled musty. In an old drawer I found a collection of swimsuits. I avoided the designer brands, with cut-out sections or high legs, and changed into a sensible red Speedo with white piping down the side and a criss-cross back. It was very tight.

The night air was chilly. My stomach growled. I reclined on the wooden slats of the sunlounger, sipped my champagne and waited for Jude. Up above me the stars glowed. A shooting star whizzed and then died. The gate clicked.

'That was quick!' I said, sitting up, salivating for my hog roast. When I saw Lucas, my empty stomach contracted, no longer hungry.

'I knew I'd find you here.'

I pulled the towel around my shoulders and hid my champagne glass. 'Elizabeth said I could have a swim,' I said defensively.

'It's okay,' he said. 'I come in peace.'

In the moonlight, his skin and eyes shone. His chinos were rolled up and his feet were bare.

'Jude's about to arrive with the food,' I warned, instinctively.

'I'm afraid I sent him off to talk to Walt Seacart.'

'He's not coming back with my food?'

'Sorry. Are you hungry?'

'No,' I said, leaning back again.

He lay on the sunlounger next to mine and linked his hands behind his head. I noted the Rolex on his wrist.

'Jude has a crush on you,' he said.

I kept staring at the sky. My heart was beating through my back and vibrating through the slats. The crack and whizz of fireworks began, obscuring the stars.

'He's a nice guy.'

'I told him he was punching above his weight.'

'That's mean!'

'I am mean.' He shot up and leant forward on his elbows. 'A swim? For old times' sake?'

'What about your party?'

'To hell with it.'

'You're drunk. Elizabeth will miss you.'

'She won't. I haven't seen her all evening. She'll be with Bo for the fireworks.'

He pulled me up by the arm. My towel slipped off my shoulders.

I wrapped my arms around my waist. He kept his eyes fixed on me as he removed his trousers, leaving me breathless. The noise in the sky shouted louder than my doubts, egging me on, daring me to reject caution. To break his stare, I ran and jumped in; a bomb. He followed suit. Underneath the water, we turned to each other. He shouldn't be here like this with me, I thought. He should be by his wife's side, chatting to his guests.

I swam away from him and ducked underwater. His hand ran up my back, tracing my spine to the nape of my neck. His touch left me powerless. He drew me towards him, cradling the back of my head, his body up against mine. When he kissed me, I took in a bubble of air from his mouth; fleetingly I imagined he was saving my life. He twirled me around and we spiralled upwards, dancing towards the surface. Under the water, the real world above us, of earth and air and wind and fire, vanished. Under the water, we were sirens and sea gods. Under the water, we were entwined and suspended in time, as if the past twelve years and all the *what ifs* didn't matter.

Above the surface, lying on the poolside tiles, the stainless steel of his wristwatch reflected the multicoloured explosions in the velvet sky.

CHAPTER EIGHTEEN

Elizabeth watched the fireworks as she and Bo lay back on one of the oversized cushions near the fire.

The spray of colour in the sky marked the finale of her night. The party could take care of itself now. She felt a wave of satisfaction and exhaustion, but she needed to find Lucas before she could relax fully. As soon as she knew he was happy, she could perhaps escape to join Jude and Heather, and maybe allow herself a swim with them, if they were still there.

Bo nudged her and offered her a drag of the marijuana-stuffed roll-up she was smoking. Elizabeth turned it down.

'You sure know how to throw a party, 'Liz'beth.'

Elizabeth propped herself up on her elbows. 'I'm glad you're having a good time,' she said absently, surveying a cluster of guests. She spotted Sarah, who was sitting on a beanbag around the fire pit, deep in conversation with Gabriel Asprey, the great-great-great-grandson of Charles Asprey's brother, on the 'poor' side of the family. Gabriel used his name to garner business for his Jacuzzi bathroom business, and partied hard, possibly helping him to forget that he sold loos rather than high-end luxury goods like his forefathers.

'I want another one of those macarons,' Bo said.

Elizabeth remembered how little time she had given to Sarah, who had delivered her macarons in the afternoon and arrived dressed up later, with her husband, as their guests.

Clare Boyd

'I'll get you some,' she said, standing up, welcoming the excuse to find Lucas.

'Find Benji Healing for me too,' Bo said.

'It's Benji now, is it?'

'I'm rather in love with him,' she chuckled.

'Jude'll know where he is.'

'Oh, your brother! I'd forgotten how damn *cute* he is.'

Elizabeth smiled.

Bo raised herself to sitting. Changing her mind, she said, 'I'm coming with you. Fireworks displays are all the same. No offence, honey.'

They moved through the crowd of people, whose necks were craned at the sky.

The marquee was empty except for Benjamin Healing, Jude and Walt. Barefoot, Bo began an Indian dance in the middle of the dance floor, beguiling in her flowing floral dress, her hair loose with flowers, the roll-up in her right hand. She was performing. Performing for the men, who were deep in conversation.

Elizabeth was surprised that Lucas wasn't with them.

Did he think the party a success? Had he noticed that the pork was a fraction overdone? Or that the salad was late to the buffet? Or that the music had been too loud at the beginning? Was he pleased with her?

Interrupting her flow of worries, Walt broke away from his conversation and stood on the dance floor, territorially. Lord William Cecil-Johnson appeared from outside and joined him.

'Fireworks give me a headache,' he bellowed.

Neither of the men took their eyes off Bo. A sly grin formed on Walt's lips. His tumbler of whisky hung limply and sloshed over William's right arm. William didn't notice. He spent most of his life drunk, hiding his quiet alcoholism behind his aristocratic bumbling. Walt might be distracted from Bo's flirting by William's stories of old money dysfunction, and Elizabeth left them to it, overhearing William explaining that his wife, Patricia, was at home, devastated after the death of one of her thoroughbreds, and that she loved her animals more than she loved her husband. Elizabeth knew this was true: Patricia allowed Shetland ponies and chickens to wonder through their vast Victorian kitchen.

As she slipped out of the marquee, smiling to herself, Leonora, a neighbour from two houses down, arrived at her side.

'Is that Lulu Guinness?' she asked, as she grabbed a half-finished glass of someone else's wine. 'Talking to that model-looking guy?'

'That's the executive director of Christie's Maritime,' Elizabeth chuckled.

Leonora flapped her hands, splashing red wine on the ground. 'Oh, how disappointing.'

She began to prattle on as they walked. Elizabeth nodded politely, wondering how she could lose her on the way to the house.

'... but Edmund will have to adjust. Just like Tom and I did. We can't take him out, can we?' Leonora said.

'No, of course not,' Elizabeth said, unsure of what she was talking about.

'His housemaster said he was having trouble making friends, but it takes time. I think I'm going to stop taking his calls. All he does is cry down the phone. I find it terribly wearing. And it can't look good if his peers see him crying to Mummy all the time, can it?'

'No, I suppose not,' Elizabeth said.

Boarding school, that was the topic. For only a moment, this punctured her happiness. The memory of her grovelling phone call to Mrs Hepburn at Channing House came back to her. She finished her champagne and looked around for another. 'I'm sorry, I've got to see to the ...' she said, trailing off, knowing that Leonora was too drunk to care what Elizabeth might have to see to.

Continuing her search for Lucas, she wandered around the fire, picking off a couple of grapes from the buffet table, swiping another glass of champagne from a passing waitress, saying hello to more guests she hadn't yet had the chance to chat to, promising to come back to them when she had found her husband.

Scenes from the party whirred around her head as the fireworks rocketed above her. Bo dancing. Walt drunk with William. She and Bo on the cushion watching the fireworks in the night sky. Jude and Heather laughing together with the children earlier. Lucas grinning with the pride of a man who owned it all. Drunk, happy people gasping at the display. Copper Lodge swirling with magic. It seemed she had pulled it off, but she wanted to hear it from Lucas himself.

As she passed the pool, the water sounded choppy. Quietly she opened the little gate and peered around the hedge.

They came up through the water, head to head, coiled together like one body. Heather's auburn hair snaked down her back, lit up by the strobing pyrotechnics above them. There was a splutter from the water, a burst of noise that hid Elizabeth's small cry. The sky cracked above her like a lightning bolt, splitting her skull open, and everything became clear. For a startling moment, time stood still. Moving into the next minute, after what she had witnessed, would be like a person seeing after a lifetime of blindness. The familiarity of a lost sense seemed preferable.

She backed away before she saw more, and ran, yanking her necklace from her neck, feeling revulsion for it, chucking it into a flower bed and vowing never to wear it again. It represented the show that she and Lucas put on for the public; as it glittered, it had throttled the life out of her.

CHAPTER NINETEEN

The swim had been short-lived and thrilling and utterly wrong. The spell of his embrace, his kiss, had been broken as soon as I reached the surface, when I came to my senses. Fury replaced any pleasure that had passed through my body underwater.

'What the hell was that?' I said, unlocking myself from his limbs. We stood facing each other in the shallow end. My lungs heaved for air. The sky had returned to black.

'A kiss?' he answered, as though it was that simple.

I hissed at him under my breath, 'For God's sake! Are you mad? You're *married*! Anyone could have seen us!'

'But they didn't.'

'Even if they didn't, it's still totally messed up!'

He swept his wet hair back, blinking too fast. 'I'm sorry! Okay? For wanting to feel good for one damned second of my life!'

'Oh yeah, your life's so *awful*,' I said.

'It's an illusion, Heather! Don't you get it? Look at me! All this bullshit. This party. This house. This deal. My marriage? Look at Walt. He's so rich and so mean. And he has all the money in the world. I've been working every hour God sends, for what? To be just as rich and mean? But when I look at you, I don't give a shit about any of it. Not one *shit.*' He slapped the water with the palm of his hands, splashing me.

I wiped my face. 'You're scared,' I said quietly. 'That's all. You're sabotaging it so that—'

'Shush a minute, I think I heard someone,' Lucas whispered, leaning in towards me.

The guests continued to party in the marquee, innocent of our betrayal. The music still pumped in the background and the smell of barbecue smoke lingered on the breeze.

Then an unfamiliar male voice from the other side of the hedge called out, 'Elizabeth! *There* you are!'

Lucas pressed his forefinger to his lips. *Stay quiet*, he was saying. *Don't move a muscle.*

The voice continued. 'Leonora and I are off! Marvellous party, thanks ever so much.'

'I'm so glad you could make it, Tom,' Elizabeth replied.

There was the sound of footsteps, away, off up the path.

Behind me, one of the baby monitors crackled. It was lying on the grass between our two sunloungers. I threw my towel on top of it to muffle the sound.

Lucas pointed to the shed. I got out and ran inside, lurking there like a criminal. I heard the gate opening.

'Hello there,' Lucas said.

'I've been looking for you,' Elizabeth said.

I held my breath.

It sounded as though Lucas was getting out of the pool. His wet footsteps slapped on the stone. 'Want to come in for a dip?' he asked.

'People are starting to leave,' she said.

'Thank God. Let's go and say goodbye to them.'

'Get dressed, Lucas,' she said.

A few minutes later, the gate opened and closed. Then there was silence.

I stayed inside the shed for five, maybe ten minutes. It seemed like days. I deserved the discomfort, and much more, for being so stupid. What had happened in the pool went against everything I believed in. I would have done anything to rewind time.

When I thought it was safe, I crept outside. My clothes were damp. As I collected the baby monitors and my champagne glass, I heard Lucas's voice again, through the hedge. I froze.

'Where are you going?' he said. To whom, I didn't know, but I could hear the panic in his voice.

'I might have left it by the pool.' It was Elizabeth.

'Why would it be there? You haven't been by the pool.'

'Yes I have.'

More voices and footsteps. One woman was singing along to the music from the marquee.

'Hi, guys! Having a good time?' Lucas called out.

'I want to go back to the dance floor!' the woman's voice replied. 'But Rupert won't—'

A man's voice cut in, presumably Rupert's. 'Bye, Lucas, I'll be in touch about Spain. Great party!'

'Prick,' Lucas said when their footsteps had died away. 'I wouldn't buy a fucking condo off him, let alone a resort.'

If Elizabeth replied, I couldn't hear it.

Lucas returned to the lost thing, whatever it was. 'I want you to find it and put it back on.'

'It might have been stolen,' Elizabeth said.

'From around your neck?'

'Maybe.'

'What's got into you?' Lucas asked her.

I considered running back into the shed. The wetness from the towel was soaking into my front. Before I could make a decision, the gate squeaked open and Elizabeth appeared.

Her hand was around her bare throat, her yellow dress twisted a little, her hair damp on her forehead. She walked up to me, so close I could smell her perfume. I wanted to die of shame. Red scratches, like fingernail marks, made lines down her neck where her necklace had been.

There was a hiss from one of the monitors.

'You can go home now, Heather,' she said in a breathy whisper, pushing her platinum hair back.

'Thank you,' I said, darting away, avoiding eye contact with Lucas.

As soon as I was clear of the gate, I ran up to the house, dumped the towel, the glass and the baby monitors onto the breakfast bar, then continued running, out onto the dark lane and back home.

I sat down on my parents' doorstep, dismayed and guilt-ridden, my knees up to my chin, gathering myself, just in case anyone was awake inside.

I heard breathing. I looked up and Lucas was right there. His approach through the dark had been silent. He still wore no shoes.

'What are you doing here?' I whispered, shocked, mindful of my parents' bedroom window a few feet away, dropping my keys as though my fingers had lost their strength.

'I'm sorry. For … before. I'm so sorry,' he said.

'Shh, keep your voice down.' I pointed at the window.

A thought fluttered through my mind like a banner: *I'm still in love with this man.* It ran in tandem with the knowledge that I could not allow it to be true.

'You have to go home,' I insisted.

'I don't know what to do,' he said, rubbing his face.

'You can't be here.'

He brought his hands to my face. 'You. Turning up after all these years. It's been hell.'

'Charming,' I said.

His lips met mine briefly, gently, lifting me off my feet. I jerked away.

He grabbed my upper arms. 'It's been over between Elizabeth and me for years. Surely you know that. Surely everyone knows that.'

I choked, incredulous. 'No. Nobody knows that.'

'She's mad, Heather. Totally and utterly mad. I'm only there because of the kids. I can't leave them with her.'

'I can't get involved,' I said, desperate for him to make it easier for me.

'I made a mistake back then. When I left for London.'

'*This* is a mistake.' I wanted to sound convincing. My words articulated what I knew I should say rather than what I felt. And he knew it.

'Please, Heather. When can I see you again? To talk. Just to talk.'

'I'm in your grounds every day if you need me,' I said.

I unlocked the front door and shut myself in, panting on the other side. Turning my back on him tore at my heart.

There was someone in the hallway. A shadow, tall and menacing, moved towards me. The light was switched on. I squinted and covered my eyes.

'What time do you call this?' my father said.

My heart thumped. I looked at my watch. It was 1.42 a.m. 'Sorry I woke you.'

'Where have you been?'

'Elizabeth wanted me to stay, just in case the kids woke up.'

'I *saw* you two.'

'Saw who?' I asked, cold with dread.

'That was Lucas,' my father said.

'No.'

'What the hell are you *doing*?'

I tied up my hair. 'Nothing.'

When I tried to walk past him, he blocked my path. 'Don't walk away when I'm talking to you.'

'I'm really tired. I want to go to bed.'

'It can't happen. Ever. You understand me?'

'Nothing happened, Dad.'

'Listen to me, young lady!' he yelled, gripping my shoulders, pressing his thumbs under the bones. 'You can't see him again!'

'I'm not seeing anyone!'

'Don't lie to me!'

He shook me back and forth until my head was banging against the plastered wall behind me, until my hair had slipped out of its band, until I thought my neck would break and my head explode.

'We do everything for you and still you throw it back in our faces!'

Through the chaos of pain and panic, I tried to think. A headache detonated inside my skull. Breathlessly, I tried to talk, 'You've got the wrong idea. Nothing is going on. I swear it. He kissed me once. It will never happen again.'

But he didn't stop until my body became limp and I lost my ability to stand up.

Then he let me go and I crumpled to the floor. I scrabbled into a crouching position, with my head between my knees, waiting for another attack.

'Don't you understand how much we love you?' I heard tears in his voice but I couldn't look up at him. I was too ashamed, of myself and of him. 'All our lives we've tried to teach you the right values and give you a good work ethic, and look at you! You're a clever, kind girl! We love you so much. I just don't understand why it's not enough for you.'

I raised my eyes to him. My vision was blurry. His fingers covered his eyes like a cage, and I felt remorseful and ashamed. I couldn't stop the next wave of tears. 'I'm so sorry, Dad. He came on to me. I didn't have time to … I just didn't think,' I sobbed.

His rage surged back. 'That's exactly it! You never think! You jump in without looking first. You've always been the same, but the stakes are too high now!'

I cowered, pleading, 'I care so much about you and Mum. I made a mistake. Please forgive me. Please.'

'I should never have asked you here,' he muttered.

Then my mother came through. Too late. Always too late. By standing on the outside, she was choosing not to see it.

'Come on, you two. Stop all this. It's two in the morning. Come on, Gordon, back to bed.'

She looked down at me and put her hand on top of my head. 'Off you go, love. Off to bed now.'

I was pitifully grateful for her affection.

'Let's get some sleep. It'll all be forgotten about in the morning,' she mumbled as they shuffled off to their room.

I let my body fall forward across my thighs. My forehead rested on the floor and I stayed there thinking about what I should do next.

I wanted to leave.

My brain rocked when I stood up. I wove about as I walked to my bedroom, where I stretched to the top of the wardrobe for my suitcase. It was feather-light. I threw it on the bed and stared into its empty cavity.

When I reached into the shelves to scoop my clothes out, the shooting agony in the muscles across my shoulders and down my arms disabled me. I stayed very still for a moment, letting the nausea and hopelessness roll through me. My whole being was sore and tender, too battered to move.

I shoved the suitcase away and crawled under my duvet wearing my clothes.

Tomorrow I would leave.

CHAPTER TWENTY

After the party, Elizabeth spent longer than usual in the bathroom, brushing her teeth, tidying her creams, refolding the towels. As she moisturised her face, her reflection in the mirror depressed her. It was as though an unhappy child stared back at her, like Isla after one of her tantrums. The tears had dried up, but she was hollow-eyed and pale. Unlike Isla, she was ugly. The innocence and plumpness of her youth had been sucked away. She was damaged goods, ravaged, empty of love. This was her real face, and she seemed to be seeing it at its true state for the first time in years.

She and Lucas undressed in the semi-darkness of one of their small bedside lights. The guests were gone, as was the pretence between them. Elizabeth had not met his eye since she had seen him in the pool with Heather.

When he spoke, he was sitting on his side of the bed, with his back to the bathroom door, buttoning up his pyjama top.

'Let's hope Gordon finds that necklace tomorrow,' he said.

'It's insured, isn't it?'

'That's not really the point. It was Mum's.'

'It's been gathering dust in a safety deposit box for thirty years.'

'I thought you'd like it, that's all.'

'I did.'

Lucas hung his head. 'I never know how to please you.'

The anger she had been suppressing for weeks rushed up and out of her.

'You could start by keeping your hands off the help, perhaps,' she said, climbing into her side of the bed.

He exhaled heavily. 'You imagine things.'

'No,' she said, clear-sighted now. 'I saw you in the pool together.'

'Shit.' He rubbed his face. 'Shit!' he said to the ceiling.

Elizabeth shuddered.

'I don't want her working here any more.'

'Please, Elizabeth. Don't go there.'

'She's not like Agata, Lucas.'

'Agata has nothing to do with this.'

'Heather sees stuff that Agata doesn't.'

'You want Heather to lose her job, her whole *livelihood*? What about Gordon and Sally? They'd have to go too? What would it achieve?'

'It would be *your* doing.'

'It's not that simple, and you know it.'

She pleaded with him. 'Lucas, if nothing else, think of Isla and Hugo.'

He glanced over his shoulder, looking down his own arm rather than at her. His profile was serene and beautiful, like a marble statue. 'You suddenly care about their feelings?' he asked.

His coldness seemed solid, right through him, and her composure fell away. When she spoke, her throat clenched and her voice was hoarse. 'How can you even question that?'

'You're the one who questions it.'

Elizabeth threw off the covers and hurled a pot of handcream from her bedside table at his back. 'You *arsehole*! When will you ever forgive me? I was ill! I was *ill*!'

He picked the cream up from the floor. 'Your brother's next door. Do you want him to worry that you're still ill?'

She lay back in bed. The last person she wanted to worry was Jude.

Rigid on her back, she stared at the cross of oak beams above her pounding head, wishing the rivets that held them together would unscrew, ending this. Pressing her temples, she said, 'You *make* me unwell.' She was telling herself more than telling him.

'By *loving* you?'

She sprang up and around the bed to face him, shaking all over. Her finger trembled when she pointed it right into his face. 'Please spare me your *love*.'

Her fury rendered her flesh jelly-like. She turned and fled. She would rather die than sleep next to him.

She stood in the doorway of the spare room in her nightie, hoping Jude was still awake, fearing he had heard their fight.

'Lucas is snoring and I can't sleep. Can I join you?'

He was still fully dressed and lying on the top of the duvet.

'Sure. Jump in,' he said, putting down his book. 'Happy?'

'Yes, happy. You?' She curled under the covers and listened to how *un*happy he was, and to his guilt-ridden monologue about leaving Heather alone by the pool. Apparently Lucas had trapped him in a conversation with Walt Seacart and Benjamin Healing about the value of his triptych. She listened half-heartedly, wishing he would stop talking, desperate to sleep off the rotation of Lucas's words, the images of him and Heather in the pool together.

'What do *you* think?' he asked her. 'Do you think I've blown my chances?'

'I expect so,' she replied drowsily, brooding about Lucas leaving her for Heather.

When Elizabeth and Jude had been teenagers, their mother had explained to them why their father had left them. She told them that Christopher – 'your father', she had clarified – had learnt how to clamp his fist around his feelings to survive the challenges thrown at him, and that his parents – 'your grandparents' – had been privileged, lazy, bored alcoholics who had left him to fend for himself. According to Virginia, their father hadn't known how to operate in a family unit. Working too hard and finding love from someone inappropriate had been predictable choices; age-old quick fixes that made it all feel better temporarily.

'Are you even listening?' Jude asked.

'I am.'

But her stream of thoughts continued. Her mother's theory might explain why Lucas threw himself into his work and made silly mistakes with young women like Heather. And Agata even? The cruelty inflicted on him by his housemaster had inadvertently taught him how to suppress his anger and how to compartmentalise in order to survive.

Jude flopped back. 'Would you give me Heather's number?'

'I can't do that.'

'I'll knock on her door and ask her myself then.'

Elizabeth had to find a way to put Jude off. 'You can't possibly do that.'

'Why not?'

She could never tell her brother the truth. 'It's rude.'

'She wouldn't think so. She's not like that.'

'You can't date Heather Shaw. No way.'

'Why not?'

She sat up, tucking the covers under her armpits, and fumbled around in her brain for a plausible reason. She was good at make-believe. When they were little, their mother had written scripts for her and Jude to act out, teaching them to method act, drawing from real-life sadnesses and bringing it into their performances. They would play characters and recreate scenes over and over until they became real in her head, when finally Virginia would clap and hand them pretend Oscars. Sometimes she would ask them to repeat lines she had written to real boyfriends or real bailiffs who had turned up on their doorstep. Often, Elizabeth had been confused about what was real and what was pretend.

'Because she's the gardener's daughter.'

'It's not *Downton Abbey*!'

'It wouldn't be right.'

Jude flew to standing. 'Are you *serious*?'

'Lucas is a very traditional man. Just like his dad. He likes things to be done properly. He likes everything to be in order.'

'Don't fraternise with the staff? Is that actually what you're saying?'

His disgust with her made her eyes sting, but she had good reason not to back down. 'That's a crass way of putting it ...'

'When did you turn into such a snob?'

'It's not about snobbery; it's about setting down ground rules for our employees.'

'She's not my employee. She's yours.'

'Think of Heather,' she urged him. 'It'll put her in a terribly awkward situation.'

He began changing out of his jeans. 'No it won't. You're the one being awkward. It's the twenty-first century, for Christ's sake.'

'Some of the old values still mean something round here. I like it that way.'

Standing in his boxer shorts, he turned and stared at her open-mouthed, then he climbed into bed and turned the side light off. Into the dark he said, 'Wow, sis, you really have changed.'

She slid down next to him, remembering how they had shared beds on holidays when they had been little, and how close they had been back then. Turning on her side, away from him, she longed for those simple days back.

She no longer knew what was right, what normal people did or thought. To survive life at Copper Lodge, her mind had adapted; its pathways had been mapped in a particular direction, programmed to think differently. She had been corrupted, while Jude was still pure; an innocent, like Hugo. If Jude had seen Lucas and Heather together, knowing what she knew about their past, what would he have done? Would he have psychoanalysed Lucas and forgiven him? Would he have insisted she divorce him? She wanted to see the situation through his eyes. Jude would have clear ideas of right and wrong.

Night night, little brother, she thought, tears sliding down her cheeks into the pillow. I'll prove to you that I'm still the same big sister you grew up with, that I'm still the girl who trapped Olly Welsh's tie in the wheelie bin. I can find that strength again, I'll prove it to you.

Instead of sleeping, she wrestled with her conscience and her fears, battling between them to find a way to prove to Jude that she wasn't lost. She ripped at the skin round her thumbnail with her teeth until it bled. It tasted metallic and chlorinated when she sucked on it. As the night wore on, spiky pieces of rag-tagged skin feathered around her nail, and she searched her soul to find the good, brave part of herself that could acknowledge the life she really led, rather than the face she showed to the public.

As dawn broke, she tiptoed outside into the garden in bare feet, checking behind her to make sure that the blinds were closed at the master bedroom window.

Discarded napkins and plates, fallen champagne flutes and half-eaten canapés littered the grass. The sun crept up behind the marquee in the meadow. It looked floppier and sadder in the daylight; used and thrown away.

As she approached the guest house, she could see that the curtains were pulled, all except one. Through the slit, she could make out a colourful shape moving inside. It was Bo, in her orange and pink yoga outfit, bent into a Downward Dog. Elizabeth ran past the window as fast as she could and crouched down by the flower bed. She shoved her hand into the 'Silver Queen' plants, underneath which she hoped the necklace would be. She needed to find it before Gordon and Heather arrived later. They were being paid double time to work on Sunday to clear up after the party.

The soil was soft and damp under her fingers.

Nothing.

She stepped into the bed, in between the plants, to take a proper look. Her feet sank, the earth pressing through her toes. Her heart rate increased. She feared the necklace had been found by someone in the early hours, stolen by them. But the chances of a guest sneaking around and finding it was slim.

She widened her search, creeping through the foliage, remembering the shock of last night and how she had tossed the necklace with abandon. It could be anywhere around here.

One more step forward – too close to the back window, through which Bo could look any minute – and Elizabeth's foot landed on cold metal. She dropped to her haunches to retrieve it. Its diamond chain was crumpled and coiled in her palm, both delicate and weighty. She brushed the dirt from the bright blue stone, shaking it off, holding onto it tightly as she walked back to the house.

CHAPTER TWENTY-ONE

First thing, before my parents woke up, I packed my bags and loaded the car. If my father was spying on me out of his bedroom window now, as he had been last night, he wasn't stopping me. He would know why I was leaving.

On the way along the high street, my headache became vicious. I felt faint and rolled down the window. I didn't think I could go much further. My concentration was impaired by the pain. It could have been concussion, or perhaps anxiety symptoms about leaving Connolly Close. Or it could have been the memory of last night that was searing through my brain's pathways like electrical currents, triggering one before it from years ago.

'Stop that!' Dad shouted.

His voice had come out of nowhere. I dropped the door knocker and held my breath high up in my chest. If I'd known I was being naughty, I would have stopped before he was cross. I didn't like it when he was cross.

'Stop that!' he repeated.

I had stopped. But I looked down at my hands. Sometimes they would do stuff that I didn't know about. They were not on the knocker. They were slid safely into the front pockets of my dungarees.

'STOP THAT!' His whole head had gone red. He brought it down to my level, close to me. I didn't know what I was supposed to stop, so I stopped breathing. I turned hot and fizzy.

'What do you say?'

'Sorry,' I said. The word came out wrong.

'What was that?'

Louder, I said, 'Sorry.'

'Now say it like you mean it.'

I would try really hard.

'Sorry,' I said.

'What?'

'SORRY!' It was a shout and I had wanted it to be.

He yanked me by the arm, inside the house, along the corridor, where his belt and his slipper lived in the bedroom.

He didn't go in there; he pushed me into the bathroom instead.

My boots left mud on the tiles. Mum would be cross. Everyone was going to be cross. I wanted to cry and I hated that pathetic feeling. I tried so hard to be happy and strong.

He held the back of my head and grabbed the bar of pink soap, which looked grey and cracked and disgusting. He shoved it into my mouth. It was too big and it tasted like vomit. It scraped along my teeth to the back of my throat. One molar was wobbly and I was terrified it would come out and fall down my throat, making me die. If I died, Dad would be sorry. Sorry! Sorry! SORRY! Stop, Dad! But he wouldn't stop. The bar hit my throat again and again, forcing me to gag, turning my tummy inside out. He shouted at me to stay still, but I couldn't help it. The jabbing went on and on, back and forth, cleaning my dirty mouth out, making me sore and tired.

When he left me, coughing at the sink, blood swirled into the water.

Later, at the kitchen table, he sat with his head in his hands. The end of the day hadn't left enough light to see him with. He was a big, sad shadow in the space. I felt ashamed.

I went to him and put my arms around his neck and I said sorry, and this time I really did mean it.

The taste of dirty soap came up from my gullet again. I made a detour to the leisure centre. I would swim. The rhythm of my body would be meditative and the thoughts of Lucas and Dad would stop. A swim would tell me whether my headache was concussion or a deeper malaise. Swimming was what I reached for when my feelings took over, when I wanted to give up on everyone and everything, when my aloneness swamped me. It had been Lucas who had given me that gift. When my father's temper had threatened to pull me under, Lucas had taught me to float. More than float; to fly. Fly through the water and cut through the chill and gulp in the evening air when I needed it, rhythmically, deep into my lungs, breathing life into them once again, strengthening my resolve to survive my father's outbursts.

The echoing sounds of the leisure centre pool lifted my mood. My towel was rolled under my arm, stuffed with my goggles and swimsuit. The lock on the changing room door was stiff and I worried I would get stuck in there. My hands started to sweat. The vision of my father closing in on me came looming into the small space. The sound of my heart began to pound in my head. I had to sit on the bench and hang my head between my knees so that I didn't pass out. The sound of the hairdryers became as loud as planes taking off. The kids' screams in the pool were deafening. The heat of the cubicle was one hundred degrees, but I couldn't take my clothes off. I couldn't breathe. I had to get out of there. The door unlocked after three frantic attempts.

I wove through the staring, dripping swimmers and out of the changing rooms. In the car park, I called my mother's mobile, trying to sound less desperate than I felt.

'Do you have time for a quick coffee?'

*

I gulped and gulped and stared at my coffee. My chin began to wobble. I wiped away an escaped tear and pulled out a rather pathetic smile for my mother.

'I was going to just leave,' I said. 'I'm so selfish.'

'Well, it might be a good idea to put some distance between you for a few days.'

I looked into Mum's bright blue button eyes and shame engulfed me.

'But what about Dad and Copper Lodge? There'll be loads to do.'

'Oh love. I'll help out if he needs me. Anyhow, I'd already thought about extending my trip to see how everyone at the kitchen was getting on.'

'But what about Auntie Maggie?'

'Brenda has said she can stay on for a few extra days.'

'Really?'

'Yes, love. And it'll give me a chance to have a look at my azaleas!'

'Probably trampled on at the party,' I said miserably.

She looked genuinely horrified. 'Don't say that!'

'There were lots of very drunk people, Mum. You wait till you see the mess.'

She checked her watch. 'Never mind that. Tell me some gossip about the party first.'

'There's nothing more to know.'

She ignored my self-pity, refusing to engage with it. 'Dad told me there was some big deal in the making. Is that true? Did you hear anything about it?'

My neck ached as I stretched it, first right, then left. 'With the Seacarts. The couple staying in the guest house, I think.'

'Yes.' Mum nodded. 'I think the Huxleys wanted to impress them. That's why they went all out on the party this year. It will make them very wealthy, he says.'

'They're already very wealthy.'

'Did you see Bo Seacart? Is she as beautiful as everyone says?'

'She is.'

'What was she wearing?'

'She was wearing a flowing dress to the floor and she had flowers in her hair.'

'Is she as beautiful as Elizabeth?'

'I think Elizabeth is much more beautiful.'

I believed this was true, but I also knew it was what my mother wanted to hear. She revelled in the Huxleys' glamour, imagining that its reflection gave her a status with her friends at the bridge club or the Rotary. It helped her to briefly escape the hardships of those she helped at the soup kitchen. There were daydreams and aspirations in her job at Copper Lodge. She was not just a run-of-the-mill gardener; she was the gardener to the millionaires in the strange-looking modern house on Bunch Lane, no less.

'Did you eat any of the food? I've heard of those caterers, what are they called again? Let me remember now … oh goodness, my memory.'

'The Foodies, yes, the hog roast looked amazing, and there was some local woman who made the most delicious macarons I've ever tasted. It was like eating clouds.'

Mum swooned. 'Did you get some of the hog roast?'

'No. Not in the end.' Tears filled my eyes. 'Jude was meant to get me some and then … Oh God, Mum.'

'Don't say God,' she scolded, looking over her shoulder as though He himself might have heard me blaspheme.

'What have I done?'

'It's nothing that can't be mended.'

My mother believed that every problem in life could be fixed by a few stitches of good sense. But the mistakes of last night were now bursting through the threads that had sewn up my feelings for Lucas all those years ago.

'Do you think I should tell Rob?'

She clicked her tongue and took a sharp sip of her coffee. 'Certainly not.'

'I think the guilt will kill me.'

'Goodness me, Heather, you want to ruin a good relationship just because of one silly little kiss?'

'What if it was more than that?'

She guffawed and then wiped a speck of coffee from her top lip. 'All this over a schoolgirl crush from way back when!'

I stirred my coffee. 'He told me he wasn't in love with Elizabeth any more.'

'What utter tosh,' she muttered, shaking her head. 'Goodness knows what he was thinking, saying that to you. He must have lost his head.'

As had I. I sighed, doubting everything about last night. 'Or he was very drunk.'

'Yes, most probably,' she said primly.

'It's so confusing,' I sniffed, wiping my nose. 'Rob and I haven't been getting on at all.'

'A few doubts are normal, love, after all this time apart.'

'You've never had proper doubts about Dad.'

'Ha! When your dad microwaves his cold dregs of tea to save tea bags, I can tell you, I have proper doubts.'

A smile crept onto my face. 'At least Rob doesn't do that.'

She handed me another napkin. 'See? Anyway, your dad and I like Rob very much.'

I massaged one shoulder, feeling the bruising from my father's grip. 'I'm not sure I care what Dad thinks of Rob.'

My mother flinched. 'That's not true.'

'He still treats me like I'm fourteen years old.'

She stacked our empty cups. 'Before you go, you two should make up.'

'What's the point?'

'Because he's your father. And because you did a very bad thing.'

I shivered. I loved my mother more than anyone in the world, and I certainly knew I had done a bad thing, but I wanted her to acknowledge that my father had done a bad thing too. Sadly, I knew she would choose him over me. The thought of her siding with him dried my tears, making the decision to leave for Rye that much easier.

CHAPTER TWENTY-TWO

Watching Lucas and Agata interact was like a sport, a tennis match perhaps. If they were hiding something, their game was flawless. A clean, expert show of detachment, its backdrop the Monday morning sun and the cacophony of birds. Nevertheless, Elizabeth would watch them until she found her evidence. Her hunch about Heather had been proved correct on the night of the party, and she was now convinced she was right about Agata too, though she suspected Lucas might have tired of Agata since finding fresh blood. Either way, her eyes were skinned for the truth. She refused to let the film of denial form again. Since the party, she had felt alert, as though a doctor had given her a shot in the arm, waking her after a long sleep.

'Agata and Piotr wanted to know if they could move their stuff into the barn now that the party's over,' she said. She took a sweet from the jar. 'Isn't that right, Agata?'

Agata nodded.

'Piotr's starting on the pool house first,' Lucas said, swallowing a mouthful of his grapefruit. He looked and smelt so clean, so clean and so groomed.

'What pool house?' Elizabeth asked, looking to Agata, whose brow had knitted.

Lucas turned a page of his newspaper. 'He's going to build us one.'

'You've talked to him about it?'

'Uh huh,' he said, sipping the last of his coffee. 'This morning.'

'We can afford it?'

'Where there's a will, there's a way,' he answered cryptically.

'But it still doesn't stop them moving into the barn,' Elizabeth said.

'The Seacarts might come and stay with us again next week.' He pushed his empty coffee cup across the breakfast bar towards Agata.

Elizabeth wanted to press and squash the grapefruit into Lucas's face until he couldn't breathe. It was Agata who blinked first and collected his empty cup, but her chin dimpled.

'Why so soon?' Elizabeth asked.

A splash of coffee spilled onto the saucer as Agata carried it over to Lucas. It was obvious she was close to tears. Elizabeth found a cloth and wiped the coffee away before taking the cup from her and giving it to Lucas herself.

'They're extending their trip to sign the final bits of paperwork and I thought it would be nice if they came to dinner.'

Elizabeth played with the sliver of lemon sherbet on her tongue, running it against her teeth. 'The party was a success then?'

He looked at his watch. 'It seems so.'

Elizabeth swallowed her sweet. 'Dinner will be fun.'

'I'll be in my study if anyone needs me,' he said.

Elizabeth whispered to Agata and squeezed her arm. 'One week until the move.'

'You think?' she snorted, a tear rolling down each pale cheek.

A couple of days ago, before the party, Elizabeth might have zoned out right here and now and retreated to her beta blockers or her sweets, and to the suppressing of what Lucas called her bad thoughts. Today felt different. No more denial, she reminded herself. She was going to ask the tough questions, find out what she had been looking at but choosing not to see. 'Why do you say that?'

'You don't … You think he … Really?' Agata laughed.

'Finish your sentence for once,' Elizabeth said impatiently.

'You think he stick to his word?'

'Do *you* not?'

'Ha!'

Elizabeth wondered if Agata was hurt that she had been tossed aside by Lucas, replaced by Heather.

'You seem cross with him,' she said.

Agata shrugged and picked some polish off her nails. Suddenly Elizabeth felt frightened of what she might be about to hear.

'There are other jobs for people with your skills. I'd give you a good reference,' she said quickly, wanting to shut it down, wishing she had never opened up the dialogue.

Agata cried, 'I not want job in this country! No more. Uh uh. I want to go home.'

'That sounds like a good idea.'

She frowned. 'But we can't with no passports.'

'You don't have passports?'

'Lucas have them!'

Involuntarily, Elizabeth's head twitched to one side.

'Why would he have them?'

'He say he keep them in his …' Agata mimed turning a key.

'In the safe?'

'He not give them back.'

Elizabeth maintained a straight back and reached for the jar of lemon sherbets on the shelf. 'Is he keeping them secure for you?'

Agata shook her head. 'When we come from Poland, yes, he nice, he say they get stolen from the van. But Piotr wants to go home now. Next week. His brother Rafal have a baby. But Lucas say no.'

Elizabeth unwrapped a sherbet. 'No. He wouldn't do that.'

Agata looked like she might spit in her face. If she had, Elizabeth would not have flinched.

'He lies to you,' she said.

'You're mistaken. You've misunderstood something here, Agata. I'll ask him for the passports myself.'

She bit down on her sweet and took another one. Old habits died hard.

Elizabeth was massaging Lucas's shoulders as he lay back in a bubble bath that she had run for him. She listened to him tell her about how tiring and frustrating his day had been. Walt Seacart was reneging on some of their agreed contract stipulations, and Lucas, at the final hour, was beginning to doubt the deal would ever go ahead. As much as Elizabeth couldn't bear the prospect of more delays, for all their sakes, his mood did not put her off. If anything, his vulnerable state worked in her favour.

'Agata said the funniest thing today.'

'Oh yes?'

'You know they want to fly to Poland next week?'

'I didn't, but go on.'

'Well, she's under the ludicrous impression that you won't give them their passports back!' She laughed.

'She's misunderstood.' He washed his face with the flannel.

'That's what I said.'

'Her English is terrible.'

Elizabeth dug her fingers deep into his knotted shoulders. 'Why not get them out of the safe after your bath and I'll pop them down to the camper van this evening? She'll be very relieved.'

'I'll do it myself.'

'Are you sure?'

'No problem at all. You're so sweet to care so much.'

She kissed his shoulder. 'I love you,' she said fervently, closing her eyes, enjoying the warmth of his skin against her lips.

'In the pool …' he faltered. 'With Heather … It's not what you think. You know how much I care about you, don't you?'

She remembered when he had once pulled her into the bath fully clothed. They had lain in each other's arms, her head on his damp chest, talking about plans for their future. At the memory, she laughed out loud, without meaning to, feeling elated and aroused all over again.

'Why are you laughing?' he asked in a gruff voice. And she was brought back to reality.

Her switch from hate to love and back again, love to hate, hate to love, was weak and worn out from over-use. Knowing someone as well as she knew Lucas was a double bind. They had become too forgiving of each other.

A reluctant creep of love re-entered her heart and a clouding-over of her suspicions about his kiss with Heather, and his midnight visits to Agata, relieved her of a burning heat building inside her. She wanted Lucas to be right; her historic paranoia had come into the mix, imprinting her bad thoughts onto innocent scenes, twisting them into what she had been programmed to expect from childhood rather than what she actually saw. What *had* she seen? Two grown-ups a little drunk, revisiting an old flirtation at a stressful time. Did it matter?

Later on, Lucas visited Agata and Piotr in their camper van, armed with their documents. Proof that he was a good man; proof that her mind was all at sea again.

CHAPTER TWENTY-THREE

Rob held my hand as we strolled along the harbour. The rich peach colours in the sky should have been beautiful but were sickly. The humidity clung to my skin like wet towels. The clink of the boats' masts was like a knocking on my brain, tapping away at my conscience.

'I called the Sports Trust about Reese,' I said, trying to move my thoughts away from what had happened with Lucas.

Rob didn't respond for a few moments. 'Did you?'

'They couldn't tell me anything.'

'Jase said something about him moving.'

'Reese? Really?'

'Yeah. I think.'

'Why didn't you say before?'

'I didn't know you were still looking out for him.'

'Where did Jason say he'd gone?'

'He said he'd bumped into him somewhere – at the chip shop, I think – and Reese told him he was getting the coach with his dad to Hastings to live. He gave him the finger when Jase waved goodbye.' Rob laughed.

Aggrieved by this news, and by Rob's nonchalance, I pulled my hand away from his to push the pedestrian crossing button.

'I hope his dad has found him a better life,' I said, but I doubted it. Quietly, like a prayer, I wished him safety into adulthood and nursed my own loss, unable to shake off the feeling that it was symbolic in some way.

Rob took my hand again as soon as I dropped it by my side. By clinging to me, he pushed at my reserve; he knew I was keeping something from him. All week he had been overly attentive and hypersensitive to my moods. As I dressed, as I ate, as I read, he had watched me. Tonight, his hand-holding, his need for this closeness, verged on aggressive.

'These shoes were a bad idea,' I said, wriggling my fingers out of his to adjust the buckle of my slingbacks. The leather was digging into my heel. It had rubbed raw in the time it had taken us to stroll the short distance from home along the seafront to our local pub.

'You'll be glad you wore nice ones when we get there,' Rob said.

'Why?' I asked, alarmed. I wanted a quiet midweek drink; keen to continue the week as it had started, to eke out more pottering, hibernating, swimming, reading, eating, recuperating. Away from everyone who might ask questions.

'Do you want me to carry you?' he asked.

Before I could object, he had swung me up and over his shoulder.

'I'm going to be sick, put me down!' I gasped, laughing.

He jogged along while I screamed and kicked my legs and pummelled his back like a kidnapped princess, realising that this was how Rob romanced me.

He slowed when he saw an old couple coming towards us, but he kept me on his shoulder. We both nodded hello politely, as though this was the most normal situation in the world, then he galloped off again.

At the door to the pub, he put me down and said, 'Are you ready?'

'For what?'

'For this lot!' He flung open the door. The long wooden table inside was filled with our friends.

The warmth and familiarity of their huge smiles was over-whelming. Their effusive hellos and kisses gave me a sense of the old me returning. Rob took my hand again and led me to the head of the table, where there was an empty chair next to Amy. She had a bright pink scarf tied around her neck and she was grinning at me.

'What are you all doing here? Have I missed a birthday?' I asked, a little disorientated, sitting down, skimming their faces, taking stock: tall Harry and his Swedish wife Catalin; eternally single Alan with his slick hair; beautiful Gerry with her long neck and boxy smile; Ben and Johanna in their trendy T-shirts; scruffy Adam and his very smart girlfriend Bex. All there. Kind of loopy-looking. Eyes too wide. Faces a little pink.

Then I caught Amy's eye again. I hadn't spoken to her in weeks. Time had flown by, peppered by the occasional text between us. Now there was an edge to her smile. One eyebrow was twitching. The same eyebrow that had twitched when I had announced my move to Connolly Close.

'How's life in Surrey?' she asked. The rest of the table listened. I wondered how I could be both honest and oblique.

I laughed. 'It's a bit like being a serf in the Middle Ages.'

There were a few chortles. 'They're that bad?' Amy asked.

'No,' I lied. 'But it's a different world, honestly. They've just thrown this insane party. The fireworks were as good as Rye's.'

'We're glad you're back home,' Amy said.

Then Johanna giggled and buried her head in Ben's black T-shirt. I glanced up at Rob, who was hovering next to my chair. His features were washed with grey. Blood collected around my heart, leaving my fingertips cold.

'What's going on, you lot?' I asked them. I looked at Catalin. She sat very tall; too tall.

'I think you should ask Rob,' she said.

Rob's Adam's apple moved slowly down his throat.

He held his champagne glass out in front of him and I noticed how the line of bubbles juddered. 'Okay. Okay. Thanks for coming, everyone,' he began, with a tremor in his voice. He paused to gulp. 'I've brought you all here today …' Then he seemed to change tack. 'To be honest, I brought you here so that I don't bottle it.' There was a tinkle of laughter around the table. 'So here I go.'

I fixed my eyes on a thick vein that was throbbing in his temple, knowing it was a sign of nerves, remembering our first date. It had been a kite-surfing lesson. Rob had been the instructor and the conversation had been limited to instructions from him and screaming from me, in both delight and terror. After the lesson, we had been joined by his kite-surfing friends, who stayed with us until we left for his flat, where we had sex for the first time. That summer, five years ago, we had fallen into a rhythm with each other: swimming and surfing and sex. We would drink tea under wide blue skies or huddle in Jason's Kiosk to shelter from howling gales. He would plait my hair as we watched the sun go down; give me fireman's lifts across the pebbles if I forgot my beach shoes; steal the bacon from my bacon baps. I had loved his strength and his humour and his excitement about the day ahead, but his shoulder injury, a year later, had changed him, and I hadn't realised quite how much until now.

'Right, I'm just going to get straight to it,' he said.

He sank to one knee by my side and my heart could have dropped from my chest. I stayed very still, just in case a sudden movement dislodged the smile that I was struggling to hold on my face, and rallied myself for what was coming.

'Heather Shaw,' he said, snapping open a black box to reveal a diamond ring, 'would you do me the honour of becoming my wife?'

Knowing that any hesitation meant doubt, I replied almost before he had finished his sentence. 'Yes,' I said, and buried my face in his neck to hide my uncertainty.

When I pulled back from him, to allow him to push the ring over my knuckle, the tears I wiped away might have been construed as pure joy.

'Thank fuck for that!' he said, to an eruption of relieved laughter and clapping and whooping. The empty feeling in my gut was filled with the force of my friends' happiness.

Once I had shown them the ring close up, and given Rob a few more happy kisses, I knew I had to get out of the room before the tears came again. Tears might have been appropriate straight after the proposal, or during it even, but not five or ten minutes afterwards, out of nowhere.

'I'm just going to the toilet,' I said, excusing myself.

'Me too,' Amy said.

She checked that the cubicles were empty.

'Those are tears of joy, right?' she whispered. She undid the pink scarf around her neck and shoved it into the oversized pocket of her flowery mini dress.

'I'm just in shock,' I whispered, twisting the alien object around my ring finger.

Amy lowered her eyes to my hand. 'It's beautiful,' she said.

'Couldn't you have given me the heads-up?' I asked.

'He swore us all to secrecy. Apparently your mum called him and said how miserable you were, and he asked her if it was the right time to ask you and I guess she said it might be.'

'You knew all this and you didn't tell me?' But that was unfair of me.

'What was I supposed to do?' Amy said. 'It would have spoilt it for you.'

'Sorry. Sorry,' I said, knowing it wasn't her fault. 'It's not quite how I imagined it all happening.'

'How did you imagine it?'

'I don't know. On the beach or something? I don't know, not in front of a crowd of people.'

'I had a feeling you'd be freaked,' Amy said, shaking her head.

'I'm not *freaked* exactly.'

'But not overjoyed?'

'I suppose I should be,' I sighed. 'Maybe it's just the shock.'

'Like a delayed reaction?'

'Maybe.'

Amy sucked in her breath and closed her eyes. To anyone else, it would have seemed like a frustrated sigh, but I knew this was her thinking pose. She opened her eyes, which were filled with understanding.

'You love him, though, right?' she asked me.

'Yes.' The tears pushed behind my eyes.

'You definitely think he's the right guy for you, yes?'

'Yes.'

'You feel it in your gut?'

'I couldn't imagine life without him.'

'Okay, well a nice long engagement then,' she said, pressing her finger on her eyebrow.

'Yes,' I sighed. Lucas's face shot into my mind, and then I felt my father's grip as though he were standing in front of me now.

'How's it been back home?'

'Great. Yeah.' I turned to the sink and redid my ponytail.

Amy stood next to me and spoke to my reflection. 'You look different.'

'In what way?'

'Remember when we went on holiday in Thailand and you dived off that ginormous cliff into the sea?'

I laughed, pretending I didn't understand. 'That's a bit random,' I said.

'You look like you did just before you jumped.'

In that moment I wanted to tell her about Lucas, but there was too much to say and everyone was waiting for us outside.

'Come on. We'd better get back out there.'

Before we walked out, Amy added one more thing. 'You're allowed to be happy, you know. We'll all survive it.'

'I *am* happy,' I insisted.

I sat at Rob's side playing the bride-to-be, letting him hold my hand under the table. Possession, more possession.

As he became drunker, I sobered up.

When I heard a text come through on my phone, I remembered the list of friends and family I would have to tell about my engagement. How would I keep up the enthusiasm to convince them I was starry-eyed in love and joyful about the prospect of a wedding? I imagined telling my parents that I had said yes. They would start pointing out houses for sale in Cobham, houses similar to theirs.

I slipped my hand out from Rob's and took a quick look at the text under the table.

When I saw who had sent it, I could have leapt up and out of my seat in shock.

'Who's that?' Rob asked, ever watchful.

I lied coolly. 'It's Dad. I'm just going to call him back and tell him the good news.'

Outside, on the pavement, I stared at the bright green text glowing in the dark.

Hi. That was all it said.

My heart swelled to twice its size.

I would not text back. I would leave it unanswered and pretend he had never sent it.

Pocketing my phone, I walked back inside and over to the crowd of hot, happy faces around the table. A wave of sadness hit me. Whether I replied to Lucas or not, I was already in a quandary about my engagement and emotionally separate from my friends; as though I were a ghost among them, loved by them, no longer part of them. To reply would set me on a path away from everything familiar. I knew I shouldn't take that path, but I couldn't help feeling that Lucas was dragging me by the hand with all of his strength.

The next morning, while Rob slept off his hangover, I found my wetsuit and towel and headed to the beach. The text sat unanswered on my phone in my bag. I knew I should delete it.

I walked through the dunes to the water and laid my towel down over my rucksack. The cord of my wetsuit was stiff. The summer wind whipped a hurricane around my neck, flicking my hair across my eyes. It was a cold day, and the chill bit into my fingers. The beach was empty. The sea spiked with white ridges and sank in grey troughs. A misty haze hung low in the sky.

The icy hit of the water was a shot of adrenalin. I swam, trying to settle down the confusion that jangled in my chest. About the world, about my father, about Lucas Huxley.

'Like a banana,' Lucas said, bending me from the middle. I no longer flinched when he touched me. 'Don't get distracted,' he said, twisting my head to face the water instead of him, shaping my hands into a point. 'Then you tip in,' he said.

His words were muffled by my arms pressed over my ears. It didn't feel natural. I couldn't trust that the water would take me. 'Go on,' he said. 'Just tip.'

I belly-flopped onto the surface. My stomach burned. I felt foolish when he laughed at me. 'I won't ever be able to do it.'

'Of course you can. You can do anything you put your mind to.'

Again I tried. And again. I wanted to cry. I was angry with him, but he wouldn't give up on me. The dusk turned to night. My jaw juddered. My fingertips pruned.

'*Again,*' he said.

'*No,*' I said, stepping back from the side.

'*Again.*'

'*No. I can't do it.*'

Gently, close to my ear, he said, '*You can do this.*' He pressed his finger up my spine, from my coccyx up to the nape of my neck, and my body curled into position.

An imaginary finger continued to roll up and down my spine as I let my body fall head-first into the pool, trusting the water to suck me in gently, trusting him. The surface was broken by my fingertips, the water swallowed me without a splash, and I shot down to the bottom, where I felt the weight of the whole pool on my eyes. I swam up to the surface and yelped.

'*I did it,*' I said, pulling myself onto the side.

He sat down next to me, dangling his legs in the water.

'*You're amazing,*' he said, pinging my swimsuit strap.

Unable to handle the surge of feeling inside me, I splashed him, soaking his T-shirt. He took it off, then slipped into the water and pulled me in by one leg. My back scraped against the edge, but the happiness overrode the pain. He wrapped his arms around me. I was slippery within them. I felt young and excited in a way I had never felt before. '*You can do anything you want to do. Have anything you want. Anything,*' he said.

Then he slid the straps of my costume off my shoulders. '*In the water, I won't be able to see you,*' he whispered. Sculling with one hand, he took his trunks off. I could see the darkness between his legs. '*Come on, take the rest off. It feels amazing.*'

Copying him, I untangled the costume from my limbs and threw it towards the side, just as he had, but it missed and floated on the surface. I set off to get it, but his hand was between my legs and I froze, startled. '*Relax,*' he whispered, '*It'll feel good. I promise.*'

*

I cut through the waves, heading further and further out. In the water, I was a fighter, thrashing out my feelings. I propelled myself forward, heading away from shore.

Perhaps I should swim the Channel right there and then, to end up in France and walk off into a new life, where nobody knew my name.

Previous swims rolled through my memory. Lightning bolts, hailstorms, jellyfish stings, dark caves, jagged rocks, hurricanes, cramps, rip tides: my fullest life. My body was branded with the scars to prove it. The safe road ahead wasn't one with my hand weighed down by diamond rings; the only way ahead was one where I could be real with myself and those around me, where I could stick my head out of that cold water and shout across the charged sea to tell the world about what I, Heather Shaw, really wanted.

I felt as volatile, unpredictable and dangerous as the sea itself. I was playing a game with the water. It had become a bully and a best friend wrapped into one. I was ready to stand up to it but I was scared of being beaten down.

My father's rhetoric flooded my thoughts. The Shaws didn't have choices! The Shaws hadn't been born with a silver spoon! The Shaws were second-rate citizens and that was okay! And so it had come to pass. It was a self-fulfilling prophecy. A self-imposed shackle. Survival had become the buzzword for fear: head down, pay the rent, bow down to the gods of money and status, bow down to the better-born, cower from the more powerful.

It dawned on me that I couldn't exist with such a heavy, bowed head. It was weighing me down and I refused to sink. Enough was enough. It was time to take responsibility for my own life. I turned my head, sucked in the fresh air – free to all – pulled my arms through the water, powerful and slick, and headed back.

My legs were wobbly and I collapsed onto my towel. I pulled my phone out and took a photo of the seascape with my Thermos propped up in the foreground and my wetsuit spread flat next to it, and texted the photograph to Lucas. I wrote as the caption:

I wanted it and I got it.

This was my life. This was what I wanted. This was where I wanted to be. This was who I was.

I always knew you would. L x

There had been a pause of an hour. I deleted the thread, thinking that that was the end of it. Then he wrote:

When are you coming home?

Home? I didn't trust myself to reply.

CHAPTER TWENTY-FOUR

Elizabeth walked through the gate in the laurel hedge looking for Piotr, to talk to him about another request Lucas had about the pool house. And to ask him when they would be flying out to see Rafal's new baby, now that Lucas had returned their documents and cleared up the misunderstanding.

Over in the corner, she spotted Isla and Hugo with their towels draped over their shoulders, hair dripping into their laps, making daisy chains. Neither of them noticed her. It was quiet. The noise of construction had stopped and she wondered where Agata was.

She didn't want to disturb the children, so she removed her flip-flops and made her way silently across the patch of grass to the building site, which consisted of four untreated oak frames covered in tarpaulin. Through the opening, where there would soon be a sliding window, she saw Agata and Piotr together, framed by the doorway as silhouettes, like a sentimental greetings card. Piotr knelt in front of Agata offering her a ring made of three linked daisies. The daisies' faces were bunched closely, like three diamonds. The pair of them giggled as he tried to slide it onto the ring finger of her left hand. It broke, but he re-threaded the delicate stems, dropping a daisy, fixing it. Agata's thin fingers dangled in front of him, waiting patiently for the big moment.

He carefully pushed the ring into place and asked her a question in Polish.

'*Tak!*' she cried.

Piotr leapt up and swung her around. They kissed, long and lingering.

The simplicity and power of their act of love left Elizabeth open-mouthed.

She stayed very still, desperate to escape but scared that any sudden movement would alert them to her presence. Transfixed, she watched as Piotr spoke tenderly to Agata. But as Agata tilted her head coyly away from him, she caught sight of Elizabeth standing there, intruding on this intimate moment like a perverted voyeur. Instantly the joy on her face disappeared. Her right hand covered her left, hiding her beautiful engagement ring.

'We get married,' she said defiantly.

'Congratulations,' Elizabeth stammered.

'Thank you.'

'You'll be able to celebrate your news with your family when you go home.'

They glanced uneasily at each other.

'We not go home. We have not passports, Mrs Huxley,' Piotr said simply.

'Lucas gave them to you last night, didn't he?' He'd had an envelope in his hand and had told her he was going out to the camper van.

Piotr said, 'You think we stay here if he gave them?'

Elizabeth reeled. 'But he came down to see you. Last night.'

'No, Elizabeth, he did not,' Agata said.

Elizabeth's diaphragm jerked. 'He lied to me?' she rasped.

Piotr took Agata's hand and kissed it. The innocence of this gesture poked deep into Elizabeth's conscience. In the face of Lucas's treachery, they loved each other more. It seemed nobody could patrol their inner lives and nobody could imprison their minds.

*

At bedtime, Elizabeth did not tell Lucas about what she had uncovered. The magnitude of what Agata and Piotr had implied
was ghastly and unmanageable, and she hadn't known how to
process it or what to do with it. She was keeping it at bay for
now, in a box in her mind that petrified her, that she could have
labelled *Warning. High Voltage. Danger of Death.*

For now, she mentioned Piotr and Agata's engagement, and
studied his reaction.

'How sweet,' he said. He dropped his rotating electric toothbrush in the sink. Flecks of toothpaste splattered his T-shirt. 'For
fuck's sake,' he said.

'I thought they could maybe get married in our grounds,'
she said, beginning to floss, knowing he would loathe this idea,
wanting to exploit his guilt, rub it in.

The toothbrush vibrated noisily against his teeth. 'Sure. They
deserve it.'

'They'll really appreciate that,' she said robotically.

He turned off his toothbrush. 'It's good to see a smile on your
face again.'

She tried to drift off to sleep by thinking of ways she could
make it better for Agata and Piotr. Planning a beautiful wedding
day for them would be a start. There would be few guests, she
imagined, if any, but she would plan it as though there might be
hundreds. In her head, she designed a garland of meadow flowers
as an archway under which they could say their vows; hay bales
for them to sit on; a tier cake that Sarah would bake.

But when she imagined this young couple being forced to live
out their future at Copper Lodge, her head began to throb.

She turned on the bedside light and took two migraine pills,
just in case the mild pain escalated.

Her sleep was broken.

A few hours later, she woke to find that Lucas was not in bed
next to her. Disorientated, she tried putting the pillow over her

head, keeping her eyes tight shut to allow herself a few more hours of sleep. Then she remembered the passports and her eyes shot open.

If she was serious about keeping them open, fully, she could not shy away from this.

She dragged herself out of bed. Her brain felt loose in her skull as she stood.

With her heartbeat loud in her ears, she headed out into the moonlight.

There was a dim greenish glow filtering through the grime of the camper van windows. The closer Elizabeth came, the more she heard. The sounds were unmistakable. Sounds she had heard from her husband in her own ear. They were sounds of anger and pleasure, of carnal lovemaking. Drawn to them with a macabre spirit clawing and spitting inside her, she moved across the grass, feeling the night's dampness between her toes, wondering if she should crawl on her hands and knees like an animal moving in on its squealing kill.

Peering through the window, grubby from moss and dirt, she could see Agata's hair, mussed up by Lucas's hand, his long fingers entwined in the peroxide strands. Her head seemed dismembered, his right hand pinning it down. The movement of his pale naked hips, raping her from behind, was rhythmic, shaking the camper van as though it were alive with his violence. Agata was not fighting back. She was not twisting and slapping and screaming, but her cheeks were squashed, distorted by his force, clamped between his hand and the table. Her eyes were blank and dripping with smeared make-up, her mouth was hanging open as though she were dead. Elizabeth almost wished her dead, so that the girl would not have to live through what he was doing to her. She knew what it felt like to be wanted and hated by him all at once, to experience his savagery and his desire in every ram of his hips.

If she acted now, she could save the girl from minutes of further torment, but she didn't move to stop him. And then it was over. A light inside was turned off and the vision disappeared.

In telling him about Agata and Piotr's engagement, Elizabeth had wanted to see him squirm, to see a flicker of jealousy perhaps, to show him that whatever he did to them, they would always find a way to be happy. But she had not considered the consequences of her petty revenge. She had not predicted that Lucas might be jealous and possessive still, might punish Agata, claim her once again.

She stepped back, frightened, suddenly aware that she had to flee the scene before he discovered her there.

An ache pulsed through her temples. She questioned what she had seen. It was too horrifying to believe. As she darted through the garden, back inside, to feel the warmth of the house cloak her goose-bumped flesh, the pain in her head spread. The doctors had once told her that migraines could cause hallucinations. And it was true that her mind, for a period, had been capable of mangling reality and distorting everyday interactions, bringing forth her worst fears like waking dreams. Experience of this delirium told her not to trust her mind now.

Back in bed, she was grateful that her headache remained low-level, but her thoughts were jumbled. She pictured Heather's face as a child, replacing Agata's like a meme that could only be found on the dark web. Heather was smiling, as though blissfully unaware she was being raped.

Sleep took the horrible repeating image away, but when she woke, she remembered it with a sickening dread, like being steeped in the lasting disquiet of a nightmare well beyond morning. Only when she saw blades of grass in between her toes did she recall how she had walked, groggy and half asleep, to the camper van. Again, like a slice through her, she relived the scene. The memory of Agata's face gaped open like a wound. It was too vivid to dismiss as a delusion – and her migraine had threatened but had never exploded in full. She had to trust in what she had seen. The doctors weren't always right.

She wiped at her lips. They had kissed Lucas's bare shoulder in the bath. She wiped and wiped and wiped. Nothing could wipe it away. Nothing could wipe away the disgust or the terrible guilt; neither could she rid herself of the sense of responsibility that reared up inside her now. It was clear that it rested on her, and her alone, to help Agata get away from him. Dread rumbled through her.

The logistics of extricating their passports and documents from the safe were complicated. A daunting prospect, rendering the party-planning a distant memory; like remembering a childhood worry that seemed big at the time but with perspective was nothing. She couldn't imagine where to begin. The potential repercussions of going against Lucas snaked inside her. She did not want Agata to suffer any longer than she had to, but she knew that her freedom, and that of Piotr, could not be gained overnight.

While she thought about Agata and Piotr, she realised that she could no longer ignore the problem of Heather, for whom it was not too late. Not yet. For both young women, Elizabeth was their only hope. Their safety was in her hands. Her dithering, indecisive, unconfident little hands. She had nobody to delegate to, nobody to defer to, nobody to confide in. For the first time in her life, she would have to be one hundred per cent self-sufficient.

A few years ago, a mother at school had told Elizabeth about her divorce, and about the jewellery shop in Mayfair where she had sold her Cartier wedding and engagement rings. After some awkward email exchanges, Elizabeth retrieved the jeweller's name and address from this woman and set up an appointment for the following day.

The premises did not have a shopfront like the elegant jeweller's below it. She rang the doorbell, twice. She was late and flustered, and unsure of what to expect.

The door opened. A young woman in a baggy pencil skirt and flowery shirt greeted her and led her up a narrow carpeted staircase and along a scuffed corridor. The woman's hair from the back was thick and dark, like purple nylon.

The room she showed her into resembled an accountant's office rather than a jewellery business. It smelt musty, like old hotels. There was a drinks bar in the corner. A man came forward. He was similar in age to the woman, dressed in a grey suit and brown shirt, and he wore a velvet yarmulke on his head. His handshake was cold and limp. 'Hello, Mrs Huxley. I'm Mr Freeman. Pleased to meet you.'

'I'm so sorry I'm late,' Elizabeth said, wishing she had never come.

'We're glad you made it,' he said. 'Would you like a beverage of any kind? We have Coke? Juice? Fizzy water? Whisky?'

'Still water would be lovely.'

She clutched her handbag on her lap and sat down in a wing-backed chair. When he placed a chilled bottle of Evian and a glass on the coffee table in front of her, his eyes flicked to the bag. He said, 'My father will be with you shortly. If you need anything in the meantime, my wife will be happy to help.'

The woman with the black hair nodded and smiled from behind a small bureau.

Mr Freeman's step was quiet as he walked across the green carpet and through a door, and she imagined the soles of his shoes were as shiny as the leather vamp stitched on top.

Before she had a chance to open her bottle of water and pour it into the glass, Mr Freeman returned. 'Come through, please.'

Mr Freeman Senior looked like a bald, liver-spotted version of the young Mr Freeman. He stood up from behind his ornate pedestal desk. His handshake was firm and warm. Elizabeth reached into her handbag for the box containing her sapphire necklace and set it down in front of him. He placed his hands wide of the box, as though giving it space to rest and breathe. Then he opened it. He did not gasp with delight at its beauty as Jude had done.

'A nice piece,' he said. He didn't move to touch it. The open lid faced him, as if poised for confrontation. 'But its Bismarck style is a little out of fashion these days.'

Elizabeth felt strangely humiliated and cheapened, as though the fusty room was an echo chamber of her home life, and of her own uselessness.

'Tell me about its history,' he said.

There was sympathy in his tone, suggesting he might want her to tell him about her own history, knowing the two were intertwined. Elizabeth refrained, lying that it had been her own mother who had given the necklace to her before she died, but that she had lost the proof of purchase. As he listened, the little finger of his left hand tapped at the gilt edging of his desk.

'And you want to sell it,' he said.

'Yes. You see, I'm leaving my husband,' Elizabeth said, testing the words out, knowing it was unneeded and untrue information, wondering if this was how she might feel if she did leave him: both empowered and defensive. And utterly alone in the world.

'Hmm. I see there are some broken prongs, and the links are worn. But I will have a closer look next door, if that is okay with you, Mrs Huxley?'

'That's fine,' she said, lacking the confidence to suggest she accompany him and the necklace next door. She reminded herself that Mr Freeman's establishment had come highly recommended, reassuring herself that it would be safe to allow him to take it out of her sight.

Over the next fifteen minutes, alone in the room, she jiggled her knee, sipped her water and worried that he would tamper with the settings and try to swindle her.

When he returned, her skin was clammy.

He sat down, setting the box in front of him in the exact same spot she had initially placed it before his inspection. 'We can offer you two thousand five hundred.'

She had been keen to be poker-faced and stalwart. 'But it's worth twice that!' Her voice was shrill.

'You are very welcome to take it elsewhere,' he said, without a hint of indignation. In fact, his eyes communicated fondness, as though he were looking upon his own daughter's dismayed, desperate face.

She thought: this is half what they need, half of what they deserve. But it was all she had.

'Do you pay cash?' she asked.

'We don't usually. But we can make an exception.'

'Thank you,' she mumbled, wiping her eyes. 'Sorry, I don't know why I'm crying. I didn't even like the necklace very much.'

He nodded. 'I will get my son to handle the paperwork,' he said, picking up his desk phone and mumbling instructions. 'While he does that, I'll show you something, if you like. Come, dear. This way.'

Having been distrustful of him before, she now followed him like a lost puppy.

He led her into the room where she suspected he had inspected her necklace. Variously sized loupes and tweezers and scales cluttered the jeweller's benches. Through another door, they walked in single file past a bank of safes to the end of a corridor. He pulled back a velvet curtain. The floor-to-ceiling shelves of the walk-in cupboard were stuffed with dozens of velvet and leather jewellery boxes, stacked higgledy-piggledy on top of one another.

'Gosh!' she said.

He took one down and opened it to show her it was empty. And another: a large Rolex box with no watch inside. Then another: a long red leather Cartier box with no bracelet. And another: a small square Tiffany box with no ring.

'We reuse them when we're brought pieces without their original boxes,' he explained.

'Can I see one?' she asked.

He nodded, and she picked out a flat velvet box from a low shelf. It creaked when she opened it. She ran her fingers across the navy satin interior, imagining what might have been inside and who would have owned it and how special it might have been to them.

'They're like my little coffins,' he said darkly. 'Every single box once had a dead body inside, if you know what I mean. Ninety-nine per cent had sad stories. But as soon as the owner lets go of the piece, their feelings for it die and it becomes worthless. Just business. You understand?'

'Pre-loved,' Elizabeth murmured, putting the box back.

'But you see, you are not alone,' he said, sweeping his hand across his collection. 'They were being resourceful. Just like you are, my dear.'

She smiled gratefully.

'Thank you for showing me,' she said.

He had overestimated her attachment to the necklace, but the point he was making was pertinent. The necklace and those empty boxes represented the worthlessness of everything material in her life.

Elizabeth returned home with a plastic wallet of cash and searched for Heather in the grounds. The garden was returning to a version of normality. The party paraphernalia had been dismantled, the ground brushed and raked, snapping it back to how it had been before.

She spotted Gordon sitting on the wall by the meadow with his back to her.

'Hello!' she panted, running towards him.

'Everything okay?' He stood up, handing his lunch box to Sally, who turned around and waved, pointing to her mouth as she chewed.

'Where's Heather?' Elizabeth asked, trying to keep the panic from her voice. 'I thought she was meant to be working today?'

'Sorry, Mrs Huxley, I'd have thought Mr Huxley would've told you that Heather's been quite poorly and is stuck in bed.'

'Next door?'

'In Rye.'

'She caught Agata's bug?' Elizabeth felt in her pocket for her tiny grain-like aniseed sweets and popped one in her mouth.

'I guess so, uh huh.'

'When should we expect her back?'

'We're not sure yet,' Sally replied, gulping back her mouthful. 'Can we help at all?'

The bulk of the money seemed to move inside Elizabeth's handbag and she clenched her arm to hold it tighter. 'Poor Heather. I hope she feels better soon.' She began walking away, with the sense of a stone falling through her. Then she heard Mr Freeman's fatherly words about resourcefulness ringing through her head, and she turned back.

'Actually, I'd like to send her a get-well card and a thank you for everything she did for us this weekend. We couldn't have done it without her.'

'Oh, that's not necessary, Mrs Huxley!' Gordon and Sally cried as one.

'Could I please have her address in Rye?' Elizabeth asked, ignoring their remonstrations, bringing out her phone to type it into her notes.

Gordon shot his wife a look, but Sally diligently relayed Heather's address.

*

Rye's main drag was busy with tourists, with their sandy feet and straw shoppers. Elizabeth's white plimsolls and gold-trim tote did not fit in. She feared she might be too conspicuous, seen by someone she and Lucas knew. Lucas thought she was visiting a yogic day spa specialising in sea algae rubs and hatha on the beach, to recuperate after the party. The spa destination was not made up. It existed near Brighton. She had booked it and paid for it and offered it to Sarah as a thank you for the macarons. Sarah, overwhelmed with gratitude, had not questioned her one condition, that she answer to the name of Elizabeth Huxley while she was there. The measure was precautionary – Lucas was busy and unlikely to check on her whereabouts this week – but she hadn't wanted to take any risks.

The street where Heather and her boyfriend Rob lived, on the edge of town, was quiet. The pastel-coloured paint on the terraced houses was peeling and the window boxes were empty. The blustery weather and caw of seagulls gave Elizabeth a sense of unease. A man on a step stared at her.

Rob answered the intercom and buzzed her in. The stairs up to their first-floor flat were covered in a brown runner. A pink door swung open and Rob stepped onto the landing. He was tall, with a sloppy posture. His deep tan couldn't disguise the dark circles under his eyes, and his white-blonde hair was pillow-ruffled.

'I'm Elizabeth,' she said, holding out her hand.

'Rob,' he said, shaking it, looking her up and down, dropping his pale eyebrows into a frown. 'Pleased to meet you.'

'I'm looking for Heather.'

He crossed his arms over his chest. 'She's swimming.'

'Oh. I was told she was sick.'

He grinned. 'The sea is very healing.'

'I understand.'

'Want to wait for her here?'

'Please. Thank you.'

He led her into their small flat. It was whitewashed and fresh, albeit messy with T-shirts hanging off chairs and old beer cans lined up next to the bin. He opened the kitchen window and reached for a tin. 'Tea?'

'That would be lovely.'

'I'd call her but her phone will be in her bag.' He sniffed a milk carton from the fridge and wrinkled his nose. 'Oops. We're out of milk. I'll nip down to the shops.'

She stood up. It felt wrong to be there. 'I really shouldn't be putting you out.'

'It's no bother.'

'You're very kind, but I think I'll go.'

He did not look offended. 'If you're sure.'

'Do you know where she's swimming?'

He rubbed an eyebrow. 'I'm not sure.'

'It's important I see her today, Rob. I've come all this way,' she added, with more transparency than she had shown him before.

He held his breath and then let it out loudly.

'Search for Jason's Kiosk on Google. She'll end up there.'

Elizabeth sat at a picnic table waiting for Heather. A polystyrene cup of tea was in front of her, untouched. The sea was uninviting, churning a white froth at the tide line. The man who had served her whistled a tune while he cleaned the counter behind her. The chorus caught on the wind.

When Heather finally picked her way over the pebbles towards the kiosk, Elizabeth was trembling, due to both the relentless breeze and pent-up tension.

She stood up too quickly and knocked over her tea. Heather's eyes matched the sea behind her, grey and churned up and spirited, and her freckles were like the pebbles on the beach, larger than Elizabeth remembered them. The top half of her wetsuit was unzipped and pulled down to her waist. A thick towel was around her shoulders. She was prettier than ever. Her looks made sense against the sea behind her.

The charged space between them was broken up by Jason, who bobbed about mopping up the tea.

'What are you doing here?' Heather asked.

Jason stopped cleaning and glanced up at Elizabeth, as though looking at her with fresh eyes.

'Jason, this is Elizabeth Huxley,' Heather said.

'Pleased to meet you,' he said, wiping his hand on his shorts and thrusting it into Elizabeth's, not letting go.

'Okay Jason, could you give us a moment?' Heather said, saving Elizabeth from his grip.

'I'll get your tea,' he said.

They sat down opposite each other. The table was narrow. They were too close.

'You're better,' Elizabeth remarked.

'Today I feel much better.'

'Might you have caught a chill from your swim the other night? Lucas wasn't himself at all.'

Heather's face reddened to her hair roots.

Jason arrived with two teas and two plastic-wrapped packets of Bourbons. 'On the house.'

'Thank you,' Elizabeth said.

Jason hesitated. 'You all right, Heather?'

'Fine, thanks, Jase,' Heather replied croakily, fiddling with her packet of biscuits.

They both waited for him to leave them alone again.

'It didn't mean anything,' Heather whispered.

'I don't care what it meant,' Elizabeth said, reaching into her bag and placing Mr Freeman's green plastic wallet on the table between them.

'What's that?'

'See for yourself.'

Heather opened the flap. A fifty-pound note fluttered out on a gust of wind. Elizabeth clamped the note to the concrete underfoot and put it back in the wallet with the rest.

'That's a lot of money,' Heather said.

'It's for you.'

Elizabeth couldn't tell her that it was guilt money. She couldn't admit that she should never have allowed Heather to return to the grounds of Copper Lodge when all along she had known about her swimming lessons with Lucas.

'Why would I take your money?'

'I want you to leave Copper Lodge.'

Heather squeezed water out of her ponytail. 'Why not just fire me?'

'Lucas wouldn't allow it.'

Heather placed both elbows on the table and covered her face. 'I feel really weird about you being here.' When she looked up, her high colour had drained away. She was pale, almost blue, and little hairs were raised across her cheeks. 'Lucas and I …' She stopped and began again. 'There is nothing between me and Lucas any more. Nothing.'

'Good,' Elizabeth said. 'We have children together.'

Heather's grey eyes filled with tears. 'I would never want to hurt anyone,' she said, plucking at the rubber sleeve of her wetsuit.

'Take it, Heather,' Elizabeth insisted, pushing the wallet towards her.

'No. I can't take money from you.'

Outraged, Elizabeth landed her fist on the tabletop, losing her patience. 'It's one and a half thousand pounds!' she yelled, unable to believe Heather's naïvety, unable to give up on her yet. 'It'll buy you enough time to find another job or pay someone else to help your parents!'

Heather reeled back and Jason arrived at her side.

'Everything okay here?' he asked.

Elizabeth curled her fingers into her palms, let her hands fall into her lap, retreating, withering inside. 'Get out while you can, Heather,' she implored.

She recognised the look of distrust and alarm in Heather's eyes. She'd seen this look on other women's faces before: Heather thought she was mad. And maybe she was. For thinking that she could do some good.

'Don't worry, I'm leaving,' she said, stuffing the wallet back in her bag, knowing it would be useless to go on, knowing she would only make it worse. Heather's refusal to take the money was a blow. It meant she was not in it for what she could get. It meant she was in love with Lucas. It meant that Elizabeth had stepped in too late to save her from what awaited her, from Agata's fate and that of many others before her.

'I'm not going to cause any trouble,' Heather said. 'I'll work through the summer and be gone. You have my word.'

'Your word?' Elizabeth laughed. 'That's irrelevant to me.'

Relevant to her had been Lucas's word, and he had broken it again and again.

CHAPTER TWENTY-FIVE

With my engagement ring like a foreign body on my finger, I opened the door to the flat. Rob was right up against me, nudging me gently in through the door as he kissed my neck, still talking about Elizabeth.

'But she seemed sooooo weird, she definitely, *definitely* had important things to tell you,' he slurred, hitting the side of his nose with his finger. He was so drunk he could barely walk.

'She's always weird like that.'

Take it, Heather, she had said.

'Nah. She must have chickened out of whatever she was going to tell you. There's no way she came all this way to give you a get-well card.'

'I keep telling you, she's mad.'

We have children together, she had said.

Rob whistled. 'You said it.'

He tripped up on the mat.

'Easy now, Rob,' I said, propping him up, unable to conceal the irritation in my voice. He wouldn't have noticed either way.

'Come 'ere, Mrs Hensher,' he said, wiping a bit of slobber from his chin. His eyes were half closed. He stank. Every day I had been home had begun with a swim in the fresh, wild air, and ended with Rob's stale breath.

'I'm not Mrs Hensher yet.'

'You will be when I'm done with you, baby.'

He launched himself at me and began kissing me with wet, beery lips. I shuddered. Not only because he was drunk, but because everything he did made me think of us doing it together for life. And I compared this to the life I had once wanted with Lucas.

It hurt. A stretching, burning hardness inside me. The laurel leaves scratched at my head as he pushed, and I thought, this is really happening. I wondered if I should groan, like the women in films, but I knew any sound I made would betray the pain I felt. I couldn't wait for it to stop. His hair tickled my shoulder, his breath was hot on my skin. When he rolled off me, I pulled my damp swimsuit back in place and noticed my fingernails were black with soil. Blades of torn grass fell onto my thighs. The stinging and the wetness there worried me.

'Come here, you angel,' he said, scooping me up and on top of him. 'Wow, look at you.'

I was straddling him. He was looking up at me and pulling my wet hair around and down each shoulder. He played with the sodden tips at my waist, squeezing out the water. In spite of being clothed in a tatty, chlorine-eaten one-piece, I felt like the Botticelli Venus *I had studied in art class – that was how he made me feel.*

'You okay?'

'Good,' I said.

'It'll get better,' he grinned, seeing through my lie. 'Soon we'll be able to do it again and again in beautiful hotels all around the world. On huge super-king beds. And afterwards I'll run you bubble baths and we can order room service and watch movies all night.'

I lay on his chest as he spoke into my ear, like the whisper of bedtime stories.

'And we'll swim in seas that have so much salt you can float, or seas that are so clear you can see your toes, as blue as gemstones. We can dive into coral reefs and shower in waterfalls. We'll do everything together.'

He was like a bed underneath me, stirring, beating, breathing, ridged, hard and soft; perfect. I wanted to sleep there all my life.

'I'm going to get a job and make us lots of money so that I can take you around the world and buy you anything you've ever wanted.'

'I don't need anything,' I said. But I was not telling the whole truth. I liked the idea of what he was offering. It sounded better than what I could have afforded by myself.

'Come on, let's get you into bed,' I said to Rob.

'Maybe …' he shouted, holding his finger in the air, '*maybe* that Huxley woman wanted to tell you she was legging it!'

I sighed. 'Where would she be going?'

'Maybe Lucas isn't such a nice guy. Maybe she's off to sunnier climes with her young lover and she wanted to say goodbye. Maybe she wanted to give you the heads-up because she likes you,' Rob went on.

'Who knows,' I said.

Get out while you can, Elizabeth had said.

Rob's fingers squeezed mine tighter and he shot me a daft smile. 'Sorrrreeeee. Now I know why you always go on about that lot. There was something about her.'

His head dropped and he mumbled something incomprehensible. I led him to bed with his weight heavy on my shoulders. I helped him take off his trousers, covered him with the duvet, and sat on the edge of the bed stroking his hair. He was snoring within five minutes.

When I knew he was sound asleep, I crept out of the room and closed the bedroom door. I looked around the shadows of the flat, unwilling to turn the light on to see the space that no longer felt like mine. My suitcase was by the door. Five days here and I hadn't unpacked it. Tomorrow I was going back to Connolly Close.

Any permanent traces of my presence in the flat had disappeared completely. Even the smell was different. Before, it had smelt of cooking and scented candles. Now it smelt of sour dishcloths and stale sofas. Rob and Jake – who was staying with his mother for the week – had not been looking after the place. The aura and the charm had completely disappeared. I wondered what it was I had thought I would miss. The happiness of a home was only kept alive by the happiness of those who lived there.

I tried to conjure up the image of moving back in, of putting my pictures and clothes back on the shelves and in the drawers, but I could not. The projection of my future as Mrs Hensher rang false.

I sat on the sofa, staring at the black television screen.

In my handbag, by the door, was my phone. My text exchange with Lucas yesterday morning on the beach had been an error, a worse betrayal than our kiss. Rob didn't deserve it. Equally, I knew there was no way I could marry him. He didn't deserve that either.

For how long I sat there in the dark, I didn't know, but my thoughts were interrupted by a text pinging through on my phone. It was from Amy.

> *You still awake?*
> *Yup.*
> *Rob was so drunk tonight. Is he okay?*
> *Think so.*
> *How are you feeling?*
> *Confused.*
> *I guessed.*
> *What should I do?*
> *Go with your heart, sweetie.*
> *I'm not sure I can. It will hurt too many people.*
> *Honey, Paul Weller once called himself an emotional coward. He now has a string of exes and seven children. Go figure ;);)*

This made me laugh out loud. Amy's mother had had a crush on Paul Weller when we were teenagers, and it reminded me of growing up, and of feeling young and carefree.

> *LOL. Okay. Promise not to be PW. Now go to sleep and stop worrying about me. H x*
> *Stop texting me then. Night, night. A x*

Her message was followed by a string of hearts and girl-power emojis.

I should have tried to sleep, but I wanted to work out a way of telling Rob, limiting his heartache, making it easier on both of us somehow. I turned on the television and flicked through the channels, stumbling on a rerun of *Tootsie*. It was about halfway through, but I knew the film well. Dustin Hoffman played the character of Michael – dressed as Dorothy – who gazed longingly at Julie as she swayed her hips to a romantic song while stirring a pot on the stove. He was transfixed. His love for her was becoming increasingly difficult to conceal. To have any hope of being with her or of being true to himself, he had to reveal his identity, lose the dress, rip his life apart, ruin his career, face up to his friends and publicly humiliate himself. He had to put it all on the line to be with her.

Like Michael, I realised that I had to find out. I was too young to stay with someone because it was the safe and sensible thing to do, because I was scared of changing my life or upsetting Rob or disappointing my father. I had no idea if I could trust my feelings for Lucas, but I didn't want to spend the rest of my life wondering if I had let him slip through my fingers because I had been scared.

As the film credits rolled, I took the ring off, tucked it back into the velvet padding and placed the box back in the centre of the coffee table. It was ready to take back. Then, exhausted, I curled up on the sofa and fell asleep under a blanket.

A few hours later, I awoke to the noise of the toilet flushing. Rob padded into the sitting room rubbing his eyes.

'Why didn't you come to bed?'

'I meant to,' I said, swallowing. The box with the ring inside was still sitting there on the table in front of me. If I reached for it, to put it on, to pretend to myself that I wasn't going to say what I was going to say, or maybe to give myself time to pluck up the courage to say it, he would be immediately suspicious of why I had taken it off in the first place. There was no reason to wait, other than cowardliness.

I picked up the box and sat with it in my hands.

At first, he smiled. Then he noticed that the ring wasn't on my finger. The smile dropped.

The guilt made me feel ill.

'Why have you put it back in the box?' Fear seemed to puncture his sleepiness. He was alert.

For a moment, I lost my nerve. I couldn't say the words. Voicing the end of our relationship would be unreal. It would be the worst thing I had ever said out loud. A destructive, shocking thing to do. Yet I was compelled to do it.

'I love you so much, Rob, but I'm so, so sorry, I can't marry you. I'm not ready to—'

'Shut up,' he said, tears in his eyes, tears in his voice.

'I'm so sorry.' My voice wobbled. I wouldn't cry. It wasn't fair to cry. 'I wanted so much to make this work. You are an amazing, amazing man but you must've felt something wasn't quite right. Surely you knew deep down that it wasn't going to work?'

'No, Heather. I have never known it. I have loved you from the day I met you. But I *do* know that I want you to get the hell out.' He hadn't moved an inch, his body rigid like a statue.

I didn't know if I had the strength to stand up, but I knew I had to find it.

My suitcase was parked by the bedroom door, ready, but as I moved towards it, Rob jerked into life, swung around and kicked it across the wooden floor. It slid to a halt right by my feet.

I took one last sheepish look at him as I picked it up, catching the terror in his eyes.

What had I done to him? It had happened too quickly. Too definitively. I had expected an in-depth heart-to-heart. He was supposed to have asked me why and I was supposed to have persuaded him that it was best for us both in the long term. The slow wriggle-out would have given me time to backtrack if it had felt wrong. If it had continued to feel right, I had imagined parting with tears and hugs and a sense of relief that the truth was out.

Now, I felt the opposite of relief. My chest had tightened and contracted.

'I am so sorry,' I mumbled again, and I picked up my handbag and lurched out as though I had been pushed.

Out in the street, with drunk stragglers lolling past me, I let my tears flow.

I was still crying as I drove back to Cobham.

There were lulls in my distress, when my salty face dried, but then the reality of what I had done would resurface, setting me off again. Stolen looks of sympathy and curiosity from a passenger in a car next to me heightened my shame. I was relieved that she didn't know the true reason I was crying. I was more sympathetic as the victim: the dumped or the sacked or the grieving. Not the person who had just ripped someone's heart out with a few simple words.

Lucas's voice was in my head, in my dream. *Are you all right, love?* Whose voice was that? I opened my eyes, wondering where I was.

My mother's concerned face was peering around the door.

'Are you all right, love?' she said. 'It was the early hours when you came in.'

I checked my watch, as if it might have the answer to that question. It was six thirty in the morning. It didn't have the answer.

I sat up in bed and Mum perched on the edge. 'We weren't expecting you until this evening.'

Dad appeared and hovered by the door.

'Sorry,' I said.

Mum's eternally cold hand was planted on my forehead.

'I'm fine. Jake – the lodger – came back from his mum's early. It was awkward, so I decided to head off last night.'

'We thought you'd be making the most of your time with Rob.' Mum's gaze darted towards my left hand.

I twigged. Of course, they knew he was going to propose. They would have been dying to see me, to hear the good news.

'I'm sorry. It didn't work out,' I said, rubbing my bare ring finger.

My mother clamped her hand over her pearly lips.

I dared to look up at Dad. 'You are having us on,' he said.

I curled up into the corner of the bed and pulled the duvet around me.

'I don't want to get married. Not yet.'

'But you're almost thirty, love!' Mum said.

'Yes, I know, but I can't marry someone I don't love.'

'You *do* love him,' Mum insisted.

'I love him in one way, but I am not *in* love with him.'

'What nonsense. You've been happy together,' Dad said. A frown had formed deep into his silvery hairline. My feet were sweating under the duvet.

I addressed my mother, as though my father hadn't spoken. 'But he's not The One.'

'The One! Och, child,' Mum cried.

'I do hope this hasn't got anything to do with Lucas Huxley?' Dad said, crossing his arms over his chest, tucking his hands into his armpits.

'He had absolutely nothing to do with my decision to end it with Rob.'

It wasn't a complete lie. He had been a catalyst, perhaps, rather than the cause, if there was a difference.

'Rob's a good lad,' Dad continued, in his lecturing voice. 'He's a bit unfocused, I grant you that, but he's stood by you and put up with all your little obsessions. I can't understand why you'd suddenly change your mind.'

'It hasn't been sudden,' I said.

'You'll regret this decision in years to come.'

My mother nodded, bunching her chin.

Dad continued. 'For starters, what are you going to do with all the stuff you've bought together for the flat? You won't be able to afford anywhere nice to live on your own, will you? I wonder if you've thought this through properly.'

Mum nodded again. 'I have to agree with your father. It's a rash decision, love.'

I felt tired all over again. The worry that was twitching through their faces made its way inside me. I tried to expel it. Couldn't they help me along and throw out some optimism for a change? Give me a positive outlook for my future? A bit of blind faith? Paint a rosy bloody picture? Did it always have to be worst-case scenario? Their expressions reflected their vision of me as an old spinster with no husband, no job, no children, no home, spending her days thinking back decades to the one shot she'd had of happiness, with Rob Hensher, the happy-go-lucky ex-kite-surfer from Rye, and how stupid she had been to walk away from him.

'Could I have some time alone?'

I didn't want any more of their wisdom, fearing I would be hypnotised by their projected fear, enough to call Rob back to beg for his forgiveness.

'Yes, love, okay. You have some time on your own,' my mother said, patting the duvet.

'Time to *think*,' my father added, before closing the door.

Or what? I wanted to ask. If I didn't change my mind, would they throw me out on the streets? Was my father capable of turning his back on me forever?

My mind slipped back to an afternoon with Lucas. We had lain on the grass, entangled in our towels, entwined in each other's arms, staring into the dying light of the domed sky above us.

'What's that flower called?' he had asked.

'*Exidopilopidus parrilibillillibus*,' I had answered.

And he had laughed – which had felt like winning a prize – and kissed my pruned fingers and told me they would never be green. And I had been terrified because I had known then and there that I would never follow in my parents' footsteps, that it was not the life I wanted, and that my father would reject me unless I did.

Gordon Shaw – my proud, stubborn, self-righteous father – held onto his principles of family loyalty with claws of steel, and I feared this latest disagreement could break us. He might turn against me and never speak to me again.

When I had turned down the place at horticultural college to start my sports science degree, the heel of his hand had met my left ear with a dull thud. It had been a small price to pay for choosing a future that made more sense to me. During that time, Lucas had become the positive voice that I had used – still used – to drown out my father's lack of faith. My respect for my father was belittled by the passions that Lucas had set off inside me, by that unique feeling of moving through water, by its healing qualities, by the ocean and its possibilities.

I loathed this power tussle between me and my father: his ruthlessness, his sporadic violence, that old-fashioned side of him that believed in a short, sharp shock of pain to knock some sense into me, to keep me in line. I guessed he would be waiting for me to fall flat on my face, looking smug at being proven right; more satisfied with this outcome than if I had found genuine happiness by following my own dreams.

Nevertheless, I couldn't help seeing it from his point of view too. There was selfishness attached to a dream, in spite of its idealist, romantic connotations. If Lucas was the dream, or part of it, the consequences would wriggle into my parents' lives, affecting their livelihood and ruining my relationship with them. Or certainly with my father.

I knew how much Dad loved me. Aside from the outbursts, he was a good father to me and a good man who gave back to society. When I thought of pushing him too far, of losing him forever, I felt abject terror. I didn't want to experience that rejection. Without siblings, or even an extended family, my parents were all I had. I loved them, I needed them. Didn't I?

Equally, I couldn't wait to see Lucas on Monday morning at Copper Lodge.

CHAPTER TWENTY-SIX

Elizabeth should have felt safe in the knowledge that Lucas would be in London all day. His study remained untouched and immaculate. He wasn't due home until late tonight, but she locked the door anyway, terrified of being caught.

The surface of the glass desk was bare, apart from the computer and a pot holding a stock of fine-tip blue-ink writing pens that Elizabeth replenished every few months in response to his Post-it note demands.

The drawer and the filing cabinet were locked. Everything was locked.

She stood in front of the Shiro Kasamatsu print of Inubo Point in Japan that hung to the right of the desk, and removed it from the wall. The built-in safe was revealed, in gunmetal grey, with its lever handle pointing down. There was a wheel of numbers that Elizabeth began to turn, trying birthdays and anniversary, dates and ages, then random combinations, angrily, back and forth, round and round. She put her forehead to the cold, impenetrable door. It would be impossible to guess the combination.

'Come in,' Agata said. Her pencil-thin eyebrows were stretched high with hope. Elizabeth was here to tell her there wasn't any.

'No luck,' she said.

'*Kurwa*,' Agata hissed.

Elizabeth resisted covering her nose and mouth to smother the smell of the chemical toilet. Her gagging reflex was sensitive and she worried she would retch.

Looking around for somewhere to sit, she began to panic. The claustrophobic space was a reminder of what she had seen through the window, as though she had stepped into a portal to hell.

Agata moved a rolled mattress and a duvet to free up the bench seats either side of the tabletop, and Elizabeth wedged herself in.

'You sure?' Agata asked, but her tone was flat. She sat down opposite Elizabeth, flipping her pink diamanté mobile phone up and down, up and down. Her long nails were painted today in blue and white stripes.

'He must have memorised the code. There's no way in.'

There was a delay of a few minutes, when Agata's expression froze. Elizabeth couldn't read it, didn't know what to expect next from her, whether there would be a bombardment of expletives or whether she would throttle her. But Agata dug her painted nails into her cheeks and began to cry. Polish sentences flowed from her lips, mumbled as though she were praying.

'Oh Agata. Shush. Shush,' Elizabeth said, wanting to press on the girl's mouth and eyelids to stop the leak of despair. 'Stop crying now.'

Agata's swollen eyes looked straight up at her, so big and brown, pushed together further by her dismay. 'I want to go home,' she spluttered.

Elizabeth felt cornered by a suffocating guilt and wanted to expel it. 'You should never have given your passports to him in the first place then!' she cried, impatiently, unfairly.

Agata stopped and raised her chin. 'Your husband. So *good-looking*. So *kind*. He say he have lawyers who say this and that, but Piotr says it's not true.'

'He's very persuasive,' Elizabeth admitted, holding her breath high in her chest, almost incapable of coping with the truth in what Agata had said. How could she, of all people, judge them for believing Lucas?

Agata continued. 'Before we come from Poland ...' She paused and mimed driving a car, beeping the horn like a child, then said, 'They tell us we get good jobs.'

'Who did?'

'The people,' she said, tapping her fingers on the table as though it were a keyboard.

'The recruitment agency?'

She nodded. 'So we save up for van and we come to a house in London. Then they steal our money.'

'They stole your money?'

'The house is terrible. Dirty mattress. Many, many people everywhere. Piotr sleep with knife under his pillow. So many bad people. So noisy. They give us food from dustbins,' she said, screwing up her face. 'I clean houses. They take my money. Piotr open a bank account and they steal from us. They ask him to open many accounts. He do it. He scared.'

'They threatened you?'

'They beat Piotr,' she said, shoving both arms between her legs as though protecting herself, looking around the van. 'But Piotr is clever. He hide this van. They not find it. And we run away one night.'

'Where did you go?'

She put her hands together in prayer and looked to the roof. 'The Army. Very godly. With the ...' She played a pretend trumpet in the air. 'They take us in.'

'The Salvation Army?'

'They say they find good jobs for us.'

'Good jobs,' Elizabeth murmured under her breath, hearing a loud screech of dismay in her head.

Agata shrugged. 'It is better here.' A lump pushed itself up Elizabeth's throat. Agata continued. 'Lucas give us money to fix the wheels.' She nodded again. 'But then Gordon say we have to pay him back and he take money away from our pay.'

'He *what*?' Elizabeth choked.

'For a borrow.'

'For a loan? You have a loan with Lucas?'

Agata picked at the blue polish on her nails. 'We have a *loan*, that's it, yes.'

Elizabeth began to doubt the solidity of everything around her. So often Lucas had talked about how he was moving his money around. One minute they didn't have any, the next they did. *Smoke and mirrors, Elizabeth. Smoke and mirrors.*

'I can't believe it.'

'Lucas is better than the bad men in London.' Agata stared back at Elizabeth as though to say, *Don't you dare judge us.*

'Your work papers. Are they legal?'

'Yes, I think,' she said. Her eyes shone. 'He say he find good work for Piotr at big houses of his friends.' She pointed towards the swimming pool. 'He say he pay a lot of money to us when his deal go through. So we can save. We can buy a house in Warsaw. Life is good then.'

Elizabeth realised that Agata believed Lucas would come through for them. 'It seems we're all invested in this deal,' she said, awestruck by how he used people to get what he wanted.

'*Tak.*' Agata nodded.

'What about Piotr's wages from the building sites?'

'He give to Gordon for Lucas!' She threw her skinny arms in the air.

'I thought you sent the money back home to Rafal and the baby?'

'No! We want to!'

Elizabeth sank her head into her hands, unable to bear to look at Agata. 'Honestly, I didn't know any of this. I thought you … I thought you and Lucas … I don't know what I thought.'

'You did not think,' Agata snorted.

Elizabeth nodded and bit her lip, deeply ashamed. She remembered the healthy, pretty young girl who had arrived. The girl sitting across from her now was hollowed out, dark shadows pressed into her eye sockets, hair thinning, body emaciated. Images of starved and abused girls chained to radiators in dirty hotel rooms and gun-toting gangsters in leather jackets came to mind. It couldn't happen in leafy Surrey. But Elizabeth had let it happen.

'You must wish you'd never come here,' she murmured.

'Do you wish you didn't love Lucas?' Agata said.

Elizabeth had never been asked this question before, and she wondered how that was possible. Anger collected in her throat. She swallowed hard. 'Yes,' she said, low and cold. 'But now we have children together.'

Agata's defiance slipped from her face. 'I sorry, Elizabeth.'

Was she sorry for asking her why she loved a monster? Or did she feel sorry *for* her? The ambiguity left Elizabeth flailing in her mind for a response. Instead, she placed her hand on top of Agata's young one and the answer came to her.

'I'm sorry too,' she whispered, unable to project how truly sorry she felt, knowing she would have to show her rather than tell her that her eyes were now fully opened to the truth. 'I'll find a way to get your passports and your papers back for you,' she said. And she meant it.

The colourful aisles of food were a blur of choice. Too much choice, while Elizabeth's thoughts were taken up with decision-making and responsibility.

'Pasta?' Agata said, waggling a tub of pesto at her.

Crazed schemes to coerce or trick or blackmail Lucas into giving up the documents rocketed through her mind. Some of the more extreme ideas involved locking handcuffs on him until he relented, threatening him with the shotgun in the closet, or calling the police. Another involved a mass email to the party guest list outing him as a monster. They all had obvious flaws. If they called the police, Agata and Piotr would never be allowed back in the UK, or worse, the trafficking ring might catch up with them.

The past weighed on her. Lucas's first assistant had accused him of squeezing her knee under the desk, but he had insisted she was a fantasist who was in love with him. She had signed a non-disclosure agreement. The babysitting agency had refused to send them another babysitter, but they had never explained why. He had promised her that nothing had happened between him and Heather when she was a child. A *child*. He had promised. How could she believe his promises now?

'Pasta's fine,' she replied, mentally blowing out a breath.

'This?' Agata showed her two different brands of ravioli.

'Either one, Agata. You have a brain in your head,' Elizabeth snapped, realising as she said it that they had trained her out of being able to use it.

A mother from school whom Elizabeth vaguely recognised reached for some pumpkin ravioli. Her disapproving look – *How could you possibly speak to your au pair like that?* – reminded her that she had to keep her cool at all times. But her mind was too full. Too many choices. Too much change ahead.

She began dumping various packets of food into the trolley, remembering to include the ingredients for the chicken Caesar salad that Lucas wanted for his lunch: chicken breasts, cos lettuce, garlic, mayonnaise, white wine vinegar, croutons. Agata trailed behind her. She began to worry that she had forgotten what Lucas had asked her for this morning. Salted caramel truffle chocolates to eat after their supper had been one of his requests, and another had been some extra-strong coffee capsules instead of his usual medium strength. There had been a third request, she was sure of it. She racked her brain for the item he had asked for. Why hadn't she written it down?

She called him, knowing it would irritate him, but he didn't pick up.

In the sweets and biscuits aisle, she dumped four bags of sugar sours into the trolley.

Her phone rang; she hoped it was Lucas so that she could ask him about the third item. But it was Jude's name on the screen. Another decision to make. To answer or not to answer.

'Hi,' she said, handing the trolley over to Agata. 'We're just in the supermarket. Can I call you back?'

'Sure, sure. Just checking in.'

'Everything okay?'

'The Seacarts are being arses.'

'About the paintings?'

'They don't like their adviser's condition report, so they want an auction house guy to do some generic piece of shit, to maintain its value. Fuckers.'

'Jude!'

'But come on! How greedy can you get? They're billionaires, for Christ's sake, but they're flipping out about the difference of a few hundred pounds when the paintings must be small change to them anyway! What is up with them?'

'Rich people are rich for a reason,' she said.

He sighed. 'I guess I should be flattered they care so much about my work.'

'More like they know it's going to be worth a hundred times more in ten years' time when you're a megastar.'

'No.'

'You will be. Look, I've got to go. I'll call you later.'

They said their goodbyes and hung up.

Agata dropped a packet of cheese in the trolley and said, 'The paintings. They worth a lot, yes?'

'Yes, why?'

'Lucas want them more than he want us? Yes?'

Elizabeth processed what Agata was saying. And then she clicked. Clever girl.

'My God. You're right,' she murmured. A plan so simple, she was amazed she hadn't thought of it herself. She called her brother back.

'Jude. Do you still have that lock-up in Clapham?'

'Yes, why?'

'Can I borrow it?'

They passed the Greek yoghurt that Lucas liked and she remembered it was the third item. She gesticulated at Agata, pointing towards the yoghurt.

'Why do you need it?' Jude said.

'I'll tell you soon. Text me how to get in, and the code and stuff.'

'You sure everything's okay?'

She opened one of the bags of sugar sours that she hadn't yet paid for.

'I've got to go, I'm at the checkout,' she said, and ended the call. She did not want him mixed up in her mess.

She chewed on her sweet. Her tongue was stinging. There were pitfalls in Agata's idea, but it was doable. Lucas had never thought Elizabeth very bright, and right now, she wondered if the plan was more than she could manage. It was easy to slip up, say something incriminating, end up in the sort of trouble there was no coming back from.

As Agata filled the conveyor belt with their shopping, Elizabeth took her pen out and ticked through the shopping list. Except for the anchovies – which she sent Agata back for – they had everything.

When Agata returned, Elizabeth said, 'We're going to need Heather's help. Is that okay with you?'

Agata looked at the conveyor belt crammed with food, as though this were what Elizabeth had been referring to. Elizabeth laughed.

'Not that. The paintings.'

Agata clicked her tongue and shook her head. 'She is back?'

'Yes.'

'But Gordon and Sally …'

'Yes. We'll have to keep them out of it somehow,' Elizabeth said.

Elizabeth waited for Gordon and Sally to leave. She had requested they go to the garden centre to pick up some extra-large plant pots and foliage to put in place on the terrace for tomorrow.

'We've got some friends coming over and Piotr's going to do a barbecue,' she had said. 'Lucas thought we could jazz the place up a bit. One big pot there, and one there?' she said, pointing to each corner of the slate-tiled terrace.

She was good at lying. Her mother had taught her how.

'Square black ones, I thought,' she continued. 'You can choose whatever you like to fill them with.'

Both Gordon and Sally were silent. She knew they did not appreciate suggestions that interfered with their designs.

'And you want these by tomorrow?' Sally asked.

'Yes please. Is that all right?' She knew they couldn't refuse.

'Of course. We'll go now,' Sally agreed, checking her watch. Gordon gave her a sideways glance that expressed how disgruntled he was.

'Thank you. You're superstars.'

It was that easy to get rid of them.

*

Large raindrops began to plop onto Elizabeth's head as she hurried to Connolly Close. It had been sunny five minutes before, and she had failed to put on her raincoat or take an umbrella. The heavens opened. She contemplated turning back. But, she thought, did it matter that she was cold and uncomfortable? Not any more. The comforts of her life were over, rendered meaningless by the misery engendered in the pursuit of them.

She ran along the lane and into Connolly Close to shelter under the small porch of the Shaws' bungalow. The rain lashed into her left side. Her summer blouse stuck to her arm. With her heart in her mouth, she pressed the doorbell. As she waited, she began shivering, but she didn't care if she died of cold, curled on their doorstep.

When Heather opened the door, Elizabeth saw how thin she had become, like Agata, and her resolve strengthened further.

'Can I please come in?' she asked, teeth chattering.

CHAPTER TWENTY-SEVEN

I stared at Elizabeth Huxley standing on the doorstep. She was almost unrecognisable, bedraggled, her small frame hunched and her golden hair smeared to one cheek. Instead of ushering her in, as I would have done for anyone else, I hesitated and began to close the door. I didn't want her money or her threats.

Her hand shot out to stop me from closing the door.

'Please, hear me out.'

'Is it work-related?' It was only Thursday afternoon. There were three more days before I had to start work again.

'Just five minutes.'

I noticed how her body juddered with cold and I weakened.

'Here, take this and change in there,' I said, handing her a jumper from the peg, pointing to the sitting room.

After a minute, she appeared in the doorway of the kitchen. The jumper – Dad's green cable-knit with the brown elbow patches – was five sizes too big for her and made her look comically small and young. Her hair was drying curlier than the tamed waves I was used to seeing tucked neatly behind her ears. She drew her finger under both her eyes in an attempt to neaten up the smudge of mascara, but it wiped stripes towards her temples, making her look wild and unsophisticated, and I had a flash of who she might be inside, behind the wealth and grooming.

'Thank you for this,' she said, rolling up the sleeves of the jumper.

I brought out the teapot and dusted it off.

As the kettle boiled, I leant back into the work surface and waited for her to tell me why she was here.

'I would like your help,' she said. Her pretty blue eyes blinked up at me, and I tried not to be drawn in by her beguiling, vulnerable face, which brought to mind Lucas and how he must have loved her once.

'I'll be back at work on Monday.'

'I need you this weekend.'

'What do you want me to do?'

'Transport Jude's paintings to his lock-up. I'm reframing them for him,' she said. 'Can you help?'

I placed her tea in front of her. 'Why not hire a van?'

'It's a secret. For Lucas. It's his birthday coming up.' She sipped her tea. 'And he'd find out if I used our joint account.'

'I'll have to ask Dad.'

'That's the thing. You're going to have to do it without telling either of your parents.'

'Really?'

'I can't risk Lucas finding out.' She laughed nervily.

'My parents are the most discreet people you'll ever meet.'

'And the most honest,' she countered. 'They won't be able to lie to Lucas.'

I crossed my arms over my chest, sensing that her request had nothing to do with a birthday surprise. 'And if I refuse to help you?'

Her light smile disappeared. 'You're contractually obliged to do as I ask. All three of you.'

'So you're giving me no choice,' I said through a tight jaw, loathing my capitulation, loathing her entitled air and her presumptuous, ill-gotten power over me.

'I'm sorry. It's just the way it has to be,' she said, standing to leave.

The following night, I parked my old car in the spot on the drive nearest to my parents' bedroom window, forcing my father to park the van on the street. This was how I wanted it to play out – the further away the van was from the house, the less likely it was that they would wake up. And they didn't.

Like a thief in the night, I drove out of Connolly Close at 3 a.m. and waited in the lane outside Copper Lodge. The engine purred. The headlights shot out into the gloom. Two diminutive figures, carrying one painting each, crept across the gravel. Their footsteps were magnified by the silence and I winced at every sound they made. I climbed out and opened the back.

Silently, wordlessly, Elizabeth and Agata slid the paintings into the back. While Agata went back for the third, Elizabeth and I wrapped the two canvases in blankets and secured them to the side with straps.

We left Agata at the house.

Once we were safely away, I turned on the radio. The noise was worse than the silence. The fast drumbeat of the dance track heightened the tension between us. The orchestral piece on the classical station added melodrama to an already hair-raising drive. I turned it off. It allowed space for me to think. I realised I had no idea what we were doing, and I became frightened.

'Are we stealing these?'

'They're my brother's paintings. How could I be stealing them?'

'Elizabeth. Please tell me what we're doing.'

'As I said, it's going to be a surprise for Lucas.'

I glanced down at my naked ring finger. I did not like surprises. I did not like driving in the middle of the night. I did not like sitting next to Elizabeth. She was highly strung, over-polite. Held-in secrets, pulled-back feelings, unvoiced grievances shimmered behind her eyes, trapped under the cool surface of her prettiness. I sensed she was changeable, unstable, as Lucas had intimated. In fact, he had said she was mad, and now I believed him.

He was only a phone call away.

'We need petrol,' I said.

'Oh, really?' She leant over to look at the gauge. 'There's enough to get us to London and back.'

When we reached the motorway, I pulled into the first petrol station we came across.

'What are you doing?'

'I need the loo,' I said, checking to make sure my phone was in my jacket pocket.

'Be quick!' she said.

The shop was empty. On the way to the toilets, through the aisles, I scrolled to Lucas's number on my phone.

'It's out of order,' the man said from behind the counter, and I jumped, too on edge to handle the smallest disturbance. My mobile screen flicked off. I pulled up my contacts again and stared at his name: *Lucas Huxley*. My finger hovered over the green button. Could I really call him in the middle of the night to tell him that I was on the A3 with his wife and her brother's paintings? Could I? Would he laugh and tell me that he knew about Elizabeth's little birthday surprise? Would he order us home? Would he call the police? Was I in too deep already? Retrospectively, would I be able to convince Lucas and my parents and the police that I had been coerced into stealing the paintings?

Could I take the risk?

Elizabeth had made it clear that she would make trouble for me and my parents if Lucas found out. The madness behind her eyes led me to believe she was capable of anything. No, I could not take the risk. I turned on my heel and returned to the van, committed to this night-time run, praying I wasn't making a decision that I could never recover from, that would have far-reaching consequences, that might ruin my life.

CHAPTER TWENTY-EIGHT

Lucas ended his call and chucked his mobile on the coffee table in front of him.

'Jesus!' he said, stretching out on the leather sofa, crossing his ankles, linking his hands across his chest, yawning loudly. The sun streamed in through the window. A shaft of light on his head, as though it could suck him upwards into the heavens like the soul from a dead body.

Elizabeth curled her legs underneath her and put the Saturday newspaper supplement down. She hadn't been reading it. She was too tired after last night.

'Everything okay?' she asked.

He sat up and leant his elbows on his knees. A chunk of his hair stuck up at the back. 'More than okay! Fuck! It's actually fucking happening. Can you believe we've almost actually done it?'

Her duplicity came down on her, heavy and hard. Panic set in. She wondered if it was possible to reverse what she had done. Bring the paintings home, carry on as before.

'It's wonderful,' she said carefully.

'Cadogan Tate are managing the logistics for the paintings after the deal's signed.'

She stood up. 'Another coffee?'

'Oh darling, you're going to miss them, aren't you?'

'No, not at all,' she said, taking his cup.

'Let's go take a look at them, shall we? Check they're in one piece. And have a swim afterwards.'

She opened the fridge for the milk and stood there sucking in its cool air. 'Later maybe.'

He came up behind her. 'Why don't we ask Jude to paint us some more?'

'I don't think it works like that.'

'Yes it does. I can commission him. After next week, I can pay him anything he wants.'

She repeated what he had said. 'Yes. After next week.' After the party. After the pool house. After this. After that. Where was the 'after' for Agata and Piotr?

'Yes,' he said. 'After next week, we'll be set for life.'

'When did you say they were coming to stay?'

'Wednesday after next.'

'I'll call Bo and ask her what she's not eating these days.'

'Come on. Join me for a naughty caffeine hit by the pool.'

She put a coffee pod into the machine.

'Where's Agata?' Lucas asked.

'She's taken the kids to Wisley.'

'Oh, okay. I'll get my trunks and then go check on those paintings.'

As soon as he had gone through to the bedroom, Elizabeth abandoned the coffee pod and began to pace, squeezing her skull until she couldn't see straight. She wanted to find Heather, send her back to the lock-up in Clapham, bring the paintings back. But oh Christ, there wasn't time! A stone of panic lodged in her chest, ready to explode. She was minutes away from Lucas discovering what she had done.

She drank from the tap as though this were her last drink, wiped her mouth, began a mental preparation for what was to come.

'See you down there!' Lucas said, whistling as he slipped out into the garden in his swimming trunks with a towel thrown over his shoulder.

Pointlessly, she made two coffees, as something to do, but she didn't follow him down to the barn. She waited as they grew cold. She waited.

Four minutes. Four minutes before the day turned. Four minutes of calm that she would never get back.

Lucas was running up the lawn, a spray of sweat flying off his head.

'They're gone!' he cried. He was holding his forehead, wide-eyed, tearful, staring at her, pleading for help. 'The paintings! They're gone, Elizabeth!'

Elizabeth gulped and her elbow knocked over the cold cup of coffee behind her as she backed into the kitchen units. She stared at him.

'I think they must've been stolen!' he shouted.

As she spoke, her voice sounded strange, as though it wasn't hers. 'They haven't been stolen.'

'What? Have you moved them?'

'Yes. I've moved them.'

'Jesus! Why didn't you say? I almost had a fucking heart attack.'

She could have lied. She could have said she had wanted them in a safer place. She could have said she hadn't wanted to bother him with it.

'They're safe.'

'Where are they?'

'Safe.'

'Stop saying that. Tell me where they are.'

The image of Piotr fixing the daisy-chain ring onto Agata's finger played through her mind on a loop.

'I'll tell you where they are when you've returned Agata and Piotr's documents.'

Lucas guffawed. 'Is this some kind of joke?'

'No joke, Lucas.'

His lips were wet. They hung open. He scratched the mole on his cheek. He didn't look angry; he looked utterly lost. 'Elizabeth?'

Her voice began to break. 'You can't hold them here against their will,' she said.

'But there's a good reason I'm not giving them back their passports and their papers.'

'There's no good reason for forcing them to stay!'

'Elizabeth! They've tricked you! They're probably halfway to Poland by now.'

Her heartbeat slowed. 'Wasn't Piotr working on the pool-house?'

'He wasn't there. You have to tell me where you took them.'

'No. I won't let you mess with my head. Piotr and Agata would never steal from us.'

'You really know them that well?'

'I trust them.'

'Think about it. *Think*, Elizabeth! Whose idea was it to take the paintings?'

'Mine,' she lied, remembering Agata dropping the cheese into the trolley and suggesting the idea after her phone call with Jude.

Lucas stepped towards her and said in a low, urgent voice, 'Where are the kids?'

'They're with Agata. At Wisley.' Saying it made it real. Anything else was unthinkable. She pictured them running through the droopy branches of their favourite willow tree and playing in the stick teepees and laughing at the naked lady statue.

'Are you one hundred per cent sure about that?'

Her palms were wet with sweat as she pressed Agata's number on her phone. 'Of course I'm sure.'

It rang and rang. Elizabeth thought she might die waiting for her to pick up.

'Where are those paintings, Elizabeth?'

'I will not tell you unless you give me Agata and Piotr's documents,' she repeated, steadfast. She blocked out his shouting and flinched when he came near her. He pointed into her face, threatening her with everything and anything he could think of. It would pass, she told herself, blinking away her fear.

Running out of steam, Lucas went outside and made a phone call. Elizabeth didn't know to whom. She watched him pacing across the flagstones. There was a redness high on his cheekbones.

A few minutes later, Gordon's tall figure appeared on the crest of the lawn. His greying brow was heavy over his eyes as Lucas talked to him. He nodded repeatedly and went away again.

Lucas came back inside and cut across the room, straight to her.

'You know Agata will go to prison for this. For theft and kidnap. Is that what you want?'

Elizabeth called Agata again, feeling the oppression of Lucas's questions, feeling the doubt crash over her in waves. She revisited her conversations with Agata, how assured she had been, how calm, how determined; how they had shared what felt to Elizabeth like a real alliance, a friendship, an affection even. How she had entrusted her with the address and code of the lock-up. Just in case something went wrong.

No, she thought. Lucas is trying to mess with my head.

'Agata did not take them,' she said, wanting him to stop accusing her.

He ignored her and stared down at his phone, as though it might have the answers. 'How could you have been so stupid?'

It was she, Elizabeth, who had the answers, and yet still he could not defer to her. Still he wouldn't allow himself to bow to her demands. In the face of his lack of respect, she became a little stronger. 'It's simple, Lucas. If you give me the passports and work papers, I'll tell you where we took the paintings.'

'We?'

'Me.'

'How did you transport them?'

She didn't answer, realising her mistake. He looked at her with narrowed eyes. 'Of course,' he said quietly. 'Heather. *Heather* helped you. You asked her to use Gordon's van, didn't you?'

'No,' she said.

For a brief moment, the tension fell from his face. What she saw, she fully understood. It was the look of a man who had been hurt by someone he had trusted, and this riled her. Historical jealousy reared up inside her. 'You don't like the idea of Heather knowing everything about you, do you?' she said, wanting him to know that Heather could never love him back.

Lucas shook his head at her. 'You have no idea what you've done.'

It felt as though his thumb was pressing on her windpipe. She staggered back and pressed Agata's number again.

As the ringtone repeated in her ear, penetrating deep into her brain, she heard Lucas on the phone.

'Meet me in the study. Now,' he said, rubbing his forehead.

Two minutes later, Gordon came into the house. He looked at Elizabeth with disdain, as though she were an impostor in her own kitchen, as though her status as his boss was null and void.

Everyone was against her. Except for Agata, who would call her back soon, armed with a cactus plant and a cuddly toy from the gift shop. Agata believed in her, unlike Lucas, who needed facts and figures to validate people. This time Elizabeth would trust her instincts. If only she had done so earlier.

She would not let Lucas keep those documents. She would not let him get into her head. Not this time. Never again. But she wasn't certain that Heather would hold out. She didn't know whether she had scared her enough to keep her quiet about the whereabouts of the paintings.

CHAPTER TWENTY-NINE

My mother was making porridge like any normal Sunday morning. My father was using fresh tea bags to make three cups of tea. I wanted to tell Mum that she was stirring it the wrong way. I wanted to tell Dad that I had developed a taste for old tea bags, microwaved.

Left and right, right and left. The devil was hovering above the pan. Auntie Maggie would be horrified. There was no way to stop it. I sensed that if I questioned anything, they would come down hard on me. Yesterday the questioning had been endless and repetitive: *Do you know anything about the paintings? Did you see Elizabeth leave with anything? Did you see Jude in the grounds? Was there a van parked outside the house at any point?* Endless questions that I had dodged and laughed at, pretending to be incredulous at their insinuations. But this morning, the atmosphere was different.

'Honey or sugar?' my mother asked.

'Honey's good.'

She poured too much. The sticky flow was like the saliva thickening down my throat.

The three of us settled at the table.

'Lucas called again,' my mother said.

'Any news?'

'Agata and Piotr and the kids have turned up.'

'Uh huh,' I said. I had always known they were safe. Not for a second had I doubted Agata, assuming that Elizabeth had blamed her for the theft of the paintings in order to wriggle out of owning up herself.

'Is that all you can say?'

I laughed, in spite of the seriousness of my parents' faces. 'They just wouldn't have taken those kids or the paintings.'

I thought about the Rolex flopping out of Agata's jeans pocket, and how it had made its way back onto Lucas's wrist. If Agata's conscience wouldn't sanction the theft of a watch, there was no way she was capable of a heist involving three paintings worth ten times the value of the Rolex.

'People aren't always what they seem,' my father said.

'Heather, if you know anything, you must tell us,' my mother added. 'We'll decide what to do together. We can help you. We won't be cross.' She smoothed her hand down my back. Her motherly voice was like the waves lapping at my toes, soothing and cooling and inviting, and I felt tearful.

'Elizabeth is the problem here,' I said, close to giving up what I knew, wanting to end this, desperate to understand why Elizabeth needed those paintings and whether it was worth it.

'What has she said to you?' my mother asked, cajoling me.

I stared at my porridge. The consistency was right. I didn't want to eat it. The address of the lock-up was dancing on my tongue and I wanted rid of it. But they didn't realise I was holding steady for their own good. I was defying them to protect them. If Elizabeth was capable of blaming Agata and Piotr for stealing her children, she would certainly be capable of pinning the theft of the paintings on me and my parents. Not only would we lose our jobs, I might go to prison. I could not divulge the details.

'She's said nothing to me. She's mad. I don't know why she's telling you I'm involved.'

My father and mother glanced at each other, and my mother sighed and said, 'I believe you.'

But my father dropped his spoon into his bowl and left the room.

On Monday morning, I skulked around the grounds of Copper Lodge, desperate to avoid seeing anyone, and climbed up the ladder to prune the side shoots of the apple trees that flanked the tall laurel hedges next to the pool. It was a hidden spot, away from everyone.

It had been swelteringly hot since the theft of the paintings. Yesterday my parents had been out for most of the day, walking with their ramblers and then helping at the Salvation Army soup kitchen. We had communicated very little. Now I was dehydrated and jaded from another night of bad sleep, having tossed and turned until the early hours. At four this morning I had woken up feeling hung-over, even though I hadn't had a drop to drink. The enormity of what I had done preoccupied me.

The heat intensified the throb of a headache. The work on the apple trees was methodical and it calmed me. The birdsong was loud and uplifting. After the third tree in the row, I was getting hungry. My lunch of crackers and cottage cheese was waiting for me in a Tupperware box in the van. But I couldn't face eating it with my father; not while he doubted me, while he suspected I was lying. Part of me felt that he had doubted me all my life, even before there was anything to doubt.

I heard footsteps.

When I spotted a head of blond curls bobbing along the path, I lost my footing on the ladder and had to steady myself by grabbing onto a branch.

'Sorry, I didn't mean to startle you,' Lucas said.

His voice was a cool rush of pleasure up my spine.

'I've got lunch. Want some?' he shouted up from the bottom of the tree.

Tucked under one of his arms was a rolled tartan rug. Jutting out from the hessian bag that he carried was a French loaf.

'I can't.'

'You can,' he replied simply.

'Where's Dad?' I held my breath for as long as it took him to reply.

'He's dealing with the mess that Elizabeth has caused. You know all about it, I guess?'

'Where is she?' I asked, looking out across the garden to the house.

'Elizabeth? She's taken the kids out. And Agata's at the supermarket.'

I glanced down. He had unrolled the tartan rug and thrown it on the ground next to the tree.

'I'll eat it all by myself then,' he said.

I made my way down the ladder to the grass and hovered at the corner of the rug, uncertain that this was a wise idea, watching him unpack a feast: hunks of cheese wrapped in waxed paper, red grapes, salami, olives, a bottle of lemonade and two plastic cups. I was ravenous.

'Sit!' he insisted.

It was irresistible. He was irresistible. Tumbling through my mind came scenes of that summer; how close we had been and how much we had shared. I sat down on the edge of the rug with my knees tucked up to my chest, as far away from him as possible, self-conscious in my sticky workman's clothes. I wished for a breeze to cool me off. My T-shirt clung to me. My hair was wet under my cap.

'I can't be long. I've got loads to do.'

'You're allowed a lunch break,' he said.

I looked behind me, wondering if I should face the direction of the house, giving me time to whizz up the ladder before anyone saw us together. I stayed where I was and reached to pluck a grape from the bunch.

'I'm sorry she accused you of being involved,' he said.

'Yeah,' I replied, feeling justified in my anger about Elizabeth's coercion, and then, in turn, guilty about deceiving him. 'I've had a roasting from my parents. It was like being a teenager again.'

'She does this. Accuses people left, right and centre to get herself out of trouble, but she doesn't think – or care – about how it might affect anyone else.'

I glanced over my shoulder again. Half of me was looking for my father; the other half wondered if Elizabeth was about to appear through the hedge.

Lucas lay back. The silence that followed reminded me of how we had once lain next to each other on the grass, easy in each other's company. How the conversation had picked up naturally, in and out of silences. Out of habit, I almost lay down by his side.

'Do you ever wonder what would have happened if I'd not taken that job in London?' he said, staring up into the sky, one forearm draped over his eyes.

There was a tug inside me, a tug towards him. 'No,' I said.

'I've always felt linked to that summer, as though everything in between, with Elizabeth, with my job, was a fill-in until I was with you again.'

'Don't say that,' I said, squeezing my knees to my chest.

Before now, the need for secrecy had compartmentalised him, put him in the background, while real life had trundled on. What we had shared was too dangerous to think about. My memories of us had become like vapours shut away in a sealed chamber of my mind, relegated there after the heartache of losing him, of realising that he would not come back to me. But he was drawing them out now, making them solid again.

He sat up and moved to sit in front of me, cross-legged, one hand on each knee. The flowers in the meadow behind him swayed in the breeze.

'Heather. It's not too late.'

'You were the one who legged it to London and never came back.'

'I needed more time and then it was too late.'

'Why was it too late? Because you met Elizabeth and forgot about me?'

'No! Not at all! Because your dad told me you were engaged!'

'*What?*'

'He told me you were getting married to some surfer in Hossegor.'

'He told you I was marrying *Frank*?'

'That's it. Frank. I wanted to get on a plane and find him and drown him.'

'I can't believe he told you that. It's a total lie.'

'He doesn't want you to have a good life, Heather. Can't you see that? He doesn't want you to get ideas above your station.'

'Why the hell didn't you ever call me?'

He rubbed his cheek. 'You know what I'm like. I'm a stubborn idiot.'

'It was male pride?' I laughed.

'Does it matter now?' he asked me, urgently. 'Maybe it wasn't our time. Maybe *now* is our time.'

However much I wanted to give in to him, I couldn't. There were too many unanswered questions.

'Why does Elizabeth want those paintings?' I asked.

He tore off a piece of bread and began pulling at the soft inside. 'They're worth quite a bit of money.'

I mentally scanned the grounds and the house, guessing, not for the first time, that the place was worth a fortune.

'Surely what's yours is hers and vice versa. Isn't that how marriage works?'

'Not ours.'

'Oh. I'm sorry.'

'Don't be. If we decided to separate, I wouldn't want it to turn nasty. For the kids' sake.'

'Why the paintings, then? She'd get a good settlement in a divorce, wouldn't she?'

'Of course. It would be fifty-fifty all the way. But she's paranoid. She thinks everyone is out to get her. She thinks the lawyers will trick her and leave her with nothing.'

'Even so, if they're her brother's paintings, why not let her have them?' This was one of the questions that had revisited me regularly over the last few days. Her brother had painted them and, I assumed, given them to Elizabeth at some point, which surely meant that she had every right to do as she pleased with them.

'Those bloody paintings have sat for five years in a lock-up because she said they were too big to hang in the house, and then Bo Seacart, who is the wife of—'

'Yes, I've heard all about them,' I interjected.

'Okay. So those three paintings were worked into the contract – which is going ahead next week, by the way,' he said, swatting a fly away from the olives before he replaced the lid. 'Bo is an art nut and fell in love with them. And what Bo wants, Bo gets.'

'Can't you just un-work them?'

He spoke through a mouthful with his hand covering his mouth, as if he couldn't wait until he had swallowed to say what he wanted to say. 'How would I explain it to the Seacarts? Sorry, I know you wanted those paintings, but no can do, my wife is insane and she's stolen them. I mean, how would that look?'

'Pretty bad,' I said, biting a small corner from a piece of salami, less hungry now, eating unconsciously as the knowledge I held about the lock-up swelled inside my brain, pushing every other thought out. Telling him where they were stored would end this torment for him.

He put the bread knife down and hung his head, pressing two fingers into the centre of his forehead. 'I've worked seven years for this deal. Seven long years. I swear, it's made me ill with stress. If it doesn't go ahead, we're ruined. My company could go bankrupt if we don't acquire new funds, and she knows it.'

'Are you serious?' Everything around me took on a picture-postcard quality, as though it were an image projected on a wall that could be switched off at the push of a button. It seemed we had more in common than I could ever have believed. Three months, they say, is how many pay cheques most of us are away from homelessness. Three months. Blink. Homeless and hungry. That was how it had always felt for me, but I had doubted very much that it felt quite as terrifying for Lucas. I had imagined that the safety cushion was there for him, always, if times were hard. They moved in a social milieu where the comfortable spare rooms in the big houses of their friends were readily available, where money arrived in envelopes, lent by those same friends. When one job came to an end, a dinner party host would provide a contact that led to an interview. But Lucas was in a different league, where the risk was giant. There were no cushions to fall back on; slipping up meant a landing of concrete and utter ruination: bankruptcy courts and public humiliation and a bottomless pit of debts for life. It would be hard to come back from. It seemed our money worries were relative, and I decided I preferred mine to his. I had been naïve to think it was simple for him.

'She wants to walk away with those paintings and ruin me. Just because she's full of hate and bitterness.'

The other night, Elizabeth's nervy fingers had tapped in the code on the keypad at the lock-up incorrectly, several times, and I had asked her if she wanted me to do it for her. She had hesitated, and a feverish sweat had broken out across her forehead. Then she had read out the code to me. On the way home, her eyes had glinted, heightening how pretty she was. In this excitable state, she had been more likeable somehow, vulnerable but alive, as though she had woken from a sleep, but now I realised that these had been signs that she was unwell. A wash of pity for her came over me.

'I'll tell you where they are if you promise me you'll protect my parents' jobs,' I said.

His tousled blond head snapped up. His look pierced me, as though the blue had shot from his eyes and entered into my soul. 'You know where they are?'

'She said she'd fire me and my parents if you ever found out,' I confessed, a red bloom of shame across my cheeks.

'Where are they, Heather?' he said, tipping over the bottle of lemonade as he stood up. He reached for his phone.

I righted the bottle. 'They're at Jude's lock-up in Clapham.'

His phone went to his ear. 'Give me the address.'

Midway through me telling him, he spoke to someone on the other end of the phone. 'Pick up your van and meet me outside the house.'

He hung up. 'Sorry, what did you say the address was?'

I repeated it, adding the code, and he tapped it into his phone.

Letting go of the secret did not leave behind a sense of relief. I had an empty feeling. Churlishly, I wanted him to sit down and honour his promise of a picnic. I began to pack away the food. But then he sank to his knees in front of me, pulled my face to his and kissed me on the lips, forcefully. 'Thank you, Heather. Thank you.'

I tasted the sweetness from the grapes he had eaten and bit my lip to taste more of it. 'I'm sorry it took me so long to tell you,' I said.

'You were scared. But your parents' jobs are always safe here. For life, if you want.'

That was when the relief surged into my system.

With a light head, I smiled. 'Go. Go get those paintings and that deal.'

'You're beautiful,' he said.

And he was gone. I fell back on the rug, lying flat on my back, wanting to scream into the blue sky above me, allowing my elation to fan out and spread through the universe, waiting for it to come down in sparkling droplets on everyone who needed nourishment.

CHAPTER THIRTY

Elizabeth was hiding out at Sarah's, away from Lucas's haranguing. Sarah had no idea of the maelstrom they had left behind at Copper Lodge.

'Put the saucer over the bowl,' she instructed Hugo. 'That's right, just like that, and drain the egg white out. Good boy.'

He beamed a smile at the yolk that was left intact on the saucer. 'Awesome!' he cried.

'That's so cool!' Isla said.

'Now for the syrup,' Sarah said. They fought over who would pour. Sarah decided they could each have a turn. Isla let the syrup drizzle onto the worktop.

'Oops, look at that!' Sarah said.

Isla hung her head and Elizabeth wondered why Sarah would be harsh about a minor spill in such a messy kitchen.

'Aren't you going to lick it up?' Sarah asked mischievously, wiping some up with her finger and sucking on it. 'Yum!'

Neither Isla nor Elizabeth had recognised her mock-scolding.

High on the relief, Isla giggled as she pressed her finger into the syrup and licked it, mirroring Sarah's face, which was in raptures at the sweetness. 'We never let anything go to waste in this house!'

Unexpectedly, tears sprang into Elizabeth's eyes. The children were never allowed to be messy at home. Lucas abhorred mess. He had expected Elizabeth to train their housekeepers to become meticulous. Before Agata, they had rarely met the required standard, leading to a fast turnover of staff. When it had been Elizabeth's responsibility to keep their home tidy, she had never been able to keep up: the pillows weren't clean enough; the children weren't quiet enough; the food wasn't hot enough; the drinks weren't cool enough; Elizabeth was lazy; Hugo was badly behaved; Isla was a disappointment. The world was wrong. When Agata and Piotr arrived, they excelled in their duties and created equilibrium in the house. Perhaps this was why Elizabeth had failed to question how they were affording to keep them.

She shuddered with anger when she thought about the documents locked in the safe. Apprehension about going home swirled inside her. She was uncertain about how long she could hold out. It had been foolish of her to expect him to roll over. It was in his personality to be unyielding. Submitting to her tough-guy tactics would be his last resort, detestable to him, part of the childhood he had left behind. As an adult, he had worked tirelessly to shed that side of him, to cultivate his new persona of success and power. Never again the victim! Two fingers to the housemaster of Winslow House!

Isla put on a large pair of cherry-patterned oven gloves and carried a tin of chocolate cake mixture to the oven.

'Careful!' Elizabeth said, watching her daughter's attempt to put the cake in the oven.

Isla hesitated and looked up at her.

'She'll be fine!' Sarah said. 'Go on, sweetie.'

Hugo was next. Just as he placed the tin on the oven shelf, the doorbell rang.

'Who's that?' Sarah asked, frowning, wiping her hands on her apron as she went to the front door.

Elizabeth heard a familiar Polish accent and shot up off her chair, but was then rooted to the spot, unable to go to her.

Sarah led Agata into the kitchen. 'Agata's here!'

'I need to talk to you,' Agata said.

'Excuse me for one second, Sarah, will you?'

'Of course,' Sarah said. 'Come on, you two. Part of baking is cleaning up.'

Elizabeth and Agata stood in the narrow hallway, almost nose to nose.

'What the hell are you doing here? How did you get here?'

'I get cab. You have to come,' Agata urged.

'What's happened?'

'Lucas make Heather tell him. I hear it. And Gordon get the van and they go. They GO!'

'Shush! *Shush*,' Elizabeth said, putting her hand over Agata's mouth in fright.

Agata twisted her head away. 'You have to get to the paintings first,' she hissed.

'Why didn't you call me?'

'You not answer your phone. I try and try! They leave half an hour ago.'

When Elizabeth returned to the kitchen, she felt slippery, as though her limbs were melting under the stress. Her arm muscles wobbled as she picked up her handbag.

'There's been an emergency,' she told Sarah with artful calm.

'Is everyone okay?' Sarah asked.

'Everyone is safe and well,' Elizabeth said, looking at her phone, seeing seven missed calls from Agata. 'Is it all right if I leave the kids with you for a bit?'

She couldn't look Isla and Hugo in the eye, but she could feel them looking up at her, could feel their searching gazes penetrate right through her. Neither of them ran to her or begged her to stay or demanded to know why she was leaving. The atmosphere at home had been bad enough for them to understand that it would be dangerous to ask. In the midst of real trauma, they knew not to cause trouble. Instinctively they were keeping themselves safe.

*

Agata pressed open the passenger-side window. Elizabeth pressed it up. 'The air-conditioning won't work if the windows are down!' she snapped, stifled by the heat in the car.

'Twenty minutes. You never catch up,' Agata said.

Elizabeth dialled Jude's number on the car phone. As they waited for him to pick up, she asked Agata, 'Where is Heather?'

Agata shook her head. 'I not know.'

Jude's line rang and rang. They tried again, with no luck.

'I don't have time to drop you off. You're going to have to walk back from the high street. Okay? You have to stay at home and keep me informed about what's going on at the house.'

'I get the bus,' Agata said.

'Good,' Elizabeth said, speeding up.

But nothing was good. Fear gripped her ribcage, squeezing the air out as she thought of the quickest route to the lock-up. She had to make it there before Lucas and Gordon. It was possible. Yes, it was possible. She prayed that her route through Roehampton would be better than theirs via Putney High Street – the way he always went. She hoped they would get lost – just as she and Heather had – around the complicated industrial estate. And she knew that her BMW was faster than their trundling old van.

She was ten minutes away, and her heart was pounding. As she ran a red light and overtook an indicating bus, Jude finally called back.

'Hi, sis,' he said.

'Jude. Is it possible to call the lock-up company and tell them to disable the keypad to stop anyone gaining entry?'

'What's going on?'

'I haven't got time to explain. Can you do it?'

'I'll try, and call you back.'

Red light after red light thwarted her journey, but the lunch-time traffic had not been heavy and she had made exceptional time, as though the gods were looking down on her favourably. She was five minutes away. Five-minute journeys in London could turn into half-hour gridlock. She took nothing for granted. But each clear road made her heart sing.

When she pulled around the final corner into the industrial estate, her jaw locked as she braced herself for seeing Gordon's white van parked outside the storage unit. She punched the air when she saw that the car park was almost empty. A hire van and a saloon car were the only two vehicles there.

As she ran past the lock-up doors, Jude called her back.

'They can disable it, but it'll take a day.'

'That's too long.'

'Tell me what's going on.'

'Lucas has found out where they are. I can't let him get hold of them. Can you get here?'

'I'm in Shoreditch. I'll jump in a cab now.'

'Shit. You're too far away.' She typed in the code and pushed up the corrugated door, closing it quickly behind her. She wondered what she was going to do when Lucas and Gordon arrived. How would she stop them from taking the paintings? How would she transport the canvases in the BMW? She hadn't thought anything through. Unable to hide her panic from her brother any longer, she said, with tears in her voice, 'What can I do? How can I stop them?'

Jude answered her with a plan that sucked her tears back.

At that moment, she heard Gordon and Lucas's voices.

'I can't do that, Jude,' she whispered.

The voices were getting louder as they moved down the corridor.

'Yes you can. Trust me, okay? Trust me.'

And she decided, with all her heart, to trust her little brother. She had no choice.

Outside the door, she heard the keypad. *Beep* – one digit. She searched the lock-up, scrabbling in the first box she saw to find a tool for the job, but it was stacked with Jude's books. *Beep* – two digits. Another box, full of IKEA pots and pans from his first flat. *Beep* – three digits. The third box, full of crockery. *Beep. Beep. Beep. Beep.* Then muffled swearing, before they started again. They'd typed it in wrong. More time. She found a set of glasses, took one and smashed it against the wall. With an old teacloth wrapped around its base, she held the sharp shard poised close to the canvases – specifically the right-hand corner of *Blue No. 3.*

Beep. Beep. Six digits, then one more. The metal door thundered up.

'Take one more step towards them and I'll destroy them,' she said.

Gordon stayed where he was. Lucas moved forward, his eyes trained on her weapon.

'I'm warning you, Lucas.'

She ripped open one corner of the wrapping, where Jude had suggested.

'You wouldn't dare.'

'This will all be over if you return Agata and Piotr's documents.'

'I will not do that.'

And with those words, she pulled the shard of broken glass down through the choppy seascape, leaving a long, straight slice across the canvas.

'Give those documents back,' she said, her voice cracking, her body convulsing, 'and I'll get Jude to patch it up for you. The Seacarts need never find out. Their condition report already cites damage in this area. This second tear will disappear if Jude's hand is the one to repair it.'

Venom and savagery destroyed Lucas's pretty face as he lunged at her.

Through a blur of terror, Elizabeth lost her head. Literally lost her thoughts and her hearing and her sight. In seconds, her consciousness began slipping away. Was there something around her throat? She flopped back, too weak to fight.

Gordon's arms were around her. 'Lucas!' he bellowed. 'Mrs Huxley, are you okay?'

'*Why*, Elizabeth?' Lucas was crying, heaving sobs, like a boy. '*Why?*' he yelled.

There was a feeling of release at her neck, and Gordon said, 'Get out of here, Lucas.'

His step faltered at the door and he turned back to look at the gash in the sea. It had been Elizabeth's hand that had sliced through Jude's beautiful brushstrokes, but it had been Lucas who had guided it.

Elizabeth ran to her car and locked the door, watching in her rear-view mirror as Gordon led Lucas towards the van.

There was nothing he could do to her now. She had finally outsmarted him. Jude was the only person in the world who could fix the tear and reproduce those brushstrokes without devaluing the paintings further and delaying the deal.

She wasn't scared of Lucas's return home. In fact, she would relish it. By then he would have calmed down and worked out that if he hurt her again, not only would Jude not fix the paintings, she would make sure he denied them, called them out as fakes. The triumph lifted her soul. She felt weightless, as though she were flying through the air above the motorway, safe from the earth's petty threats.

CHAPTER THIRTY-ONE

I bent hesitantly over my parents' bed. The flowery pink duvet was pulled high up over my father's head. The bristles of his face were squashed into the pillow. The cotton was pretty and bright next to his ravaged skin.

'Do you think you might be able to get up for some breakfast now, Dad?' I asked quietly.

'I need to sleep,' he growled, and turned away from me. The mound of his body under the duvet was large and indeterminate. Even in bed, the power of him scared me. I took a step back, almost expecting him to throw back the duvet and leap up at me.

'Mum says breakfast is on the table.'

I had been instructed by Mum to be gentle but firm. I didn't feel firm.

'I'm too tired.'

I sat down on the bed and waited.

'Dad, what happened yesterday?'

He was still and unresponsive. He could have been asleep again. I felt my heart speed up as I waited for his response. Nerves fluttered through my stomach. I had sent a text to Lucas yesterday:

Just checking everything at the lock-up was okay. I hope I remembered the code correctly? H x

There had been no reply. I had regretted sending it.

'Did Lucas get the paintings back?'

'Get out!' my father yelled.

The force of his anger propelled me off the bed and I backed out of the room.

In the kitchen, I found Mum pouring boiling water into a cup without a tea bag.

'Want one?'

I dropped a bag into the cup. 'Might need one of these, Mum.'

She didn't smile. 'He won't get up, will he?' she said, dunking the tea bag over and over. I followed her as she drifted out of the kitchen and into the sitting room, sagging into an armchair. The under-eye circles showed through her make-up like dark paint under a wash of white.

I sat down next to her. 'No.'

'I can't miss my train,' she said, staring at the mantel clock as though challenging its relentless momentum. I didn't want her to leave for Scotland.

'Don't worry, Mum. I'll deal with him.'

'He has to go in today.'

'Would one day off matter?'

'Absolutely, yes, it would matter.'

'Why? Because of yesterday?' I asked. My curiosity felt like a crawling creature inside me scratching for answers.

There was a long silence. She held the tea in front of her, poised to drink it, but she didn't put it to her lips. 'How did you get mixed up in all this? What were you *thinking*?' she asked.

'I told you, Elizabeth threatened me. She said she'd fire me, and you and Dad, if I didn't help her take them. I didn't know what else to do.'

She laughed and shook her head. 'That stupid woman has no power over us.'

Never had I heard her speak with such disrespect about anyone, let alone Elizabeth Huxley, the woman I had believed she admired, wished in another life to be like.

'You know what happened, don't you, Mum?'

She slammed the mug onto the coffee table, 'Your dad did nothing but try to help.'

'Have they fallen out? Lucas and Dad?'

Mum said nothing; tight purple lips. There was no pearly lipstick to soften her face. I saw the lines that crowded around her mouth, spiky and mean in the morning light. 'To fall out, you have to have been friends in the first place,' she said with a strange smile.

Unsettled, I said, 'I'm sure they'll work it out.'

Her expression hardened. She shot me a look, almost sneering at me. 'You really believe that, don't you?'

'You don't think they can work it out?'

'I think you're distracted by Lucas's handsome face.' Her words blew out of her mouth like a hot odour. The leaking of bad feeling, lying in wait underneath her meekness, underneath her agreeable, wholesome nature.

'It's not like that,' I said.

'What is it like?'

'I like him, Mum,' I admitted, hoping this would appeal to her, hoping her softness would return.

'Well, you mustn't.'

'I know it's complicated with Elizabeth.'

'You think Elizabeth is the problem?' she laughed.

'I know she is. She's totally crazy.'

'Ha!'

My father had got to her. She would not be behaving like this if he hadn't. 'You think I'm not good enough for him? Is that it?'

'You're *too* good for him, you silly child.'

I stood up. 'I'm not a *child*.'

She picked her tea up and swallowed a mouthful. 'You're happy to split up a family, are you?'

'They're not happy together.'

'Who told you that? Him?'

After all the years of reverence, I was astounded by her distaste. After all the years of her aspirations for me, she was now pulling back, U-turning. Perhaps it was the prospect of me being with him that somehow diminished him in her eyes, ruined the fantasy she had enjoyed.

'Nothing will happen between us unless it is over between them,' I stated calmly.

'Nothing will *ever* happen between you two if I have anything to do with it!'

'This is about Dad, isn't it?'

My mother would do anything to pacify my father's temper. Say anything to keep him happy, to make home life easier. My father's power had grown and his word had become gospel. When I looked at my mother now, I thought she looked wrapped up, as though cellophane had been wound around her face. I wanted to rip it off her and allow her to breathe, but I knew she would just bind her head again herself. She and my father shared a perverse co-dependence, a warped sense of neediness: he needed her, and she needed to be needed; her needs were subsumed by his. Always second in line, she could not live a day without contemplating his contentment first. If he was unhappy, she could not locate her own happiness. If he was sad, she was too. But their love, albeit unhealthy, ran deeper than the more prosaic, run-of-the-mill bonds of mutual respect and equality that the majority of people shared.

'It's not about Elizabeth or your dad or the kids or me! It's about Lucas,' she shouted.

'You think he's not serious about me?' My voice was small.

The bitter edge to her face melted away. 'I think he is probably very serious about you. Lucas is all-or-nothing. There is no in-between.'

My mind dived into a warm Mediterranean Sea, where the sun lit up the bubbles around each stroke, turning them silvery, as though I had magic cascading from my fingertips.

'Why are you so against it, then?'

She stood up and walked to the window, twitching the curtains to look outside, as though someone out there might be listening. 'Your father has debts,' she said.

'What kind of debts?'

'He owes Lucas money.'

A surge of blood rushed to my head; my face felt burning hot and my extremities freezing cold. 'How much?'

'He used to like a flutter in the betting shops. Not like an addiction or anything, but he got himself into trouble, just once.'

'What kind of trouble?' I asked, baffled by the idea that my father had been anything but sensible with his money.

'We lost our van, and we didn't have the money to replace it.'

I was stunned. All my life I had presumed they had always been thrifty and cautious, and self-righteous.

'And Lucas lent him the money?'

'He did. Yes.'

I swallowed hard. 'That was good of him.'

My mother let out a snort. 'Good?' She dropped the curtain and stared at me, agog. 'This was ten years ago, and we're still paying it off.'

Clutching at Lucas's goodness, I asked, 'Because you only pay back small amounts?'

'Because of interest. That old van out there,' she said, pointing, 'has cost us sixty-two thousand pounds.'

'That's not true.' I had heard her but I couldn't absorb it.

'I'm afraid it is.'

My mother had never lied to me, and yet here she was, lying to me. 'You're saying this to put me off him.'

'I wish that were the case, love.'

My father appeared in the doorway, tall and forbidding. 'What are you telling her, Sally?'

'Nothing.'

'She doesn't need to know.'

I stood up. 'Stop talking about me as though I'm not here!' I yelled.

'We thought we were doing the right thing,' he said.

My mother said sharply, '*Gordon.*' There was warning in it, but he didn't seem to hear her. His pupils were large. His stare was edgy, trained on me.

'They were supposed to have a good life at the Huxleys',' he said.

Who was 'they'? I wondered. We were at cross purposes. I looked at my mother, her face ghostly white, her lips hanging open as though she had done something terrible and was waiting for my admonishment. She reverted to what we had been talking about before, leaving my father's babbling – sleep talk or Nurofen-addled – hanging in the air, waiting for it to dissipate into nothingness.

'Why would he charge so much interest on a loan? He's totally loaded.'

My mother answered. 'That's the thing. He's broke. Lord only knows how he's hidden it from Walter Seacart. We probably have more money than him. Or we would have, if we weren't paying him half our salary every month.'

'Half your salary?' I spluttered. I didn't want it to be true. It couldn't be true.

'At least we have *half*,' my father said, sitting down.

'What are you talking about? You're not making any sense, Dad,' I said tearfully.

That was when he told me another of their tales from the soup kitchen. This time, it involved a young, aspirational Polish couple who had been lured to England by a recruitment firm with promises of good jobs and a better life. Foot soldiers had guarded them in a cramped, overcrowded dwelling in London, where they had been beaten and starved and saddled with debts. It was the story of Agata and Piotr.

'And you helped them?' I said, wiping my eyes.

'We thought we were helping them,' my mother said.

'I told Lucas about them and he said he'd give them jobs,' my father added.

'Which he did,' I said.

'Yes, he did,' Dad confirmed. 'But he won't give them their weekly pay packets.'

My mother closed her eyes and turned her face up to the ceiling, as though wanting cool rain to fall on her and wash it all away. She said, 'On Sunday, Lucas called and asked me to drop round, to see if I could get some information out of Elizabeth about the paintings.' She sighed. 'She gave nothing away on that front, but she told me other things. She was distressed, and talking so fast, I could hardly keep up.'

'What did she say?'

'She told me that Lucas visits the camper van at night when Piotr is away in London.'

Acid saliva pooled under my tongue.

'You think that's true?'

'He's always had an eye for young pretty girls.'

'How do you know that?'

'We've seen more than you can imagine over the years.'

'I need …' I said, tripping over my feet in my haste to get to the toilet, where I found tissues to wipe my mouth as I stared into the eyes that stared back at me from the mirror. A stranger's eyes.

When I returned, my parents were both sitting in exactly the same positions. My father was hunched over his knees. My mother was upright, rod-straight, staring ahead of her.

'I'm so sorry, but it's really hard for me to take in,' I said. I hovered, unwilling to sit down with them again.

My father's words tumbled from him as he looked up at me. 'We never wanted you back here. We wanted you to stay away from us forever. But when Aunt Maggie fell ill, you were the only one Lucas would accept as a replacement, or he wouldn't have let your mum go to help your auntie. And we truly believed you could serve your six months and get out without ever finding out what was going on.'

My mother let out a sob, and then inhaled, holding it at bay. 'We wanted to keep you safe.'

'We never thought this would happen. We never dreamt it would happen. But how stupid we were! Look at you! You're beautiful and full of life, and I've been such a terrible father. How could he not fall in love with you?' Dad spluttered.

I began to cry. 'Don't say that, Dad.'

'You never deserved this,' he said.

'You deserve better,' Lucas said.

My wrist was stinging from where my father had twisted it away from my rucksack, packed with my swimsuit and towel. He had told me I wasn't allowed to go to Amy's tonight. He had told me he wanted me to stay in for a change. He had said I was too young at fifteen to go out every night.

Lucas kissed the bracelet of red before touching me between my legs. 'When you're old enough, I'll get you away from him.'

'Okay,' I said, not really wanting to get away from my father, but eager to keep Lucas happy. Confused by the prospect of adulthood, keen that it should remain in the distance. A brain swimming with contradictions. Swimming with Lucas, terrified that he would abandon me if I told him I didn't want to go so fast, wishing we didn't have to keep secrets.

'It'll fly by,' he said, wrapping his arms around me.

'There are boys at school who like me, you know,' I said coyly, grinning over his shoulder. I knew he could feel my smile without looking at it. 'I might not wait,' I added.

He laughed and said, 'If any of them come near you, I'll kill them.'

It'll fly by, he had said. But it had not. He had lied. He had never come back, and our summers had spawned a lifetime of secrets.

'He wasn't just a crush,' I said.

My parents looked at each other before they looked at me.

'What did you say?' my father asked.

'Lucas and I used to meet up.' The words were so hard to say, and I realised it was why I had never said them before.

'When Elizabeth was out?'

'No. Back when I was a … when I was …' I began, but my throat constricted.

'When you were still living at home?' my father rasped.

I spoke falteringly, through tears that heaved from the depths of me. 'All those times you thought … All those times I was at Amy's, I wasn't … I was next door. I was with … Oh God …' I was gasping, trying to pull in more air. 'I was with Lucas. He taught me to swim. He—'

My mother interrupted. 'But Amy's parents moved. She went to sixth form college in Rye. When you were going to Amy's, you were only …' She stopped, as though someone had throttled her.

'I was only fifteen,' I said.

She let out a terrible wail.

'I'll kill him,' my father said, lurching from his chair. 'He's gone too far this time!'

My mother pulled him down by the arm, begging him to stop and think. 'Please, don't go over there, Gordon.'

'He'll pay for what he's done! Let go of me!'

'And then *you*'ll go to prison!'

'I'd go to prison happily if I knew he was dead!' he thundered.

'But then he's won,' she cried, clinging to him as he tried to walk with her dragging behind him.

I watched them in stunned silence, as though viewing the scene from above. Through their eyes, I had not been in an equal relationship with Lucas. He had been a twenty-five-year-old man and I had been a child. A child whom he had enticed into having sex.

'Dad. Stop,' I said.

And he did. Obeying me for the first time in his life.

'This isn't helping,' I told him, which was not entirely true. Seeing his protective rage was gratifying, as though it were the natural order of things, setting everything right inside me, and I couldn't bring myself to tell them the full story, to tell them that I was to blame too.

He dropped his large frame into the chair and began to cry. 'I'm so sorry,' he said, over and over.

'It's not your fault, Dad. I'm the one who's caused all this.' I wiped my face with the sleeve of my fleece, trying to stem the tears that kept falling.

'You were a child!' he said.

Mum spoke. 'You were supposed to have got away. We wanted you to find your own way in life.'

'But Dad's always made me feel guilty for it.'

'There was a time when I wanted you to follow in our footsteps,' he said. 'But then we found out what Lucas was really like.' He paused, then added, 'You must know how proud we've been.' He let out a choked-up laugh, then broke down again.

Seeing his distress was unbearable.

My mother began to mutter, wringing her hands. 'Now you're trapped in this job.'

'But we can't go back there!' I cried.

'If we leave, Dad says Lucas will go to the police about you taking those paintings,' she said.

'Agata and Piotr are on our side. They'd tell the police the truth,' I said.

My father rubbed his face dry and cleared his throat. 'Piotr believes we recruited them knowing what Lucas would do. They think we're part of the trafficking ring that brought them to England. They don't trust anyone except each other. And I don't blame them.'

'So,' my mother continued, in a pragmatic tone, 'if we don't go to prison for procuring Agata and Piotr, you'd go down for theft.'

'No,' I said. '*No*.'

She rose, slowly, and wiped her hands down her trousers.

'You're going to be late if you don't leave soon,' she said. 'I'll call you from Aunt Maggie's.'

It was only then that the true horror of what we now had to go through dawned on me. My father would have to take orders from a man who'd had sex with his fifteen-year-old daughter. I, too, had my own conflicts. The man I had been secretly in love with for most of my life had been transformed into a man I did not recognise.

'What did I do wrong?' I asked Lucas after a failed tumble-turn. I sculled in the water waiting for his instruction.

'I don't know,' he said.

'What?' I laughed.

'I can't teach you any more.'

'Why not?'

'I've got a job.'

'Where?'

'In the City.'

Illogically, I tried to stand, my toes scrabbling for the bottom. 'You're moving to London?'

'Yes,' he said.

I swam away from him, fast and efficient, my stroke honed after a long, happy summer in the pool, now over. I couldn't believe it.

'I knew you'd be upset,' he said, pulling himself out of the water and sitting on the side.

Upset? I thought I might bleed on the outside from a broken heart. 'No, it's cool,' I said.

'I'll drop a note through your door when I'm next home.'

'Okay,' I said, my voice quavering, betraying my feelings.

'Promise,' he said.

'Promise, promise?' I laughed.

'Cross my heart, hope to die.'

And he made a sign over his heart, where water rolled down his skin like tears.

My belief that the note would appear had never wavered. The following year, I had pounced on news that I thought explained its absence, convinced it was why he had broken his promise to me. The female head of mergers and acquisitions at the German bank he worked for had faced an employment tribunal following Lucas's accusations of sexual discrimination and bullying. The story had made the newspapers. His whistle-blowing had uncovered a back catalogue of employment abuses in the firm, and many other victims had come forward. When the story broke, my mother had overheard Mr Huxley Senior talking to his wife – Mum had been weeding by an open window – about how much money Lucas had won in damages and how he was coming home to set up a property investments company. Lucas and I had taken up where we had left off, as though no time had passed between us. We had grabbed moments whenever we could, meeting in secret, swimming together, dropping the pretence of lessons. He called me his 'stress-buster' when the teething problems of building his property portfolio threatened to overwhelm him.

Now, it seemed our summers and weekends and evenings spent by the pool together had been a sham. My parents' information had capsized him, revealing the barnacled, slimy underbelly that slid beneath the surface. He had played on my naïvety and my hero-worship, pretending the rest didn't matter. He had used me and lied to me, and I had no idea how I would cope when I saw him later.

CHAPTER THIRTY-TWO

It was 10 a.m. Elizabeth had not seen Lucas since the incident at the lock-up yesterday. He had failed to come home last night, and Gordon and Heather had still not turned up. She should have tried to enjoy the peace, the respite; should have had a leisurely morning. Drunk two coffees at breakfast, read the newspaper online, reclined on the sofa, twiddled her thumbs. Not this morning. This morning she checked her watch too often, prowled the kitchen while Isla and Hugo watched cartoons and ate their breakfast.

'I'm bored,' Isla said, ripping off her headphones and discarding her iPad. 'Me too,' Hugo said, copying his sister.

Of all times to get bored on their iPads!

'Neither of you has finished your croissant.'

The children hadn't noticed their father's absence, so disengaged were they from him and his disinterest. But Elizabeth had been awake all night, resisting the urge to call him. His well-being and whereabouts hadn't bothered her; she had simply wanted to get the exchange done, get Agata and Piotr out. She feared every minute of the delay, wondering what he was plotting, whether there was a loophole she hadn't considered.

'What are we going to do today?' Isla whined.

'What about some tennis?' Elizabeth suggested, knowing they couldn't leave the house.

'Boring.'

'How about a swim?'

'Agata said she's too busy.'

Elizabeth had instructed Agata to start packing up the camper van, to be ready to leave at short notice. Jude would be returning the paintings next Wednesday morning, on the day of the Seacarts' arrival. At the latest, Wednesday was to be the day their documents would be returned to them, the day of their liberation. Exactly seven days away.

'I'll go swimming with you,' Elizabeth said.

'Really?' Isla jumped down from her stool and threw herself at her.

'Yeah!' Hugo cried, shoving the end of his croissant into his mouth.

The weather wasn't ideal for swimming. A light rain pattered on the water's surface. Hugo's blonde curls lifted as he ran at the pool and bombed in, sending half the water onto the side.

'No splashing!' Elizabeth said, wading in, not wanting to get her hair wet, not wanting to get wet at all.

Isla slipped in and grabbed her legs.

'Don't do that! You frightened the life out of me!' Elizabeth shouted, overreacting, too tense to be playful.

Gingerly she began to swim breaststroke to the other end. It was warmer inside the pool than outside. Hugo jumped in again, sending a wave of water over her head. A flop of hair covered her eyes and she heard Hugo and Isla burst out laughing. Their mirth untwisted the tension from her heart.

'You rascals!' she said, bobbing underwater to tug at Hugo's toes, pretending to be a shark. Instinctively he pulled his knees to his chest. She surfaced to his giggles and he clipped his arms around her neck. His slippery, skinny little body reminded her of when she had held him as a baby in the shallow, tepid baths she had run for him. She remembered how fragile he was, how ill-equipped she had felt to be in charge of him.

'Come here, you,' she said to Isla. 'Group hug.'

Isla hurtled over to them in a splashy front crawl. Goggles on, she wrapped her arms around both of them and sat on Elizabeth's lap under the water. Her blonde tresses were tangled into brown clumps, and she looked younger somehow.

'I'm going to start doing this with you more often, okay?'

'Okay,' Isla said.

Hugo stroked her hair. 'You're so pretty, Mummy.'

'You two are the pretty ones,' she said, kissing them some more.

'I'm not pretty, I'm a boy!'

Isla and Elizabeth laughed at him.

'How about some handstands?' Elizabeth suggested.

The handstands turned into a synchronised swimming routine that Isla was in charge of. Elizabeth had so much water up her nose and in her ears, she didn't hear the gate open.

'Room for one more?' Lucas said, throwing his towel onto a sunlounger.

'Daddy!' the children cried in unison. 'Do a bomb!'

Elizabeth began swimming to the side. 'Come on, you two. Time to get out. It's a bit rainy now.' Her instructions were ignored. Lucas performed a perfect racing dive, skimming the surface, shooting towards the other end like a missile.

Hugo pulled himself out and tried to copy his father. He dived in too deep and his legs flopped about.

Isla watched from the side, her feet dangling. 'I want to dive, but I can't.'

'I'll teach you now,' Lucas said.

Elizabeth climbed out and covered herself with her towel. The uncontrollable shivers that had broken out across her flesh were not from the cold.

'Where have you been?' she asked.

'Bend like a banana,' he said to Isla. 'And tip yourself in.'

Isla flew like a fruit bat and landed flat on her stomach.

'At the club,' he replied casually, slipping into the water. He held two plastic floats on the surface, leaving a space in the middle. 'Dive in between these.'

She stepped off the side, jumping in instead, coming to the surface. 'I can't.' She was kicking her legs to stay afloat, her little face barely out of the water, her purple goggles tight around her head.

'Yes you can,' he said. 'Come on. Again.'

'My tummy hurts,' she said.

'Like this,' Hugo said smugly, diving in again with even less finesse than before.

'That was rubbish!' Isla screamed at him.

'Come on, sweetheart, you mustn't give up,' Lucas said.

Isla's chin wobbled as she held her arms above her head. Again she belly-flopped. Elizabeth imagined her purple goggles filling up with salty tears. She blinked and blinked, as though clearing her daughter's tears away for her. But as her sight cleared, she saw Lucas holding his large hand over Isla's little head, dunking her under. Her legs and arms flailed and Elizabeth's mind was wiped by a white flash of horror.

'What the hell are you doing?' she screeched, running, flying into the water, yanking his hand off Isla, who squirmed to the surface. 'Are you fucking insane?'

'Just having a bit of fun,' Lucas said. 'Weren't we, Isla?'

'Yes, Daddy!' She coughed up some water.

'A little party trick I picked up at school.'

Elizabeth lifted Isla onto the side and yelled in her face, as though she were the one who had tried to drown herself, 'Grab a towel and go inside *now!*'

Isla began to whimper, but she did as she was told.

Before Elizabeth could gather herself, she sensed that the pool was quieter and the water stiller. *Hugo.*

She swivelled around and saw only Lucas's head above the surface. A sickening panic surged through her, and she screamed Hugo's name, bobbing under to look for him, choking on chlorine.

'He's swimming a length underwater,' Lucas said. His eyes were bluer than the water. She realised she had drowned in them many years ago; dead.

A murky shape moved towards the shallow end, and seconds later, Hugo popped up. 'I did it!' he gasped.

'Well done, son,' Lucas said.

'Get out of the pool!' Elizabeth screamed, swimming towards Hugo before Lucas could get to him. 'Get out!'

'What's wrong, Mummy?'

Lucas said, 'You're scaring him.'

She thought fast. 'There was lightning,' she told Hugo. 'It's dangerous to be in the water. It conducts electricity, remember?'

Hugo scrambled out onto the side and stared down at his parents, chin dripping. He frowned up at the white sky, then down at them again. 'You have to get out too, Mummy. And Daddy!'

Elizabeth waded up the steps. 'Don't worry, I'm getting out now. Here's your towel and your glasses; off you go, into the house, please. It was a silly idea of Mummy's to swim today.'

As soon as Hugo had scampered through the gate, Lucas shot out of the pool and blocked Elizabeth's path. Holding her by the upper arms, he said, 'Don't go.'

She twisted her face as far away from him as possible, from the smell of his sweet breath and his unfamiliar aftershave.

'You understand what that deal means to me. You can't forget that. You mustn't forget. Not now, not when we're so close.' He continued urgently, as though their lives depended on the information he was imparting. 'Agata and Piotr can't leave. You know that and they know it.'

She squeezed her eyes shut and clamped her lips together, wishing she could close her ears. If she looked at him and spoke her mind, she would say the wrong thing and put her children in danger. She nodded instead, waiting for her rage to subside.

'Nobody believed I would be able to pull this deal off with Walt Seacart. *The* Walt Seacart. I've been a laughing stock in the City,' he said. 'All those pricks with their trust funds are so fucking superior. Working there was like being back at Winslow House. None of them had any faith in me.'

Through her fear, she wasn't sure whether he was actually kissing her closed lips and eyelids, her ear lobes where the diamonds he'd given her were pinned, or whether she was imagining a time when he had, when he'd loved her, before their money had changed them.

He murmured, 'After next week, nobody will be able to dismiss me. You understand that, don't you? I know you understand that.'

She remained silent and rigid in his embrace until she finally trusted herself to speak.

'I'll call Jude now and get the painting fixed,' she said.

He squeezed his arms tightly around her and exhaled over her shoulder. 'I'll always love you, you know that, don't you?' he said, but she detected sympathy in his voice.

Jude heaved the warehouse doors open to reveal his studio. Streams of sunlight poured in and turned to dust as they bounced off the encrusted jam jars and paint pots and rags, and the flotsam of household goods: dismembered chair legs, stacks of bathroom tiles, an iron bath, a pile of old clothes. Parked in the middle of the space – it was too big to call a room – in a clearing that seemed temporary rather than stage-like, was his easel.

'You need a cleaner,' Elizabeth said.

Settling down on a chair that looked like it might stain her trousers, she looked around for a place to put her handbag. There was nowhere. She kept it on her lap. She sneezed.

He laughed, at her comment, she hoped, then clicked on the kettle and peered into a mug, wiping the inside with his fingers.

'I feel more relaxed in mess,' he said.

The clutter was solid, ingrained, part of the fabric of her brother's working life, as though he had made peace with the chaos of his thoughts, made friends with the uglier, pre-loved facets of his own being. Each strange item, some unidentifiable, looked like it might serve some kind of purpose to him at some point, collected randomly, like treasure found in the gutter. She imagined that it all somehow contributed to the beauty of his work.

He only made one cup of tea, for her. As soon as he had poured the milk, he picked his way to the clearing and pulled the damaged painting onto his easel.

'Can it be fixed?' she asked, holding her breath.

She noticed a familiar photograph Blu Tacked to the wall near the kettle, tucked in between other photographs and various postcards. It was of the two of them lying on a pebbled beach, sheltered by a stripy windbreak, fully clothed in coats and wellies and sunglasses, pretending to sunbathe as the late April wind howled around them. His black hair was wild, obscuring his laughing face, and her blonde curls whipped around her head. It had been her birthday and she had been happy. On that beach, chilly and wishing for sunshine, she hadn't realised how lucky she had been and how soon her fortunes would change. That same summer, she had met Lucas.

'Hmm,' he said, running his fingers across the back of the hole. 'The glass left nicks in the canvas. Makes it a bit tricky.'

'Oh God,' she said. Without meaning to, she let go of her handbag. It slid off her lap and onto the floor, scattering its contents at her feet. She stepped over them and joined Jude. 'Have I made everything worse?'

'Don't despair. It's in exactly the right part of the painting. When are Lucas's people collecting them?'

'He wants them back at Copper Lodge by Wednesday latest. The Seacarts are coming that evening.'

'Should be okay.'

'They'll not notice, will they?'

'No. Not when I'm done with it.'

'They made such a fuss about the damage before.'

'Lucas was right to come clean about that. They'll trust you now.'

'All this for nothing,' she said. Her stomach seized up and her shoulders rounded over the cramping pain.

'Are you okay?' Jude said, noticing her flinch. 'Sit down.'

He stood to let her sit on his stool. Her toes were a few inches off the floor and the seat swivelled. He put a hand on each of her thighs, steadying her.

'You can't give up now.'

'He always wins.'

'Not if you let him. Not if you *leave* him,' he said.

Elizabeth indulged in the fantasy. 'How would I leave him?' she asked.

'There are lawyers you can go to.'

None expensive enough to win against Lucas, she thought.

'You'd get custody and a good settlement,' he continued.

I'm an unfit mother, she thought.

'You could rent a lovely flat, around here maybe. Find yourself a job. Get the kids into the local school. Make some friends. Go to Beigel Bake every day.'

He would find us, she thought.

He wiped a tear from her cheek. 'It could be a good life, Elizabeth. A better life,' he concluded.

Smoke and mirrors, she thought.

'You *know* you can do this.'

But who would I be? she thought.

'The Elizabeth I grew up with is in there somewhere. *She's* the one you have to find, underneath all his bullshit indoctrination,' he said, answering her thoughts.

In a small voice, she asked him, 'What if she's gone?'

'If she's gone, why were you putting everything on the line to help Agata and Piotr?'

As she sat there feeling like one of the pre-loved curiosities that surrounded them, she tested how it might feel to let go of Lucas and the armour of their wealth. Even thinking of it was frightening, as though a balloon had slipped out of her hands and was up and away into the blue sky. There was a pinch of loss and self-recrimination for letting it go, but also a weightlessness in her soul, a freeing of a tie she had been clinging to for reasons she was no longer sure of. A glimmer of her old self re-emerged, bringing her back down to earth gently but assuredly, as though a bird had the balloon's string in its beak and was pulling it down to safety.

In the studio, the sound of bristles dabbing on canvas was a perfect substitute for absolute silence, for clear thinking. London's traffic and bustle seemed far away. Surrey even further. But as her brother worked with energy and precision, with a concentration and skill she both admired and felt alienated by, fear crept back into her heart, bigger and more frightening than ever. How could she even contemplate the life that Jude had so flippantly put forward for her? How could she explain to him the risks involved in pursuing that simple existence of independence and normality?

Assuming Lucas would let her go without a fight – which was a far-fetched concept on an optimistic day – they would share custody, which was utterly petrifying. The scene in the pool played out again. If she was not there to keep him happy, to stabilise his moods, to catch the emotional fallout of a bad day at work, the next in the firing line would be Isla and Hugo. They would be vulnerable to his obsessive routines, his paranoia, his pathological self-centredness. And when he wasn't there, when he was at work, to whom would he entrust them? She wouldn't sleep at night while a stranger, someone she hadn't vetted, was in charge of them, while *he* was in charge. Finally, she could not guarantee that he would hand them back at the end of his weekend, or week, or whatever the courts had carved out for them. They would be his playthings and he would bash them around like a toddler with a favourite cuddly toy, one minute clutching it for dear life, the next ripping its head off. She would fret every minute of every day that they were in his so-called care.

Any freedom she gained would be rendered meaningless when – not if – he decided he wanted payback for her decision to divorce him.

For now, she knew they were safe across town, sitting next to their grandmother in the darkened auditorium of the cinema, where their faces would be turned up to the screen, lit by the moving pictures, ringlets dangling in Isla's popcorn, cartoons flickering across Hugo's spectacles, below which his mouth would be open in concentration, just like his Uncle Jude now. Miles away, in west London, she knew Lucas was in meetings with his lawyers and Walt's advisers, fine-tuning clauses, with his mind fully switched off from his family. Agata would be at home, preparing supper for the children and dinner for her and Lucas later. Piotr would have made progress on the pool house, and their move into the guest barn would be one day closer. Gordon and Heather would be tending the garden, ensuring Copper Lodge was tamed and beautiful. A working team.

This state of equilibrium for Lucas would function if Elizabeth continued as his wife, the delegated main carer to their children and the gatekeeper to Copper Lodge. As it stood, everything was in its rightful place, just how he had designed it. If she interrupted his plan, changed an iota of their family life, he would become volatile once again. He had too much to lose. For Lucas, it was all or nothing. As he had proved in the pool two days before, which she couldn't think about without a wrench of terror that obscured and mutated the actual memory. Sometimes she implanted Isla's laughter and a game between them, sometimes her crying and their fight; sometimes she saw Isla dead.

Leaving Lucas was inconceivable.

CHAPTER THIRTY-THREE

Agata and I were sitting side by side on the wooden platform that would become the floor of the pool house. I had poured her a cup of black coffee from my flask. The vibrations from Piotr's hammer went up my spine and into my teeth. The sharpness of it kept me alert, readying me for Lucas's inevitable approach.

'Mum and Dad told me everything,' I said.

Agata took a small sip from her cup, without replying.

'Agata, I'm so sorry. I had no idea what was going on.'

My words sounded pathetic. By giving Lucas the location of the paintings, I had prolonged their suffering, and we both knew that my apology couldn't begin to cure it. I went on to explain how I had fallen for Lucas's lies about Elizabeth's poor mental state, and tried to convey the full force of my regret. Then I attempted to exonerate my parents from blame. 'When they met you at the soup kitchen, they really believed Lucas could help you.'

'I understand,' she replied, putting her finger in the way of a procession of ants at our feet. They were carrying crumbs of food many times bigger than their bodies. Instead of going over Agata's finger, they rerouted around it.

'Another cup?' I asked tentatively.

She nodded.

We sipped our drinks and stared at the water in the pool. It was so still, it looked solid, like a block of glass. For the first time ever, I had no desire whatsoever to dive in. Earlier, I had caught a brief glimpse through the hedge of the Huxley family in there together, dive-bombing and splashing each other and laughing as though nothing out of the ordinary had occurred.

I glanced across at Agata. I guessed this was what broken looked like: beyond anger or hope, she knew it would be a waste of energy to exercise a protest or shout me down. She was resigned to her fate, and perhaps Elizabeth was too. After this last effort to hold the paintings hostage – ruined by me – it seemed she had lost her appetite for a fight, just as my parents had become jaded and afraid.

I wondered if I would become as resigned as they were. I supposed I was already heading there. Since my arrival here this morning – a capitulation in itself – I had worked conscientiously, pruning the hydrangeas and mowing the lawn, as I had promised my mother I would. The threat of seeing Lucas loomed large, but he had not sought me out. He would not know that my parents had accused him of holding them and Agata and Piotr in debt bondage, and of coercing Agata into having sex with him. Following my text yesterday, which remained unanswered, he would assume I was still on his side. He wouldn't know I had been restless throughout the night, thinking of ways to get my parents out of their domestic servitude and to express my disgust.

I shuddered at the thought of the Rolex, guessing Agata had been his latest little stress-buster.

As I worked, I imagined Lucas visibly deformed by what I had heard, but of course when I eventually saw him coming towards me, the sun backlighting his tall frame, he possessed the same physical presence as before. His eyes were blue and his hair was golden and his smile was white. The history between us had spanned over half my life. His influence ran deep. The recent negative information was so new it was barely embedded. On first sight of him, gut instinct told me that my parents' accusations had been absurd.

The conflict of emotions fought inside me, thrashing and ducking and reeling and screaming, close to bursting out of my head in one thick, angry, confused sentence. I held it in and wiped my soiled hands on my jeans, down my thighs, as though pushing the fury off my lap. Channelling Agata's dignity, I looked up, straight into his eyes, momentarily caving in, then hardening again, steeling myself for his usual compliments and flattery and kisses.

'I want you to read this,' he said in a flat, businesslike tone, shoving something at me.

It was a blue file with the flap opened, showing a stack of paperwork. On the top was a letter with an NHS hospital header.

'I know your parents have got to you, just as Elizabeth has got to them, but I wanted you to see this. I didn't want to have to share it, for Elizabeth's sake, but I have to now.'

My fingers resumed their task of tugging small weeds from the soil, intent on keeping up my barriers. 'It won't change anything.'

'Read it for yourself. It's all here in black and white.'

'So if I read it, I'd see that Elizabeth is as screwed up as you are. Do you think that makes any difference to Agata and Piotr?'

'Didn't your parents tell you where they would end up again if I let them go? They're so fucking naïve! They have no idea what they could face. I've been on to human rights lawyers and they say their work documents aren't worth the paper they're written on and their passports are fakes. They've seen cases like theirs over and over and it never ends well. The trafficking gangs are ruthless criminals who'll catch up with them here or back in Poland. But Piotr is stubborn. He refuses to believe me. And Elizabeth thinks I'm lying and that the lawyers are lying and she's convinced Agata of it. She's so damn paranoid she doesn't realise I'm just trying to protect them. That's all.'

'Even if that was true, isn't that *their* mistake to make?' I yelled.

'If they went to Poland to visit Piotr's nephew now, they'd end up dead! You think that's what I want? Wouldn't you ground your teenager if you knew he was about to go out and rob someone's house and end up in jail? That's all I'm doing, being cruel to be kind. I don't care if I look like the bad guy, as long as they're safe.'

'What about their money? Dad says you don't pay them.'

'I pay their wages monthly into a bank account I set up for them. But Piotr refuses to have anything to do with it. He says it's controlled by the people he was brought over by.'

'Then how do they live?'

'Piotr gets paid a wage from his construction job in London. They eat here, they don't go out. What do they need money for? What I pay them is effectively savings. Maybe it'll benefit his family back home one day.'

I was running out of questions, finding it hard to dismantle his side of the story.

'What about my parents' loan?'

'Why, what have they said?' he asked cautiously.

'A loan for that van can't have cost as much as sixty-two grand!'

'Sixty-two thousand pounds is half of what your father owed the bookies. I paid a lump sum back to them on his behalf, and he insisted on paying the rest. I have begged him to stop the repayments. A few hundred quid every month is nothing to me. Why would I need that?'

'Why would they lie?'

'You think your dad wants your mum to know how much he fucked up? He's hiding the full extent of the debts from her, don't you see? It's easier for him to lie to both of you and to vilify me. For fuck's sake, Heather, your dad brought me Agata and Piotr in the first place, as a way of making up for all the money he owed me. He said I didn't have to pay them! He used them! I'm sorry to say it, but if anyone's the villain here, it's your father. I'd guarantee he's still gambling.'

'No, no, no,' I said, jumping up and storming away. I couldn't hear any more of his lies.

'Heather!' he called after me.

Why was he going to such lengths to lure me back to him? Nothing would change what had happened between us when I was fifteen. He couldn't lie about that.

When we reached the meadow, I ran out of steam. He grabbed my arm and I swivelled around, yanking myself away from him, hissing, 'Don't you dare take advantage of me again.'

He reeled back, putting one hand flat on the top of his head in utter dismay. 'I know what we did was wrong back then. But I was in love.'

'You knew I was underage!'

'You told me you were sixteen!'

'You should have stopped it when you knew.' But I felt guilty. I regretted not telling my parents that I had lied about my age. When Lucas had found out the truth, he had backed away, but I had been crazed by the loss and begged him to come back.

'There's not a day goes by that I don't regret that. But I knew I would hurt you if I ended it, and I knew I wanted to be with you anyway.' He shook his head. 'I don't know what I'm saying. It was wrong. I should have known better. I should have waited. I'd wait forever.'

'Don't give me that crap. I've heard about what you force Agata to do!'

He shook his head again, as though shaking off a thought, and his frown deepened. 'What the hell are you talking about?'

'Sexual favours?' The words were bitter on my tongue.

'That is a *lie*!' he bellowed. 'I've never laid a finger on that girl! Elizabeth's jealousy is out of control. I can't actually believe what I'm hearing.'

As though his legs had given way, he dropped onto the stone wall, wrapping his arms over his head.

'The way you speak about Elizabeth doesn't add up, Lucas. You forget, I'm here, seeing stuff, hearing stuff. And only today I saw you playing in the pool with her and the kids. All happy families and splashing about. You're not leaving her for me! You're a fantasist!'

His head snapped up and he glared at me. '*She's* the fantasist! She's deluded. She sees things that don't happen! And I'll do or say anything to keep her happy so the kids are safe. *Anything!* What choice do I have? One minute I'm playing a game with Isla and the next she's accusing me of trying to kill her! Look what she did to those paintings. They're her brother's paintings and she cut through his work with a piece of glass, on purpose. Who the fuck does that?'

'Stop! STOP TALKING!' I clamped my hands over my ears.

'You don't have to listen to me, you just have to read this. It says everything you need to know, written by an independent expert in the field of psychiatry. Look at all the letters after his name, for Christ's sake! Do you think *he's* making it up too?'

He backed away and left the papers on the wall. 'Read them, that's all I ask.'

They fluttered off the wall and into the breeze, landing around my feet. If I left them there, at the mercy of the weather, they might blow away. I considered letting them go, making up my mind without having to read them.

'What if I let them fly away?'

He shrugged. 'I don't need them to prove my wife is ill. I live with her every day. All I'll say is this, that after this Seacart deal is closed, I'm going to divorce her. Earlier this year I begged the authorities to keep the kids in her custody, promising that we would consider boarding school to make sure Isla was protected from any further episodes, but I can't do it any more. I can't fight for her any more. I want out. I want more for them. Is that so wrong?'

His voice cracked and I thought he might cry. Instead, he turned and jogged away. My instinct was to run after him and comfort him, until I remembered my parents' warnings, Agata and Piotr's unhappiness, Elizabeth's desperation, and my own memories. None of that made sense in the face of his tears. Or did it?

When I thought about it, I surmised that my parents' information had come from Elizabeth, and from Agata and Piotr. With that in mind, I raked over the last few weeks, re-analysing events.

Had I myself not questioned Elizabeth's sanity on the day she had turned up in Rye with an envelope of money? Had I not seen the craziness dancing in her eyes on the night we had stolen the paintings? Had I not been slapped by her? Was her point of view to be trusted?

Even earlier today, I'd wondered if I had misunderstood Agata's low mood. I had assumed she had been resigned and depressed about their entrapment at Copper Lodge, but it was equally plausible that she had been wrestling with Lucas's information about their forged documents, unsure who to trust. The language barrier between us had made communication spare and open to interpretation. In the light of Lucas's information, I could imprint a different theory onto both Agata and Piotr's behaviour: disbelief and denial perhaps. Having discovered that they had been duped, Piotr might feel responsible and guilty and Agata quiet and resentful. Piotr's non-stop hard work on the pool house could be a self-imposed punishment rather than a manifestation of sub-servience and fear; a show of stubbornness perhaps, as he blamed himself for the situation they had found themselves in, too proud to accept that Lucas was right, too humiliated to accept his help.

Before I had even read a word of the file on my lap now, I realised that Lucas's story held up. Believing him meant dismantling much of what my father had told me. It meant that Dad was covering up far more than I dared think about. It meant he had lied to my mother about his gambling debts and had hidden behind the saintliness of the Salvation Army to recruit vulnerable adults for his own gain. My head and heart ached; it suddenly seemed easier to demonise Lucas than to believe that my own father was a bad human being. He was my flesh and blood. He was the man who had shaped me. The man my mother worshipped.

As I stared at the escaping pages, I reminded myself that the truth was more important than misplaced loyalty. I had to find out who was lying to me and who was genuine. Regardless of blood ties, loyalty should be earned.

Quickly I gathered the loose papers, then I sat on the wall that I had sat on with my father every lunch break, and read the contents of the blue file.

CHAPTER THIRTY-FOUR

She said goodbye to Lucas and hung up the phone, unable to believe what she had heard. In the searing heat, her mind might have been playing tricks on her. She flapped her shirt, trying to cool herself down, and considered calling him back to double-check, to reconfirm that finally, after years of waiting, Huxley Property was now officially merged with Seacart Capital Management to create Seacart–Huxley Investments.

It meant they were likely to become multimillionaires in the next few years; rich beyond their wildest dreams. It meant they could have anything they had ever wanted. For a fleeting moment, admiration for Lucas tweaked at her heartstrings as she remembered how bowled over she had once been by his charisma and ambition. His potential had been almost visible, like an aura around him. Everything he touched had turned to gold. Agata, Piotr, Heather and Elizabeth herself had been incapacitated and possessed by him; his Midas touch a curse rather than a blessing.

She reflected on Heather's future. What Elizabeth had planned for everyone tonight would inevitably send Lucas running into her arms. But it couldn't be helped. Heather's trust and naïvety reminded her of her own. It might take her years to fully comprehend that she was trapped.

Barefoot, wearing the lightest dress she could find, she ran down the garden to the pool house site to ask Piotr for a hammer and some nails. She was going to fix up the garlands on the beam above the dining room table for tonight's dinner party with the Seacarts.

Her whole body jolted to a stop, stunned by the sight of Gordon snatching a thick envelope from Piotr. The exchange was followed by angry words. In response, Piotr hung his head. Anger rose in her. It seemed Gordon had adopted the role of Lucas's foot soldier.

She cleared her throat, making herself known.

'Give that back,' she said, feeling beads of sweat pop onto her top lip and the tip of her nose.

Seeing her, Gordon's sturdy expression collapsed. Piotr took a step back, standing on one of his power tools, losing his footing. He shook his head and held his palms up, fingers splayed. 'No, no.'

'You owe Lucas nothing, Piotr. Gordon, give the money back to him now.'

Gordon fondled the envelope and looked down at her. 'I don't think Lucas would like that.'

Even as the sun beat down on her head, Elizabeth experienced a shiver up her spine, but she recalled how Gordon had come to her rescue in the lock-up last week. She knew he was only following Lucas's orders to collect Piotr's debts. And, perhaps wisely, he was cautioning her. Lucas's phone call about the deal came to mind. She thought of the dinner party later. Today of all days, none of them needed any trouble. A small incident might ignite Lucas's suspicion, and her own plans for the evening could be compromised. She had to consider the bigger picture.

'Okay,' she conceded.

'Let me know if you need any help with anything today, Mrs Huxley,' Gordon said, before striding off.

Elizabeth gathered herself, feeling the perspiration pool at her lower back. 'Piotr, could I please borrow a hammer and some nails?'

*

As she pinned up her garlands, she processed what she had seen in the pool house. It proved that Lucas was still taking money from Agata and Piotr, further embedding her certain knowledge that he would never change, that he would never improve their living conditions. Unless she followed through with her plan tonight, they would never be free.

A nail slipped out of her sticky fingers and clanged on the concrete. She wiped her hands on her jeans. The newspapers had predicted record temperatures today, which would work in her favour tonight, but the thick air was tiring now, slowing her down while she prepared the house. She pictured Isla and Hugo holed up in Jude's small London flat, stifled and sweaty, wishing they were at home by their pool.

They would have to get used to having less, she thought. After tonight, everything was going to change for them.

The four of them stood staring at Jude's three oil paintings on the wall. Lucas had insisted they hang them on the oak partition between the bedrooms and the living area, replacing a series of Tracey Emin line drawings that Lucas had bought in a charity auction a few years ago. They took up the space with a magnificent sense of belonging, adding a dimension and depth to the room that Elizabeth hadn't realised was missing.

'I've finally decided which house they're going in,' Bo said, sipping her cocktail of gin and lime and fresh mint, which Agata had prepared with extra ice.

Earlier, they had pulled back the sliding doors, hoping for a breeze, but the wall of hot air outside had collapsed into the cool interior of the house and they had closed them again, hoping to keep the heat out. The reflections of the dozens of candles with which Elizabeth had decorated the room bounced off every surface, setting the blackened windows alight with gold.

'You sure about that, honey?' Walt snorted, rolling his blood-shot eyes at Lucas, who chuckled with his new best friend, taking a larger-than-usual glug of champagne.

'For real,' Bo said. 'It's been a head-fuck, seriously.'

Fighting back the urge to commiserate with Bo for having to wrestle with a decision only a hedge-fund billionaire could relate to, Elizabeth said, 'Bridgehampton?'

'Oh, you guessed already!' Bo cried.

'It's by the beach,' Elizabeth said. 'Where I would have put them.'

When she imagined the paintings on Bo's wall, as disturbed and rousing as the sea that would churn only a few feet beyond where they would hang, she felt a sting of regret. Letting them go was going to be hard.

'Correct! They'll look phenomenal against the whitewash, won't they? You'll just have to come out there next summer to see them. The ocean is as wild as they are.'

'One day you'll want to buy your own beach house there,' Walt drawled. 'The realtors on that strip are *snakes*, but I'll know if a property comes on *before* it goes on, if you catch my drift.'

'I've always dreamed of living by the sea,' Elizabeth said, as something to say, knowing it was what other people wanted. Lucas raised an eyebrow at her. Bo took up the cue and elucidated the pleasures of beach life. Her wittering was peppered by too many swear words – perhaps she thought it brought her down to earth – and a self-conscious confession of how they had sponsored the twin daughters of their Filipino maid for immigration to the USA.

As Elizabeth listened, she placed herself there, in the Hamptons, with Isla and Hugo, a few houses down from Bo, whiling away summers, sandy and salty, reading on a swing seat, drinking fresh lemonade, away from home, maybe even away from Lucas. Swearing too much. Laughing more. Happy. Happier.

She stood next to Bo, with all her wealth and beauty, shoulder to shoulder as an equal, and comprehended that the exclusivity of Bridgehampton was now within their reach. Or perhaps Cap Ferrat in the South of France – the European equivalent of the Hamptons, where the super-rich spent their summers. Before today, she had not wanted more than she had, but now it seemed her desires were ever-evolving, shifting up a notch when presented with a lifestyle change she hadn't previously considered attainable. Within hours of the ink drying on the contracts, she was imagining how the money could work for her, how this new house might solve all their problems.

This line of thought ruffled her, and she wondered whether there was a cap on wanting more, whether there would be a moment when they knew they had everything they needed, or whether, at that point, they would be dead. Dead inside? A spiral of greed that lead to nothingness?

'Excuse me, I'm just going to check on supper.'

The open-plan space did not allow her to talk to Agata alone, but she would have to take her aside and warn her of what was ahead of them.

There was still time.

The brittle flower garlands, weighted by a smattering of shells, hung low over the table centrepiece of dried flowers and reeds. The napkins they had rolled into the rustic burlap napkin rings were made of paper, not linen, breaking one of Elizabeth's key hostess rules. The origami seagulls acting as place cards had wings that flew close to the heat of the fifty jam jars, each decorated with starfish emblems that glowed hot orange. It had taken Elizabeth and Agata twenty minutes to light them, leaving them with burns on their wrists. The overall effect was glorious, fitting; and nobody had noticed how precarious it was. Like tongues, the flame tips of the tea lights flicked hungrily at the centrepiece.

As the potatoes boiled in the pot, Elizabeth seared the halibut and Agata seasoned the dill sauce.

'Go fill up everyone's glasses, Agata,' she said, dissociating from Lucas and their guests' spending sprees, focused on the show she had in mind for them.

When the idea had first come to her, her palms had sweated and her heart rate had picked up. Over the past few days, the minutiae of the pre-planning had smothered her initial anxiety and excitement, too busy with the technicalities to be emotional about the consequences. Now the agitation was rising inside her again, and she worried about how she would conceal her nerves. Wet patches spread in the silk under her arms. Damp tendrils pinged out from her blow-dried hair.

She pictured the line of lit torches leading the way to the pool, where they would end their evening, and hoped the cloud cover would trap the warm air. Even in the height of summer, it was rare for their garden to retain its heat beyond sunset. But tonight, the weather was working in her favour. Still, she had asked Gordon to prepare a fire pit under the tree next to the sunloungers, just in case the temperature dropped.

'Okay, everyone, time to sit down,' she announced.

She instructed Agata to serve them, which she wouldn't usually ask of her, but she couldn't trust her own limbs to respond correctly to the messages from her brain. Plates would be smashed on the concrete, dollops of food would end up on laps, glasses would be knocked over. Her neurological pathways were being short-circuited by the terror that shot through them every time she pictured her plan succeeding.

They sat down.

The talk of New York art shows moved on to the Seacarts' excitement about their son starting at Yale.

'We're so lucky we can pass on our legacy to him. Some can't do that for their kids,' Bo said.

'He must be very bright. To have got in,' Lucas said.

'He does okay,' Walt said, chewing his fish, picking out a bone, adding, 'The new Seacart bursary scheme helped.'

'Walter. That's unfair, honey. Julian's a smart kid.'

'I paid for him to be smart,' he snorted, scraping up the jus on his plate with his dessert spoon and dribbling it onto his forkful of fish before piling it into his mouth.

Bo laid the back of her hands flat either side of her plate and exhaled. 'You're so competitive with him.'

'Competitive? With that couch potato?'

Elizabeth wanted them to simmer down. If the evening turned sour, they might go to bed early. 'Isla's the same. She's capable academically, but her teachers say she's bone idle. Sometimes I think I should throw her into the local school and see how she gets on.'

'We should make it tougher for them, like we had it, right, Elizabeth?' Walt said.

'Right,' Elizabeth agreed, relieved that she had steered him towards a topic she knew he responded well to. At the summer party, she had discovered that Walt had not come from money. He had grown up in a crime-infested neighbourhood in Cleveland, Texas, and his mother's determination to home-school him and keep him off the streets had driven him to succeed. Hearing about Elizabeth's education at a failing London state school – although she had concealed how well educated her mother had been – had fired him up that night.

'Maybe Isla can learn how to tie bullies to wheelie bins,' Lucas laughed, taking the baton.

'What's that?' Bo asked, her interest piqued.

Elizabeth refilled their glasses to the brim. 'He had it coming.'

'A side to you I haven't seen?' Walt asked, winking. 'Go on. I wanna hear this one.'

Enjoying herself suddenly, Elizabeth described her one heroic moment at school. After witnessing one of the skinheads in Year

9 making fun of Jude's dyslexia, she had grabbed the lanky bully by the tie in front of the whole playground, dragged him to the bins and fixed him there. It had felt like a film scene, in which everyone should clap and cheer. Not that anyone had. Her peers had slouched off giving her sideways glances, wary of her gallantry rather than celebrating it.

Walt began sharing stories of his own childhood, some of them funny, some of them heart-wrenching, and the evening was kicked into life. By the time they had scraped the last smears of cream from their pudding cups, they were all drunk and over-sharing. Or at least Lucas, Walter and Bo were.

At the perfect point, before offering coffee, Elizabeth grinned and said, 'I saved some pot from the party. How about a sneaky smoke, a shot of sambuca and a swim?'

Bo's face lit up. 'Let's get this party started!'

Elizabeth flicked Walt a persuasive smile. All evening he had been flirting with her, and she had hoped that the idea of her frolicking half naked and stoned around the pool would be a turn-on.

'You English girls are so *naughty*,' he said, taking a toothpick from his top pocket and inching it between his capped teeth.

Bo clapped. 'All set? I'm so *hot*.'

'I'm up for it,' Lucas said stiffly, plainly not up for it at all, which tickled Elizabeth. His discomfort was only going to get worse.

'You guys get your swimsuits on. I'll bring the drinks down to the pool.'

She nipped down to the camper van and knocked on the door. Agata was awake, ready and waiting for her. Elizabeth explained what was going to happen.

'No, Elizabeth. It is not good. Not good at all.'

'It's the only way.'

'You get in big, big trouble.'

'How? Accidents happen, Agata. I can't be blamed for that.'

'You crazy. You *crazy!*' she repeated. Her hands were squeezing the sides of her head.

Elizabeth was used to being called crazy. It didn't mean anything. Crazy simply meant she thought differently to other people. Perhaps Lucas had driven her beyond normal.

'Just promise me you'll stay away from the house. For your own safety,' she said, unmoved by Agata's remonstrations.

Agata nodded, dropping her hands, realising there was nothing she could do.

Elizabeth returned to the house and headed for the bedroom, where Lucas was changing.

'I really don't feel like a swim,' he grumbled, stumbling as he tried to aim one leg into his trunks. 'I might drown, I'm so drunk.'

'It'll be fun,' she said, locating the Tupperware box in a shoe at the back of her wardrobe. She opened it to check that the vaporiser and the lump of hash were still inside. 'Take that down to Bo. I'll bring the sambuca shots,' she said.

'I hate pot,' he said, taking the box and padding off.

Within a few minutes, there were sounds of shouting and splashing from the pool.

Carefully, so as not to disturb the candles, Elizabeth made room on the dining room table for a tray. She poured the sticky drink into four shot glasses, licking it off her fingers where it had spilt. She would use long matches to light the coffee beans she had dropped into each glass.

Her hands shook. This was the moment of truth. She still had the opportunity to change course: light the drinks, swim with the others, get stoned with them, and buy a house in the Hamptons. That would be the path of least resistance.

The image of Lucas's hand on Isla's head, pushing her under, blocking her airways, was fading; if it disappeared, she would weaken and nothing would change.

She struck the match along the side of the triangular box printed with a strip of 1930s dancing ladies kicking their legs high.

'It's only a bit of fun, Lucas,' she said under her breath.

The first sambuca shot was lit. The blue flame danced about on the liquid's surface. The match burnt down to her fingers. She struck a second and glanced up at her brother's three paintings.

'I'm sorry, little brother,' she said, hoping Jude would understand.

With one last glance around the house that she had built, she held the shot glass under the dried flowers for longer than she should. They caught instantly. She dropped a napkin on top of a cluster of tea lights, then another, watching for a second as the flames took hold. Then she darted off into the toilet behind her, sat on the loo seat and started the timer on her watch. The smell of smoke was already permeating the room. The smoke alarm was not sounding, as she knew it wouldn't, having swapped the batteries. She began to cough. Stubbornly she focused on the timer on her wrist, fearing that five minutes was too long, determined to make sure the fire had taken hold.

When her watch beeped, she opened the door. The handle was already hot. A magnificent bonfire rose above her where the dining table had been. She could see the black shadow outline of the chairs, eaten alive. She held a wet towel to her face and ran to the glass doors, catching sight of the flames crawling along the garland that hung from the beam, all the way to the three paintings on the wall.

She saw the seawater in the pictures sloshing out of the canvases, trying to dampen the fire that had begun charring the top corner of painting No. 3. She laughed at herself, setting off a coughing fit, bursting outside into the garden. Five minutes had almost been too long.

Before she ran down to the pool, she eked out as many minutes as she could bending over her knees, knowing that if she was seen, she would have to look like she was in the throes of a coughing fit. The laurel hedge by the pool was thick and tall, but she wouldn't have long before they would see or hear or smell that something was wrong. She didn't want them to try to put it out too soon.

When she heard a smash of glass, as though the heat had blown something out, she began to run, glancing back only once. Behind her, the inside of the house glowed like a huge lantern in the dark.

'Fire!' she screamed, charging through the pool gate. 'There's a FIRE!'

Lucas stopped swimming. Walt and Bo jumped up from their sunloungers. 'Are you serious?'

'Call the fire brigade!' she yelled at them.

Lucas was out of the pool, phone in hand.

Bo dropped the vaporiser and reached for her own phone. 'What's the emergency number in the UK?' she cried.

'I've got it,' Lucas said, running from the pool towards the house.

Elizabeth followed him. 'Don't go too close! It's too late.'

Confronted by the sight ahead of him, Lucas stopped in his tracks. The house was engulfed in flames. The heat could be felt from where they stood on the lawn.

'Oh my fucking God,' he murmured. His wrist fell limp. A voice spoke from the handset. As he stared slack-jawed at the blaze, he put the phone back to his ear and gave the emergency services their address with a calm that sent goose bumps up Elizabeth's arms. It was clear he knew it was too late.

When he hung up, he turned to her and said, 'You started it?'

'*What?* I almost died in there!'

Then his skin whitened. 'Where's Agata?' he shouted, taking a step towards the house.

'It's okay. She's in the camper. I just saw her there.'

He frowned. 'Did you plan it?'

'It was an accident, Lucas! I swear!'

Walt appeared next to them. 'What the hell happened?' he asked, eyes wide.

Elizabeth spoke breathily, full of angst and confusion. 'I don't know. I lit the sambucas … and then … I don't know … I was so stupid … I left them there on the table for a few minutes while I went to the loo. I'm so stupid. Oh my God, I'm so stupid.'

Bo's arm was around her. 'It's okay. We're all safe. We're all safe.'

Lucas brought his hands together with his fingers pointing towards Bo and Walt. 'The paintings are in there.'

Bo let out a cry and jerked forward instinctively towards the house. 'Our paintings!' she screamed.

Walt pulled her back, offering soothing words. 'They'll be insured, honey. It's just stuff.'

Elizabeth knew that they weren't insured, that Lucas had not been able to afford to insure them; knew that he had risked it, aware that he only had to keep them safe for a couple of days.

As though hearing her thoughts, he hurtled towards the house. She dived at his legs, tripping him up, saving him from doing something stupid – she didn't want his death on her conscience too.

'What have you done!' he yelled right in her face, wrestling her onto her back.

She felt his hands around her throat and the weight of him on top of her. His pumping flesh pressed the life out of her. She relished his touch, knowing that she had broken him. He hadn't held her like this in years, not with such passion and intensity. Sex had been mechanical. A need rather than a want. A stress-reliever. Before the summer, when he had lifted her from the shower rail, saving her life, he had cradled her like a child, not like a lover. At the lock-up, she had covered her neck to protect herself from him, pressing her own fingers into her throat in abject fear of his attack, imagining his hands were there, willing them to connect with her. Gordon had come to the rescue, but she wondered who would help her now. Perhaps she wanted to die like this, in his arms.

'LUCAS!' Walt bellowed, yanking him away, pulling him off her.

Her head fell back as Lucas let go. He collapsed next to her, panting.

A window blew out. Bo screamed. She and Walter backed off from the house, but Lucas and Elizabeth stayed there on the grass, deaf to the warnings of the others to move away.

'We've lost everything,' Lucas said quietly, the reflection of the flames turning his golden hair red, as though it too was on fire.

'Not everything. You have Isla and Hugo.'

He let out a guttural wail.

Sirens rang out, drowning his cries.

Before long the house was swarming with firemen and white bolts of water.

Elizabeth listened to his blubbing. Everything he cared about was gone. Everything she cared about would be intact. She pictured the blaze encircling the fireproof safe, unable to dominate and destroy the vulnerable papers inside, however furiously it tried.

CHAPTER THIRTY-FIVE

In my sleep, I heard sirens. An acrid smell filled my head, waking me up. Bleary-eyed, I climbed out of bed to get some water. A strange glow, like the sunrise, edged my blind. I checked my clock, which rested on top of the blue file that Lucas had given me, and saw that it was only an hour after I had gone to bed. I pulled back the blind, almost yanking it off its rail. A thick cloud of smoke piled into the sky, and I dropped the blind as though it were hot.

Grabbing a sweater and shoving my feet into shoes, I ran out of the house, not stopping to wonder if my father had woken up.

From around the side of the house, I crawled through the hedge, just where I used to sneak in as a child, and emerged into the horror show of Copper Lodge on fire, green flames licking from the roof.

I thought my chest would burst open with fear when I thought of the children and Lucas inside. The noise of the hoses blasted my eardrums as I made my way around to the back, past the camper van and the guest barn. When I reached the back lawn, I spotted people far down at the bottom of the garden. Dark shapes wrapped in foil. There were no small children amongst them. The smoke filled my lungs and I coughed as I ran towards the figures. I counted three, four, five people. Still no children.

'Where are Isla and Hugo?' I screamed, seeing random faces in a blur as my eyes stung, unable to recognise features, viewing them only as mouthpieces that could tell me the children were safe.

'It's okay, Heather,' Lucas said, stepping forward. 'They're safe. Everyone is safe.'

My head fell into his shoulder and I cried, 'Oh! Thank God. Thank God.'

His arms were around me and I remembered we were not alone. I pulled away.

Elizabeth, Agata and the Seacarts – whom I knew Lucas had been hosting tonight to celebrate their merger – stared at us.

'Bo. Walt. This is Heather,' he said, holding his arm around me still, as though introducing his girlfriend at a party.

We exchanged handshakes; grave smiles, nervous glances.

The strange circumstances could explain Lucas's possession of me, but not for long. I took a step away from him.

Elizabeth's eyes were burning as brightly as the flames behind us.

The blue file had been filled with documents that provided a timeline of the deterioration of her mental health, taking me back through the years to her childhood. There was no doubt that she was unstable, and that she would be unable to cope with her jealousy at the sight of Lucas's affection towards me.

The clinical psychologist's letter dated 22 July 2013 had described her as a delusional and narcissistic patient suffering from pathological jealousy and hallucinations triggered by severe migraines, for which she had undergone MRI scans. He had diagnosed her with a borderline personality disorder and referred her to a psychiatrist for treatment. The social workers' letters of earlier this year had built a picture of Isla as a traumatised child who was deemed at risk after being forced by Elizabeth to watch her multiple suicide attempts. They had recommended a conference to discuss further action. There was a letter from Elizabeth's mother, dated 10 January 2015, a heartfelt scrawled plea to Lucas begging him to restart her monthly payments, pleading for forgiveness, racked with guilt after the discovery that her live-in boyfriend had molested Elizabeth as a child. An old school report from Kensal Rise Grammar was full of complaints about Elizabeth's 'active imagination', her violent outbursts and poor attendance.

At the back of the file, there was a yellow legal pad filled with pages and pages of dialogue written in a child's hand. It was a play about a bailiff and a young girl arguing at the door. The bailiff wanted to come in and seize the family's television set, but the girl told him that her mother was at work. Inflections and underlining had been scribbled in Elizabeth's mother's handwriting, with instructions on how to act the scene out. Another role play, written by her mother this time, was set in the hallway of a block of flats, where a girl told a man that her mother wanted to break up with him. Further dialogue and scene direction covered the A4 sheets. Each play starred a young girl called Elizabeth who ended up in altercations with various unsavoury characters. It explained why she might have trust issues, and why she might struggle to distinguish between reality and fiction.

I had read this personal file as I sat on the low wall that overlooked Elizabeth's beautiful wildflower meadow, and I had cried. In spite of all of her wealth and beauty, her life had been one long battle to stay ahead of her paranoia and her fantasies. Sometimes winning, sometimes losing. Lucas had been like a firefighter tackling the blaze at Copper Lodge; he had tried to control the spread of her neuroticism, tried to mitigate the damage on the children and protect Elizabeth from the bad influences in her life. Sometimes winning, sometimes losing.

When I looked across at the burning house, it seemed that they had both finally lost that battle. I could not imagine that the fire was an accident. It would fall to Lucas to decide Elizabeth's fate now.

'How kind of you to show such concern,' Elizabeth said, stepping towards me, shedding her foil blanket. She pushed a wave of blonde hair up and away from her forehead, and it stayed sticking up in an angular shape.

'I'm just glad nobody was hurt,' I murmured, backing away from her.

She moved close, holding my forearm. 'Thank you, Heather,' she said, but she was looking at Lucas.

'I'd better go tell Dad. He seems to have slept through it. Ear plugs, I'm guessing,' I said.

I left them, hurrying away, avoiding eye contact with Lucas.

But Lucas ran after me, catching up with me behind the guest barn.

Out of sight, he began to cry. He covered his face and said, 'Heather.' That was all. There were no words big enough to encompass his loss.

I put my arms around him and let him sob into my shoulder, stroking his hair, which reeked of smoke.

I wondered now how little he had consciously processed about his own childhood. Elizabeth's psychiatrist's letter had talked of her childhood experiences informing her behaviour as an adult, suggesting they were integral to her paranoia and her suicidal ideations, and to the emotional trauma she inflicted on Isla specifically. In isolation, her behaviour was unacceptable, could characterise her as a monstrous mother. In context, it was a logical chain of events when preceded by a trauma that had remapped the pathways of her tender young brain. The same for Lucas, perhaps. His housemaster at Winslow House – his name escaped me now – had been *in loco parentis* for boys from the age of seven, and he had abused his position, humiliating Lucas, undermining him, inflicting a grinding routine of bullying and cruelty, drilling him to believe he was worth nothing, that he would amount to nothing. The stories had shocked me at the time. And the housemaster had got away with it, been celebrated at an assembly when he had retired. 'He didn't break me. He wanted to, but he didn't,' Lucas had said to me one evening by the pool, after some good news about a new commercial property investment. He had believed he had successfully exorcised the housemaster, but the man's legacy perhaps lived on in Elizabeth.

When his crying abated, I asked him the more pragmatic and immediate questions that had been gathering in my head.

'Where will you all sleep? Does anyone need to stay at ours? We've got camp beds in the loft,' I said, pulling away from him, knowing he had to go back to the others. 'And do you need clothes?'

'That's kind, but no. Bo and Walt are going to lend us some stuff to wear. They've ordered a car to take them to a hotel in London, and Elizabeth and I will stay in the guest barn. And Agata's okay for tonight. The camper's untouched, ironically.'

'Why ironically?'

'If there was anything that needed to burn to the ground, it was that,' he said, shooting it a dirty look. 'They refuse to let go of the bloody thing.'

'Really? But why?'

'It was how they escaped their traffickers. Symbolic of their independence, I guess.'

'You know, you're wrong about Dad bringing them here to pay for his debts. I know he's made mistakes, but he'd never do anything so awful. You must know that.'

'I'm sure you're right. It was probably a misunderstanding. Your father has been very loyal to our family, which is why I never took it any further.'

I tried not to hear the mechanical edge to his voice as he said these conciliatory words. If I was wrong about my father, if he was capable of lying for so long, and doing evil to others less fortunate than him, what did my own blood run with? What legacy had I inherited?

I said, 'I'd better get back.'

His voice was croaky when he said, 'Yes. Take care.'

*

When I reached home, I couldn't bring myself to wake my father. Not simply because letting him sleep would be kinder, knowing how upset he would be, but for another reason too. If I woke him, everything I had learned about the Huxleys would come tumbling out. After reading the blue file, I was eager to set the record straight about Lucas: show my father the psychiatrist's letter, ring my mother, prove to them that Elizabeth was the one to distrust, that she had developed delusions about Lucas sleeping with Agata. In turn, I hoped that Dad would come clean to my mother about the loan on the van and confess to his ongoing gambling debts. Lastly, I wanted to hear him verbally counter Lucas's claim about Agata and Piotr, prove to me that he had brought them to Copper Lodge in good faith.

But now wasn't the time for any of that.

The desolation of the blackened ruins and the stench of toxic embers was far worse than the fire itself. My father stood on the sooty, puddled gravel of the drive staring through the wreckage. The copper roof had survived, held in place by the concrete pillars. It was mottled purple and black and green and gold, still sheltering the grey powdery remains of the Huxleys' lives.

Lucas and Elizabeth were standing where the study had been, staring down at what looked like a large blackened fridge at their feet.

I waited for my father to exclaim or cry, even to speak, but he was silent, holding his emotions together with the strength that characterised him.

'It's horrendous, isn't it?' I said stupidly, filling the gap.

He walked off towards Lucas and Elizabeth, and I followed. It felt disrespectful to be stepping across the detritus. A metal sign that said *Love* was in one piece, covered in ash. A desk lamp was tipped over, its bulb blown out. I had the urge to pick it up and set it upright.

After last night's uninhibited display of affection from Lucas, I dreaded seeing Elizabeth. Her voice rang out, higher and clearer than I had ever heard it before. 'Lucas doesn't need your services today!'

At first I thought she was talking to me. Before I could respond, she began running towards us, her yoga pantaloons flapping and a hoodie dropping off her head, revealing wet hair combed back.

'Come to collect Lucas's debts, have you?' she yelled, pointing her finger right into my father's face. Her eyelids were pink and swollen.

My father looked down at her. His fists were clenched into large balls at his thighs.

'Elizabeth, please,' Lucas said. 'This isn't the time.'

'Don't worry, I understand,' my father said.

'You understand everything, don't you, Gordy?' Elizabeth said. 'You certainly understand who's boss. But when you're taking envelopes of cash from Piotr, do you understand that his baby nephew is ill in hospital because they can't afford damp proofing? Because Uncle Piotr hasn't been able to send any money home?'

'Elizabeth, Gordon isn't taking envelopes of cash from Piotr,' Lucas said.

My father still didn't speak.

'You *would* say that, wouldn't you, my darling husband? Look at you both, protecting your own backs. It's disgusting,' she spat.

I remembered the psychiatrist's detailed explanation of Elizabeth's delusions, but I also remembered what Lucas had said about my father luring Agata and Piotr to Copper Lodge, and my bones seemed to bleed with fear.

'I don't know what you saw, but you're mistaken,' my father said.

'Ask Agata, then! Where's Agata? Agata! Agata!' Elizabeth screeched, running towards the camper van.

'Neither of us slept a wink last night,' Lucas explained.

My father nodded. 'I'm so sorry this has happened to you.'

Lucas shrugged, putting his hands in his pockets. 'It's only stuff.'

'Stuff you've worked bloody hard for,' I piped up, remembering his tears the night before.

'It's a good excuse to start over again,' he said, smiling almost giddily, and I realised how little I had seen of this childish, light-hearted side of him over the past few months. He crouched down beside the large black object that sat in the middle of us and heaved it onto its side, revealing a safe dial.

'If there's anything we can—' my father began, but his offer of help was interrupted by Elizabeth, who was dragging Agata across the rubble.

'Agata! Tell them,' she said. 'Go on. We might as well have it all out now.'

Agata looked haggard, as though she hadn't slept either.

'What do I tell them?' she said.

'Tell them about Gordon doing Lucas's dirty work for him!' Elizabeth shouted.

Lucas stood up from his haunches, abandoning the safe.

'You mean the money?' Agata asked.

'Yes. The cash. How much does Piotr have to give Gordon every week?'

'One hundred pounds,' Agata replied, looking at the floor.

Lucas stepped towards her. 'What are you talking about?'

'You borrow us money and we pay it back!' she yelled, losing her cool.

Lucas turned away from her and looked at my father. 'But Gordon, I've never asked Piotr to pay back any of the money I've lent them. Not a penny.'

'Gordon take it every week! Every week!' Agata screamed.

Like Lucas, I was fixated on my father's face, on his pallor, on his look of distaste. 'She's talking nonsense,' he said, and began walking away.

I ran after him. 'Dad! Dad! Where are you going?'

Behind me, I heard Lucas say to Elizabeth, 'Let him go. I never want to lay eyes on him again.'

'Dad! Why didn't you defend yourself?' I gasped, jogging next to him as he strode on, my breathing too fast for my lungs to keep up. I tugged at his jumper to hold him back, but he was impervious to my questions and to my attempts to stop him.

As we turned into Connolly Close, I slowed down, worn out by his guilty silence, and trudged behind him. I wanted him to tell me the truth, but that wasn't going to happen. Admitting to his daughter that he had lured a vulnerable young couple to Copper Lodge and extorted money from them would be too much to concede. My respect for him would disintegrate into an ashy ruin, like the house next door, as though the substance of him had been a similar illusion to the luxury and desirability of the Huxleys' life.

I stopped walking in his footsteps.

Standing still in the middle of the close, I watched how his steel-toecapped boots crashed into the tarmac, one step after another, and how they came to a stop. He shuffled around slowly, his shoulders hunched. His eyes were hangdog, his lips slack.

'Don't tell your mum, please, Heather, I beg you,' he murmured. It was not the tone of a begging man; it was that of a defeated man, a guilty one. I saw bitterness and disappointment behind his eyes. I saw his mistakes. I saw that he was a bully: weak and insecure.

Silently he was admitting to the crimes he had been accused of: procuring slave labour to service his gambling debts; taking money from Piotr while pretending Lucas had ordered it; accusing Lucas of increasing the loan payments so that he could hide the truth about his ongoing habit from my mother. My poor mother! The truth was going to destroy her.

I mulled over the ramifications of that horrible reality and I thought back over my childhood. My father's silences had not been inner strength and his beatings had not been discipline. I wanted nothing more to do with him.

I wanted to wash him out of my mouth with soap.

CHAPTER THIRTY-SIX

Lucas turned the dial of the safe and Elizabeth held a hand to her chest in anticipation.

The devastation of their home and the hatred she felt for Lucas and his web of lies dissolved into the background. All she cared about was retrieving the documents inside.

Her vision was tunnelled towards that one goal. Nothing else mattered.

'There you go,' he said, opening up the safe. The inside was clean and neat, untouched and whole, contrasting with the mess around them.

She dropped to her knees and scrabbled around, searching for the documents she needed. Two passports fell into the dust, but she left them there.

'Where is it?' she screamed at Lucas.

'They're here,' he said, picking the passports up out of the charcoal, blowing the ash off and handing them to her. 'Their work papers are in there too. For what they're worth. Which is nothing. At least Agata has finally accepted they need legal help.'

'Where's the blue file?'

He put both his hands on his head. His elbows stuck out like wings. A strange cough or laugh, Elizabeth couldn't tell which, spluttered out of him.

'*That's* what you wanted?' he asked.

'I want to read Mum's letter,' she said, looking up at him.

'Is that what you've really wanted all this time?'

'No,' she said, picking up the passports. 'Not just that.'

She pressed her fingers to her lips to stop them crumpling, but two streams of tears made stripes through the soot on her cheeks.

Lucas approached her and she cowered from him. He was undeterred. His arms encircled her in a firm hug. 'That letter brings up too much. It took you days to recover last time.'

Sobs heaved from deep inside her. 'But I didn't read it properly last time,' she cried through her tears. 'I need to check it. Everything gets scrambled in my head and that letter tells me all the facts and then I know that I'm not going mad. It tells me what is real and what's not.'

'What happened to you back then was real. Very real and very horrible.'

His words were familiar. For a moment, they were soothing. She began to feel the panic subside. Then she thought about the fire and surveyed the charred remains of her life.

'Is all this real?' she asked him, tasting the soot on her tongue.

'This is real,' he said. 'I'm real, right here, holding you now.'

She blinked her blue eyes at him. 'Was there a fire?'

'I'm afraid the fire was real.'

'Yes.' She hung her head.

Now that the material gains were gone, the false construct of a functioning life had been destroyed and the reality of the state of their marriage was evident all around them.

She had one more question to ask, to clear up one last thing.

'Is Heather real?' she asked.

He sighed and kicked at the dust.

'Yes. Heather is real. But I've been straight with you about that.'

'No more smoke and mirrors, Lucas?'

'No, Elizabeth. What you see is what you get.'

She smiled at him. It seemed the smoke had cleared but the reflection was still ugly.

And she knew exactly what she had to do.

CHAPTER THIRTY-SEVEN

The gathering storm blew a dustbin over. It scuttled towards the car. I righted it and slammed the boot, worrying about the drive to the coast. The reports on the news showed tidal waves over promenades and sandbags outside riverside cottages. My father had warned me against driving south in this bad weather. It was the only sentence he had uttered since we had returned from Copper Lodge.

I was clearing the crisp packets and old water bottles from the back seat when I saw Lucas staring at me through the car windscreen. He smiled goofily, and stuck his thumb out to the right, like a hitchhiker. He was dressed in a seersucker jacket and a pair of beige slacks that were, respectively, too short in the arms and legs for him. I shuffled out of the car and bit the side of my mouth to stop myself from laughing.

'Any chance of a lift?' he asked.

'Where to?'

'London.'

London had not been in my plans.

'What's in London?'

'Isla and Hugo.'

I imagined their distraught faces when they heard about their house.

'What happened to your car?'

'They all blew out in the fire.'

'Oh Lucas. Is there anything left?'

'Nothing but the clothes on my back.'

I chuckled. 'And they don't even look like yours.'

'Walter Seacart's. The last thing he'll ever give me, no doubt. After last night.'

'Do you need anything from Dad? A jumper or toothbrush or anything?' I asked, looking back at the house, not relishing the thought of nipping back in.

Lucas stuck his hands in his pockets, letting the wind blow through his hair, closing his eyes as the raindrops fell on his face. 'Nope. I have everything I need.'

'Except a lift,' I said.

He laughed. 'Except that.'

'I'll meet you in the lane outside Copper Lodge in half an hour. I won't drive in.'

'Give me an hour,' he said, striding off, his hair bouncing from the top of his head.

When I closed the red front door of Connolly Close for the last time, I thought of my mother, who would be returning from Scotland next week after Aunt Maggie's funeral. She would clean the house from top to bottom and make a pie for the Huxley children next door, and pretend that life could continue as normal.

Before pulling away, I saw the front door open.

My father stepped out and ran with a heavy step towards me, motioning for me to wind down the window.

I did as he asked, and looked down at his huge hands, which he had hooked over the open window, as though holding onto me. A gust of wind blew through the car.

He said, 'I'll miss you.'

His earnestness broke my heart. The power of his contrition seemed to swipe the storm out of my path. It cleared out my brain, sweeping it of all the indecision and self-doubt. He was a man of few words and I had been a child with many. He had disciplined with his strength and I had fought back. My life under his roof had been complex and controlled, yet there had been happiness.

'I'll miss you too, Dad,' I said, and held back my tears: a rip tide in shallow waters.

He paused on the doorstep. 'Drive safe in this wind,' he shouted, and walked back inside.

Before pulling out of the close, there was another knock at my window and I rolled it down again.

'You leave now?' Agata said.

'I am leaving. Yes. I'm sorry I haven't said goodbye.'

'It's okay.'

Her ponytail whipped around her head. The millions of tiny muscles in her pretty face were pinched and wrinkled. I waited for her to speak.

'Bye then,' I said, turning on the ignition and placing my hands at ten to two on the steering wheel, steady and sure, ready to go and collect Lucas.

'Wait,' she said, holding onto the wheel. 'I see you and Lucas. Last night. You are together?'

I looked her directly in the eye. 'Yes. We are.'

She put her hand over her mouth. 'I did not want to believe it.'

'I know it will hurt a lot of people.'

She shook her head, as though I had misunderstood. Then she said, 'I did not steal his Rolex. He took it off before … And then afterwards,' she swallowed, 'afterwards, he left it in the van.' She touched the gold cross on a chain around her neck and looked up to the sky, and my right foot slammed on the brake as though I was driving at two hundred miles an hour.

'Afterwards? After what?' I asked, barely recognising my strangled voice.

'After the *sex*,' she whispered.

I clutched the steering wheel, holding on to something solid while my heart and soul shattered into tiny pieces. My fingers shook as I unclenched them to open the car door, finding this simple, familiar task almost impossible to manage.

Face to face with Agata, I touched her hand, both of us trembling, and said, quietly but urgently, 'You and Lucas had an affair?'

She shook her head. 'No.'

A swirling feeling engulfed me. I dropped my head into my hands and breathed in, savouring the semi-darkness my fused fingers created; then I looked up again, into Agata's blinking eyes, ready to ask the question I couldn't bear to ask. 'He forced himself on you?'

Her whole body twitched with a shudder. 'Yes. I am very sorry.' She grabbed both my hands. 'I did not want it. I never wanted it. I'm so sorry.' A tear rolled across her nose, blown horizontally by the wind.

'You have no reason to apologise,' I said, wrapping my arms around her as she cried, biting back my own tears. 'I'm sorry I had to ask.'

Her chest expanded into my embrace and a ragged sigh followed.

Before I let her go, I saw, over her shoulder, a hooded figure under the tree on the street corner. Elizabeth's unmistakable blue eyes shone out from the shadows. She tucked a strand of blonde hair back into her pink hoodie. Agata turned around to see what I was looking at.

'Elizabeth,' I said, under my breath, remembering the blue file in my rucksack. Its private contents didn't belong to me. By giving it to me, Lucas had exploited Elizabeth's vulnerable state, just as he had exploited Agata in the dead of night. And me, too, in the past. Elizabeth had tried to warn me against him, had even given me money to get away from him, and I had thrown it back in her face.

I ducked back into the car to get the file. But when I emerged, ready to run to her with it, she had vanished.

'Here,' I said, giving it to Agata. 'Return it to her. And tell her that I'm sorry.'

'Yes. She be happy,' Agata said, hugging the file. 'She said you believe me.'

I frowned. 'She knew you were coming?'

Agata looked surprised. 'She sent me.'

Shame ate into me. Elizabeth had sent Agata to deliver a message, knowing I would not have believed Elizabeth herself, knowing that Agata was a pure and genuine source; knowing the information would save me from Elizabeth's fate with Lucas. 'Tell her thank you,' I murmured, looking over to the place where Elizabeth had stood. 'Is she going to be okay?'

'With this now,' Agata said, patting the file. 'Yes. She get lawyers. She get help. Good help. Not from Lucas and his *doctors*. You know?'

'Yes.' I thought about Copper Lodge, burnt to the ground, and I felt a flicker of admiration for Elizabeth. It seemed she had some fighting spirit. 'And thank you too, Agata.'

'Go,' Agata said, pointing at my car, reminding me of the urgency of my departure.

I climbed into the driver's seat and closed the door.

Through the open window, I said, 'Look after yourself. Find your way home, won't you?'

She nodded. 'Yes. You go, Heather.'

My forefinger was poised on the indicator. Turning left would take me to the sea. Turning right would take me to Lucas. In five minutes' time, he would be waiting for me in the lane outside the entrance to Copper Lodge.

My foot lifted the clutch.

Agata stepped back onto the kerb. She looked young and innocent, like a teenager waiting for a mate on the street corner. *I did not want it*, she had said of Lucas's advances. And neither had *I* wanted it. At fifteen years old, I hadn't wanted anything more than his attention, until he had touched me and shown me what more there was to want.

I clicked the indicator left. To the sea. Away from Lucas, away from a lifetime of my delusions about him.

As I drove off, I glanced into my rear-view mirror and caught Agata's small wave and a smile.

I focused on navigating through the storm-beleaguered roads, bumping over loose branches, creating bow waves through floods and U-turning at fallen lamp posts.

The charred remains of Copper Lodge were etched on my mind. I grieved for it. I had believed in its prettiness and its promises of a better life. But its destruction had exposed its dark heart. The myth of Lucas now blew like a wind across its grounds, unsettling the feather-light ash in swirls, his beautiful smile having melted away in the heat, along with everything else he cared about.

Three hours later, I climbed exhausted out of my car at Amy's sea-view apartment block. It had fallen still outside. The wind had changed.

I took my shoes off and left them by the open door of the car and padded across the road to the water's edge. The foamy tide rushed in and touched my toes, like a kiss hello.

I listened to the sea's brush over the pebbles. My skin tingled. The waters were calm. And I realised that my best life was right here; right under the soles of my feet.

A LETTER FROM CLARE

Dear Reader,

Thank you so much for reading *My Perfect Wife*. I am always very excited at this stage of the publishing process, when I'm finishing up the last bits and bobs of editing and writing this letter to you. In a few weeks' time, I'll be seeing the cover design. Then there's the prospect of the book going out into the world. In this respect, I'm a split personality. Part of me wants to delete every word I've written and the other part of me is desperate for readers to get stuck in. I have no idea who I am!

Whoever I am, I'm very grateful you are still reading! I'd love to hear from you. Please keep in touch by clicking on the sign-up link below, where you'll hear what I'll be writing next:

www.bookouture.com/clare-boyd

Did any of you fall in love with Lucas, secretly, guiltily, just a little bit? I'm ashamed to say that *I* did, even though I knew exactly who he was and what was coming. I loved Lucas and then I hated him, and I loved him because I hated him. He wasn't all bad. They never are.

His paternalistic promise to look after and provide for Elizabeth – *his* woman – was appealing to me. Perhaps this is because

I am a victim of the historical repression of my sex, or because of the complex male role models in my life, or because there is an atavistic comfort in the idea of the male hunter-gatherer. I don't know. I'm not proud of it. All I know is that, as I wrote him, I was lured in by his chivalry and charm.

When I think back to my teenage years, I am staggered by what I put up with in the dating game. If I'd put my younger self into a book, all you readers would be crying, 'She'd never go back to him if he did that!' But there were so many times when I went back again and again to be used and thrown away. The worse they behaved, the more obsessed I became – which I imagine, for the men I lusted after, was a complete power trip. You're probably now thinking: you need therapy! This is definitely true. As it was true for poor Elizabeth. Being maltreated was the norm in her childhood, and so she normalised Lucas's abusive treatment of her. Sadly, those feelings of shame and worthlessness sat more comfortably inside her than love and respect did. The default position of childhood has a powerful continuation into adulthood until you break the cycle (as explored in my second book, *Three Secrets*). For a vulnerable woman, Lucas's wealth was the perfect tool for manipulation and corruption. The world today is perhaps a macro example of that.

My Perfect Wife was a personal vent for me to express how upset I get about the rich getting richer and the poor getting poorer. In this book, I wanted to tell a simple tale about how money can corrupt morality; how the motivation to gather more and more wealth at the expense of the vulnerable in the name of choice feels like upside-down logic to me. I'm certainly not dying to up sticks and leg it over to communist China, but I do feel shocked by how much money there is out there in the UK and how appallingly it is distributed. Obviously, I have zero clue about how to address the problem – and little faith that our politicians will sort it out any time soon – but perhaps Lucas can be my tiny contribution to disincentivising gratuitous greed!

At the very least, I hope it's a good story that will keep you turning the pages. For those of you who have enjoyed *My Perfect Wife*, please do write a review, and follow me on social media. See below for details.

With very best wishes,
Clare

clare.boyd.14

@ClareBoydClark

claresboyd

ACKNOWLEDGEMENTS

What a journey this book has been for all those involved! There have been highs and lows, and I'm seriously appreciative of those people whose good hearts and professionalism got me through. Jessie Botterill and Broo Doherty, my dream team, thank you.

I'm also filled with gratitude for everyone at Bookouture who was able to offer me flexibility and faith, allowing me precious time to turn this book around.

There are a few other people who offered me some major help on the fact side of this fiction.

Firstly, a huge thank you goes to my wonderful brother-in-law, Julian Clark, who talked me through the basics of the finance world and didn't laugh at me when I asked him stupid questions. Any mistakes I have made are mine alone.

The same thanks and caveats go to Lucy-Anne Garnett, whose expertise in the art world helped me to build the storyline of Jude's paintings. Thanks, Luce!

And many thanks to Nick and Jane Davies whose story of a pawned Rolex made me laugh on holiday and enabled me to build a true-to-life account of Elizabeth's trip to Mayfair with her diamond necklace.

Always and forever, I thank my family for their endless wrap-around love and support.